JANINE

TALE OF AN ABANDONED
WIFE AND MOTHER

JANINE
TALE OF AN ABANDONED WIFE AND MOTHER

MARK ERIC JOHANSEN

ARPress
ILLUMINATING IDEAS.
EMPOWERING VOICES

ARPress
45 Dan Road Suite 5
Canton MA 02021

Hotline: 1(888) 821-0229
Fax: 1(508) 545-7580

Ordering Information:
Quantity sales. Special discounts are available on quantity purchases by corporations, associations, and others. For details, contact the publisher at the address above.

Printed in the United States of America.

ISBN-13:	Softcover	979-8-89676-532-5
	eBook	979-8-89676-533-2

Library of Congress Control Number: 2024926165

TABLE OF CONTENTS

THE DELLS

Janine and Brent returned to their vacation chalet from early morning tennis. The weather in Wisconsin Dells is sunny, warm, and inviting. They planned to take the kids to the waterpark for the day. While Janine organized the kids, Brent checks in at the resort office. Since all their phones and laptops were stolen, all their messages are being forwarded.

Brent says he will have to go home early. Charlene from the office is coming to pick him up. He must prepare for a big meeting. He says Jan should take the kids to the waterpark and the Ducks for the day. They had promised and still have a day's rental. Jan can drive home tomorrow.

Janine showers quickly while Brent organizes the kids. Olivia, her sixteen-year-old, is sketching birds on the porch. Brent Jr., her twelve-year-old, and Monica, her eight-year-old, are watching *The Little Mermaid* on TV.

Janine embraces Brent. "Love you. Be good. When you get home, get some phones for the kids." She loads the reluctant kids in the Mercedes and drives off.

She never sees Brent again.

After the waterpark Janine parks near the Duck Landing. They had purchased tickets for both amusements earlier in the week. When she tried a credit card to buy refreshments, the card is declined. Thinking no more about it, she digs in her purse for cash. In the bottom of her purse, she found her phone. She thought it, too, had been stolen.

As the Duck ride was loud and wet, she waited to call Brent about the card. Back in the car she tried calling him. It was then she realized that her phone had no service. She thought there was something wrong with her phone.

Back at the chalet, she wanted to call the credit card company. No service.

It was earlier in the week when most of their electronic devices went missing. All the laptops and kid's cell phones were stolen from the chalet. The policeman looked all around the chalet and made a report. He found it strange that there was no sign of a break-in.

Janine wanted to put pictures of the kids at the waterpark and the Ducks on her Facebook page. No service.

They returned to the chalet with take-out food bought with cash. When night fell, Janine directed the kids to start packing. She began organizing her room. She collapsed into a chair with a glass of wine.

In the morning, Janine planned to take the kids to breakfast after closing out the chalet. When she was sure all their belongings were out, Janine went to the office. When she checked out, the clerk handed her a bill for in-room movies. All of Janine's credit cards were declined. She dug in her purse and brought out an envelope of cash. She paid the clerk red faced.

Back in the car, Janine held the wheel and cried. Olivia, in the passenger seat, asked her mom if she was alright. "Fine. Fine," she said, wiping her tears away. "Let's get something to eat."

On their long drive home, she wanted to call Brent several times. At a rest stop they ate and gassed the car. None of her credit cards were good.

Janine had a sinking feeling all the way home but tried to be outwardly positive for the children. What had Brent done?

HOME

As she drove, Janine watched the sky turn grey then pink then crimson as the sun rose. The kids were quiet. Olivia and Monica were asleep. She could not hear Brent Jr. but checked him in the rear-view from time to time.

The closer she came to home the more she dreaded it. What was going on? Why did Brent leave early? Why hadn't Brent paid the credit cards? She went over the questions again and again. Anyway, a nice hot soaking bath in her own tub would be welcome.

The traffic was almost non-existent. It was early Sunday. The kids began to rouse the closer they came to home. Janine felt an easing of her worries as she turned the corner. Home, her castle. A showplace of affluence and elegance.

As the house came into view, the horror show commenced. Janine felt a virtual knife in her heart. There, on the darkened house, was the signpost to oblivion, big and bold. This was the sign that would drop the bottom out of her world. She would never forget it. EVICTION NOTICE.

Janine stopped the car in the drive and stared at the sign.

Olivia pointed at the sign. "Mom, what's going on?"

"What's wrong?" asked Brent Jr. "What's that sign mean?"

Janine sat stunned, unable to speak for some seconds. "I...I...don't know." She shut off the car and got out. She approached the porch, leaving the car door open. She did not hear the beep, beep, beep of the warning. She stood staring at the house with her head swirling. She was unaware of anything until her daughter touched her.

"Mom...Mom...where's Dad?" asked Olivia. "What's going on?"

Janine stood frozen in front of the house. All her fears solidified in that moment. She was standing at the gates of perdition with no escape.

Olivia crossed the porch and unlocked the front door. Entering, she yelled, "Dad! Dad!" She disappeared into the house.

Brent followed Olivia. "Dad?"

Janine was still frozen in place when she felt Monica's small hand take hers.

"It's alright, Mommy," said Monica. "We're home." She pulled her mother toward the door.

Suddenly Janine was jerked back to reality. "Yes, we are. Come on."

Hand-in-hand with Monica, Janine stepped into her home. It was eerily familiar yet foreboding. The air was hot and stale. No lights or sounds came from anywhere. It was like a cave with her furniture in it. She could hear Junior and Olivia upstairs.

Janine led Monica through the hall into the kitchen. There were discarded food containers and plates, signs that Brent had been there. Instinctively she opened the refrigerator. The putrid odor of rotting food overwhelmed her. "Oh my God!" she choked, slamming the door on the fridge.

Janine turned to find Monica frozen in place. Her eyes locked on her mother.

Janine stepped over and knelt down, taking Monica in her arms. "It's okay, baby. I've got you."

The four met up in the front hall. Olivia's expression told Janine that she too understood the situation. It was Brent Jr. that clung to the notion of normalcy.

"Mom, nothing works here," said the boy. "Let's go to a motel. I'm hungry."

Janine thought about the dwindling amount of cash in her purse. She thought about all the possibilities before an idea came to her.

"Kids, there's a party at the country club. Get your swimsuits. We'll go over there for the picnic, and we'll decide about where to go later. We can stop by the ATM on the way."

At the ATM Janine requested $500. When the machine denied her, her heart sunk again. She tried $200: no deal. She tried $100: no deal.

Janine arrived at the country club expecting some shelter from the storm raging around her. Once she led the kids to the patio cookout, she knew the storm had followed her. As the kids were served hamburgers, she felt that everyone was staring at her. When she casually waved at people, they half-heartedly waved back. She ushered the kids to an open table. Janine kept up the mommy conversation with the kids, hoping they would not notice their notoriety.

Saundra, Janine's tennis partner, hastened up to the table. She struggled to cover her swimsuit with a wrap. "Janine, are you okay? I've been worried about you." She pulled up a chair and sat, giving an acknowledgment to the kids. "I've been calling you."

"We just got back this morning," said Janine pleasantly. "My phone's not working."

"What's going on?" Saundra asked with concern. "I saw the house…" She looked at the children and back to Janine. "Are you kids going for a swim?"

"The house? It's some kind of mistake. We'll get it straightened out tomorrow," Janine said with bravado.

Chase, Saundra's husband, came up to the table. "Janine," he said coolly, "is Brent with you?"

"No, no he isn't," Janine replied with a half-smile.

Chase nodded affirmatively. "Saundra, don't forget you have guests by the pool." He turned and walked away.

Saundra put her hand on Janine's. "Look, I have to go. I've got Chase's boss today. I'll catch up when I can." After she left no one talked to them.

Janine led the kids to the locker room. Monica and Junior changed into their suits. Olivia and Janine found an empty table with a shade near the pool.

"Livy, honey," said Janine, "you shouldn't let people bother you. Don't let them body shame you. It was alright in the Dells."

"Mom...I don't want to swim," she whispered. "I feel like I should hide somewhere. They all know."

Janine and her daughter sat in silence. No one acknowledged them. She felt a pariah in a place she had been so comfortable in. She tried not to let the kids see her discomfort.

When the lifeguard signaled that the pool was closing, Janine instructed her children to shower there. "No hot water at home."

On their way home they stopped at the 7-11 for milk, soda, and ice. They reloaded the cooler in the back of the car.

They reentered a dark, stale house warily. Janine felt she had to keep things upbeat. "Okay, kids, let's open all the windows and doors. We'll get out some candles and camp out here in the front room."

They munched on fast food that they'd brought home. As the darkness fell, the house became gloomier. They lit candles and sat quietly. The kids all looked at their mom in the flickering candlelight. There was no laughter, no ease, just growing bewilderment.

"I want Daddy!" burst out Monica. "Where is he? Where's Daddy?" She came over and plopped in her mother's lap, crying. "Why isn't he here?"

"I don't know, sweet thing," she said, putting her arms around the weeping child. "I don't know. Something must have happened to him." She looked at Brent Jr. and Olivia. They too were crying.

Janine motioned her children close. When they cuddled up next to her, she tried to soothe them. "It's okay, kids. We'll figure this out."

They sat for some time hugging and crying, oblivious to the noises outside.

"Hello in there. This is the police!" A flashlight beam blazed in the hall. "Hello?"

"Hello," replied Janine. "We're in the front room."

Slowly a figure behind a bright flashlight entered the room. The beam shone all around the room before focusing on the four huddled together. "Just you four?" said the disjointed male voice.

"Just us four," replied Janine. "Is there a problem?"

A second figure behind a bright beam walked down the hall toward the kitchen. Janine could just see that this officer had a gun drawn.

"Is this your house?" asked the male officer, moving into the front room. "Are you living here in the dark?"

"Yes, it's my house," said Janine, rising. "We just got back from Wisconsin. What's going on?"

"Sorry, ma'am," said the male officer. "We got a report of a break-in. We thought the house was abandoned. We thought you might be squatters."

"We're not squatters!" said Olivia. "This is our house."

The female officer returned from a first-floor inspection and holstered her gun. "We're sorry, folks. If we could just verify some identification."

"Get out of our house!" said Olivia.

Janine held Monica who was now crying. "Mommy, I'm scared."

"If we could just check an ID, we'll be out of here," said the female cop calmly. "We have a job to do, and it looks like you have troubles enough."

"Sure, sure," said Janine. "My purse is over there." She pointed to a pile stacked on a chair.

The female cop found the purse, opened it, shone her flashlight in, and produced a wallet. "Here."

Janine took the wallet with shaking hands. She found her license and handed it to the male officer.

"Janice, what are your childrens' names?" asked the cop.

"It's Janine. This is Monica, that's Brent Jr., and this is Olivia."

The cop handed her ID back. "Janine, when is the power going to be back on?"

"We just got back today. I'll have to call them in the morning."

"Okay," said the male cop. "But maybe you should close and lock the doors tonight."

The cops left. Monica kept crying. Brent and Olivia locked the doors.

NEW DAY, NEW TROUBLES

The early morning birds woke Janine. She extricated herself from Monica, stretched, and went to the bathroom. When she returned to the front room, Olivia was awake. Olivia plodded off to the restroom. Janine flopped into an easy chair. She scanned the room making a memory.

"Now what?" asked Olivia, returning.

"Cereal and milk for everyone," replied Janine. "Today we get some answers."

"What about school?" asked Olivia. "Can I go with you?"

"Sure, Livy. Let's get these two ready for school." Janine looked around. "What time is it anyway?"

While Livy roused the children, Janine went up to her bedroom suite. The room was gloomy half-dark, but she memorized the image. She surveyed Brent's dresser, his drawers uncharacteristically left open. In the closet she touched one of his suits. She ran her fingers over one of his fine dress shirts.

As she assembled her clothes, she noticed their fire-proof safe open. She took it to the light and examined its contents. Gone were Brent's passport, all the jewelry and the safety deposit key. Now she was sure that she had been abandoned.

Janine sat on the bed and wept. This too was going to be a bad day.

With the two youngest off on the school bus, Janine and Olivia went to the mortgage bank. They were at the door when a woman unlocked the entrance. They were seated at a desk with the branch assistant manager. "Hi, I'm Stuart Wilson. How can I help you?" he said with a half-smile.

Calmly Janine said, "I'm Janine Piersen. I'd like to know why I'm being evicted from my home."

"Oh…" Assistant Manager Wilson said. He punched in several lines on his keyboard. "And what is your account number?"

"I don't know."

Wilson stopped dead. "I see…Give me your social security number, please?"

After Janine repeated her number and Wilson had punched it in, he began reading something. He reached for a Starbucks to-go cup and sipped. "Uh ha…I see…uh ha. Well…" Wilson looked at Janine stone faced. "It seems that you were given a thirty-day final notice and a court date. The property has been foreclosed. You have been given a ten-day notice of eviction." Wilson turned from the screen and faced Janine. "There is nothing I can do." Wilson leaned back in his chair. He reached for the telephone and punched in a number. "Yes, it's Wilson in my office. Right now, please."

Janine struggled to find her voice and a coherent thing to say. "What…what can I do? I don't know anything about this. How can I fix this?"

"I don't know," said Wilson. "It's out of my hands. You're going to have to leave now," he said, rising. As he left, the office a security guard came in.

Janine sat flabbergasted. Olivia held her hand.

The security guard motioned them out of the office. "I'm sorry. I'm going to ask you to leave now." The guard followed them to the car. He watched while Janine calmed herself behind the wheel.

"Where do we go now?" asked Olivia.

"We go to the bank," said Janine through her tears. "I don't want to, but we'd better."

At their bank, Janine asked for an agent. They were shown to a cubicle marked Alice Wilson.

"How can I help you?" asked Alice. She sipped a Starbucks to-go cup.

"I need to know the status of my accounts," said Janine, handing Alice her ID.

"I see. Just a moment," said Alice. She sipped her coffee and punched in some numbers. "Ms. Piersen, would you like a printout?"

"Yes, I would."

Alice excused herself and returned with several sheets a few minutes later.

Janine, fearing the worst, found it on the paper. The account had $100 in it. The sheets showed a steady reduction of funds over six months. She closed her eyes and felt like a runaway elevator was descending rapidly. She regained reality when Livy touched her.

"Mom?" The girl had sat silently so far. She then addressed Alice. "Can I check my account, please?"

"Ms. Olivia, your account was reduced to $100 in January," said Alice. The bank official, sensing the panic in her office, made a quick call.

"Mom, that's my college account," said Livy, perplexed.

"No…the kids' accounts too?" Janine struggled to find her voice. "What about Brent Jr. and Monica?"

Olivia had Alice check the other two accounts. They too were at $100.

Janine sat clutching the account reports. Her head was swimming. "Can…Can I close this account and get the $100?"

"I'm sorry. Only Mr. Brent can close the account. You are an add-on to the accounts," said Alice apologetically. "Is there anything else I can do?"

Janine shook her head negatively. "Okay…I'd like to open the safe deposit box."

"Do you have the key?" asked Alice.

"No, I can't find it."

"Well," said the bank officer, "you can you fill out a lost key form. You can get a replacement in thirty days."

"Thirty days...sure."

While Alice was printing out the form, Janine noticed a uniformed bank guard a few feet away.

Alice handed Janine the form. "Do you want to fill it out now?"

"No," said Janine crestfallen. "No, I'll take it with me."

"Is there anything else I can do?" asked Alice.

Olivia followed her mother through the bank lobby. The guard followed them to the door. Janine froze at the door. The guard opened the door. "Thanks for coming in. Have a nice day."

Olivia ushered her mother through the lot. Janine moved like a zombie. At the car she stood motionless until Olivia spoke. "Mom, open the car."

Seated in the car, Janine still had the bank statements clutched in her hand. She stared out the windshield at some far away spot.

"Mom," said Olivia plaintively. "Mom! What do we do now? Do we look for Daddy?"

Janine slowly turned toward her daughter. "Where?"

"What about Dad's office?"

Olivia sat silent as Janine drove the expressway to downtown Chicago. She negotiated the tangle of cars, buses, bicycles, and pedestrians jerkily. When she found the high-rise building, she had Olivia scout parking lot signs.

She pulled into a drive that took her down two levels. An attendant came over to the car. His name tag read Wilson. "Are you going to stay more than four hours? No. That'll be $45."

"What?" Janine pulled her purse open. She pulled an emergency $100 bill out from behind her ID.

They parked two levels further down. They rode the elevator up to the ground floor. They crossed the street and found the entrance to the building. They approached the lobby desk. They needed a pass to access the elevators.

"Gawn Associates on twenty, please," said Janine automatically.

The women hesitated. "Sorry, there's no one up there."

Janine's attention focused sharply on the woman. "My name is Janine Piersen. My husband works here. I have to speak with him. Gawn Associates on twenty," she said forcefully. "Of course, they're there."

A man in a jacket came over. "There is no reason for raised voices, madam. There is no one there, trust me. But if you wish, I'll take you up."

The man led them through the barriers and to an elevator. The man stood perpendicular to Janine and Olivia, back against the wall. His name badge read Wilson.

When the elevator doors opened, Janine moved out with purpose. She turned left at the hall and left again at the T. She froze there within sight of the door.

The entrance was taped over with yellow tape marked Crime Scene. A large sticker on the door read "Law Enforcement Only Beyond This Point!"

Janine stepped forward and touched the door with her fingertips. Her lips moved but no words escaped.

Wilson began talking to Olivia. "The feds were here all weekend. They can't find any of these guys. It was all over the news." He pointed to the door. "No one can go in."

Tears began running down Olivia's face. She reached out and touched her mother. "Mom, we should go." Olivia pulled her mother back to the elevator.

As they waited, Wilson spoke into a radio. "No, it's okay. We're coming down."

Olivia directed her zombielike mother through the lobby. Wilson interacted with two police officers who watched them intently.

Olivia got her mom back into the car. "Mom, we should get home. Monica should be home soon."

Suddenly Janine came to life. "Monica…yes, we'd better get home."

Olivia studied her mother all the way home. Although she had to keep wiping the tears in her eyes, Janine showed no emotion. When they pulled into the drive, Saundra was waiting in her car.

"Jan, thank god you're alright," said Saundra breathlessly. "Everyone's been trying to reach you."

"What, who?"

"Brent's been in a fight. They called me because I'm your back-up number. And the school won't let Monica on the bus. Something about fees." Saundra looked at Janine questioningly. "I was going to collect Monica. You can deal with Brent. Okay?"

"Yeah, okay. Thanks," said Janine. She looked at Olivia. "Now what?"

Janine pulled up at the school. Brent and a young teacher sat on a bench outside. They came to the car. Brent had dried blood on his lip and a bruise by his eye. Janine inspected him. "Are you alright?"

"I'm suspended," said the boy with a sigh.

"Brent started a fight with another boy," said the teacher. "You will have to see Mrs. Carmichael to get him reinstated."

"Okay," said Janine. "Brent, get in the car. Thank you, Miss…?"

"Wilson. Jean Wilson."

Janine drove to Saundra's home. Saundra gave her a hug and led the three into the kitchen.

"Why don't you kids play in the yard while your mom and I talk?" Saundra showed the kids to the yard where Monica was. "Glass of wine?" she asked Janine.

Janine sat on a high stool. She nodded affirmatively and rubbed her forehead.

Saundra poured two glasses out. She moved next to Janine and rubbed her back reassuringly. "Okay, Jan, what's going on?"

Janine took a gulp of wine. She stared out the patio doors as she talked. "He took everything. Brent took everything. There's nothing left.

He even got the kid's college funds. I don't know what we're supposed to do."

"Oh honey, no," said Saundra sympathetically. "We knew something was wrong. First the eviction sign went up. Then I couldn't reach you. Your phone kept rejecting my calls. Then the stories on the news. I asked Brent what was going on…"

"What! When?"

"Brent was at the house, what, Saturday? I asked him what was going on. He said everything was alright and he had to get back." Saundra had a sip of wine. "Honey, what are you going to do?"

The sound of the garage door opener caught Saundra's attention. "Chase is home. Maybe he'll have some ideas."

Chase entered and froze at the sight of Janine. "Saundra, honey, she can't be here. They can't be in the house. I've already had to talk to the feds. They're toxic. Janine, you and the kids have got to go!"

Saundra took Chase by the arm and led him to the den. "Honey, do you know what she's going through?"

"I don't care what they're going through. Do you know what I've been through?"

Through the closed door of the den, Janine could hear them arguing. She rose and motioned the kids in. "We have to go."

Janine drove to the country club. "Alright, everybody shower up. We'll eat after."

"Can't we go to a motel?" Brent Jr. asked plaintively.

"C'mon, let's go." Janine ushered them into the locker area. She was happy no one was around.

Janine lingered in the shower. She let the hot spray soothe her until she heard Monica's voice.

"Mommy, we're hungry."

As Janine and the girls exited the locker room, the club manager approached. "Ms. Piersen, may I see you for a minute?" asked the red-faced man. "Alone?"

Janine gave the keys to Olivia. "Get the others to the car. I'll be there in a minute." She looked at the red-faced man. "Your office?"

She followed the man to an office near the entrance. She had never spoken to the man before. She sat at his desk. The name plate read W. O'Connor.

"Madam, your accounts are seriously overdue. I have no choice but to suspend your privileges as of today." He handed Janine a billing.

Janine was numb. She did not look at the billing in her hand. She stared at the manager without emotion.

"I'm sorry to do this," said the man, expecting some response.

"Privileges," replied Janine quietly. "Privileges…I'll take it up with my husband when I see him." She rose to leave.

"I'd appreciate that. Please get back to me as soon as possible." The manager reached out a hand to shake hers. She did not respond.

At the door she stopped and faced the man. "Is your first name Wilson?"

He nodded. "Yes, yes it is."

"I thought so."

When she got to the car, the kids were agitated. "Aren't we eating here?" asked Olivia.

"No. How about the chicken place? We'll get a family meal."

Janine picked at her food. Junior and Monica fussed with each other. Olivia ate while studying her mother intently. Aware that her eldest was focused on her, Janine tried not to make eye contact.

At the Quick-Mart, Janine bought milk, soda, batteries for the flashlights, ice for the cooler, and cereal. By the time they returned to the house the shadows were falling.

Janine settled into a chair on the rear patio. The wind brought the rustle of dry leaves. The yard was quiet. She surveyed the yard remembering the children playing, the BBQs. As the sunlight faded, the clouds took on a pink hue. She sat immersed in memories until it was dark.

The kids were playing a game of Monopoly in the front room. Olivia invited her mother to play. Janine declined and sat in a chair watching them.

Janine was roused from sleep by a thunderclap. The wind was blowing the drapes wildly. Flashes of lightning showed the kids draped on the furniture sleeping soundly. She moved to the window to close it a little.

She noticed a strange car parked at the end of the drive. She went out the front door to scrutinize the car. The car started. The headlights came on, blinding her. The car drove away.

She turned back to the house. The lightning reflected off the eviction sign. She went back in and locked the door. She went up to her bedroom. The lightning illuminated her room in flashes. She sat down on the bed. She put her hands to her face. She began to weep.

EVICTION

"Mom, Mom, wake up." Olivia shook her gently. "Mom, we're going to be late for school."

Janine roused. She had fallen asleep on her own bed. "Okay," she said automatically.

The kids were having cereal in the kitchen.

"No school today," she said with as much composure as she could muster. "I need you here with me today."

The kids froze. "Are you sure, Mom?" asked Olivia.

"Yes, I'm sure."

A knock and "Hello" came from the front door.

"Who is it, Mom?" asked Monica.

"I don't know. Let's look."

At the door was a grey-haired man. He was vaguely familiar to Janine.

"Oh, hi. I'm glad I caught you. They've been delivering all your mail and legal papers to me again." He pointed to two boxes with assorted mail. "I wanted to get it to you before…"

Janine stepped out onto the porch. She remembered that the man had stopped by before with some mail misdirected to him. "All this is for us. How did that happen?"

"Well, we have the same last name and the same street address," said the man apologetically. "This guy came with some papers. My first initial is B., B. Eric Piersen. I thought the papers were for me. After Peggy died, I haven't been myself. I didn't realize the papers were for you 'till after he'd left. I came over here, but you've been gone for weeks. More guys served me papers and then the post office forwarded all your mail because of the…notice."

Just then Saundra pulled up. She got out of her car with two coffees. She came up on the porch and looked at the boxes of mail. "What's this?" She handed Janine a cup.

Janine focused back on the man. "Papers? What papers?"

The man reached down and handed her a packet of legal papers. Saundra moved around to look over Janine's shoulder. One packet was a demand for forfeiture of the property. Two were a bank's demands. All of them were in Janine's name. She had a sinking feeling.

Janine walked into the house, stunned. She clutched the papers in her hand.

"Where do you…" The man picked up a box and followed. He stacked both boxes in the front hall.

Janine and Saundra sat on the couch looking at notice after notice, demand after demand.

The man asked Olivia, "Where are you going?"

Olivia shrugged her shoulders. "I don't know."

A sheriff's deputy appeared at the door. She was middle aged, dressed in black with a vest, monitor, gun belt, and large star. She stood sideways, left hand out with papers. Her right hand, back, resting on her pistol. "You Mr. Brent…" She looked back at the paperwork.

"No," said the grey-haired man. "But his wife's over there." He pointed to the front room. He stepped back into the hall.

The deputy stepped slowly into the hall. Another deputy stepped in behind her. He, too, had a hand on his pistol.

"Are you Ms. Janice Piersen?"

"It's Janine. But yes, it's me."

"I'm here to execute the eviction." She thrust papers into Janine's hand. "Why don't you and your family gather up what you're going to take with you? I need you and your family out of the house in fifteen minutes." She looked around the room. "Okay?" She turned and left.

Janine sat immobile, staring at the eviction papers. Saundra sat staring at Janine.

"Kids," said the white-haired man, "go gather up everything you need that you can carry. Put it in a backpack or something. Quickly, go!"

"Ladies!" said the white-haired man. "Go gather up important family things. Pictures, papers, whatever." He emptied the mail into one box. "Here use this. Get it out of the house now!"

Janine and Saundra were suddenly brought to life. The white-haired man watched them go upstairs. He picked up all the legal papers, stuffed them in his box. He carried the box back to his car. He watched as a county van pulled up. The doors opened and seven men with orange vests got out. A pickup truck appeared towing a portable toilet trailer. A local police car pulled up with two officers. Several people gathered across the street.

The grey-haired man watched it all while leaning on his car. "The circus is in town." He checked his watch. The cops had given them fifteen minutes.

The two deputies reentered the house. "Alright, let's go! Everybody out!"

The grey-haired man moved to the doorway to help Monica. She had a large stuffed giraffe that kept falling. He helped her put her things by his car.

"Geoffrey can't sit in the grass," complained Monica.

"Okay," said the man. "Let's put him in the back seat of the car." He opened the door and helped her place the doll on the seat. "He'll be safe there."

Janine and Saundra carried armfuls of clothes to Janine's car. Janine ran back in for a box. She put the box in her car. She leaned on the hood and wept. Monica and Olivia held her and cried. Brent Junior stood silently and watched as the workers moved the furniture out of the house.

Saundra walked over to the grey-haired man. "I'm sorry. I'm Saundra."

"Eric," said the white-haired man. "I use my middle name. It's Broadrick Eric actually. Aren't they going to try to save anything? Why don't they get a truck and a storage space?"

"She doesn't have any money. Her rat of a husband left them penniless."

"Where are they going to go?" asked Eric.

"I don't think they know. They can't stay with me."

"I'm going to get a truck," said Eric. "We can save some of this stuff."

Janine, Saundra, Olivia, and Monica sat in the grass crying while the house was emptied out. Brent sat silently nearby.

It seemed like a long time had passed until Eric returned with a truck. He backed the truck up on the grass. He pulled out a ramp. He opened up the rear of the truck. He came over to Janine. "Pick out the things you really need and let's put them on the truck."

Janine looked at Eric and moved her hands in frustration. Her mouth opened but no words came out.

"Where are they going to go?" asked Saundra.

"Look," said Eric, "they can stay with me for now. We'll figure something out later. Right now, we have to save what we can. The scavengers will be here by nightfall."

Eric looked at Janine and Saundra who sat immobile. Eric shook his head in impatience. "I'll go talk to the deputy."

Saundra looked Janine in the face. She wiped away tears from her eyes. "Honey, let's try to save something?" Getting no response from Janine, Saundra got up. "Come on, kids. Let's decide what we can keep."

Saundra found Eric engaging with the female deputy.

"...Look, Officer. I know that they're on community service. But if they clear out the house early let them work for me until they have to go. You don't have to be party to the negotiations. This poor lady and her kids have been abandoned. Give them a break. They will not interfere with the job you have to do. Let me buy everyone lunch?"

The two deputies moved off to consult.

"Do you think she'll cooperate?" Saundra asked Eric.

"We can only hope."

The female deputy came over. "Okay. They work for me until the house is empty. What they do on breaks is their business. We leave here at 3:30 sharp. No issues: you got me?" The deputies moved away.

Eric and Saundra went into the now empty front room. Eric addressed the laborers. "Hey guys. If you hustle all the things out of the house, and there is time, I'll pay everyone $100 to load my truck. The deputy said you're leaving at 3:30." Eric opened his wallet. He pulled out several $100 bills. "Anyone who'll help me gets one of these."

Eric put his wallet away and strode out of the house. Saundra caught up with him by the truck.

"That was something," Saundra said. "What can I do?"

"Take lunch orders for a really good take-out place," said Eric. "Get the cops whatever they want."

While Saundra dealt with food issues, Eric had the kids put Janine's clothes in the car. Eric directed items near the truck if he thought it was worth saving. All the while Janine sat immobile, watching.

When Saundra returned, she began passing out cold water. When she offered a bottle to the female deputy, she reluctantly accepted. "I don't like this, you know. Nobody likes this. It was my turn." She looked in the doorway. "This must be hard for them."

Janine sat silently watching as her possessions accumulated on the lawn. When she saw Eric and her son trying to load a mattress on the truck, she roused. She came over and helped the boy push the load on the truck. Suddenly she became part of the team.

"What's next?" she asked Eric.

"We'll need beds and dressers. We can put TVs in, last on top. You decide if anything is too important to leave," said Eric. "Right now, see about clothes. Get some of yours and the kids in your car."

Janine began rifling through piles of clothes.

"Okay! Lunch break!" called out the deputy.

As the crew collapsed on the furniture they'd put on the lawn, Saundra gave them lunches. They ate gratefully.

Janine fell into tears again.

Two men went over to Eric. "Is the deal still on?"

Eric held up two $100 bills.

"Can we eat as we go?"

Eric nodded. He directed them to load a couple of dressers. Three of the other five joined in. Eric directed the loading. They kept loading. Janine pointed to an antique dresser. Eric helped her load it onto the truck.

Eric finally told the workers to stop. "I don't think we can take any more. Thanks. Good luck." He gave each that helped a $100 bill. He then gave the other two $50. "Thanks for what you did."

Eric was thanking the officers when Chase pulled up. He jumped out of the car to confront Saundra. "What the hell are you doing here? I told you to stay away from them. Do you have any idea what…?"

The male deputy moved up next to Saundra interrupting, "Sir, I'm going to ask you calm down."

Chase glared at the officer. "I don't give a rat's ass…"

"Sir!" said the deputy. Now, all the uniformed officers were there. "Sir, I am obligated to keep peace at this site. It doesn't really matter who I arrest." The officer stared at Chase. "It's been a peaceful day here. This lady has helped this family at a time of need. Please don't make me arrest you. Why don't you get back in your car and leave?"

Chase was red faced. He looked at the faces of the officers. They all had a hand on a pistol. He slowly put up his hands. "Okay. Okay." He returned to his car and drove away.

The female deputy looked at Saundra. "Are you going to be alright, honey?"

Saundra shook her head. "Yeah, I'll be alright."

"Okay. We've got to go."

As the county crew left Janine, Saundra and the kids hugged. Saundra led them over to the front room sectional now parked on the lawn. When they sat, Janine became aware of the people gathered across the street. Although they gawked no one came over.

Eric joined them on the couch. He surveyed the belongings strewn across the lawn. He looked at Janine.

"What do we do now?" Janine asked the man.

"Well…I guess we go to my house," said Eric. "We'll figure things out later."

"I'll follow," said Saundra. "We'll have to unload my car before I go home."

Eric looked at Brent Jr. He was sitting quietly. "Young man, why don't you help me secure the truck. You can ride with me, okay?"

Brent nodded.

Janine followed the truck. Her girls were barely visible amid the piles of clothes. The truck turned and headed across the invisible border from the suburb into Chicago. The truck turned on a street with a familiar name. It pulled up in front of a ranch-style home like all the others on the block.

Eric got out of the truck and motioned Saundra into the driveway. He propped open the front door. Saundra and Eric began the parade of trips from her car. Eric directed them to stack the clothes in a side bedroom. In a few minutes her car was empty.

Saundra and Janine met in the front room. "I'm so sorry, Jan," she said, hugging her. "I'd take you in if I could. You know that."

"I do know that. Thank you for the help. I'll never forget," said Janine, hugging her. "Will you be alright?"

"Yeah. Good luck."

Eric looked at Saundra. "I need you to drop me at the truck place to retrieve my car."

Eric got in Saundra's car. The woman was weeping.

"Will you be alright? Your husband was…furious."

"I'll survive," said Saundra. "It's a good thing you showed up when you did. Will they be alright?"

Eric was silent for a minute. "Their odyssey is only beginning. It will either make or break their spirits."

Saundra reflected for a minute. "If Chase throws me out, can I come stay with you?"

"Ha," said Eric with a laugh. "Sure. Why not?"

SHELTER AND REASSURANCE

When Eric returned, he found them sitting in the front room. Eric produced the stuffed giraffe and handed it to Monica. "He said he missed you." She hugged the toy.

"Alright," said Eric cheerfully, "I put a casserole in the oven. It won't be done for a while. But first we have something to do." He looked into Janine's eyes. "This is important."

Eric moved a small table into the center of the room. He took a large candle and holder from the mantle. He lit the candle in the middle of the table.

"Okay, everyone. It's the truth circle." Eric motioned them to their feet. "Now hold hands in a circle. C'mon."

"Now everyone close your eyes and take a deep breath. Exhale slowly. Now breathe again. Exhale again. Now repeat after me: I am homeless. It is not my fault."

They hesitated. He insisted. "Say it. I am homeless. It is not my fault." They repeated it. They continued:

I am homeless. It is not my fault. We love each other. We trust each other.

Brent has deserted us. It is not my fault. We love each other. We trust each other.

Somethings will change. It is not my fault. We love each other. We trust each other.

Some people will not like us. It is not my fault. We love each other. We trust each other.

I am homeless. It is not my fault. We love each other. We trust each other.

Eric then added himself to the circle. "I will make a bond with you. So long as you stay in this house, I will do all I can to protect you. I will share what I can with you. We love each other. We trust each other." He kept them there in the circle for some seconds. "So may it be. Let's eat."

Eric doled out casserole for everyone. The kids picked at it. He poured out milk for the kids. Janine opted for a hot tea.

"Where are we all going to sleep?" asked Janine. "Good casserole. You make it?"

"No," replied Eric. "I have a widow lady who's keeping me fed. Look, there's a double bed in my son's room. And there's the couch. We'll have to make do tonight." Eric looked at their faces. "You all look tired. Why don't you all wash up and make sleeping arrangements. I'll clean up."

Eric finished cleaning up in the kitchen. He put a cup of coffee in the microwave. When he went into the front room, Janine and Monica were asleep on the couch. Brent was asleep in a chair. Olivia came out of the bedroom.

"Can I take a shower?" she asked.

"Of course," replied Eric. "Let's see if some of Peggy's clothes will fit you." He led her to Eric's bedroom. He opened a drawer. "I haven't cleared away all her things. If something will fit you, take it." He went to the closet. "Here is a bathrobe." He handed her the robe.

"Thanks," said Olivia. "Thanks for everything." She stepped forward and hugged Eric.

"That's alright," said Eric, hugging back. "Let me know when you're finished. I'm going to have a cup of coffee."

When Olivia finished her shower, she found Eric at the kitchen table. He was using a laptop, an empty cup of coffee nearby.

"Is there more coffee?" asked Olivia. She kept the bathrobe tightly closed.

"Help yourself," said Eric. "I'll take my shower now."

"Can I use your computer? I've been off-line for a while."

"Sure," said Eric. "Let me generate a new user." After a few moments he stood. "It's all yours."

When Eric finished his shower, he plodded to his room. He closed the door. He looked at his late-wife's picture for several seconds. He touched her picture. "Good night, love." He settled down and fell asleep immediately.

PHYLLIS, JANINE'S MOTHER

Eric awoke with a start. He looked at the clock: 4:45. He found his slippers and headed for the bathroom with some urgency. Startled by his bedroom door being closed, he plodded his way, in his underwear, to the bathroom. He was startled again when Janine, wrapped only in a towel, exited the washroom.

"Oops," said Janine, darting into the bedroom.

Eric finished his bathroom routine and retreated to his room. He donned a pair of shorts and a T-shirt. He went to the kitchen. He started a pot of coffee.

Janine came in, now dressed. "Hi, Eric. I'm sorry."

"Nothing to be sorry about."

"Can I join you?" asked Janine.

"I wish you would," said Eric, sitting at the table.

Janine talked as the coffee maker gurgled. "Your truth circle hurt me. I mean, it drove the whole thing home. Brent hurt us. He didn't just hurt me; he hurt his children." She poured out two cups of coffee. "Cream?" She sat down facing Eric. "If you hadn't come along, we'd be on the street. You saved us yesterday and I don't know anything about you. Who are you?"

Eric assessed Janine for a moment. He nodded his head in assent. "Okay. I'm a carpenter. I retired a year early to nurse Peggy, my wife. You met her before when we got your mail. Anyway, she slipped away pretty fast. Now I'm all alone. My son is grown and married. I'm all alone in this house. I've been clearing up and deciding whether to sell the place.

"When I saw you there drowning, I had to do something. A couple of Peggy's friends got deserted over the years. It was totally devastating to their lives." Eric looked at Janine earnestly. "What will you do? Do you have a plan?"

Janine smiled at him. "Eric, thank you, thank you, thank you." She reached out and touched his arm. "You...were a godsend." She looked off and pursed her lips. "I guess I'll have to call my mother and see if she'll help. Other than that, I have an aunt in South Bend. Maybe we'll go there." Janine's attention drifted off.

"Janine," said Eric, bringing her attention back. "We should make some short-term plans." Eric brought out a pad and pencil. "Today you should call your mother and your aunt. Also, you should call Saundra; she was a big help yesterday. You should stop at the post office and see if there's anything else for you. You should get the kids to school yourself."

"Okay," she said. "Anything else?"

"Yes. Long term plans. Your things can stay in the truck for a couple of days. We can access clothes and things later. You need to see a lawyer post haste. You need to protect yourself and the kids."

Janine's eyes welled up. "How can I do that? I don't have any money. You must know that."

"I know," said Eric with a sigh. "I'll stake you the money. You can pay me back later. If your mom can help you, so much the better. But you need some legal protection. Let me call my lawyer."

"What about Brent's lawyer?" she asked. "Oh, maybe not." She touched Eric's arm again. "Anything else?"

"Yes. Is your car leased or do you own it?"

"Leased, I think."

"If it is, they'll want it back soon. Don't leave anything of yours in it. Use it while you can, but the repo-man doesn't care."

By the time Janine roused the kids, Eric had made pancakes for everyone.

She dropped off Monica and Olivia and their schools. She had to take Brent Jr. to see Mrs. Carmichael to get reinstated.

The principal had Brent Jr. wait outside while she met with Janine. "I know that you've been evicted. Here are the resources available from the school district." She handed a piece of paper to Janine. "You are required to keep us informed of your current domicile. I'll reinstate Brent Jr. this time with just a warning. He has no previous incidents on his record. Let's keep it that way. Good morning."

Janine calmly kissed her son. "Everything is going to be alright. Please don't fight. Have a good day."

When Janine closed the car door, her anger boiled over. "Condescending bitch!" she yelled.

Janine stood in line at the post office for an eternity. When she asked for her mail, the clerk asked for her ID. The clerk disappeared into the back. Janine waited for another eternity. When a man with a cart appeared, she gave him no notice. He tapped her on the arm. "Ma'am, do you want your mail or not?" The cart was brimming with mail. He pulled the cart up to her car. He helped load the trays of mail into the car. "Have a good day," he said routinely.

When she returned to Eric's home, she dropped a pile of mail on the couch.

He was on his phone. "Is that it?" he asked.

"Not hardly. There's a ton more in the car."

Eric helped Janine in with the mail. "You were right about that. I think it weighs a ton." They looked at the piles of mail for some seconds. "Let's have a cup of coffee first," said Eric.

Eric poured out two cups of coffee at the kitchen table. Janine collapsed into the chair opposite Eric. "That condescending bitch principal...I had to sit through a lecture about my situation. She'll let it go this time. This time?" She hung her head. "This time?"

"Janine, you will survive."

She focused on Eric across the table from her. She took several breaths, preparing to speak, but could find no words. She closed her eyes and nodded yes. "Okay, I'll survive." She looked into Eric's eyes. "I'd like to call my mother. But I can't."

"No phone?" replied Eric.

"No phone. I grabbed my old phone with my contacts. But I have no service."

"I figured," said Eric. "I charged up my wife's phone for you. I never cancelled the service. Use it for now. We'll figure that out later. I made an appointment with my lawyer for tomorrow. We need to go through the mail and find out where things are at."

She looked quizzically at Eric. "How am I going to pay him?"

"Obviously, I'm going to have to pay him."

"How am I ever going to pay you back?"

Eric sighed. "I don't know." He smiled at her. "Go call your mother. I'll sort mail."

It took almost an hour for Janine to track down her mother. After her mom's story of a pottery class disaster, Janine began her tale. Her mother was silent except for an occasional gasp.

"Janine, honey, your father always thought he was a rat. He did not trust him at all."

"Mom, is there anything you can do to help?"

"Well, dear, I guess I have about $200 in my account. I only get a little a month. I can send it to you."

"Mom, that won't help. We have no place to stay."

"Well dear, you can come here for a week or so. But I don't think you can stay longer. This is a senior's village. There are visitation rules."

"Mom, we've lost everything, and Brent is gone."

"Dear, your trust fund should have plenty to help you out. You just have to see the lawyer."

"Mom, he took that too."

"Well dear, I can't say I didn't expect it. We warned you."

"Mom…"

"Honey, I have to go. It's bridge this afternoon."

When Janine entered the living room, Olivia was helping Eric sort the mail. "When did you get home?"

"Just a few minutes ago. I got dropped off," said the girl. "Is Grandma going to help?"

"No," replied Janine with resignation. "How was school?"

"Terrible," replied Olivia. "Either they avoid me, or they ask what it's like to be evicted. Tomorrow, I have to see a counselor."

The room was silent for some seconds.

"Okay," said Eric. "This pile is for banks and credit cards. These are legal demands. These are catalogs and come-ons." Eric looked at the dejected face of Janine. "Did you get ahold of your aunt?"

"No. I left two messages on her machine."

"Look," said Eric, "let's talk." He motioned Janine to sit. "You won't be going anywhere tonight. We need to unload a couple of mattresses and some of your clothes. We can all pitch in when Monica and Brent Jr. come home. In the meantime, let's start organizing bank statements."

When Janine picked up Brent Jr. from school, he was glum. "I had to see the counselor today. She said I should ignore the other kids calling me names."

"What names?"

"Evicted and homeless."

Janine pulled the car over, turned, and touched her son. "You are evicted and homeless. But you know I love you. We will stick together, okay?"

Brent Jr. gave a reluctant nod. "Okay."

Monica was in tears. Janine got out and hugged her daughter. "It's okay, honey."

"No," blubbered the girl, "it's not. They keep teasing me: Homeless, homeless, homeless. I hate them."

"I know it hurts, dear," Janine said, still hugging the girl. "We can't change the truth. It hurts me too. We have to live with it." She raised her face by the chin. "But we love each other and we're together. Now come on."

At the house Eric organized the kids. They climbed into the truck. They gathered clothes and bedding. Eric and Olivia muscled a double mattress into the house. They set the mattress on the floor of the second bedroom next to his son's bed.

Once they had things removed from the truck, he locked it up again. "Everyone get to their homework," said Eric. "I'll start the grill. We are going to have a picnic in the yard. Hamburgers and hot dogs. After dinner we'll have a family meeting, okay?"

Eric called everyone out to the yard for dinner. He had set up a table and chairs. He had a spread laid out. The sunlight was fading and the breeze was warm. They all seemed to relax for a bit.

"Before we go in, everyone is going to report on the day. Let's start with Monica. How was your day?"

Monica started out talking about how mean the kids were and then broke down into tears. Brent Jr. started talking about all the taunts but abruptly stopped. He was holding back his tears. Olivia recounted her tale of avoidance or uncomfortable questions. She too fought back tears.

Janine tearfully recounted her call to her mother. "We just are not going to get any help from her. I hope Aunt Sarah can help.

"For now," she looked at Eric and smiled, "I hope Eric will help out."

"Okay," said Eric, "it's time for some house rules. I will protect you all as much as I can. If you are somewhere and you need to get out, you call me. No questions asked. I'll come get you. There will be no drinking, smoking, or drugs. If there is, you're out of here. Everyone contributes to the home. There will be chores for everyone. From now on you kids will call me Uncle Eric.

"Tomorrow I will hire some guys. We'll set up dressers and beds here. The rest your things we have to put in storage. Does everybody understand?" Eric looked at all of them. "Okay. Let's circle up."

They stood in a circle. Eric led them. "I am homeless. It is not my fault. We love each other. We care for each other. We trust each other. Brent is gone. It is not my fault. We love each other. We care for each other. We trust each other."

They stood looking at each other for some seconds.

"Okay, chores start now. Uncle Eric says carry all the dinner things into the kitchen. Monica, you get your bath in first. Olivia, help me with the table."

Janine supervised the baths and homework assignments. She came into the front room to find Olivia and Eric sorting papers.

"I think we've finished sorting out the mail and papers," said Eric. "Why don't we grab the important piles and set up at the kitchen table. We can make a list for the lawyer."

The three stacked piles on the table.

"Can I start a cup of tea, Eric...Uncle Eric?'" asked Olivia.

"By all means. Any time you want."

"Where do we start?" said Janine.

"Let's start with the creditors. These have filed actions against you two." Eric put the pile forward.

Monica came in with her giraffe under her arm. "Mommy, can you tuck us in?"

"Of course, pumpkin."

Monica came over to Eric. "Goodnight, Uncle Eric." She reached out and hugged him.

He hugged her back. "Good night, sweetheart." He tweaked the toy's nose. "And good night to you too."

Janine led Monica out.

Olivia sat down opposite Eric. "What's going to happen to us? Are they going to put us in foster care?"

"I don't know what's going to happen," said Eric. "If your mom can find a secure place for you to live, she can keep you together."

"Can we stay with you?"

Eric and Olivia locked eyes for a few seconds. "Your water's boiling."

Olivia rose and poured it into the tea pot.

Janine came in and sat opposite Eric. She looked at her daughter and Eric. "What?"

"Olivia wants to know if you can stay here with me," said Eric. "She's worried that she'll end up in foster care."

"Oh, honey," said Janine.

Olivia brought two cups of tea to the table. She set one in front of Eric. He pushed it over to Janine.

"I don't generally drink tea," said Eric. He pointed Olivia to an empty chair. "Look, this has all happened so fast. I was not thinking of adopting a family. I've been fending off widows." Eric paused. He looked into both sets of eyes. "Your mother and I would have to talk about a lot of things before anything is decided. I wouldn't want you going to foster care. But I don't know that I can support five. We'll have to talk. That's a ways off. Right now, it's your legal situation I'm concerned about."

"Livy, honey, why don't you let us talk?"

"Okay, Mom." She hugged Janine. She came to Eric's side of the table. "You too, Uncle Eric." She hugged him.

Eric and Janine made the lists and decided on the papers she would take to the lawyer.

"I guess we should talk," Janine said.

"I guess we should," replied the man. "I'm going to have a scotch. I have bourbon and brandy. What's your poison?'

"I usually just drink wine, but scotch is fine."

Eric brought two glasses, two waters, and a bottle. "Lady, you're in a heap of trouble. You should understand the options ahead of you. I've given your situation some thought. Firstly, let me say this, I like you and your kids. But if you end up staying here it means big changes for all of us. Let me say this up front, if you can get a better deal somewhere else you should take it. We can square up down the line." Eric sipped his scotch while she nodded her assent.

"Secondly, there is the matter of finances. As I see it you have to do two things. First, you have to get a job."

Janine rocked back in her chair. "Job?"

"Yeah," said Eric, assessing her reaction. "When's the last time you had a job?"

"Well…" she said, biting her lip, "my dad made me work in his office a couple of summers. I was a volunteer lifeguard at school." She looked at Eric and shrugged her shoulders. "I got married right out of college. I didn't have to work."

Eric assessed her for a minute. "Okay. Well, let me say that you did do an admirable job raising your children. They are mannered, respectful, and polite. But getting back to job experience, you have none? Is that correct?"

She shrugged and nodded no.

"Okay, we'll find a starter job." Eric sipped his drink. "Item two. You will have to apply for welfare and food stamps."

Janine closed her eyes and began to weep. "Oh…oh my god. This is a nightmare."

Eric reached out and held her hand. "Yes…yes it is."

As Janine continued to weep, Eric noticed Olivia peeping around the corner. Her eyes met Eric's. He smiled at the girl but spoke to the woman. "Go ahead. Have a good cry. You've earned it."

Janine sat up and extricated her hand from his. "More scotch?"

"Sure," said Eric with a smile. "But let's go to the front room."

Eric and Janine settled on the couch. He poured from the scotch bottle into both their glasses.

"I was a good wife," said Janine. "I stayed fit. I raised our good kids. We belonged to that stinking club. What did he want?" She downed the scotch and poured more. "I kept fit. I exercised. I'm a good-looking woman."

"Yes, you are," replied Eric. "And you have stayed…fit."

"Damned right! How could he do this to me? He left us, he left me! Did you know that?"

"Yes, I did. It's terrible."

Janine drifted off to sleep.

Eric took the glass out of Janine's hand. "Get some sleep." He took the glasses and the bottle to the kitchen.

A crash of thunder and the rumble woke Janine. She had been asleep in a chair in Eric's front room. Another clap of thunder brought a flash of lightning that illuminated the room. Asleep on the couch was a threesome: Eric, Monica, and Geoffrey, the toy giraffe. Eric had his arm around the girl. Monica had her arms around the toy.

Janine's mind was foggy. Her head hurt. Suddenly she was angry. She bounded over and snatched the girl up. "Keep your hands off my daughter!" she snarled.

"What?" said Eric, half asleep.

Another crash of thunder shook the house.

"Mommy," said Monica, waking, "I'm scared."

"It's alright, baby. Mommy's got you." She carried the girl to the bedroom. She hollered back, "Keep your hands off my children."

When Janine awoke, she was alone in the bedroom. The sun was well up. Suddenly she was aware of a blinding headache and hangover. The sunlight hurt her eyes. "Oww."

Janine padded into the kitchen and made for the coffee pot. Olivia had gotten the kids ready for school. "How long do I have?"

"Uncle Eric's going to drop us off, Mom," said Olivia. "You two go get your things." Olivia herded the children out.

Eric began clearing the table.

Janine leaned against the counter. "How much scotch did we have?"

Eric did not answer.

"Look," she said. She focused on Eric. "I'm sorry. That was…that was…"

"It's okay," said Eric. "Why don't you shower and get dressed for the lawyer?"

"Lawyer? Oh shit." She sipped the coffee. "Eric, really, I'm sorry."

"Okay."

THE LAWYER

Janine was shown into an office lined with books. The lawyer, Levi, was middle aged and warm. He sat at his desk while she recounted her tale. He made notes on a large yellow pad. He asked her a few questions to clarify a few points.

When she ended her story, Levi sat back in his chair and gazed upward in thought. For a full minute they were silent. "Missus Piersen."

"Janine, please."

"Janine, let's recap. Your husband of eighteen years has cleaned out all your financial resources. His company has been raided and closed. He has deserted you and your children. You have been evicted. You four are living with Eric, a stranger to you. Is this the situation so far?"

"Yes."

"And," said the lawyer, "in the box you have legal demands?"

"Yes."

He looked Janine in the eye. "What do you want me to do?"

"What?" asked Janine.

"You have to tell me what you want. Do you want a divorce? Do you want to keep your children? Do you want support? I need you to direct me."

"I don't know what to do," she said with tears. "I need you to tell me what to do. I must keep my children. I guess that means…divorcing Brent? He left us. He stuck me with this mess. He deserted me."

"Alright," said the lawyer. "It sounds like your husband left you with his debts. We must separate you and your children from your husband's liabilities. You will have to do several things to accomplish that. First, you have to legally separate with the intent to divorce. Secondly, you will probably have to declare bankruptcy. You say you've been evicted; are you going to a shelter?"

"For now, Eric has taken us in."

"I am concerned about you keeping your children. You will have to reestablish residency to ensure the state won't take your children. If your friend can keep you, you'll be safer. The state will do what the state wants."

"Another thing," asked the lawyer, "you did report your husband missing, didn't you?"

"No. It never occurred to me."

"You had better do that right away." Levi looked at her sympathetically. "You have had a tidal wave come down on you. You are holding up pretty well. Your friends are helping you. That's good. It's probably going to seem a lot worse in the future, but I think you're going to be alright.

"I have other appointments to deal with. We will contact you next week when I have examined your box full of documents." Levi rose. "Your assignments are this: a missing person's report and establishing a residence."

Back in the car Janine turned the phone on. There was a missed call from Saundra. When she called, her friend picked up. "Jan, honey, are you alright?"

"Okay, I guess. I'm just leaving the lawyer's."

"Well, tell me all about it tomorrow. We'll have an early lunch and a foursome at the club. I gotta go, bye."

Janine returned to the house. Eric had given her his wife's keys. She found Monica's dresser and single bed set up. The dresser from Eric's son was empty and open. In the bedroom opposite, Brent Jr.'s bed and dresser was in place. She sat on Brent Jr.'s bed and called Eric.

"Eric," she said, "how did you get all this done?"

"What, the beds and dressers? I hired day laborers. We're putting the last of your things in a storage space now. I'll be home in the next few hours. Can you pick up the kids?"

"Sure. Okay."

Janine drove back to their old house. She parked at the curb. There were work vans in the drive. On the lawn was a sign, Foreclosed-Bank Sale.

Janine drove to the police station. She waited until an officer was free.

"Missing person," said the officer, showing her to a cubicle. He fed her information into a terminal. "Brent Sr., you say. Hmm…" He read the screen before looking at her. "Can I see your identification, please?"

"Well, Janine," the officer said. "Your husband is a wanted man." He assessed her reaction.

"Well, Officer," she said as matter-of-factly as she could, "he's wanted at home with his family." Janine struggled with her composure. "Officer, my lawyer insists I file a missing person report. Can we just do that?"

"Sure, when did you see him last?"

"When?" Her mind went blank.

"When? Did he leave the house and not come back?"

"No, no. We were in the Wisconsin Dells. It was six days ago."

"And you haven't seen or heard from him since?"

"No. I think he wanted it that way."

The officer assessed her for another few seconds. "And this is your current address?" He held up her ID.

"Yes, I mean, no…We've been evicted."

"Where can we reach you?" He handed her the ID.

Unable to control her tears any longer, she blubbered Eric's address.

"Ma'am, can I put you with one of our Community Service officers?"

The officer escorted Janine to another cubicle. "Ms. Wilson will help you."

The woman had files stacked deep on her desk. "Ah, I saw the notice of your eviction. Have you found accommodation anywhere?"

"I'm staying with a friend," said Janine tearfully.

"Do you need to find a shelter?" she asked as she shuffled files. "Just you?"

"No, my son and daughters too."

"Ooh, a son. If it was all girls, it would be easier. A son? Let's see?" She talked as she accessed her computer. "Family shelter...family of four...one son, two daughters...ah ha." She pursed her lips and addressed Janine. "Well, there is room in a shelter downstate. I don't recommend it. In the six-county area, not at this time. I can put you on a waiting list, but it could be months."

"Months?" said Janine. "Sure, go ahead."

When Janine finished at the police station, she picked up the kids from school, and she was determined to remain upbeat. All three of her children had seen their school counselors and all three wanted a parent meeting.

A man was waiting as she parked the car. "Are you Janice Piersen?"

"Janine Piersen."

"Yeah, Janine." The man thrust papers into her hands. "Just sign here."

She did and he handed her the papers.

As they entered the front room, Eric was snoozing in a chair. She put a finger to her lips and the children crept past.

Janine kept her children in the kitchen talking while she organized dinner. She dispatched Monica to wake Uncle Eric for dinner.

Janine did not recount her meeting with the lawyer to the kids. She kept the conversation light. She had the kids thank Uncle Eric for the beds and dressers. After dinner she banished all the children from the kitchen. She poured out coffee for her and Eric.

Janine spoke quietly to Eric recounting all the day's happenings. He listened without comment or reaction. She spoke with urgency about retaining her children. She spoke of the pain of divorce.

All the time Eric listened. When she stopped, he took a deep breath. "Janine, I don't see how you can get around divorcing Brent. He screwed you and the kids big time.

"You must keep your children together. You should go down to South Bend and see if your aunt can take you in. If not..." Eric broke his gaze. "If not, we could set up an agreement for you to stay here. There would have to be conditions."

"Conditions? What kind of conditions?"

"Well, for one you'd have to get a job or some kind of income. But let's see what your aunt says."

"Okay. Tomorrow I'd like to have lunch with Saundra. We're playing tennis at the club."

"Okay with me."

THE LAST TENNIS GAME

Janine met Saundra in the country club lot. Saundra signed her in, and they went to the courts. Char and Denise met them there. Saundra agreed to partner with Janine. Janine noticed several people averted their eyes.

After the game and a shower, Janine headed for the dining room. Saundra was waiting. She led her to a table near the corner. "Let's sit here," said Saundra.

Janine looked for the other girls.

"They're not coming," said Saundra. "They left while you were in the shower. What's going on? Tell me everything."

Over salads and iced tea, Janine recounted her visits to the lawyer and police station. Saundra listened intently.

"You are going to divorce him," stated Saundra emphatically. "He robbed you blind. And he abandoned you." She hesitated for a few seconds. "Did you say he's a wanted man?"

"That's what the police said."

"I know that Chase and his partners are circling the wagons over this. I don't know how Chase is involved, but they took lawyers to an FBI interview."

It seemed like everyone in the dining room took turns staring at them. Janine barely tasted the food.

In the parking lot Janine's car was being loaded on a tow vehicle. The "repo" man watched her approach warily. "I don't want any trouble, lady. I got orders to repo this car."

When she dug in her purse the man froze. She pulled out her key ring and removed the car key. "Here." She threw him the key.

She felt Saundra's hand on her shoulder. "C'mon, honey. I'll drive you home."

Olivia came in as Eric was readying for the school pickup run. "You're early," he said.

"I got dropped off," she said. "I'm going to take a quick shower while you're gone."

"Okay."

Ten minutes after Eric left and five minutes into Olivia's shower, Eric's son Paul let himself in the front door. Hearing the water running he called out, "Dad!"

Startled, Olivia let out a yelp. "Don't come in here! I'll scream!"

Paul, now totally confused, repeated, "Dad?" He peaked in his former bedroom. There were now two beds and multiple dressers. He walked into his father's room. This looked normal. He walked back toward the bathroom where he ran into a girl in a bathrobe and towel. "Who are you?"

"Olivia. Who are you?"

"This is my father's house. Why are you here?"

"You're Uncle Eric's son?"

"Uncle Eric? Okay, he's my dad? Where is he?"

"He's picking up the kids from school."

"Kids? What kids?"

"Your dad…"

Just then Janine came through the door, pushed past Oliva and Paul, and disappeared into the bedroom.

Saundra came in and closed the door. She assessed Olivia in bathrobe and towel. "Olivia, who's your friend?"

"What's going on?" said Paul, exasperated. "What are you doing in my dad's house?"

"Oh," said Saundra. "You must be Eric's son. It is a pleasure to meet you. I'm Saundra."

"O…kay," said Paul.

Olivia pushed past Paul and disappeared into the bedroom. "Excuse me."

The front door opened, and Monica bounded in. She ran up and hugged Saundra. Brent Jr. and Eric followed.

"Paul!" greeted Eric. "It's good to see you son."

"Dad…who are all these people?"

"These are the people who got evicted," said Eric. "That's Monica. That's Brent Jr. I see you've met Saundra. She's not staying here."

"Dad?" said Paul calmly. "What are they doing here?"

"Right now," said the man calmly, "they're living here."

"Dad, what are you doing?"

"I'm helping. You were worried that I needed something to do?"

Exasperated, Paul pulled his father into his bedroom. Paul closed the door.

Janine came out of the bedroom. Saundra was still in the hall. "What's going on?"

Saundra nodded toward Eric's bedroom. "Family drama." She pulled Janine toward the front room. "Come on."

The women sat in the front while Eric and Paul argued in the bedroom. The kids came out and sat around their mother. "Will we have to go?" asked Monica.

"I don't know, honey."

Eric led his son out of the room. "You were impolite to these people. You should apologize."

"I…ah," said Paul.

Monica sprang from the couch and hugged Paul's leg. "Don't make us leave."

"Mon," said Janine with a gasp.

"Hello," said Paul. He reached down and touched the girl's head. "You must be Monica." He came down to her level. He looked her in the eye and touched her shoulder. He smiled. "You want to stay here with my dad?"

"We're so thankful to your dad," said Janine. "It is just temporary. We should be moving in with my aunt soon."

Just then the doorbell rang. Brent Jr. bounced up and opened the door.

"Hello, Brent. Is Saundra here?" Chase stepped into the front room. He was clearly angry and had fire in his eyes. "Saundra, I told you to stay away from these people!" He stepped forward to confront the woman.

Eric rose and stepped in front of the angry man. "Just a minute. You don't come into my house and threaten anyone." Eric stared back.

"Outta my way!"

Now Paul stepped up behind his father. "Really? Not here. I'm going to ask you to leave now."

Chase stepped back. "Saundra, this isn't over."

Chase stormed out.

Eric looked at Saundra. "Are you going to be okay? We'll find room here if we have to."

"I'm so sorry," said Saundra tearfully. "I'll be okay. Really." She wiped her eyes. "Jan, I'm so sorry about today. I should go." She picked up her purse. She hugged Janine and the kids. "I should go." She moved to the door.

"Are you sure you'll be okay?" said Eric. "We can find room for you too."

Saundra waved and left.

"It sure is exciting here, Dad," said Paul. "I thought your life was dull."

"Well, that was the excitement for the day," said Eric. He looked at Janine. She was still in tears. "What did happen today?"

Janine was crying and wiped her nose. "Everyone at the club hates me. No one talked to me. And then…and then…and they took the car."

"What?" asked Eric.

Janine put her head back and looked at the ceiling. "They repoed my car. Did you know that? Right there at the country club." Janine hesitated. "That'll give those bitches something to talk about…repoed… right there."

Eric, Paul, and the kids sat quietly trying to understand Janine's story.

"Who took the car?" asked Eric. "The repo-man?"

Janine nodded yes. The kids hugged their mother.

Paul and his father looked at each other for a few seconds. Eric broke the silence. "So, do you want to stay for dinner?"

AUNT SARAH

It was early Saturday morning when they set out for South Bend. Eric's sedan seemed cramped with five, although the youngest children were small.

Janine felt comfortable with Eric's driving. He was less aggressive than her husband. He did play classic sixties music, which she found comforting. Eric was beginning to remind her of her father.

The children seemed agitated and restless in the back seat. It took Janine a while to realize that they had never been in the car without their phones or iPads.

Three plus hours and a rest stop later, Janine guided them to Aunt Sarah's house. The property looked a bit untidy, and the house needed paint. Not the bright, gleaming place she remembered.

Janine bounded from the car and up on the porch. She rang the bell and waited breathlessly. She rang again. Finally, an elderly figure approached the door. The woman who opened the door was not Sarah. "Yes?"

"Is Sarah here?" she asked, peering behind the woman. "I'm her niece, Janine."

"You want Sarah," said the elderly woman. "You're her niece, you say?"

"Yes. I'm her niece, Janine."

"Oh, you'd better come in." The woman opened the door.

Janine stepped into a house that was familiar and yet strange. The house had a musty and an antiseptic smell. "Is Aunt Sarah here?"

"Yes, yes," said the woman. "I'll get her."

Janine's excitement at seeing her aunt was beginning to sour. She could hear the two women talking in the bedroom. Finally, Sarah came out.

Aunt Sarah was dressed in a faded, torn bath robe. Her hair was wild, grey, and frizzy. She was clutching a framed photograph to her chest. "My niece. My niece Janine." She scanned the room not recognizing her.

"Aunt Sarah, it's me, Janine." She hugged her aunt.

Sarah looked at her relative without recognition. "You are not my niece." She showed Janine's framed high school photograph. She pointed to the picture. "This is my niece." She retreated to the bedroom.

Janine looked at her children and Eric in exasperation.

"This can't be good," said Olivia.

They could hear someone on the porch. The door opened. "Who's here? Who's in here? I'm calling the police."

"It's Janine, Sarah's niece."

The woman stepped into the room. She was in her sixties. Her greying hair was cut short. She was stocky. She held a bag of groceries. "Cousin Janine," she said ironically. "What brings you here?"

It took Janine a second to recognize Aunt Sarah's cousin. "Naomi? Is that you?"

"That's right."

Janine rose to hug the woman. She recoiled. "You've got a lot of nerve coming here," said Naomi. "After all this time."

"What's going on?" said Janine. "What happened to Aunt Sarah?"

"You did it to her, robbing her that way."

"What? I didn't rob anyone."

Sirens preceded a police officer at the door. "What's going here?"

"That's her," said Naomi, pointing at Janine. "That's the thief!"

"Ma'am, is that right?" asked the officer. "Are you Janine Piersen, Sarah's niece?"

"Yes, yes I am."

"I'm placing you under arrest. You have the right to remain silent…"

"Mommy, Mommy," cried Monica, hugging her mother's leg.

"What's going on?" asked Janine.

"Monica," said Eric, calmly pulling the girl back. "We have to let the policeman do his job." He wrapped his arms around the girl. "Kids, why don't you go wait in the car." He looked at Olivia and motioned toward the door.

"Let's go, lady," said the officer, pushing Janine out.

Eric looked at Naomi. "Please tell me what happened here? I'm trying to understand."

"She's a thief, that's what," said Naomi haughtily. "And who are you anyway?"

"What is this all about?" implored Janine. The officer pushed her into his squad car. We closed the door. She found herself in a virtual cage. She saw Monica and Brent Jr. crying. Olivia moved them to the car.

"Officer?" implored Janine.

"Tell it to the judge," he said. He called in on his radio, but she could not focus on the words.

With her hands cuffed behind her, tears rolled down her face. All she could see was the image of her crying children. Detached from all feeling, she let the policeman push her wherever he wanted.

"Put your fingers on the card one at a time," came a distant voice.

"What?" Janine suddenly became conscious.

"Your fingers. On the card, please." The officer grabbed her hands and pressed her inked fingers on a card. He handed her a wipe. He pushed her toward the wall. He took pictures of her front and side. "Okay, lady."

She was led to a holding cell. The cell smelled of urine and disinfectant. A woman snoozed on the bench head back.

Janine perched on the steel bench waiting for something to happen. Her heart and head pounded. Her mouth was dry. This was a nightmare. Suddenly she realized she had to urinate. The urge was growing. There was a steel toilet on the back wall. No walls. No privacy. She waited as long as she could. Finally, she could wait no longer. She pulled down her pants and panties, hovered over the steel seat, and peed. There was some paper. She struggled to dress. She returned to her perch.

Finally, an ununiformed female came to the cage. "You, come with me." She was led to an interrogation room. "Sit," said the woman.

A man came in and sat down. He, too, was wearing a badge on a lanyard. "I'm Detective Wilson." He pointed to the woman officer. "That's Sargent Jones."

Wilson opened a file. "It says here that you authorized the transfer of funds from your Aunt Sarah's accounts without your Cousin Naomi's consent. You drained away the old woman's funds."

"I did not," said Janine. "What money? I never touched her money." She looked into the eyes of the detectives. "This is some sort of mistake."

Officer Jones spoke next. "We have authorizations with Naomi's forged signature on them." She placed a plastic enclosed document on the table.

Janine picked up the document. "I've never seen this before." She looked at both officers. "You have to believe me. I have never seen this."

Detective Wilson leaned toward her. "Well, if you didn't sign this, who did?"

Suddenly, Janine knew the architect of this fraud. "Oh my god, he got her too." She hung her head and began to cry. "It was my husband, Brent. He and his company cheated everyone in Chicago. He cleaned out all our assets." She pulled out a Kleenex and wiped her eyes. "He took everything and left me and the kids. I've been evicted for god's sake. He must have forged this…thing."

"Your husband?" asked Officer Jones. "Isn't he with your children?"

"What? No, that's Eric. He's a friend."

"What was the name of your husband's company?"

"Gawn Associates."

Detective Wilson rose. "I'll be back in a minute."

After half an hour Detective Wilson called Officer Jones out of the room. The two returned after a few minutes. "Ms. Piersen, how can we contact your friend, Eric?" asked Wilson.

"You have my phone. He's speed dial #2."

After twenty minutes Eric came in.

"Eric, thank God. Are the kids alright?"

"They're alright," said Eric.

Detective Wilson cleared his throat. "Ms. Piersen, tell me about the transfers from your aunt's account?"

"I don't know. I wouldn't take her money. Brent must have scammed her too." She broke down into weeping. "If I ever catch him, I'll…" More weeping.

"Janine," said Eric calmly. "They want to release you into my custody. We will have to stay here until at least Monday. We have to meet some people. But if we stay in town, you can be out of the jail. Is that okay?"

"We can go?"

"I'll get us a couple of rooms at a motel. I'll get us some things at Walmart. But…" Eric handed her a tissue. "It will take some time to process. They will drop you off later. Okay?"

Officer Jones escorted Janine back to the holding cell. She perched on the bench and waited.

An eternity passed before Officer Jones came for Janine. "C'mon, honey. Let's go."

Eric was waiting at the desk when they entered. He wrapped his arms around her.

"Alright, sir," said Wilson, "she's yours. Don't let her leave the motel. Okay?"

When she got to the car, she froze. "Where are my children?"

"I left them at the pool. Olivia's got her eye on them."

As Eric began to drive Janine's mind kicked into gear. "They went swimming? They don't have suits."

"They do now."

She began to weep. "I'm so…I'm so…"

"Ashamed?"

"My kids saw me arrested."

"Yes, they did," said Eric. "I talked to Naomi after you left. I think Brent cleaned them out."

"I know he did. How could he do that? How could I be so stupid?" She snuffled for a second. "What do I tell the kids?"

"The truth. You have to. It may get worse."

"Yeah," she said. She looked at Eric for a few seconds. "Hey, you've been really good about all this." She reached out and touched his arm. "Thank you."

Eric smiled at her. He thought for a moment before replying. "My wife had a friend whose marriage broke up badly. He threw her out in the middle of the night in a snowstorm. I picked her up and we let her stay for a while. He would call and they would talk. Eventually she went back. The next time he beat her up. We took her to the emergency room. We helped her file for divorce and a protection order. She went to live at a shelter." He paused. "He followed her from a court hearing and shot her." He paused again. "I owe it to her to help you."

After a few seconds Eric said, "The kids had some dinner. Are you hungry?"

"I'm starving. I haven't eaten since this morning. Is that a Steak & Shake?"

Janine was met with a group hug when she entered the motel room. "You guys. I love you so much." She smelled Brent Jr.'s hair. "But you all smell like the pool. Baths for everyone."

"But Mom, are you okay?" asked Olivia. "With the arrest and all?"

Janine explained that there had been a misunderstanding. She believed that Brent had stolen some money. She would have to stay in South Bend until Monday for a court appearance.

"Can we stay here until then?" asked Brent Jr. "The pool is really neat. You can swim outside or inside."

Janine had not considered the situation.

"Sure," said Eric. "It's my treat. We'll stay here. I have the next room." He nodded toward the door adjoining the suites.

"Alright, everybody get your baths in. Eric, can Brent bathe in your room?"

"Sure."

Janine awoke on the couch with Monica in the crook of her arm. Exhausted from the day's commotion, she had drifted off to sleep. Olivia was watching the TV. The clock radio said 2:45 a.m.

"What are you watching?"

"This guy who paints landscapes with putty knives. He has this weird afro hair."

"I've seen him. He's good." Janine picked up Monica and put her on the bed. "Where's Brent?"

"He's in Uncle Eric's room. He declared it men only."

Janine crept into the other suite. Brent Jr. had been watching the TV. He was asleep on the floor. She picked him up and put him on the empty bed.

Eric slept in the second bed.

She crept out.

"Livy, are you okay?" she asked her daughter.

"Mom," said the girl, "did Dad steal the money?"

"I don't know," came her automatic response. She looked into her daughter's imploring look. "Yes, I think so."

"I'm sorry," said Olivia. "I don't understand." She struggled for words. "You trusted him, didn't you?"

"I did."

"How do you know who to trust?"

"Honey...I really don't know."

Olivia thought for a minute. "Can we trust Uncle Eric?"

Janine let out a sigh. "Well, I guess right now we have to." She hesitated for a minute. "Why? Did he do something?"

Olivia smiled at her mother. "No. Nothing like that. He's been nice like a grandpa."

Janine thought for a second. "Yes, he has. Now I'm going to bed."

Eric ushered everyone to the complimentary breakfast area. When they were all seated Eric addressed them.

"We are going to a ballgame at one o'clock. I called and reserved us tickets. We should be back in the early evening, so we can go swimming then."

"The Cubs," said Brent Jr., surprised. "I've been to Wrigley Field."

"No," said Eric. "The South Bend Cubs. Minor league ball." He looked around the table at the lack of interest. "C'mon. It will do us some good to get away from things for a couple of hours."

"Alright, kids," said Janine, cutting off any discussion. "If Uncle Eric wants us to go to a ball game, we owe him that much."

Eric seated them on a bench at the ballpark. He handed each of the kids $10. "Go explore the park. We'll be here."

The youngest kids got up, but Olivia hesitated. "You kids stay together. Olivia is in charge," said Janine. Olivia reluctantly led the kids to the concourse.

Initially, Janine had sat apart from Eric. Now she slid over next to him. Eric was watching the players.

"Why are we here?" she asked.

"For the next couple of hours there are no troubles. There is just the ball game. No one knows you here. No one cares. Just relax. Let your guard down." He looked at her askance. "It's a beautiful day. Just enjoy."

Janine let her mind wander. At first, she relived the jail cell experience. Then she recalled how Aunt Sarah seemed addled. The cheering and clapping of the crowd caught her attention. Men were running around the bases and the cheering went on. She looked at Eric.

"You've been gone a long time," he said.

"What? Where are the kids?"

"They were here a few minutes ago. They're fine."

"I guess I...zoned out."

"I'll say," he said with a laugh.

"Eric, did you and Livy have some sort of conversation?" She hesitated. "I mean...You got her in a swimsuit."

Eric spoke while watching the ballgame. "Yeah. We needed overnight things. I thought that we'd all like to use the pool. Good catch. Yeah, I told Olivia that I needed her to step up. We needed her to lifeguard the kids. She helped me pick out suits for everyone. Catch it, catch it...yeah. We had to guess at your size."

"She doesn't like swimming."

Eric looked at her over his glasses. He smiled at her. "Are you hungry? Pizza? Hot Dog?"

"No thanks, not right now."

Eric's attention returned to the game.

Her thoughts turned toward Eric. What's his deal? Brent seldom talked to Livy. Brent, that bastard.

"Mom? Mom!" Brent Jr. was in front of her.

"Yes, Brent?"

The boy held out a baseball. "I got a foul ball," he said excitedly.

"Oh, that's great," she said, hugging the boy.

A cheer came from the crowd.

Eric was clapping. "Well, that's it. We won."

Janine hugged Monica and Olivia in turn. "Let's go."

On the ride back to the motel, Brent Jr. repeated his foul ball capture several times. Janine was momentarily insulated from the issues pressing her.

In the motel room the youngest kids scrambled into their bathing suits. Olivia hesitated.

"C'mon, let's get our suits on," said Janine.

Olivia had picked out a modest one-piece suit for her mother. Janine put it on.

Janine led her family to the pool. The younger kids jumped in and began splashing around. Janine waded in from the shallow end. Olivia followed.

Janine swam an easy breaststroke. She didn't have a swim cap and didn't want her hair wet.

Eric appeared a few minutes later. He jumped in and began swimming laps.

After a while Janine left the water and found a deck chair. Olivia followed.

"Are you alright, Livy?"

"I'm okay," said the girl. "We're not going to stay here, are we?"

"I don't think so."

"Where are we going to go?"

"I…I don't know."

A pair of tween boys loudly entered the pool.

Olivia seemed to shrink into the chair. "Can I go back to the room?"

Janine nodded. Olivia left.

After a few minutes Eric sat down, dripping wet. "They're wearing me out." He dried his hair. "Is Livy alright?"

"She wants to know what's going to happen to us."

"Well," said the man, "you're not going to move in with your aunt. You are not moving in with your mother. If you moved in with Saundra, you'd both have to kill Chase." Eric gave a little laugh. "Wow, you're in a bad spot."

"Eric, can we stay with you for a little longer?" Janine watched for a reaction.

"Janine," he said with a sigh, "let's cross that bridge back home. Right now, we must keep you out of jail here." He looked at her and smiled.

"You've been very kind. I don't how I'm ever going to repay you." She broke her gaze and focused on the children. "I guess I haven't been the best niece or daughter. I must have failed as a wife. I really failed at taking care of my kids."

"You haven't failed your kids," said Eric. "Not yet. They are loving, thoughtful, and well mannered. Despite the shitstorm around them, they are cooperative and concerned. They must be as terrified as you are. Your husband, their father, betrayed all of you. You loved and trusted him. That was what you were supposed to do. As for the rest, I don't know."

After dinner and showers Janine had Brent and Monica ready for bed. She put them to bed in her room. Olivia was using Eric's laptop on the internet.

Eric invited Janine to his room. "I'm making coffee or tea if you wish."

They sat at a table with hot drinks.

"I've been thinking," said Eric, "if you stay at my house, I can't support all of you. My pension won't support a young family. You'd have to find work. We can set up expenses and a budget. I can find a cheap car for you. We'd have to divide up the work." He looked at her. "I can't throw you out."

Janine's eyes welled up. She threw her arms around Eric. She couldn't find the words.

"Okay," he said. "Look, it's not going to be alright for quite some time. You have to be strong for yourself and the kids. You can do it."

She released her hug and wiped her eyes.

"Now tell me about your Aunt Sarah's place?"

"Well…" she said, wiping her eyes, "my dad was concerned about her living alone down here. She would not move because her husband and son are buried here. She had my dad set up some sort of trust fund. I was an alternate power of attorney for Sarah. Naomi, her husband's niece, and I were supposed to inherit the property when she died.

"We saw her last summer. She was a bit forgetful, but I did not think much of it. Brent stopped here a couple of times since then. He said she was alright." She began to weep. "Oh god, he set this up too. That... bastard." She blew her nose. "God damn it."

"Janine, can I suggest something that might get you off the hook here? It seems to me that you cannot move in with your aunt without her cousin prosecuting you. Neither of you can touch the house until she dies. Maybe you should sign away the house to Naomi and let her have it. So long as she takes care of your aunt, she will have earned it. She can try to sue you, but you don't have anything left but your stake in the property."

"Do you think that'll work?" she snuffled.

"Look, if you did have power of attorney and proved she was incompetent, you could have syphoned her money away. Lots of relatives have. By all means, tell them it was forged but it makes no difference." Eric thought for a second. "Will Naomi take care of her aunt?"

"I think so. They were always close."

"You can tell them that you are in no position to help anyone. That is true. Tell them that Naomi will do a better job of caring for Sarah."

"I just want to die."

"How do you want to handle tomorrow?" asked Eric. "You can't keep your children with you at the court's building. Someone has to watch them. I'd like to be with you for moral support but what about the kids?"

"Can you keep an eye on them for now?"

"Look, I'm not related to anyone. You'd be trusting your children to a stranger. They are all you have."

She smiled at him at touched his arm. "We already have." She cocked her head. "You're not a pervert, are you?"

"Certainly not!" he replied with a start. Slowly he smiled. "A little late for that question, isn't it?"

Eric dropped Janine and Olivia off at the courthouse. Olivia insisted on accompanying her mother.

Janine reported to the district attorney's office. She and Olivia were shown to a conference room. They were offered coffee and sweet rolls.

After a while a young woman came in. "I am Clare, Junior Assistant District attorney. I'd like to go over the facts with you. Do you have an attorney?"

Janine replied that she had no attorney. They reviewed the incident. Clare left.

Janine went through the same rig-a-marole twice more with Detective Collins and Assistant District Attorney Wilson.

ADA Wilson summed up: "Detective Collins reports that your husband Brent is missing and wanted. He has been charged with grand theft. You claim that he forged documents diverting funds from your aunt. Is this correct? And you further claim that you had no knowledge of these actions. Is that correct?"

"My husband…deceived everyone," said Janine with tears in her eyes. "He took everything and left us homeless. We have nothing."

"Homeless?" asked ADA Wilson. "You have been evicted?" Her attention shifted between Janine and Olivia.

"Yes. We are living with a friend."

"I see," said the ADA.

"Look," said Janine, "I don't want to hurt my aunt. I didn't hurt my aunt. But I cannot help her anymore. I'd be willing to sign over all my claims to Aunt Sarah's property to Naomi if she cares for her."

ADA Wilson sat back and looked at Janine. "That does not answer the charge that funds were taken from your aunt."

"I know. I have power of attorney, but I did not take her money."

ADA Wilson was still looking at Janine. "And you contend that your husband, Brent Piersen, forged bank documents?"

"I do, he did."

ADA Wilson began shuffling papers. "And that you have no knowledge of the funds?"

"I do not."

"And you are prepared to sign over the property to…" ADA Wilson referred to a file.

"Aunt Sarah's niece Naomi. Yes, I will."

"Stay here." ADA Wilson led her group out.

Janine looked at Olivia. She was crying. "Oh, Mom."

Several hours passed.

"Olivia, maybe you should go outside and call Eric? Check on your brother and sister? Tell him what's going on."

"Okay, Mom. Will you be okay?"

"Yeah," Janine replied. "And honey, I appreciate your being here."

While Olivia was gone, Detective Collins and Clare came in with two more men. Clare introduced them as Special Agent Trask and Attorney Yoder. They all sat down at the table.

"Ms. Piersen," said Clare, "I have prepared a statement that says that your husband, and not you, signed and/or forged a document diverting …"

Janine was hearing the words detached from reality. It was when Olivia returned that her mental fog lifted. Olivia's entrance stopped the proceeding momentarily.

"…and if you sign away rights to your aunt's property the criminal complaint against you will be suspended. We reserve the right to reinstate the criminal complaint if we find evidence of your complicity." ADA Clare pushed a paper in front of Janine. "Ms. Piersen, do you understand?"

"I do."

"At this point I would like to say," said Attorney Yoder, "that my client is reluctant to believe that Janine is not complicit in this matter. It is only after discussions with Special Agent Trask that we believe a shred of truth exists here. My client will accept Janine's removal from all aspects of her aunt's affairs in good faith. She must have no further contact with her aunt."

"Is that necessary?"

"I'm afraid so," said Clare. "It's part of the deal."

Janine looked at the documents in front of her. "Part of the deal." She hesitated. "It says here that I did not take Sarah's money?"

"That's right."

"And I can go home now?"

"You'll have to inform us of your whereabouts, but yes, you can go."

She began signing documents. Clare, Detective Collins, and Attorney Yoder signed them too. "Wait here for your copy of the documents," said ADA Clare. She left with the attorney and officer.

Special Agent Trask remained. "We should talk for a couple of minutes."

"I thought we were done?"

"They're done." He waived at the empty seats at the table. "The agency has a few more questions for you." He looked at Olivia sitting silent along the wall "Do you want her to hear this?"

"Why not?"

"I believe that that you have been terribly naïve. Your husband and his associates have been planning this for a long time. That you had no knowledge seems implausible." He waited for Janine to react.

Janine was too numb to respond.

The agent looked between Janine and her daughter. "You've had no contact with your husband in the last week?"

Janine just shook her head no. Olivia shrugged her shoulders and shook her head negatively.

"I see," said the agent. "How about any of Brent's associates?"

Janine was struck by the question. "No. No one."

"Are you aware of any place out of the country that he might go?"

Janine's mouth was dry. She felt trapped. "He...he kept talking about the Cayman Islands."

The agent pursed his lips. "Cayman Islands? Did he ever talk about anywhere else?"

"Windsor," said Janine. "We drove there once for a meeting. A meeting that didn't happen. We drove there, stayed overnight, and came back."

"I see," said the agent. "I assume that we will be talking to you again. How can we reach you?"

"Right now, we're staying with Eric."

"Okay," said the agent. He got up and left.

When Eric picked them up, Janine sunk into the passenger seat exhausted. She let out a deep sigh. "Thank god that's over."

"Mom, are you okay?" asked Monica plaintively.

Janine perked up and turned to face her daughter. "Oh honey, it's so good to see you guys. What did you do today?"

"We went to the zoo!" replied Monica. "Until it started raining."

"You did? That's great," she replied enthusiastically.

"Then we went to this old car place," said Brent Jr. in a monotone.

"The Studebaker Museum," chimed in Eric. "It was raining too hard to stay at the zoo."

"It was raining?" asked Janine. "I didn't know." She focused on Eric. "Where are we going?"

"It's late," he said. "I thought we could get some dinner. Then we can all go swimming, get a good night's sleep, and drive home in the morning. That okay?"

"Yeah, sure."

"You can go home, can't you?" asked Eric.

"Yeah, sure."

After dinner and time at the pool, they returned to the rooms. Eric insisted on a circle of truth before bed. Still in their swimsuits, Eric had them hold hands in a circle.

Eric had them say it twice: "I am homeless. It is not my fault. We love each other. We trust each other." They fell into silence. "Janine, tell us what happened?"

Janine took a deep breath. "Brent took all of Aunt Sarah's money. Everybody is blaming me. We can't stay here." She fell quiet.

"Mommy," asked her son, "will you have to go to jail?"

"No, no honey," she tried to reassure. "We go back to Chicago tomorrow."

"Where will we go?" asked Olivia.

"Well..." said Janine.

"You'll be staying with me for now," said Eric. "Now, we'll say it again: I am homeless. It is not my fault. We love each other. We trust each other.

"Good night, children," said Eric. "Janine, why don't you and I go down to the bar for a drink?"

Eric brought two drinks to the table.

"Before you say whatever it is you want to say," she said, "you were a massive help today. Thank you."

"Okay, well, you are welcome." He paused. "Janine, you are a good person. You are an excellent mother. I like you. But...I think I've earned the right to say, you've been...careless? Naïve? I don't know. You've heard of women being taken by their husbands. And you were warned."

Janine sunk her head. "You mean Dad?"

"Yeah, your dad. He went to extraordinary lengths to protect you and your aunt."

"I'm sorry," she said, holding back tears.

"Look, you don't have to be sorry for my sake. You've done nothing to me. But you've got to be heads-up from now on. For you and for them." Eric reached out a hand and took hers. "I'm not upset or angry with you. This is just a pep talk. Okay?"

"Okay. Heads-up."

They smiled at each other. They finished their drinks.

Two guys at the bar had been giving Janine the eye.

As Janine and Eric left one of the guys said, "Atta way!"

"Well," said Eric, "at least they think I've still got it."

Eric and Janine walked up the hallway with a laugh.

They had all been quiet at breakfast. They piled into the car with little discussion or enthusiasm. Janine settled into her seat and let her mind drift.

It was Brent Jr. that broke the silence. "I don't want to be Brent anymore. I don't want to be like dad."

"What?" said Janine, trying to focus. "Honey, you are not your dad."

"I don't want to be Brent anymore. I want to be Eric."

"Oh, honey," she said in mom sympathy voice.

Eric looked at the boy in the mirror. "Son, you should be your own person. You should not be Brent or Eric. What's your middle name, son?"

"Alan."

Janine smiled at her son. "Sure. From now on you are Alan. Everybody, this is Alan."

DOMESTICITY

Janine reentered Eric's house with mixed emotions. She was relieved that, for now, she wasn't going to jail. Certainly, she was dejected that they weren't going to live with her aunt. With no options left, they were now truly homeless. She had to keep her family together—that was paramount. She had to convince Eric to let them stay.

Eric purchased a family chicken meal on the way home. The kids were unusually quiet at dinner. Everyone could feel tension in the air.

Janine directed the kids to clear the dishes. "Can we talk?" Janine asked Eric.

"Sure," replied the man. "How about coffee in the living room?"

Janine stopped to straighten her hair and clothes. She put on lipstick. She brought in a tray with coffee. Eric was looking at a collection of mail in a chair. He put it aside when she handed him a cup.

She sat on the couch and poured a cup for herself. "You know my... situation." She began to choke with emotion. "I've got to keep my family together. I...I don't know how." She began to weep. "I don't have...we don't have...anything." She could no longer speak.

Eric had watched her descent into tears without emotion. He now moved next to her on the couch. He put an arm around her and drew her into a hug. "Go ahead and cry. Let it all out. You've earned it." He handed her some tissues.

Janine continued to cry, pressed against his shoulder. "We had it so…nice. And he had to…And Aunt Sarah…He took our lives." She blew her nose. She looked at Eric. "My dad was right!" She began sobbing again. She leaned against his shoulder again.

"Easy, Janine, easy." He held her for a few seconds. "How about if I talk for a little bit? Okay?"

She sat back. She wiped her eyes. She nodded yes.

Eric reached out and took her nearest hand. "Janine, you have been so…brave, so courageous. No one could have done better with the hand you were dealt." He smiled at her. "Did you think you had to beg to stay here?"

She nodded and began crying again. "I…I…"

He drew her to his shoulder again. "It's okay. Of course you can stay. We'll work it out."

She leaned back and looked at him. "Can we?"

"Yes, you can. You just stay strong." He held out the tissue box for her.

"Eric, thank you so much," she said between snuffles. "Really, you're a godsend."

Eric gave a little laugh. "I've never been called that before."

"You are for us." She stayed against his shoulder.

"Well…I've been thinking, there are three things. First, we have to set up the bedrooms."

"Okay."

"Second, you apply for welfare."

"Do I have to?" she said, still huddled against his shoulder.

"Sorry, yes you do."

"Okay. If you say so." She sat back. "What's the third thing?"

"Can we have coffee now?"

Janine got the kids ready for school. Her plan for the day was getting birth certificates for the family. She ushered the kids out the door. They all froze there. Janine had no car; it had been repossessed. She went back in. Eric was reading the paper.

"Eric, I'm sorry. We have to use your car."

"What? Oh, yeah sure." He handed her the keys. "Let me know how you are doing. Do you have cash for the clerk's office?" He looked at her puzzled face. "I thought not. Wait here."

Eric disappeared into his room. He returned with an envelope. "Here. Now get going."

Janine was uncomfortable driving Eric's sedan. After dropping off the kids, she headed to the county clerk's office. She had to park in a large lot at the courts building. She waited in a line that snaked across the room. She finally saw a clerk.

"Let's see here," said the clerk, looking at the call sheet. "You need four birth certificates and a marriage license. One for Janine, Olivia, Brent Jr., and Monica. These are their birthdays? This is date of marriage. Okay. This may take a while. Sit over there, please."

Janine waited in a sitting area. She read from a purse-sized paperback. She monitored the parade of people coming through. Finally, they called her name.

"Well, we have certificates for Brent Jr., Monica, and Olivia. We have the license. But we have no record of you." The clerk looked at her questioningly. "Where and when were you born?"

"Waukegan…" As soon as she said it, she knew.

"Ma'am," interjected the clerk, "Waukegan is not in Cook County. You'll have to go there to get your record."

"Of course," she said. "I'm having a rough time. I'll take the ones you have."

"Okay, that's alright." She handed Janine the call sheet back. "Pay the cashier and come back." She pointed perfunctorily at another line.

As Janine neared the cashier, she produced the envelope Eric had given her. She was floored to find $200 in it. She paid for the certificates, collected them, and headed out of the building.

She was struck by the cash. She had rarely kept more than $50 over the years. She had depended on credit cards for everything. Except for her $200 emergency money she rarely used cash. Another new life reality. She had no credit.

Another thing struck her. It was as if Eric, a substitute dad, had given her an allowance. She could not become dependent on another man.

She exited the building into the parking lot. She was disturbed by the thought of dependence on Eric. She went to her car. It was then that she realized that she didn't have her car. She had used Eric's sedan. She did not know the type or color of the car. She went up and down several aisles hoping to recognize the car. In a sea full of cars, she didn't know which she came in.

"Goddamn it!" She stomped. She worked at composing herself.

A security car pulled up. "What's the problem? Can't find your car."

"No." She shook her head.

"Happens all the time," said the guard with a smile. "Get in. We'll find it."

Janine got in as the guard called in: "Lost car."

"Okay, what kind of car is it?'

"I don't know."

"Okay…what color is it?"

"I don't know."

The guard started to laugh. "Well, lady…No wonder you can't find it. You did come here in a car, right?"

"Yes. I borrowed Eric's car."

"You borrowed his car? Can you call him?"

"Sure." She called. Eric did not answer.

"Let's give him some time and call again. In the meantime, when did you get here? Maybe we can narrow the search."

Eric called. The guard wrote down the info.

As they cruised the aisles the guard reassured her. "I'm Sam, by the way. Did you have traffic court?"

"No. I had to get birth records for my divorce."

"Oh, sorry to hear that. That can be rough." He stopped the car.

"It is." She looked at the guard. "Why have we stopped?"

"Because that is your car."

She looked. "Are you sure?"

"According to Eric. Good luck, lady."

"Thanks, Sam." She went to the car. When she opened the door, she waved at the guard.

He waved back and pulled off.

She called Eric from the car. "I feel like such an idiot. I have to go to Waukegan for my birth certificate. And I lost your car."

"No harm done. Come on home. You can go on safari to the wilds of Lake County tomorrow."

Janine laid out coffee for her and Eric at the kitchen table. "Eric, you put $200 in the envelope for me."

"Yeah. I didn't want you to get caught short."

"You've laid out a lot of money for me, for us. I never used to think about the money. I mean I always had it. I never thought much about having it."

Eric nodded. "You were very lucky."

"Did your parents give you money?"

Eric shook his head no. "They barely got by. Everything I have we earned, Peggy and I."

"My dad." She shook her head and gave a little laugh. "I can't believe I'm saying this. My dad said that if I borrowed from a friend, I had to pay it back."

Eric nodded his head in agreement. "Okay."

"I…I can't afford to lose you as a friend. And I can't afford to pay you back right now."

"Okay. What can we do about that?"

"Well…" She shrugged. "I don't know."

"How about if we keep a log of expenses, you and me. When you get a job, you can start paying me back."

"Okay." Janine reached out her hand. "We'll shake on it."

"Alright," said Eric. "Have you given any thought to what kind of work you can do?"

"I haven't thought about it."

"You never had a job with a paycheck?" Eric closed his eyes and rubbed his forehead. "Do you know your Social Security number? Or where your card is?"

She shook her head. "No."

Eric looked at her quizzically. "When you left your house did you grab Social Security cards for you or the kids?"

"No. Brent cleared out all the papers from the safe."

Eric closed his eyes and rubbed his head again. "You can't work without it. Scratch the birth certificate, tomorrow you go to Social Security."

"What kind of work do you think I could do?"

Eric closed his eyes and rubbed his head again. "Okay, so you have no job skills. Can you type well? Or take steno?"

"No, sorry."

"Well, they are always looking for people at the casino. Maybe they could take you there?"

"You mean, like a cocktail waitress or something?"

"Okay, sure. While you're out, go apply."

Saundra stopped by that afternoon with a bottle of wine.

Eric let Saundra in. Janine joined them in the front room. The two women hugged.

Eric excused himself to let the women talk.

"No, no. Stay please," Saundra entreated him. "You are part of this story too. Janine, all kinds of things are happening. But first tell everything that's been happening to you."

They settled in the living room. Janine told the tales of banks and lawyers. She recounted the odyssey of South Bend and her mother's empty offer. Finally, she stopped. "That's all so far."

"Are you going to stay here?" Saundra looked between Janine and Eric.

"For now," said Eric.

"And you haven't heard anything about the club?" Saundra took a breath before going on. "Apparently your hubby was a busy guy. Several of the men invested in whatever he was up to. Your hubby also was screwing a few of the wives. Did you know?

"Oh, sorry. Anyway, my man was working a side deal with Brent over some property in Canada. Last week the FBI, no less, came by the house to interview Chase. After the feds leave, Chase says he's leaving the country. He packs a bag and leaves. I ask where I contact him. He says he'll call me. Next morning a divorce lawyer rings the bell. Hands me papers."

Saundra stops for effect. "Chase thinks I'm helpless. I've been stashing away money for years. I got my own lawyer. The feds have put a lien against the house."

Saundra looked at Janine. "You didn't stash anything away, did you? You don't have anywhere else to go, do you?"

"No," said Janine. "We are homeless. We…rely on the kindness of others."

Saundra looked at Eric. "Will they be able to stay here?"

Eric seemed startled by the question. "Well…No one's going to take my house away. I do have the room. And I do need a project." He looked at Janine and smiled. "But they will have to earn their keep."

"We haven't worked out all the…arrangements yet," stammered Janine.

"Honey," said Saundra, "you should marry this man. He has to be the last decent man around."

"I think I'd better go get the kids from school," said Eric, red faced. "Why don't you stay for dinner? It's just pasta and salad. Plenty to go around. You girls talk."

After Eric left, Saundra shared the gossip from the country club. Janine had once been in the thick of the club gossip. She now felt detached like hearing about distant relatives. But it was good to hear Saundra.

When Eric returned with the kids, they all hugged Auntie Saundra.

As Janine and the kids put dinner together, Eric sat with Saundra.

"Brent cleaned them out?" she asked.

"Yeah, they're penniless. We were just talking about what kind of job she should look for."

"A job?" Saundra seemed startled by the notion. "What kind of work can she do? Now Eric," said Saundra devilishly, "Janine would make an excellent wife. She's young, younger than you. She's attractive, many men have said so. And," she said with emphasis, "she's available."

Eric adjusted his glasses while considering an answer. "Well, some of that is true. She's got a lot of legal issues to iron out. I don't intend to entangle myself with legal liabilities. Not to mention she's still another man's wife." He hesitated. "So, while you are a guest in my house, I would appreciate it if you would not mention that again. Okay?"

"Well, I was just talking," she replied.

"Look, Janine and the kids are bruised and stunned. They need to lick their wounds and find some sort of normalcy. Let's not set any expectations on them, okay?"

The dinner was pleasant. Saundra spent most of the conversation with the kids. The kids were happy to interact with her.

Eric and the kids cleaned up after dinner. Saundra and Janine settled in the front room. Eric and the kids disappeared to let the women talk.

Every time Saundra brought up Brent, Janine changed the subject. Every time Saundra brought up Janine's relationship with Eric, she changed the subject.

Finally, Saundra stopped Janine. "Look, honey, I was there when they threw you out of your house. Please tell me about Brent?"

Janine took a deep breath. "Okay. But I need your solemn oath that it's just between us? I don't know who to trust."

"Honey, I'm Monica's godmother. I'm on your side."

"I think Brent and Lance from the office cooked this whole thing up. I think Brent and this Charlene Wilcox are working together too. She's the twenty-something bitch all the men are hot for. I think Brent took all the laptops and phones in Wisconsin to keep me in the dark.

"Dad warned me about him, but I didn't take his advice. I signed a bunch of papers for Brent without asking enough questions." She looked at Saundra and shook her head. "I was a fool."

"Oh, honey," replied Saundra, "you are not alone. That bastard fooled a bunch of people. You do love him?"

Janine laughed. "Yeah, enough to cut his balls off."

They both laughed.

"Honey," said Saundra, "you know I would take you in, but I have to vacate the house by next week."

"You too? Where will you go?"

"I'm going to stay with my son and his bitchy wife. At least I'll get to see my grandkids."

They both descended into silence for a few seconds.

"Seriously, Jan, when are you going to throw yourself at Eric? He's…a steady man. Would make a good father. You could do a lot worse."

"Saundra!?" Janine choked.

"Well?"

"It's like this. Sometimes he's like my dad. I hear Dad's voice. Other times he's very tender. He is great with the kids." She thought for a second. "Actually, he's better with the kids than Brent ever was. He's…"

"He's what?" said Saundra devilishly.

Janine hesitated. "He's been better to me than my husband was." Then she looked at Saundra. "Excluding the sex!"

They both laughed.

"Honey, what are you going to do?"

"I don't know."

The next morning after dropping the kids at school, Janine went to the Social Security office. By plan, she returned home after applying for new cards. Eric was waiting.

"What's today's plan?" she asked him.

"Car shopping."

Eric directed her to a car lot. They talked as they drove.

"I'm glad you and Saundra had a good talk," he said.

"Yeah, it was nice. It was nice to talk."

"She's going through a rough time too. Is she okay?"

"I think so. She…put money away. I guess she didn't trust Chase." She pulled into the car lot. "She thinks we'd make a nice couple."

"Really?" He unbuckled. "Let's go get you a car."

"Me?"

Eric led her to the SUV's. "Let's see what will work for you?"

"I'm used to a Mercedes," she replied.

"I'm sure you were. Think Buick. Think Chevy. More in my range."

"Will this do?" Eric asked after they test drove a Buick.

"You're buying me a car?"

"Well, actually, I'm buying a second car that you will be using. If something changes, I can always sell it."

While they waited for the SUV to be ready, they sat in a waiting area.

"Eric, how am I ever going to pay you back?"

"I told you it's payback for my wife's friend."

"Come on, be honest. You've gone way past helping out. You're… subsidizing our lives."

Eric was silent for a few seconds. "Maybe you're a good investment. At any rate you will pay it forward. Promise me you will help another drowning woman."

"That I can promise."

The saleswoman came up. "Your car is ready." As she walked with Janine, she remarked, "Your dad is really taking care of you."

Rather than explain she just replied, "Yes he is."

As Eric and Janine returned to the house, Eric's phone rang. He took the call outside. Janine readied the tea pot. Eric stepped into the kitchen. "You'll have to deal with the kids yourself," he said. "I've been roped into a bridge game tonight."

"Really? That's short notice."

"Yes, Harold's had a stroke. I've got to shower right away."

When Janine returned from the school run, Eric was coming out the front door. He was in good slacks, a polo shirt, and a sports jacket.

"Hi, Uncle Eric," the kids said in succession.

"Well," said Janine, "you got all dressed up." She hooked an arm around his. "You're going to knock those widows out!"

"Yeah, yeah," he replied.

As he got to his car Eric waved at the lady across the street. She waved back from her porch.

By the time Eric came home, only Olivia and Janine were awake. Eric joined them at the kitchen table.

"I think there's some tea in the pot," said Janine.

"No, no thanks," said Eric with a wave. "I've been plied with cake and coffee all evening. All the women were whispering. One of the guys told me that he didn't believe I had a young lover move in. He thinks my daughter-in-law moved in."

Both Janine and Oliva giggled.

"I had to eat everybody's cake while they tried to get me to talk."

"Oh, you poor dear," said Janine mockingly.

"One lady had it right though. She's a social services counselor. She knew all about you. She'd like to stop by to talk to you." He smiled at them both. "I'm tired. I'm going to bed."

"Oh, one thing," said Janine. "I have to see the lawyer. He wants to see us both."

Janine and Eric sat at a table in the law office. The attorney, Levi, came in with a flourish. "Ms. Piersen, hello. Eric, how are you?"

"Okay," said Levi, not waiting for an answer. "So, I need your approval to place notices in the papers denying your husband's debts. Secondly, I need your signature on the bankruptcy papers. Thirdly, what have you done about residency?"

"They're staying with me," said Eric.

"Okay. Thirdly, I need you to sign the divorce complaint. Your reasons are desertion and theft. Right?"

"And adultery."

Levi nodded his head. "And adultery." He sat back and assessed Janine. "How are you holding up?"

"Well, I'm not on the streets." She reached over and took Eric's hand. "And I have my children, so, it could be a lot worse."

"Good. I'll process forms for you to sign. Be back in a minute."

"One thing?" asked Eric. "How can she establish residency in my home?"

"Good question," said Levi. "Usually if someone pays some kind of bill, that works."

On the way home Janine brought up the question. "Bills? How can someone with no money pay bills?"

"I've thinking about that," replied Eric. "The kids don't have cell phones, right? How about if we get three cheap cell phones on a plan and have it charged to you? That might work."

"Cheap phones? The kids are used to smart phones."

"Maybe so," said Eric. "They're going to have to get used to disappointment."

Janine went to the casino to apply for work. There are assigned hours for applicants. She wore a nice dress. She spent a lot of time on her hair and makeup.

Janine filled in the application as neatly as she could. When she came to the section about previous employment, her heart sank. She tried to decide if she should walk out. Support the children or run. What to do?

Janine turned in the forms. She was sent in to see an "Interview Specialist." "Hello, I'm Marsha Wilson. Let's have a good look at this." She scanned the form. "You have no job experience?"

"I've never had a job. I never had to…I never had to until now."

"Okay. What changed?"

"I…" Janine hesitated. "My husband left me. In fact, he took everything and left. I mean everything."

"I see," said the interviewer. "We can't take your application seriously without some kind of work record. Go get six months' job experience and come back and see me."

Dejected, Janine walked back to the car. This time she had carefully noted where she had parked. Exiting the casino however she got turned around. Heading in the wrong direction she was stopped in the left turn lane. She looked to her right and saw a Denny's. A sign in the window said Now Hiring-All Positions.

At the counter she asked for a job application. They had her wait at a table near the front.

A woman came over and put an application in front of her. She shook Janine's hand. "Hello, I'm Elaine Harris, assistant manager. I understand you're looking for work. I sure hope so because we really need some servers. Why don't you fill out the application, and I'll be back with you in a while?"

Janine filled out the application. She watched the genial quality of Elaine with the customers. She had rarely eaten at Denny's. Brent had usually opted for high-end eateries.

Elaine came and sat with Janine. She went over the form and stopped at the section marked Previous Employment. "Janine, is this right, you have no previous employment? You never worked anywhere?"

Instinctively Janine rubbed the spot on her finger where she used to wear her wedding ring. "I never had to before." She looked Elaine in the eye.

Elaine assessed Janine with her jaw slightly agape. "I see. Well, we need servers. We can train you to do the job. You would have to work nights at least three times a week. We need help on Sundays. Is that acceptable?"

"Ah…I guess so."

Elaine sat back and assessed Piersen. "Do you have kids at home?"

Janine smiled. "Yes, three."

"I ask because when I said nights, I mean graveyard. Eleven to six in the morning. Will someone be available to tend your children?"

"Yes, I think so. I mean I'm sure he will help with the kids."

"And you have a dependable car?"

"Yes."

"Look," said Elaine, "I'm not supposed to ask about your personal life. Are you recently separated?"

"Recently deserted."

"Oh, oh my." Elaine looked stunned. "I'm sorry." She regained her pleasant demeanor. "I have to submit your application through channels. Unless they find something, I would guess that they'll hire you."

"Really?" replied Janine. "I hope so. I've got to do something."

"Okay, well, thanks for coming in."

Janine left the restaurant upbeat. A job! Serving tables, how hard can that be?

Over dinner Janine recounted her day. She seemed excited that the job interview at Denny's went well.

The kids were not so excited. "Denny's, Mom? Really?" said Alan.

Olivia looked at her mom questioningly. "The casino said you weren't qualified?"

"I have no job experience."

"Isn't being a mom a job?" asked Monica.

Janine looked at her and smiled. "Yes. It's the most important job." She reached out and touched her daughter. "But…that doesn't count."

"But Denny's, really Mom?" said Alan.

Eric had listened but not said anything. "Well, that's some good news. You can hone some skills as a waitress. It's good honest work. Learn the job, do it well. It'll pay off in the long run. Good experience job."

"If I get the job, I'll have to work some nights. All night. The graveyard shifts." She looked at them all for reaction. "Eric will have to get you up and ready for school. Is that okay?"

"You have to work all night?" asked Monica. "When will you sleep?"

"I'd have to come home and sleep while you're at school. It means Uncle Eric will be in charge a lot." She looked at Eric for reassurance.

Eric nodded ascent.

Janine kept the kids talking about their school day through dinner. The kids did not understand that the restaurant had thrown her a life jacket.

After dinner Eric suggested they all play a game together. Eric brought out the card game Skip-Bo. They played with cheerful competition until bedtime for Monica and Alan.

Janine, Olivia, and Eric settled in the front room with coffee.

Eric looked at Olivia. "You are unhappy with your mom working as a waitress, aren't you?"

"Mom, do you have to go to work?"

"Honey, I've got to get a job. We have nothing anymore." She smiled at the girl. "At least Eric is letting us stay here. But it's still expensive. You kids are going to need clothes and shoes."

"Denny's, Mom?"

"What's wrong with that?" asked Eric. "There's no shame in doing any job well. Earn your pay with your head up. My first job was working in a kitchen after high school. It was hard and hot. But it was honest work."

Eric and Janine went shopping for cell phones. Eric insisted on the cheapest phones, call and text only. Communication without internet brought the lowest priced plan. Janine's credit check denied her an account. It was only a joint account with Eric that was approved. It was actually a senior's plan. But the kids would have a phone.

As they were leaving, Janine's phone rang. The restaurant wanted a second interview. Could she stop by in the afternoon?

Janine was met by Elaine and the unit manager. Edward was plump with a stained tie and shirt.

"Ms. Janine Piersen, there are…I have some questions about your application. The address on your ID is your former address. Is that correct?"

Suddenly Janine felt a sinking feeling. "That's right. I now live here." She pointed to the address on the form.

"You moved from there, but you haven't updated your license?"

Janine took a deep breath. "I can't."

The man cocked his head and blinked his eyes. "Why not?"

"I can't because we were evicted. I have no home. I'm…homeless. I'm currently staying with a friend. Until I have some bills or paychecks, the state won't allow me residency. I can't register as homeless because I want to keep my children."

"Oh my god," said Edward. "I'm so sorry. I understand now why you…I understand." He looked out the window. "You aren't living in your car, are you?"

"Thankfully, no. As I said I'm staying with a friend."

Edward looked at Elaine. She nodded yes.

"Ms. Janine, I'm going to push your application through to my district manager. I expect he'll approve it. Elaine explained that we need graveyard and Sundays. Good. I would expect you here next week for training, but we'll call. Okay?"

"Okay," said Janine. She realized she had tears in her eyes. "I… thanks."

Elaine handed her a tissue. She smiled.

EMPLOYED

Janine reported for work at Denny's in the late morning. She spent time filling out forms. She got a uniform top. She received a booklet from human resources. She felt like a kid on orientation day.

After a while she was paired up with her trainer, Emma. Janine guessed that the woman was older than her. She had an easy way with the customers and a quick laugh. She called everyone honey.

"Remember, honey, keep the coffee cups full. Get the food out quick, they're here for food. Just follow along with me for now. Honey, you'll get the hang of it."

Before she knew it was time to go. "Jan, honey, I'll see you tomorrow night."

Janine drove home exhilarated and mind numb. She was pretty sure she could do this.

At dinner she patiently listened to the kids' stories of their day. When it was her turn, she recapped her experience.

Janine sat with Eric after dinner. "Eric, things are looking up. I'll start paying you back with every paycheck."

"I appreciate the thought," he replied. "But let's cover two things first."

She sighed. "Okay, if you must."

"Firstly, I'll take you tomorrow and get you some good work shoes. You'll die in those."

"No, really Eric, I'll be fine."

"No, you won't. Trust me. It'll be my treat."

"Okay. What else?"

"Something's not right with Alan at school. He's holding back something."

"I didn't hear anything."

"I know you didn't. Livy is holding back too."

"You think so?"

"I do."

"Okay, I'll ask them separately." She sipped her coffee. "You think I need new shoes?" she said.

."Trust me."

When Janine got to the restaurant about 9:45 p.m., the place was bustling. Emma came in right behind her. "Honey, we got a full house tonight."

Janine shadowed Emma through the first half of the shift. She filled coffee and served plates of food. She noted how Emma dealt with the customers. Emma handled complaints with the aplomb of a diplomat.

Janine was startled when Emma said, "Honey, why don't you take your dinner break now. It's quiet." Janine looked at the clock; it was two a.m.

It was not until she sat down that realized her calves were killing her. She scanned the room. The crowd had thinned out. Only two tables had customers. There was only one man at the counter. Emma would be going on break. She could handle it. When she stood up, she realized how tight her legs were.

Two drunks came in. They were loud. She showed them to a table. She returned with coffee. "Can I take your order?"

The first drunk ordered a burger and fries. The second drunk was moving the menu back and forth. "I don't seem to have my glasses." He pointed at something on the menu. "What's that say?" When Janine stepped forward and leaned in the man put his hand up the back of her skirt. She jumped up and bolted behind the counter.

"Roving hands?" said Emma. "You've got to keep your distance, honey. If you want, I'll take those two. Why don't you start servicing tables?"

Janine began filling salt, pepper, and sugar containers. She kept a wary eye on the drunks. About 4:30 she met up with Emma at the counter. Suddenly she felt very tired.

"You done alright, honey. I knew you'd last. The last one left at midnight. Never saw her again."

"I need this job. I've got to support my kids."

"We all do, honey."

"I hope I didn't mess up too bad. I got a couple of orders wrong." Janine reached into her pocket. She retrieved a wad of cash. She held it out. "This must be yours?"

"Honey, I took mine right away. That's yours. You earned it. You did okay for a first night." Emma laughed. "You've just got to stay out of reach of those men. Tonight wasn't that busy. Friday night will be busy." She spied a customer waiving at her. "More coffee?"

Janine drove home as dawn was breaking. Traffic was scarce but frantic. She pulled up in front of the house. She'd done it. Her first shift. Things will be getting better.

"Mom?" Olivia was tapping on the car window.

"What's going on?" she asked.

"We're on our way to school. Did you fall asleep in the car?" asked Olivia with a laugh.

"I guess so." She waved goodbye. Getting out of the car was hard. Her legs were very stiff.

She made it to the front room and collapsed on the couch. When Eric came in, she stirred. "I thought you were going to drop off the kids?"

"I did. I've been gone an hour." Eric let out a small laugh. "This is as far as you got? Let me use the bathroom. Then I'll draw you a hot bath. You can have a nice hot soak and get to bed. Okay?"

Eric roused her. "Come on. Your bath is ready."

"Let me die here!"

"Sorry, no dying in the front room." Eric helped her up by pulling her arms. He pushed her into the bathroom. "Take your clothes off before entering the water. I'll round up a bath robe."

She dropped her clothes on the floor. The hot water was soothing. Eric knocked on the door. "You okay?"

"I'm never coming out."

Eric opened the door a crack. He hung a bathrobe on a hook and closed the door.

Janine soaked and added hot water a couple of times. When she came out, she looked for Eric. His bedroom door was closed. She laid out on her bed still in her bathrobe.

"Mom?" Olivia entered the bedroom. "Mom, are you going to have dinner with us?"

"Dinner?" She rubbed her eyes. "Sure, I'll start dinner."

"No, silly. Dinner's ready. We're waiting for you."

Janine kept the usual routine during dinner. She let Monica retell her day. Then Alan. Then Olivia. Clearly, they all wanted to hear about "Mom's job." She recounted her night without mentioning the free-handed drunk. She admitted that she was not ready for eight hours on her feet.

After desert Eric, Janine, and Olivia settled in the front room.

"Mom, are you going to be alright?" Olivia asked.

"Livy, honey, I'll be alright. I just haven't worked a shift like that before." She looked at Eric. "Is this going to be alright with you?"

"I'll be okay. We'll make it work."

"I made you some money in tips," she said to Eric. "Livy, go check my pockets."

"Never mind that," replied Eric. "Keep your money for now. We'll settle accounts at a later date."

"I haven't the strength to argue." Janine looked at her daughter. "Livy, you've been awful quiet. Is everything alright at school?"

Olivia looked uncomfortable. "Well…I have to see the counselor twice a week now. It's kind of creepy talking about these things to a stranger."

"I know, honey, but it's necessary. Have the kids been giving you a hard time?"

"Well…this guy Bo started to give me a hard time. Then these cheerleaders told him to shut up. I couldn't believe it. They never talk to me." She hesitated a moment. "I think a made a friend in art class. Julie and I are in history too. She wants me to come over one day."

"That's great. You should do that. Just call." She smiled at Livy. "What kind of hard time did he give you?"

"He called me Out-of-the-house-Olivia. It wasn't so bad."

"Olivia," said Eric, "I know it sounds funny, but he may like you. It's a way of getting noticed."

"Naaa," said the girl, making a face. "Boys!" Olivia rose. "I've got homework. Good night." She left.

"I think you may be right about Brent Jr., sorry, Alan too. He is sitting on something. I'll have to find out. But," she said with a stretch, "it'll have to be tomorrow. How about a round of cribbage?"

Emma was right, Friday night was extremely busy. Multiple customer groups kept coming in until about two. She felt she was keeping up pretty well. She and Emma would gab in short moments. In the early hours a couple of middle-aged men came in inebriated. She had learned to flirt with the customers. But these drunks were aggressive. They tried to touch her every time she passed by. She was getting frustrated. Emma called her over to the register where Elaine was.

"Elaine," said Emma, "we've got a couple drunks with grab hands. They keep lunging at Jan."

"Those two," said Elaine. "Alright, I'll talk to them."

Janine watched as Elaine went over to the drunks. The manager's caution only seemed to inflame the pair.

Janine tried to ignore the men. She avoided going near them. She was wiping down a table when she felt a hand on her bottom. Surprised, she jumped back. "Hey!"

"Nice," said one of the drunks. He leered at her. "Nice ass, honey!"

"Keep your hands off!" she growled. "Don't touch me again."

The drunk leaned toward her. "You liked that. There's more where that came from."

Janine fled the area and ducked into the kitchen. She put her back against the wall. She tried to ease her shaking.

Emma came up. "Jan, honey, are you alright?"

"I can't go out there."

"It's okay. The cops are taking them out now." Emma led her out into the dining room.

Two policemen were ushering the men out of the restaurant. One man noticed Janine.

"There's the bitch!" He pulled away from the cop.

"Whoa, big fella!" said the cop.

The drunk turned and swung at the cop. The policeman forced the drunk to the floor. He was handcuffed in a second.

"Now you're goin' in," said the officer.

"Come on, honey," said Emma. "We have work to do."

Janine watched as the police put the drunk in the car. She looked around the restaurant; people continued with their meals. Emma was already pouring coffee. Elaine was at the register. No one seemed seriously concerned. "Okay," said Janine to herself.

When Janine came home early Saturday morning, Eric was there to greet her. "How'd it go?"

"I'm doing better, but it was a wild night. My calves are going to be like iron. I'd like a hot bath. How are things here?"

"Okay. Quiet." Eric hesitated. "It may be crowded in there. Livy's friend, Julie, stayed over."

"I know. I got the update. Are you sure it's not too much for you?"

"Naaa, the kids are great." He hesitated. "Before you tell me all about work, I'd like to organize a family movie night tonight. Popcorn, soda, and a comedy. Have the kids seen *The Pink Panther?*"

"I don't think so. I haven't seen it in ages." Janine had rarely brought the family together in that way. "Sounds great. So let me tell you about my night. I got groped and I got him arrested!"

Janine slept until the late afternoon. When she padded into the kitchen, Olivia appeared.

"Hi, Mom. It's okay if Julie and her mom come over, right? I mean Uncle Eric said it was okay?"

Janine was delighted that Livy had a friend. "Yes, sure. Do you need me to call her mom?"

"No, Uncle Eric already did. I just wanted it to be okay with you?"

"Livy, honey," she hugged her daughter, "it's fine. I love you."

Olivia reciprocated, "I love you too."

Eric invited Julie and her mom, Allie, for dinner. Olivia, Alan, and Monica helped Uncle Eric with dinner. The two moms talked together over salad and pasta.

"I'm so glad Olivia has found a friend," said Janine.

"I'm so glad too," replied Allie. "Since the separation we seem to have lost all our friends."

"Me too."

"I like Olivia. She's a sweet girl. I hear they bonded over art class. We all heard about you being…evicted," said Allie in a whisper. "We heard your husband left too. I'm so sorry."

Janine considered explaining but let it go. "That's why we were evicted."

"Oh," said Allie. "The girls said they'd like to visit the Art Institute downtown. Your Uncle said he'd take them."

Janine thought about explaining about Eric but let it go. "Did he? He's a gem."

"Don't you think one of us should…chaperone?"

Janine assessed Allie. Although it was fairly warm, she wore a turtleneck, long sleeve sweater. She was plumpish, had no makeup, glasses, and adorned by only a large cross. Allie had insisted on saying Grace before dinner. She had declined wine. Janine thought Allie to be an inhibited, born again divorcee. She would be over-protective of her daughter.

"Allie, I trust Eric completely. He has acted like a father to this family. If you are uncomfortable, I can't help that."

They all settled in the front room for the movie. There were bowls of popcorn and bottles of soda. The moms sat together on the couch with their daughters at their feet. Eric settled into a chair. Monica wanted to sit in Eric's lap. When Eric declined, Monica sat between the moms. Livy had Alan next to her.

As *The Pink Panther* theme played, Janine had a flashback. She remembered sitting in the den with her parents. She snuggled next to her mom. Dad, who usually fell asleep in the chair, roared with laughter. It was a warm, happy memory.

Janine focused on everyone in the room for a few seconds. She wanted memories.

She watched the two tween girls, budding with womanhood. Young Alan laughed and pointed at the hijinks of the movie. Monica seemed to hang on to her mother. Allie seemed to repress all emotion. Even her laughter was stifled.

When she looked at Eric, he was looking at her. He nodded an acknowledgment and then smiled. His gaze returned to the movie. His focus on her made her wonder. What exactly was he thinking?

About one hour into the movie Eric called an intermission.

"Are you enjoying it?" Janine asked Allie.

"Yes. I never really watched it before."

While intermission was on, Janine cornered Eric. "Why were you looking at me like that?"

"It was a moment of perfect motherhood. You were relaxed and soaking in your family. I wish I'd had a camera."

"Oh," she replied. She felt flushed. "You know that you're a part of my family now too."

He looked into her eyes. "Yes."

Suddenly she felt uncomfortable. She looked away. "Maybe we should get back to the movie."

Immediately after the movie ended, Allie announced that it was time for them to leave. "Come on, Julie, there's church in the morning." She looked at Janine. "Are you going to church tomorrow? You could come with us?"

"Sorry, I have to work tomorrow. Maybe another time?"

Olivia walked the guests to their car. Eric and Janine stood at the door.

"She thinks you are a sex maniac with eyes for her daughter," Janine said wryly.

"The poor woman," Eric replied, straight faced. "That turtleneck was driving me wild." He watched as the car pulled away. "She seems so sad. Is it anger, hurt, and disappointment rolled into one?"

"Probably. I don't know. I don't have time for that."

Eric began straightening up the front room. "Maybe you should. That could have been you."

When Olivia came back in, Eric signaled that she should sit down. Eric motioned Janine to sit as well.

Eric addressed them. "Ladies, our friend Allie has bought out an issue that we need to discuss. Sooner or later a counselor or social worker is going to examine this…family we've set up here. I am not related to any one of you. That puts me roughly in stepdad category.

"Olivia, it is really important that you and I keep a discreet distance. You are a maturing girl. Too many stepdads have taken advantage of young girls in their households. You and I must refrain from all physical interaction. No hugs, no touching. If you are ever asked, you can truthfully say no, we never touch, hug, or kiss."

"Really, Eric," said Janine, "I trust that you can behave yourself."

"Thank you. But that is not enough. If one social worker asks Livy if we hug, the children could all be removed by the state. Now we would have to employ lawyers to get your children back. I am sorry, the most stringent modesty must be maintained."

Eric looked at Olivia. "You must understand that the rules here have changed. I know that you understand what I mean. I feel a kinship toward you like a daughter. But you are not my daughter. And you are a mature young woman. Do we all agree?"

"Would the state take my children away?" Janine asked skeptically.

"I understand," replied Olivia. "A girl at school was taken from her mom because of her boyfriend." She nodded at the man. "Okay, Uncle Eric, I'll be careful."

"Wait a minute," said Janine. "If someone complains, they'd take the kids?"

"That's right. And we have to be careful when the social worker inspects the house. If they feel that any compromise of the children's welfare, they're gone."

"Okay," Janine said skeptically. "What about us? You and me?"

"You are an adult. They figure that you can take care of yourself."

THE INTERROGATION

Janine dropped her children at school oldest to youngest. Before heading home, Janine wanted a treat. She had enough money for a latte and scone at Starbucks. She sat and mused about her idyllic past. Her cell phone broke the spell.

"Come home now," said Eric. "There's trouble here."

There was an argument in front of the house. Two Chicago policemen stood by as Eric argued with two other men.

"There is no one of that name living at this address. This warrant is invalid!" Eric pointed his finger at one of the men.

Janine walked up by one of the uniformed police officers. "What's going on?"

"This guy won't let the FBI search his home. He is right, the warrant is bogus."

One of the two men arguing with Eric spotted Janine. "There she is!" He pointed to her. "Officer, detain that woman!"

Janine stepped forward. The cop put a hand on her shoulder.

The man, in jacket and tie, addressed her. "Are you Janine Piersen…?"

"Yes, I am."

"And he is your husband Brent Piersen?" pointing at Eric.

"No. His name is Eric. I have not seen Brent."

"What's he, your father?"

"No. We just happen to have the same last name."

The man closed his eyes and shook his head. "And you are going to tell me that there is no Brent in that house?"

Janine looked back at the house. "I don't know who is in the house. But my husband, Brent, is not here."

Eric and the other man came over. "I'm still gunna search that house!"

"Not with that warrant you won't," said Eric forcefully. "But I tell you what," said Eric more calmly, "I'll let one of Chicago's finest search the house with me."

"Come on, Wilson," said the calm agent. "A new warrant would take hours. If this officer will search the house, we can go."

"Alright," said Wilson grudgingly.

Eric led the officer into the house. After a few minutes he emerged. "No one's home."

Janine was cuffed and put in the back of a car.

Janine was brought in through a guarded entrance in a fenced-in yard. Agent Wilson guided her by the arm. She was still handcuffed. After an elevator ride, they proceeded down a long corridor. She felt like she was in a mausoleum headed toward Hades. Ahead were some chairs against the wall. A woman was sitting dejected, head down. Wilson opened a door immediately in front of the woman.

The woman raised her head. "Janine Piersen?"

"Miriam, Miriam Porter?" she responded.

Janine recognized her as another of the "Gawn Wives Club." They had often commiserated at company events.

She was led into an interrogation room. Her handcuffs were removed. Janine was told to sit.

"Ms. Janine," said the official, opening a file. "I am Special Agent Odom. You know Special Agent Wilson. We would like to ask you some questions and get a statement from you. Can we get you anything?"

Janine assessed the two men across the table. This was getting too familiar. "Yes please, some water. And a cup of coffee if that's available?"

Wilson's partner was standing by the door. "Cream and sugar?"

"Just black, please."

The man left. Odom was an older man, balding with glasses. He focused a steely stare on Janine. "Now madam, please tell me what you know about your husband's dealings. Let's start with Gawn Associates. What do you know about them?"

Janine thought for a few seconds. "I really don't know much. I've been to the office. I've been to a few parties. Brent went out of town occasionally. I've met a few of his partners." She thought for a few seconds. "I guess that's all I really know."

"C'mon," said Wilson impatiently, "you don't know what they were up to?"

She knew that they were trying to get her rattled. Maybe in tears. She had no more tears. She responded calmly. "Sir, do you think I would be homeless, bankrupt, and begging for shelter if I was in on the scams? Brent took everything except my underwear."

Both men stifled their amusement. The agent returned with coffee and water.

"I see," said Odom, composing himself. "I understand Mr. Brent also scammed your aunt in Indiana. How do you explain that?"

Janine sipped the coffee. "I feel really bad about that. That bastard robbed an old lady. He forged my signature on some documents or something." She looked at the man across the table. "If I had the money at least I could afford a lawyer."

Agent Odom assessed her. "And yet you have enough money to sue for divorce and bankruptcy?"

"No, I don't," she replied. "Eric put up the money for that."

"Yes," said Wilson, "and what is your relationship to Mr. Eric Piersen?"

Janine sipped the coffee. It was bitter. "He's just a friend."

"A friend with the same last name? A friend who's put up, what, $10,000?" Wilson leaned forward to intimidate her.

She sipped more again. "This is…shitty coffee." She leaned forward to meet his stare. "That's right, just a friend." She sat back and slumped for effect. "Right now, the only friend I have."

Agent Odom took over. "What do you know about your husband and Canada?"

"We drove to Detroit. We drove across to Windsor. He couldn't find his friend. We had dinner. We drove back to Detroit and then home."

"And he met with no one there?"

"Unless he met him in the men's room, no."

"I see," said Agent Odom. He turned over some papers. "What can you tell us about your husband and the Cayman Islands?"

"He had some brochures. He said we should go there next winter."

"That's it?"

She tried to assess the agents. "Yeah, that's it."

"Did he ever discuss Cuba with you?"

"Cuba?" She thought for a second. "Cuba? No, I don't think so."

The two men whispered between themselves.

Janine realized that she was very dry. She opened the water bottle.

Agent Wilson spoke next. "You mean to tell us you signed a bunch of papers giving away your legal powers and never checked anything? You trusted Brent with everything? I think you're lying to us."

Janine was wrong. She had tears left. "Things were so good. I trusted him with everything. And no, he's robbed me."

"I think that you'd take him back in a minute," said Wilson, baiting her.

The tears in her eyes blurred her vision. "I'd take him back long enough to castrate him!" She was crying now.

"Let's take a break now," said Odom.

The men rose and left. A few seconds later the door opened, and Miriam came in.

"Janine, are you alright?"

Both women hugged and cried. Miriam had a box of tissues. They sat at the interrogation table.

"What happened?" asked Miriam. "Lance is gone with all the money. They've impounded the house. I had to withdraw the kids from school." She wiped her tears.

"Brent is gone too. He stole all our money, even the trust Dad left for me. He scammed my aunt too."

"What have they done?" said Miriam through tears. "I did everything Lance wanted. And now he's gone. He left me with this?" She looked at Janine. "And Brent's gone too?"

They both sobbed and hugged.

"Are you still in the house?" asked Janine.

"For now. They say that they're going to foreclose on it. I'll have to find somewhere to go."

"They already threw us out," said Janine. "How are the kids taking it?"

"Not too well. I packed them up and sent them to my sister in St. Paul."

Agent Odom returned. "Sorry, ladies. Ms. Porter, can you go across the hall?"

"Okay." She hugged Janine. "Come see me tomorrow."

"I will."

The next several hours dragged on for Janine. Agent Odom drafted a statement for Janine stating her story. After she altered the statement several times, she finally signed it.

Then another agent handed her a document. "You are hereby required to furnish a copy of all financial records for the previous three years," he said. She signed that too.

Agent Odom had her wait in the interrogation room. Finally, Agent Wilson came for her. "You're free to go."

"Where's Miriam?" she said, looking down the empty hall.

"She was released hours ago."

Eric was waiting for her in a lobby.

Janine walked up to Eric without emotion. "Let's get out of here."

Eric helped her to the car. "Are you alright?" he said.

"Not here." She refused to break down within sight of the agents.

When Eric had driven a while, she could hold it no longer. She began to weep.

As she cried, she looked outside the car. It was dark out. "How long was I there? What time is it?"

"About 8:30," replied Eric. "Are you hungry?"

"I suppose you took care of my kids?"

"All fed and watered, ma'am," he said humorously. "They're ready for bed when you get home."

She reached out and touched Eric. "Thanks again. You're the best friend I ever had." She relaxed a bit. "You want to know what happened?"

"Why don't you tell us all at one time? The kids will want to hear something."

After a minute of silence Janine spoke up. "One of the other wives from Gawn Associates was there. Miriam. Her husband, Lance, took off too. She doesn't know what hit her. I'm worried about her."

Eric said nothing.

"I feel like I want to help her," she said.

"That's noble of you. Especially as you're barely able to take care of yourself."

"I know. But she's…vulnerable. Lance walked all over her. He treated her like…she should be grateful he married her. He dismissed her totally."

"Okay," said Eric. "What can you do to help her?"

"I don't know yet."

Janine told her tale over a meal. She reassured the children that they were all okay. After dinner she asked if Eric would have a drink with her.

She joined Eric with a scotch.

"Before I go to work, I want to go see Miriam." She looked at Eric for reaction.

Eric took a long breath. "Why?"

"I've felt sorry for her for a long time now. She was…really used by Lance."

"So…" said Eric, "you'd like to help her. I can understand that." Eric assessed her for a moment.

"I'll stop by there on the way to work."

Janine pulled into the crescent-shaped driveway at Miriam's house. She rang the bell several times with no answer. She decided to go into the backyard. She had been to pool parties there a few times.

The pool was empty and full of debris. A couple of deck chairs were laying on their sides. She peered through the sliding doors into the kitchen. She saw nothing unusual there. She knocked on the glass. No answer.

On a whim she tried opening the sliding door. It opened. She called out Miriam's name several times. She continued calling Miriam's name as she searched the ground floor. On the desk were a pile of legal papers. She peeked in the garage. Miriam's SUV was there. She stood at the stairway and called Miriam again. Suddenly she had a bad feeling. She walked up the stairs. The bedroom lights were on.

Miriam was laying on her side on the bed. Her back was to the door. In front of her were pictures of her children. On the nightstand was a bottle of wine and an empty jar of pills.

"Miriam?" Janine walked around the bed.

Miriam's eyes were open and dull. Janine reached out to touch her. Miriam was cold.

"Oh, honey." Janine collapsed into a chair. "Oh god."

Janine let two cops into the house. "You called about…"

"She's up in the bedroom."

"Did you touch anything?"

"I didn't move her," she replied.

"How did you get in?"

"The back door was open."

The police asked her to stay while they processed the suicide. She sat in a chair and cried.

A female officer came over. "Honey, how did you know the deceased?"

"We were friends. Our husbands worked together."

"Oh, yeah. I remember you. You were staying in the house with no power. You got evicted, right? Janice something?"

"That's right. It's Janine Piersen."

An officer in jacket and tie came over. "I'm Detective Collins. You found Ms. Porter. I'm very sorry. I'm afraid I have to ask you some questions."

The detective asked her some general questions. Some she had no answer for. They stood in silence as the coroner removed Miriam's body.

"Is there anything else?" Janine asked the detective.

"Just one more thing." He handed her an envelope. "Your friend left you a message."

Janine took the envelope but did not open it.

The female officer walked her to her car. "Are you alright, honey? Do you need someone to drive you home?"

"I'll be alright. I just want to go home."

When Janine went home, Eric was out. She made herself a cup of tea. She sat at the table and opened the envelope.

Dear Janine, I can't take any more. Lance ruined everything for me. I worked so he could finish school. I was supposed to go but then the kids came. I know he slept with other women. He told me I was fat and ugly. I loved him so much. He hurt me so much.

I guess Brent screwed you too. He was sleeping with that secretary.

I just want to die.

Please tell my children I love them. Miriam

When Eric came home, Janine was sitting on the couch. She barely moved as he entered. Eric looked at the letter in front of her. "Bad news?"

She nodded her head slowly. "Yes. Very bad news."

"Do you want to talk about it?"

"No."

"Do you want me to get the kids from school?"

"Yeah, would you? I'm going to lay down."

Eric shrugged his shoulders. "Sure. Okay.

Janine rose and moved toward the hall. She stopped long enough to say, "Miriam committed suicide."

Eric read the note. He folded it and placed it in the envelope. He put it aside for her.

UNSETTLING INCIDENTS

The weeks that autumn were a blur for Janine. She and Eric had come to agreements about house use, chores, and responsibilities. She maintained a work week of three nights and Sundays.

Janine's legal encounters continued. Her attorneys had filed for separation leading to divorce. She was notified that the case against her in South Bend had been dropped.

Janine hoped for a few weeks of calm. Unfortunately, four issues would disrupt the fragile calm.

The first unsettling issue. A phone message came while Janine was resting after work. Miriam's sister Miranda informed her of an upcoming memorial service.

Wanting her entire family in attendance, Janine consulted the group. They all agreed to join her for Miriam's memorial service. The event would be held on a Saturday afternoon, so it did not conflict with anyone's schedule.

On the Thursday before Miriam's service, Janine received a call from Detective Collins. He asked her to stop by the police station. He had some questions pertaining to Miriam's death.

Janine went to the police station suspecting trouble. Detective Collins and another detective reviewed her statement from the scene.

Twice they asked how she had gained access to Miriam's house. Twice she repeated her story.

"What's going on?" she asked impatiently. "Do you think I killed her?"

"Oh, no, Ms. Piersen," replied Collins. "But the family believes that certain things are missing. Things of value."

"Did you notice the safe open in the den?"

Janine felt her boat descending into hell again. "No. I did not go into the den. I went through the patio doors, through the kitchen. Then I went upstairs. After I called you, I waited in the front room."

She repeated her story several times. Each time the detectives referenced other objects from somewhere in the house. Each time she denied knowing about it.

"Ms. Piersen," asked Collins, "you opened a bank account and deposited $300 in it? Where'd you get the money? Selling objects from your friend's house?"

Janine was now angry. "I did not steal anything from my friend. I deposited pay checks. Check it out."

"We will," said the other detective. "We have some more questions."

Janine quelled her anger. "Ask away. I'm done answering."

The detectives asked more questions. Janine was silent.

After a few minutes Detective Collins said, "Okay, Ms. Piersen. You're free to go."

Janine returned home angry.

Eric tried to soothe her. "Okay, calm down. What happened? They can't think you killed her?"

"No! They think I stole items from the house. They think I opened the safe! What am I a safecracker?"

Eric burst out laughing. "Yeah, you're a cat burglar. What's missing?"

With the tension eased Janine shook her head. "I don't know. Some art objects and a laptop. Why are they blaming me?"

"Maybe the family is boosting its insurance claim?" Eric hesitated. "Do you still want to attend the memorial?"

"Yes, of course."

"Okay, but be ready for a scene from the family."

"I don't believe that," she said. "I've known the family for years."

Janine set the dress code for the service: jacket and tie for the men, nice dresses for the ladies. She ushered them all into a pew near the back. No one interacted or made eye contact with them. Janine suddenly felt like a pariah. She only recognized two faces in the crowd.

As the service progressed Janine noticed no mention of Miriam's husband by name. That she had been married was only mentioned.

Eric pointed out two groups of men on opposite sides of the church.

Toward the end of the service the congregation was invited to the mic for personal tributes. When Janine began to stir, Eric thrust a hand out. "Don't," he said forcefully. "Don't do it."

At the conclusion all were invited to the church basement for refreshments. The congregants began to line up in the central aisle of the church. There was pleasant head-nodding between strangers. The family was shaking hands in the foyer.

Janine nodded toward a woman greeting people. "That's Miranda."

As Janine approached, Miranda's expression changed. "You! You thieving bitch! How dare you show up here?" She looked through the crowd. "Hal, call the cops!"

Shocked, Janine froze.

Eric took her by the arm. "Let's get out of here. Kids, go to the car, now!"

Eric tugged Janine through the crowd and out the door. "Let's go."

Janine kept looking back over her shoulder. "I just wanted..."

Eric purposely guided them to the car. He helped Janine into the passenger seat.

Janine had tears in her eyes. "I just wanted to say goodbye to my friend."

All the kids had tears in their eyes.

"I know," said Eric. "Why don't we go for a drive? We'll find a nice place for dinner. We're all dressed up any way."

Eric drove to the Forest Preserves. He pulled into a scenic wooded area. At a spot overlooking the lake, he parked. Everyone else in the car was crying.

Eric began to speak, "What everyone else thinks is not important. We know that Janine would never steal from her friend. Some day they will realize it too. But until then we stay strong. It is not my fault. We love each other. We trust each other. Right?"

Olivia repeated the words. "It is not my fault. We love each other. We trust each other." Then Alan repeated it. Then Monica.

Finally, Janine repeated it. Then she wiped her eyes. "Anyway, who's she calling a bitch?" They all laughed.

"Okay," said Eric, admiring the view, "where should we eat?"

The second unsettling issue, the visit. It was after dark on Sunday. They were gathered in the front room. Janine was back from her shift, feet up. Olivia was reading. Alan and Monica were doing homework.

Eric was organizing coffee. He brought a tray in with drinks and cookies. His phone rang. "Yes, oh hi." He listened for a while. "I see. Why don't you invite them over for coffee? I'll open the door."

"Kids, I need you to go to your rooms right away." He looked at Janine. "We have company coming. Two guys have been watching the house. They're scaring the cops down the block. The cops are going to send the men over."

Janine ushered the kids out of the front room.

Eric opened the front door and waived the men in. "Come on in, gentlemen. Sit down, there's coffee."

The two men came in and sat on the couch. They said nothing.

Eric and Janine sat in chairs opposite. She sank into the chair, intimidated by their presence.

Eric offered them coffee again. One shook his head no.

"You don't remember me, do you?" said the other man. "Eric, we went to school, remember?"

Eric looked at the man. "It's…Tony, right?"

"Hey, nice place, Eric," he said without smiling. He nudged the silent man. "This guy got me through high school."

"Are you are looking for Brent?" asked Eric.

Slowly they nodded yes.

"He is not here. We do not know where he is." Eric looked at the stone-faced man. He showed no emotion. "But I can tell you what we know."

"Why don't you do that?" said Stone Face.

"Well…the cops thought that Brent and the girl crossed into Canada from Detroit. But Brent was obsessed with the Cayman Islands. He had info on the Caymans."

"Man, that's bullshit," said Stone Face. "The islands are south. Canada is north."

"Naaa," said Tony. "Eric is a straight shooter. Is it Canada or the Caymans?"

"I've been thinking about that," said Eric.

He looked at Janine. "Please find the brochures from the Caymans for me?"

Janine left the room.

Eric faced Tony. "These guys planned their getaways in different directions. I think Brent did go to Canada. He talked to his wife about Cuba. He could have travelled to Cuba from Canada easily. From Cuba he can charter a boat to the Caymans."

Janine returned with papers. Eric urged her to give them to Tony. She sat down after.

Eric addressed Tony. "Did Brent borrow from you guys too?"

Tony did not answer. He gave Eric a wry smile. "I think we should be going."

Both men moved toward the door. Tony looked back at Eric. "Maybe you'd better walk us out. Those cops were kind of...snotty."

"Sure, sure," said Eric.

The three men walked to a car. Eric waved at a neighbor sitting on his porch. As Tony entered the car, Eric addressed him. "Nice to see you again. And listen...If you find Brent, we don't want him back."

"Yeah, sure. See ya."

When Eric returned to the front room, Janine threw her arms around him. "Are you alright? I'm so scared!"

Eric hugged her back. "It's alright. You're alright. Shush."

"Eric, they were..." She was panting. "I was never so scared! They were really scary." She stepped back from the hug. "Was Brent...I mean... And you knew that guy?"

"It's okay," said Eric. "Let's sit and have coffee." Eric moved her into a chair.

Janine sat obviously shaken. Eric poured coffee.

"If they find him, what will they do?" she asked.

"I don't know. Let's have coffee," said Eric in a soothing manner.

The doorbell rang. Eric answered. It was his neighbor. "Hello. Yes, everything is okay here. Thanks a lot."

The third unsettling issue. As autumn changed the landscape, Janine felt they were settling into their new routine.

The kids were quickly getting used to their school schedule. Their extra activities had to be curtailed because the family had little funds to spare. Alan seemed the most disgruntled. There was no money for his sports activities.

The lawyer had recommended Janine establish residency at Eric's address. The lawyer created a rental agreement for Eric and Janine. Armed with the agreement, a couple of paychecks, and the cellphone bill, she went to the DMV. Janine felt uncomfortable with the scrutiny she encountered. After an hour of red-tape officialdom she had an updated driver's license.

With her new license, a lease, and paychecks, Janine went to the bank. She created a checking account for herself. She had never before had an account solely in her name.

Janine was starting to feel better about things. With the paychecks from the restaurant and the tips, she bought the kids some new clothes. She paid the gas for the car herself.

Janine and Eric planned meals together. Eric introduced Janine to coupons and weekly grocery flyers. They calculated how best to use her SNAP food benefits. She did go far from home when using the benefits card.

As Halloween approached, Janine was feeling that things were in control. A social worker, Ms. Parker, scheduled a visit. She was assigned to Alan and Monica.

Ms. Parker toured the house. She asked how the kids were doing. She asked about Brent Sr. She asked why Brent Jr. now called himself Alan. Janine gave Ms. Parker an update on her legal situation. Ms. Parker told Janine that she was lucky to have a relative like Eric. Janine did not correct her.

Janine felt relief that Ms. Parker had not found any glaring issues. Or so she thought.

It was the in the following week that Janine got a call to see the principal at Alan's school. At dinner she asked Alan if there was an issue at school she should know about.

Alan shrugged his shoulders and said, "Nope."

Janine was shown into the principal's office. There she met with the principal, a senior administrator, and Ms. Parker. As she sat Janine had a foreboding feeling.

"Ms. Piersen," said the principal, "we have to speak to you about Brent Jr., now called Alan."

"Oh, what's he done?"

"It's not like that," said the principal. "It's not that Brent, or Alan, as you call him, has done anything. The issue here is your residency. Do we understand correctly that you have established residency in...in Chicago?"

Janine looked at them. "I had to establish…I had to go somewhere?"

"I see," said the principal. "Of course. Can I see your current ID please?"

"Sure," said Janine. She accessed her wallet. She handed the card to him.

"May I make a copy for our records?" he asked.

"Okay."

The administrator took the ID and left the office for a minute.

Janine looked at the other two. They didn't make eye contact.

The administrator returned with several copies. He handed Janine her license. "Well, there it is," he said. "There it is in black and white."

"I'm sorry. What's going on? What's black and white?"

"You have established residency in Chicago," said the administrator.

"Yes, I said that. So what?"

"You're out of district," said the principal. "Your three children will have to register in Chicago schools. Ms. Piersen, you are no longer residing in this district." He looked at the administrator. "Please have Brent, or Alan's, records ready on Friday."

"Out of district?" Janine felt the bottom drop out.

"That's right. Friday will be the last day for your children in our schools." The principal rose. "Thank you for coming in. Good luck." He motioned Janine out of his office.

Stunned, Janine looked at the other two women. "What…?"

"I'm sorry," said the principal. "It's out of my hands."

Janine looked at Ms. Parker. She said nothing.

Janine gathered herself up. With as much dignity as she could muster, she said, "Friday."

Janine returned to the house. She found Eric at the kitchen table. He had lain out tea for two.

"What's the bad news?" he asked. He poured tea.

"They've been thrown out of school."

"What? What'd they do?"

"We are now…residing…out of district. They have to go to Chicago schools."

"Ooh, I didn't think of that."

"Me either." She took a deep sigh. "There is one thing though."

"What's that?"

"The social worker thinks we're related. So, she wouldn't be too concerned with my children living with a strange man."

"Well, I guess that's a good thing," said Eric. "We should reinforce the Uncle Eric title if it helps." He looked at Janine and smiled. "It's not the end of the world. You are all still together. Have faith."

"Okay," she said with a smile.

"And just for the record," he said with mock sincerity, "I'm plenty strange!"

That night Janine called for a circle of truth after dinner.

Janine began by explaining that she had to change their address. She explained that change of residence meant that they were out of district. Janine apologized, but they would have to change schools. Janine regretted being forced into change. But it had to be.

She wanted each of them to express something about the change.

Olivia said she would miss Julie. She said nobody else really mattered.

Alan said he'd miss his team. He'd miss John and Billy. But he really wouldn't miss Egan.

Monica was crying. She'd miss everybody: her teacher, her room, everybody.

Janine ended with their chant:

We are homeless. It is not my fault.

We love each other. We trust each other.

It took a long time for the kids to settle down. Janine found Eric in the front room reading. She brought coffee.

"I thought you might be watching the ballgame?" She poured out cups for them.

"Your lives are way more entertaining than the game," he replied wryly. "That must have been hard."

"It was the last link to their old life. I didn't want it to end. I thought that they'd have their old life a little longer.

"Where I grew up, living in Chicago meant the bottom of the barrel. It was a cool place to visit sometimes but living there?" She looked at Eric. "I'm sorry."

"Why? Because you grew up a privileged suburban kid? What is it they call it now, entitled?"

"Yeah. I was never supposed to earn a living. We used to mercilessly ride the kids who had jobs. It never occurred to me that we could lose everything. That I would have to use food stamps, no way."

"You were living a fantasy dream," Eric said stoically. "My parents and grandparents warned us over and over about overextending. You get what you earn, and you keep it."

"My dad was so right. He warned me about Brent and the easy money guys. He must be rolling over in his grave."

They sat in silence for a few minutes. "If those guys, Tony, find Brent, will they kill him?"

"I don't know," replied Eric. "I don't think we'll know if they do. You must have loved Brent very much."

"You know, I've been thinking about that a lot. I thought we were Barbie and Ken. We looked like a photo spread of perfection. I even had the dream house. But…We never talked. Not like this. Not to the kids. We had thirty second discussions about things. But never about how we felt. He never asked what the kids wanted or how they felt. We were just…window dressing. I had the house, the kids, and the country club."

She shook her head. "We used to pity the abandoned wives, the divorcees. The men got trophy wives, the divorcees disappeared—most of them. They got fat or tired or old and the husbands moved on. Like sharks to their next meal." She fell quiet. After a long silence she said, "I hope they kill him. He killed my dream, my life."

"Yes, he broke your bubble, but not your life," said Eric. "You're stronger today than the day you were evicted."

"I'm not so sure," said Janine quietly. "I loved him so much, but…I don't think he ever really loved me. He gave me the house, the kids, the life. All I dreamt of. But I never had him, really had him. I knew he boffed Sylvie. I think lots of them did. She was such a flirt, the skag.

"When we played tennis with Bob and Linda, he couldn't keep his eyes off her ass. That's when I started yoga, to trim up my ass. You don't think my ass is too big, do you?"

Eric seemed startled by the question. "I think it's very nice."

She smiled at him. "Thanks for that. Have you been ogling my ass?"

Eric tried to evade her look. "Well…I ain't dead yet." He tried not to look uncomfortable. "Are you up for a game of cribbage?"

The fourth unsettling issue. Eric woke Janine in the late morning. He stood at the door knocking and calling "Janine!"

"What? Are the kids alright?"

"I think so," said Eric "There's a phone call from the police."

"Police? What do they want now?" Janine grabbed her robe and met Eric at the door. She took the phone from him. "Hello, yes, this is…"

Eric retreated to the kitchen. He started some coffee.

Janine padded in with a pale look. "I've got to go to the morgue. They think they've found Brent."

"I see," replied Eric. "Do you want me to go with you?"

Janine had tears in her eyes. "Oh, yes please. Could you?"

"Sure. I'll be ready when you are. I'll write a note for the kids."

"Okay," she said, choked up.

"Why don't you use the bathroom and get dressed. We'll have a cup of coffee and go."

"Shouldn't we go right away?"

"There is no hurry. The dead can wait."

Eric drove them to Cook County Morgue.

Janine was crying for most of the trip. She kept blurting out incomplete thoughts: "Do I bury him? Where has he been? They can have him, I don't want him…"

As they pulled up, she looked at Eric. "Why should I do this? I don't want him!"

"Janine," he said calmly. "If your husband is dead, it makes a couple of things easier for you."

"Like what?"

"Well, firstly you do not have to wonder where he is. He can do you no more harm. Secondly, you do not have to divorce him. It saves some legal bills. Thirdly, as a widow you can claim social security benefits for you and the kids."

Janine dried her eyes. "Really?" She blew her nose. "Okay. I can do this for the kids."

Janine and Eric waited half an hour before they were summoned to a cubicle. It seemed garish to have the morgue decorated for Halloween.

"I'm Detective Voss with the coroner's office. I'd just like to go over a few things. Can I see your ID, please, Ms. Piersen? I see by your missing person's report that you last saw your husband in Wisconsin in August; is that correct?"

"Yes."

The detective looked at both of them. "And you haven't heard from him since?"

"That's right."

"Well, the body is badly decomposed. We'll have to view it through a window."

"Okay," said Janine.

"Can't you match dental records?" asked Eric.

"Have you visited your dentist in the last few months?" asked the detective.

"No, we haven't," said Janine. "I think there was a fire."

"That's right. Your dental office burned down a week before you reported Brent missing." The detective looked at them for a reaction.

Eric shook his head. "They are thorough. You've got to give them that."

"What?" said Janine.

"This way," said the detective.

They entered a small viewing room. Beyond the glass in the next room was a body under a sheet.

"Are you ready?" asked the detective.

Janine nodded. The detective nodded. A masked worker unveiled the corpse.

Janine gasped. She looked the bloated, discolored body back and forth. "I don't know," she said. "Can you hold up his hands?"

The masked worker held up the hands one at a time.

"Anything?" asked the detective. "Anything at all?"

"Wait," she said. "Brent is missing two toes on his right foot. He cut them off with an axe."

The worker held up the right foot; five toes.

"Are you sure?" said the detective. "There's nothing in the report about missing toes."

"I'm sure. I try not to think about it. It never seemed to matter."

"Alright," said the detective. "I'll need you to sign the form that this is not your husband."

She looked at the body. "Whose husband is it?"

As they left the viewing area Janine asked for the lady's room. Eric stood outside while Janine wretched.

When they got back to the car she cried. "I guess he did not want to be found."

"I guess so."

"Why did he want to dump us so badly?"

"I don't know."

"Yes, you do. You're a man."

"Do you think that there is any way you could have lived with him, knowing he cheated your aunt? Or drained your trust? He burned his bridges leaving the carnage behind." Eric was silent for some time. "I'd be shocked if you ever hear a thing about him again."

"What do we tell the kids?"

"You tell them the truth. The coroner thought he had their father's body, but it was not."

"Do I tell them I hope we never find him?"

"If they ask you in the truth circle, tell them the truth. It is all you have."

A VISIT TO MOM'S

It was the Wednesday before Thanksgiving when Janine took her kids to visit her mom. She deliberately went without Eric. Her mom's phone calls made Janine think her mother was no longer sharp.

The "Home" was decorated in Hallmark Thanksgiving. Mom's room was neat with a bed and sitting area. Meals were served in the dining room. Janine had arranged for a family dinner.

"Hi dear," said Mom. She was in her good dress. "I'm so glad to see you. And you all together. Where's Brent? I like him."

"Mom, Brent's gone."

"He died! I'm so sorry, dear. When's the funeral?"

"No, Mom. I mean he left. He took off."

"Oh, okay." Janine watched as her mom rose and hugged Monica. "You're getting so big Janine."

They ate a table set for the five of them. Her mom talked on about nothing. The kids giggled quietly at the absurdity of Grandma's conversation.

As the meal ended an administrator introduced herself. She asked if Janine could spare a few minutes before leaving.

Janine had the kids return Grandma to her room. She found the administrator's office.

"Please come on in and sit down. I'm Rhonda White."

Janine knew this was not going to be a happy meeting.

"Ms. Piersen, your mother's dementia is increasing. She will not be able to stay in a room unattended. She will soon need full time monitoring." Ms. White waited for a reaction but got none. "Phyllis's care will need an increase in funding to continue at this level."

"Mom's trust is paying for her care," said Janine. "I have no control over it."

"Yes, I know what the trust is supplying. However, her care increases require additional funding."

"You are saying that the trust can no longer support Mom's care? I don't know what you want me to do about it. Have you contacted the lawyer?"

"I have. The new law firm says that they can only authorize funding at this level. I have prepared a proposal that meets her increased needs." Ms. White tried to hand Janine a packet of papers.

Janine did not take the papers. "I'm sorry, I'm in no position to fund anything. You'll have to make do with what you're getting."

"But you see, your mom's care will have to be adjusted. There isn't enough funding for increased care." Ms. White held the papers out for Janine again.

Again, Janine refused to accept them. "Send those to the lawyer. I'm done here." She rose to go.

"Just one more thing," said Ms. White, "I need an updated contact number."

Janine returned to her mom's room. She was looking out the window. The kids were nowhere to be found.

Mom greeted her. "Jan, honey, sit down." Mom settled into a chair. "I'm sorry, dear, I've been a little foggy today. Did you say that Brent took off with all the money? And he got Sarah's too?"

"Yes, Mom. We're penniless. We've lost the house too. I get food stamps now. We're living with a stranger. I had to put the kids in Chicago schools. I'm working as a waitress, Mom." Janine started crying.

All the while her mom sat expressionless. "I'm so sorry, dear. I always hoped to spare you these kinds of things. Your dad set up your trust so that this wouldn't happen. He wasn't much of a father, but he was a provider."

"What do you mean, Mom?"

"Jan, dear, did he ever hug you? Or me? Those trips we took, did he ever join us? I took the trips with you. He worked at the office and worked at home. He made your college graduation a business trip for gosh sakes. I don't miss him at all."

"Mom, they want to reduce your care here. They say that there isn't enough money in the trust fund."

"Well, dear, it seems unlikely your father didn't account for that. But if it's true, it's true." She looked at her daughter and smiled. "Don't worry, dear. I'm just waiting here to die."

Janine went over and hugged her mother. "I love you."

"I know, dear. I love you too. But you have to take care of my grandchildren. That's what's important now. Them, not me. I'll be okay. But Jan, honey…be happy."

Janine looked at her mother with tears in her eyes. "We've got to be going. I'll have to round up the kids."

"Sure, sure," she said. "I'll see you soon."

Janine found the kids outside. "Go up and tell your grandma goodbye. I'll be in the car."

In the car Janine cried some more. The kids piled in. "All okay?"

"She was asleep," said Olivia.

On Thanksgiving Day Janine worked a full shift. Management wanted everyone in. She was glad for the extra money.

Eric took the kids to his son's house for the day. Paul and Sheila had a houseful. Janine's kids mingled with relatives in Sheila's family. Olivia even had a tween to talk to.

Alan tossed a football around with several boys. Paul came out and played a little. When the games broke for dinner, Paul engaged Alan.

"Is you mother working today?" he asked.

"Yeah, at Denny's. She's a waitress."

"Do you like Uncle Eric's house?"

"It's okay. I liked my other house better."

"Do you miss your father?"

"Yeah. I guess, sometimes. He left us and took everything."

Paul smiled at the boy. "Do you like Uncle Eric?"

"He's okay." Alan looked at Paul. "He's your dad. Did he ever run away?"

Paul smiled. "No. No, he never ran from anything. Do you think he likes your mom?"

"I guess so. They talk a lot."

Paul noticed that Olivia was watching him.

They were all called to the table.

After dinner Olivia sat next to Paul. "Do you want to ask me if my mom sleeping with your dad?"

Embarrassed by the question, Paul could only manage an "Ah."

"Do you think he's hitting on me?"

"No!" replied Paul emphatically. "No, no I don't. I think he's taken you in the way my mom would have."

Olivia looked at Paul and nodded. "He said that too." She looked away. "He made us face our homelessness. He made us believe in ourselves. He's kept us together. He even made mom get food stamps." She looked at him. "He's been more like a father than mine was. Don't be mad at him? Please?"

Paul looked at the girl. He smiled at her. "I'm not mad at him. He is a good father. I think he misses Mom. And I'm glad he found you guys. It's given him…purpose."

Paul looked at the girl. "Tell me about your mom."

In the car Olivia asked Eric in a hushed voice, "You want to know what your son asked me?"

Eric kept his eyes on the road. "Only if you want to tell me."

Again, in a hushed voice, "He asked if you're hitting on Mom."

Eric looked at Olivia briefly. "No, he didn't. He knows better."

Olivia looked at Eric quizzically. "Isn't she pretty?"

Eric kept his eyes on the road. "Yes, she is a lovely woman. She is also a married lady. Gentlemen don't hit on married ladies."

"But if Mom's divorced?"

Eric broke his focus to look at Olivia briefly. "A gentleman doesn't comment on his relations with a lady."

"Dad was always saying 'he'd like to tap that.'"

Eric's eyes stayed on the road. "As I said, a gentleman never comments on his relationship with a lady."

Eric suggested a family outing for the Saturday after Thanksgiving. He was met with surprised silence. Eric suggested a trip to the Art Institute. Again, surprised silence.

"When's the last time you guys went?" he asked.

Again, stony silence.

"Never?" He shook his head. "Okay, the Art Institute it is."

"I don't want to see a bunch of silly pictures," blurted Alan.

"Shush," said Janine.

"That's alright," said Eric. "I'll bet we find somethings that you like."

Eric looked at Janine. "Everybody dresses in nice-casual. Uncle Eric will take everybody to dinner."

Eric had a plan in mind for the museum. He would sit in a galley and ask the kids to report what they'd seen in every portrait. Monica and Olivia were moderately engaged, Alan less so. Janine was caught between watching the children and the pictures.

Eric led them through a few galleries. Again, he sat. "Tell me what you see." He motioned Janine to sit next to him. "Let's see what their reaction is."

Monica and Alan raced back to where they were sitting.

"It's the farmer with the pitchfork!" said Alan.

Janine watched Olivia. She was mesmerized in front of *American Gothic*.

"That's right," said Uncle Eric. "But what do you see?"

The two raced back to where Olivia was standing.

Eric pointed at another painting. "There's the *Night Hawks* over there."

Janine looked at the painting of the diner with its lonely customers. She thought about those solitary people who came to the restaurant in the wee hours.

Eric led them to a gallery of Old Masters. "What do you see?"

Alan rushed back to Janine's side. "There's naked girls," he whispered.

"And naked men too," she replied. "It's art."

Janine watch Olivia through the galleries. She seemed to absorb every picture.

Eric brought them to the food court. He suggested snacks. While the kids wolfed down a snack, Eric suggested Olivia take the kids to the hall of ancient arms and armor. The adults wanted a longer coffee break.

Once alone Eric asked, "You never visited the museums?"

"No. Dad never went anywhere but work and company parties. Mom was afraid to go into Chicago alone. We never went anywhere."

"I think Olivia likes it here."

"I think she does too."

Janine was taking in her surroundings. "Thank you for dragging us here. It's different than I imagined."

Eric took them to a steakhouse for dinner. Eric maneuvered seating between Janine and Olivia.

Janine was engaged with Monica and Alan about the museum.

Eric talked to Olivia. "You liked it there, didn't you?"

"It was…" Livy could not find words.

"I've seen some of your drawings. Maybe we could arrange Saturday classes at the museum."

Olivia could find no words.

Janine hit Eric's arm. "We can't afford that."

"We'll talk about it later." He looked back at the girl. "Which pictures did you like the best?"

As the Christmas season started, Janine was a little depressed. When Eric pulled out his Christmas decorations Janine realized her need. She wanted some of her family's cherished decorations. She realized that all their family's decoration had been in a storage locker. The storage place had sold off her belonging's months ago.

When she talked to Eric about it, he suggested that they each pick out one new decoration apiece for the tree. It would be a symbol of their new life. At their weekly family meeting, she brought it up. The kids reluctantly agreed.

Janine was a little depressed that she would have to work Christmas Eve and New Year's Day at Denny's. She had always enjoyed the holidays with the kids and Brent. But she needed the money and holidays got bigger tips.

Eric wanted to host his son and wife for Christmas Day. Janine could not turn him down.

It all seemed to fit on the schedule until the casino called. Was Janine still interested? Could she come in for an interview?

Janine talked it over with Eric. He counseled, "See what they're offering. We'll go from there."

Janine arranged an interview in the hours before her shift at Denny's.

She was sent in to see "Interview Specialist" Marsha Wilson again. "Oh, hello. I've been trying to remember what you looked like."

"I was surprised to get your call," replied Janine. "I'd given up on you."

"I see," said Marsha. "To be honest a recruitment initiative began when an immigration sweep took several of their employees. Your application came to the surface. Your background check was clean. You have a college degree. You don't have any immigration issues, do you?"

"No. Born in Lake County."

"Good. Anyway, we are looking for some part-time help for the holidays. Cooks, servers, janitors, waitresses, and cocktail servers."

"Well, I'm working as a waitress at Denny's now. I could not do kitchen work. I would not do janitorial work."

"I see," said Marsha. "Let's concentrate on waitress and cocktail server. As a waitress you'd be issued a uniform and work in one of our casual eateries. As a cocktail server you'd wear your own dress and wear heels. That seems to be a no-go with some people."

"What do you mean by part-time?"

"You'd be filling in the schedule where we are short-handed. Peak hours mostly. We usually have a pool of people for fill-ins." She smiled at Janine. "If you are interested in both, it would be an asset. Here are the pay scales." She handed Janine a chart.

"How soon do you need an answer?"

"As soon as possible. We need people this weekend."

"Look," said Janine, "I'd have to keep my other job too. I'd have to mesh them together."

"I see. Of course. If you'd like to try it, that'd be fine. There might be a full-time spot open in the future."

"Look, I have to go home and talk to my family. Can I call you in the morning?"

"Please do," replied Marsha. "I have others to reach as well."

"Two jobs!" said Alan. "How can you do two jobs?"

"Only with your help, honey," Janine replied. "I know it's a lot, but we owe so much money."

"Mom, it seems like a lot," said Olivia. "We need you here."

"I know, my loves. But if we all pitch in and help Uncle Eric, we can make it. Besides, I might get a better job at the casino. I have to work there so they can see how reliable I am."

"We can help you, Mommy," said Monica.

"And you do. I think it's something I have to try." She looked at Eric.

"I worked two jobs for a long time," said Eric. "I had help at home. If everyone pitches in, we'll make it."

Janine went in for new employee training at the casino. She spent a whole day on procedures. They gave her a large notebook full of papers. She sat with a scheduling manager. At first, she was assigned to two nights in the restaurant. She would now be working a forty-hour week between the two jobs.

Janine trained in the restaurant. It seemed very similar to her work at Denny's. She still had to deal with inebriates. The tips were generally better.

She now seemed to be on a night schedule. She would come home, rouse the kids for school, shower, and sleep. She managed to have dinner with the family most nights.

With a bit more cash in pocket she proceeded with the Christmas ornament plan. She took Alan and Monica shopping for basic clothes at JC Penny's. Then she led them to Christmas decorations. "Pick one for yourself," she told them. Monica found her new favorite, Snoopy. Alan settled on a baseball ornament.

Getting together with Olivia seemed more difficult. She resisted the shopping trip. Janine told her she needed new underwear. Janine also wanted her daughter to have a nice dress for the holidays. Livy refused to look or try on anything. When she wanted her to look at ornaments, she refused again.

At their weekly discussion, Janine remarked to Eric about the changes in her life. "I always shopped high end stores for everything. I bought designer outfits for Livy. I never thought about whether their clothes would last until spring. I never worried about money. I guess I should have.

"I never gave a thought about the homeless. I thought the people who needed assistance were druggies or careless. I never even considered having a real job. How can somebody support themselves this way?" She reached out a hand and touched Eric's. "How can I ever thank you helping us? I don't know."

"You can pay it forward. When things are better you can help the helpless. Please don't worry about me." He smiled at her. "About Olivia, let me talk to her. We seem to have a rapport these days."

THE HOLIDAYS

The weeks before Christmas were a blur for Janine. Work, breakfast with the kids, sleep, dinner with the kids, and work. Off days were crammed with laundry and shopping.

Eric organized the kids into grocery, cooking, and house cleaning patrols. They got a tree and set it in the front room. Alan self-deputized himself keeper of the lights.

Eric laid out a schedule of activities for the kids' winter break. Janine was scheduled to work Christmas Eve and Christmas night graveyard at Denny's. Eric planned to host Paul and Sheila for Christmas dinner. Days before the feast, Eric invited his niece, Alice, to join them.

Janine worked the Christmas Eve shift with as much cheer as she could muster. There were a couple of groups happy to be together. Lone people, eating alone, tugged at her heart. She tried to engage with them as cheerfully as possible. No one seemed happy on the staff. Everyone wanted to be somewhere else.

Near the end of her shift Emma came in. "Hey, girl. How ya doin'." They hugged briefly. "Merry Christmas."

"Okay, it's been slow. We're down a bus boy. I have tables to clean and prep in the back."

"Okay," said Emma up-beat. "You clean bus and prep. I'll handle the customers."

Janine rushed through her chores like a horse headed for the barn. She looked at the clock; fifteen minutes to go.

"You can go ahead and leave," said Elaine. "We'll see you tomorrow night."

Janine waited until she talked to Emma. "Hey, I'm going to leave. Have a good holiday. I'll see you next week."

"Sorry, honey. I'm taking my man down south to meet the family. I'll be off 'till New Year's. Have a good holiday, honey." They smiled at each other.

Janine waived at the cook smoking in the lot. Her car seemed really cold. The streets were virtually empty. There had been no snow. Everything, unlit by holiday lights, looked grey and dead. The bank sign read 10 degrees. She wondered how the homeless were coping.

Eric's house was decorated outside. Alan had used every string of lights in the basement.

Everyone was waiting for Janine to come home. They all sat at the table for fruitcake and coffee.

"Before bed, everyone gets their ornament and puts it on the tree," said Eric.

They met in the front room. Monica went first. She hung her snoopy near the bottom. Alan went next. He hung his baseball player as high as he could reach. Olivia hung an ornament. It was Princess Leia in white. Eric hung an ornament that said Peace.

They all looked at Janine. "I...I didn't get one for myself."

Eric nodded at Olivia. She handed box to Janine. She unpacked an ornament that said Best Mom Ever.

Janine began to cry. She motioned for a group hug. "Thanks, you guys. I love you." She handed the decoration to Monica. "Please hang it for me?"

After a few minutes of appreciating the tree, Eric spoke. "Okay troops, we all have duties in the morning. Let's get some sleep."

Janine awoke to find two strange things. First, she recognized the drone of the vacuum cleaner. Secondly, she recognized the smell of baking.

After a bathroom stop, she padded into the kitchen. Monica, Alan, and Eric were peering into the oven.

"Oh hi, you're up," said Eric. "Merry Christmas. You missed breakfast, but we kept a cinnamon roll for you. Hot coffee coming up."

"Merry Christmas!" said the kids with a hug.

"No hurry, Jan. You have about two hours until anyone gets here. The bathroom is clear and all yours." Eric poured coffee. "Okay kids, let's start setting the table."

"You need my help?" she asked Eric.

"Na," said Eric. "I think we've got everything here."

Olivia walked in. "Merry Christmas, Mom." They hugged. "Anything else?" she asked Eric.

"I think we're good. Thanks, Livy."

Janine had a leisurely bath. Both of the girls left her alone to dress. She was apprehensive as she'd only met Paul once. She wanted Eric's family to like her. She decided on a sensible dress and simple jewelry.

When she came out, she was surprised to find Olivia in a dress. It was simple and black, but it was a dress. "You all look so nice," she said.

The doorbell rang. As Eric went to answer it, Janine whispered to Livy, "Nice dress, honey. You look great."

"Uncle Eric said I needed to look nice for his family."

Eric brought a woman into the room. She was in her sixties. "Everybody this is Alice. This is Janine and her children Olivia, Alan, and Monica."

"It smells nice in here," said Alice. She looked at Janine and said, "Are you making turkey?"

"I'm not cooking," said Janine. "Eric is."

Eric sat in the chair next to Alice. "I haven't seen you many years now. What brings you to Chicago?"

"Well, I came to visit my husband's brother. He's in the Jewish home down by the lake. And I thought since it was Christmas, I should see you. I'm sorry I couldn't make it to the funeral…"

Janine motioned the kids to the kitchen. "Let's let Eric talk to his guest. We'll put dinner on the table. Okay?"

"Mom," said Alan excitedly, "there's presents under the tree for us!"

"Really? We'll deal with that later. Now, dinner." She found Eric's meal plan on the counter. She put on an apron.

The doorbell rang. A few minutes later Paul appeared. "Hi, kids." He shook hands all around. He looked at Janine. "Smells great. I brought beer."

Paul and Sheila talked to Alice while everyone else put food on the dining room table.

"Everyone, I don't want to rush, but Janine has to work later. The food is ready. Why don't we get seated?" Eric directed the places.

At the head of the table, Eric had Alice on his right. He put Paul next to her. Sheila was on Eric's right with Janine next to her. Eric explained to everybody that Alice was his wife's niece. Eric spent most of the meal conversing with Alice about relatives.

When Eric went to the kitchen Alice asked Paul, "When did your father re-marry?"

"He didn't," replied Paul, amused. "They only live here."

After dessert Eric said, "It's time for presents!"

Everyone settled in the front room.

Paul and Sheila began handing out presents. They gave Monica a Hello Kitty purse. They gave Alan a football. They gave Olivia a sketch pad. They gave Janine a box of chocolate. They gave Eric a six pack of beer.

Eric handed out presents. He gave Monica a small ceramic unicorn. He gave Alan a baseball glove. He gave Olivia a water-color paint set. He gave Janine a sweater. He gave his son a mug with the Cubs logo. He gave his daughter-in law a crystal vase.

And then Eric handed a box to Monica, Alan, and Olivia. They each opened a laptop.

Janine was choked up and tried to thank them.

Alice watched the present giving with a quizzical expression.

"I'm sorry, Alice, I didn't have time to get you anything," said Eric.

Alice motioned Paul to sit next to her. "I haven't seen you so long. I'm glad to meet your wife…"

"Sheila," said Paul. "Aunt Alice, I'm a little confused. Dad called you his niece?"

"I am your mother's niece. We grew up together in Lansing." She pointed at Janine. "How are they related?"

"They're not," replied Paul. "Dad found them out on the street. They'd been evicted. The dad ran off."

"The dad ran off and left them?"

"That's right."

"And your dad took them in, just like that? In my aunt's house?"

"That's right."

Alice fell silent watching Janine. Paul vacated the chair without her notice.

Janine watched the kids clean up the Christmas wrappings. She took her present and placed it under the tree.

Alice's eyes followed Janine the whole time. Janine wondered what she was thinking. Alice motioned Janine over to the empty seat. "Sit down, dear."

Janine and Alice looked at each other.

Alice spoke first. "Did I hear that your husband left you?"

Janine nodded.

"And these lovely children?"

Janine nodded.

Alice reached out and took Janine's hand. "Oh, dear, I'm so sorry." She patted her hand. "And you were evicted?"

Janine nodded.

"Are you going to marry Eric?" she asked earnestly.

"I…I don't think I can." Janine was totally flummoxed.

Alice summoned Eric over with a wave. She still held Janine's hand. "Why won't you marry this nice girl?'

"Alice?" said Eric, stunned.

Paul, Sheila, and Olivia found it embarrassingly humorous.

"Why not?" asked Alice earnestly.

"Alice," said Eric patiently, "it's complicated. For one thing, she's still married. But most importantly, it's none of your business."

"She's taken my aunt's place here in the house. You ought to marry her. She deserves that."

Paul, Sheila, and Olivia were stifling their amusement. Janine was red with embarrassment.

Eric took a deep breath. "Alice, I loved your aunt as much as anyone could. You know that. It seems kind of soon for me to remarry. But for right now they're just living here. I couldn't let them live on the streets."

"No, no. I see that." Alice nodded. She looked at Janine. "Don't let him take advantage, dear."

"Alice!?" said Eric.

Janine looked into the woman's earnest expression. "Eric has been very kind and very generous. He's been…a gentleman."

"Well, I should hope so."

Janine smiled at the woman. "You'll have to excuse me. I have to go to work. It was nice to meet you."

"You work?" asked Alice.

"That's right. I'm a waitress. I have to support my family."

Janine left the room, still embarrassed. Olivia followed her into the bedroom.

"Mom, are you alright?" asked her daughter.

"Sure, sure," she said, sitting on the bed with her daughter. "She just…hit a spot."

"Mom, would you marry Uncle Eric?"

"Oh, honey, I don't know. I can't think about that right now. There are so many issues. You know that."

"But you like him, don't you?"

"Yes, of course I do." She took her daughter's hand. "But marriage? I can't deal with that right now." She hugged Olivia. "But I do need to go to work."

Janine's phone rang. It was the casino.

"Janine, this is Pauline. Can you come in to work drink hostess tomorrow evening?"

"Sure. I'll be there."

When Janine came home after her shift at Denny's, Eric was waiting. The house was strangely silent. With the kids off school the usual buzz was silent.

Janine sat with Eric at the kitchen table.

"I'm sorry Alice put you on the spot."

She smiled at him. "Eric, it's okay."

"She shouldn't have embarrassed you that way."

"She just caught me off guard. It is an unusual situation. I don't want you to be uncomfortable."

"Me?" He looked at her quizzically. "I gave up worrying about what others think a long time ago. I just don't want you to feel pressured to leave."

"Eric," she said earnestly, "we couldn't feel more…welcome. You and your son gave the kids presents. We don't have anything for you."

Eric gave her a slow smile. "I don't need anything. Just knowing the kids are safe and warm is all I need."

They both looked at each other for a moment.

"I'd better get a shower. I have to work cocktails at the casino tonight."

"Sounds like a promotion?"

"Sounds like a new group of gropers."

Janine found drinks hostess not unlike waitressing. It was more lucrative as tips were better. In general, the customers were less difficult. She had chosen her clothes wisely; she smelled of beer by night's end. She had picked out comfortable low heels, but her calves were aching.

Around midnight Janine noticed a three-couple group. One on the men she knew from the country club. He had his arm around young woman that was not his wife. Luckily the party was seated in a different section.

Janine sneaked a peek at the group from time to time. She tried to remember if the man had an older daughter. When the three women got up the man stroked her rear. The young woman sashayed to the lady's room with as much wiggle as possible.

Janine lingered at the order station for a minute. Another hostess came over. She guessed the woman to be her age. Her ID said Marlene.

"First time, honey?" Marlene asked.

"Yeah. Does it show?"

"You're doing okay, honey," she said. "Want a suggestion? Wear a low-cut top, honey. Show a little cleavage. It's worth at least $50 a night."

"Ah, okay," replied Janine. She watched the three women return to the group. She watched Marlene engage the group. When Marlene cleared the table, she bent forward to show her cleavage.

"I see," said Janine to herself.

The evening went with just one incident. One inebriated customer spilled beer on her staggering to the men's room.

When Janine came home Eric was waiting at the table.

"Did you have a good night?" he asked. "Whoa, did you bathe in beer?"

"Yeah, somebody spilled on me. It was okay. My feet hurt and my calves are tight. But it was alright. Are the kids okay?"

"Sure. Olivia is spending the night with Julie. The other two are tucked in bed. Hot tea?"

"Please. But let me shower first. I smell like a brewery."

Janine returned to the table in her bathrobe fresh from the shower. Eric poured out tea.

"I saw a guy from the country club tonight. He was in a cozy group with some young thing. Not his wife." She stirred sugar into her tea. "Are all men pigs? He has young daughters. And there he is with hands on some young thing."

They both sat in silence for a minute.

"I haven't thought about Brent in a while. I haven't had the time. He always found some young thing to charm. He could really turn it on." She sipped her tea. "I ignored the truth about him. I really did. He was cheating but I…ignored it. We were comfortable. I was comfortable. I did not want to face it. I should have watched him, but I didn't. I should have checked out the accounts, but I let him charm me. Dad warned me. Mom warned me. But we were so…" She looked at Eric is sincerity. "We were Barbie and Ken in the dream house, country club, and Cadillac. I let it happen."

Janine looked down at the table. "And I let my children down. I was so foolish, I let my children down. I didn't protect them." She looked Eric in the eye. "Didn't I?"

Eric's gaze locked into hers. "It's not my place to judge you. You trusted your husband. He was supposed to be dedicated to your family. Your dedication to those kids cannot be questioned.

"As for men being pigs," Eric hesitated, "I believe some are." Eric hesitated again. "If the job is going to upset you, maybe you should let it go."

"Ha," she replied. "My not taking the job won't change their behavior. The tips are good. And the security won't let them touch me. I'll be okay. I think I'll get to bed."

"Oh, by the way, Saundra called. She'll call back tomorrow."

Janine invited Saundra over for dinner. She was jovial and interacted with the kids personally. Saundra brought each of them a stocking full of Christmas candy.

Saundra also brought a bottle of wine. The two ladies settled into the front room together.

Saundra told of a divorce settlement that left her an income. Chase wanted to sell up and leave the country. Apparently, he had dealings with Brent that he wanted kept quiet. Saundra was now living with her daughter's family in Cleveland. She had come to Chicago over some legal thing.

Saundra told Janine that Brent had caught several men in the country club in his scam. That triggered two divorces, which brought out several of Brent's peccadillos.

"But really Jan, honey, how are you doing?" Saundra asked.

"I've been busy working. Between waitressing and keeping house I haven't had time for much."

"Keeping house? Have you moved into Eric's bedroom yet?" said Saundra devilishly.

"No. I mean we do the chores here and he lets us stay."

Saundra laughed. "He'd let you do more than that!"

"Shhh," cautioned Janine. "He'll hear you."

"Listen, honey, you'd better take as much as you can. Everybody does."

"It's not like that."

"Oh, yes it is. Do you think he'd let you stay if you were old and fat?"

"Stop it! You're drunk."

"I better use the bathroom," said Saundra.

When Saundra left the room, Janine closed her eyes. She was startled awake by the sounds of voices in the hall.

"Yeah, yeah," said Eric. "The bathroom is over here."

"I'm so sorry," said Saundra.

Janine heard footsteps in the hall.

Saundra reentered the room. "I got lost there."

Janine laughed. "Maybe you should sleep here on the couch if you can't find the bathroom?"

"Maybe I should."

Janine woke up in the front room with a headache. After a bathroom stop, she went into the kitchen. Olivia and Saundra were having coffee.

"How's your head?" asked Saundra.

"Pounding," replied Janine. She poured coffee.

"Uncle Eric had to go out," said Olivia.

"Okay," said Janine. She looked at Saundra. "What are your plans?"

"Honey, I have to go. I have a meeting around noon and a three o'clock flight. But it's been great seeing you." Saundra hugged Janine. "I think you should take advantage of the opportunities in front of you. Anyway, I'll be in touch."

Saundra hugged Olivia. "Say goodbye to the kids, okay?"

Janine slid into a chair, clutching her cup of coffee.

Olivia returned to the kitchen. "Mom, that was so weird."

"What was?"

"Aunt Saundra going into Uncle Eric's bedroom like that."

"Like what?"

"And then using the bathroom while he was shaving!"

"She did what?"

"Yeah, she walked right in on him."

"I don't understand?"

"Mom, she's making her moves on him."

"Eric?"

"Yes Mom, Uncle Eric."

"Where is Eric?"

"He went out. He said something about the hardware store."

"Really?"

"What did Aunt Saundra mean about opportunities? Did she mean Uncle Eric?"

"You know, I think she did."

When Eric returned, Olivia and Janine were still lingering over coffee. Eric poured himself a cup and sat down.

"How was your night?" asked Janine.

"I had just dozed off when your friend Saundra climbed into bed with me," said Eric matter-of-factly.

The women began to laugh. "She was lost," said Janine, laughing.

"Well, she was searching around for something."

They all laughed.

"And this morning she wanted to help me shave!"

Janine clocked in at Denny's at ten p.m. on New Year's Eve. The restaurant was fairly quiet. She hoped it would stay that way.

Eric had taken the kids to a children's arcade New Year's party.

Janine had usually gone to the party at the country club. She had usually dressed to the nines to outshine the other women. Tonight, she had on her waitress uniform.

Janine heard fireworks go off as midnight came. Few in the restaurant seemed to notice.

She was talking to an elderly couple when she noticed her kids outside. Eric brought them in for a treat.

Monica and Alan rushed over to hug their mom. Elaine seated them in Janine's station.

"Did you guys have a nice time?" she asked.

The enthusiasm waned as the age increased.

"We missed you, Mom," said Olivia.

Janine served pie, coffee, and milk to her family. She lingered with them for a few minutes. Alan and Monica excitedly recounted a mini-golf game and various skill games. Janine stayed with them until she noticed a couple of incoming groups.

The customers were now loud, obnoxious party goers. Janine had confidence she could handle them.

Eric led her kids out. "It looks like time for us to leave. Happy New Year."

"Thanks for bringing them in. I appreciate it."

The early hours of New Year's Day were not easy. The customers were difficult. The staff was reacting to the mood of the house. Several large groups left little or no tip behind. Buoyed by her childrens' visit, Janine maintained a positive attitude through the shift. She left the restaurant about an hour late.

When Janine returned home, no one was awake. She missed having Eric to greet her. Her schedule showed the next forty-eight hours off. It seemed like a vacation ahead. She had a hot bath. She went to the bedroom. Monica was asleep in her bed, clutching her giraffe toy.

Olivia was in the double bed. She stirred as Janine got in. "You okay?"

"Go back to sleep, Livy," she replied with a whisper.

Janine lay awake. Happy New Year? Husband gone. Her beautiful home gone. Sharing a bed with her daughter. Living in a stranger's house. Working two menial jobs. New Year's yes, but happy?

She listened to the sounds of the house. She listened to the breathing of Monica. She listened to the breathing of Olivia. She had her babies safe. Right now, that would have to do.

Eric organized a day trip for the family. They would visit the Museum of Science and Industry. Eric particularly wanted them to see the hall of Christmas Trees. Twenty plus trees were decorated by different ethnic groups.

In the museum Janine let the children roam. Olivia drifted off, following a mixed group of girls and boys. Alan ran off to find the submarine.

Monica stayed near to her mom. Both Eric and Janine watched Monica's enthusiasm with amusement. She went from tree to tree pointing out particular ornaments.

As they walked Janine unconsciously took Eric's arm. Once she realized it, she held on anyway. He did not resist.

After the museum closed, Eric drove back along Lake Michigan. He exited Lake Shore Drive and headed toward the planetarium. He drove out the peninsula and stopped when they could look back to the city. The vista was aglow with buildings and streets lit against the darkness. "One of my favorite views," he said.

Eric took them to the Olive Garden for a meal. He situated himself between Alan and Olivia at the table. When Janine tried to engage Eric's gaze, he avoided it. She engaged the children in conversation throughout the meal.

Janine noticed that all of Eric's responses to her were monosyllables. On the way home his attitude chilled her happy day. She hoped that she had not damaged their relationship.

At home Janine invited Eric for coffee.

"Sure," said Eric.

Eric sat with Janine at the table. "Eric, are we alright?"

"Sure," said Eric. "Why would you ask that? Nothing has changed."

"I…" She struggled for words. "I didn't mean anything by taking your arm. It just felt…comforting."

"I know. It was comfortable for me too. It reminded me…of Peg. That's all. Sorry?"

"Don't be sorry. You loved her."

"Yes, I did, I do. You remind me of her sometimes."

"Is it difficult?"

"It is sometimes. Is it difficult for you? I mean about Brent."

"Yes, sometimes. But I think I could kill him most of the time."

He looked at her and smiled. "I'll just bet. But I don't think you could kill anyone. Not even him."

THE DATE

The man came up out of the crowd at the casino. "Janine? It is you, isn't it? Janine, right? It's me Roger, Roger Preiss." Seeing non-recognition on her face, he continued. "We met at a couple of parties at Lance and Miriam's."

"Roger? Oh yeah, Roger. How are you?"

"Me? Fine. Just fine. But how are you? I've heard some things."

"Okay," replied Janine. "Nice to see you. I've got to get back to work."

"Sure, sure," said Roger. He hesitated. "Listen, how about if I take you out for dinner sometime soon?" He smiled at her. He fished a calling card out of his wallet. "Call my office. Please?"

Janine raised the issue with Eric over after-dinner coffee. "Roger was a friend of Brent's and Lance. He was always very nice. He offered to take me out." She sipped coffee. "I haven't been out in so long. Besides he might know something." She avoided looking him in the eye.

Eric put his coffee down. "Janine, I have told you many times if you can get a better deal, take it. If you want to see this guy, you don't need my permission."

"Yes, yes I would." She smiled. "If you don't mind. I mean you've been watching the kids a lot."

"No, I don't mind." He hesitated. "One thing does occur to me…"

"What?"

"If he was a friend of Lance and Brent, how trustworthy is he?"

"What do you mean?"

"I mean, just be careful. Do you really know this guy?"

"Oh, Eric, you sound just like my dad."

Janine arranged to see Roger on an evening off. She spent extra time on her hair and nails. She had kept a party dress tucked away.

Olivia appeared after school. She watched her mother's routine. "You haven't worn that dress in a long time. I didn't know you had it."

"I didn't feel up to wearing it," she replied. Her statement surprised herself.

"Is this man important?"

"Not really," Janine replied. "I just felt like dressing up." They both knew she was insincere.

When Roger came to the door, Olivia let him in. He politely shook hands all around.

Roger helped Janine into his car. "Wow. You really look great tonight."

She smiled. "Do you think so?"

"Yes, yes, I do. I mean you have every right to be…"

"Depressed? Sorry, I'm too busy to be depressed."

Roger drove for a bit. "I'm sorry. It's just that I ran into Miriam after Lance disappeared. She seemed depressed."

"She was," replied Janine. "And then she committed suicide."

"No, really?"

"Really."

"I take it that you don't know where Brent is or what he's up to?"

"No, I don't. Do you?"

"No, I don't," he replied. "Let's agree to not discuss Brent, Lance, or Gawn Associates for the rest of the night. Agreed?"

"Agreed."

Roger pulled into a high-end steakhouse. He had them seated in a half-round booth. They sat fairly close to each other. He ordered a bottle of wine. Roger talked about his trip to Switzerland. He talked about a car trip to Luxemburg.

The food, the surroundings, and the wine led to a warm comfort for her. She saw two young guys checking her out. She felt great.

Roger's phone broke the mood. "Sorry. I have to take this." He left the table.

Janine took the moment to check her makeup.

Roger returned. "I'm so sorry, my dear. I've got to go home and send off some info asap." He looked at his watch. "I'll have to drop you at home."

Janine felt warm and comfortable. "That's alright. I'll go with you."

"If you're sure?"

Roger turned on the lights of his apartment. "C'mon in." He moved to the desk. "Make yourself comfortable."

"I'd better visit the bathroom."

"Down the hall," he said, pointing. "I'd better check my messages." He sat at the desk and opened his laptop.

As Janine left the restroom, she dropped her purse. Her lipstick rolled into the bedroom. She stepped into the room. She turned on the light. She picked up her lipstick. And then the bottom fell out.

There on the dresser was a crystal art piece. She knew that piece. She had admired it many times. It was Miriam's. Miriam, who had committed suicide. She'd have never parted with the piece. Why was it here?

Janine remembered a party long ago. She was talking to Miriam when Roger approached. "I love that piece," he said, pointing at the crystal. "And what are you two lovelies talking about?" said Roger. Miriam stiffened and shrunk back. Roger ignored her. "You and Brent should come over some evening or maybe just you," said Roger.

Then Brent came over and Roger disappeared. "I don't like that guy," said Brent.

Then Janine noticed Miriam had her back against the wall shoulders hunched.

At the time Janine thought it seemed an odd reaction.

With all this going through her mind, Janine turned off the bedroom light. She moved into the living room. She sat on the couch and asked, "All done?"

"Yes. Yes, I am." He walked over and placed a glass of wine in front of her on the table. He placed another glass in front of himself. "Janine, of all the women I know, you are the most desirable." He eyed her reaction.

"Really?" she said coyly.

Roger's computer signaled. "I'd better get that."

When he rose, she exchanged the wine glasses.

When Roger returned, she was sipping the wine.

"You really are beautiful," he said, sitting near her. He leaned over to kiss her neck. He put a hand on her leg.

She pushed his hand off her leg and pushed him back. She finished the wine.

He sat back a little. "At those parties, I was jealous of Brent. I told him so."

"You were always flirting with me."

"I wasn't just flirting. I wanted you then and I want you now."

She noticed that he had not touched his wine. Suddenly she wondered if she should have drunk his.

"What's the matter? Are you getting a little sleepy?"

The computer dinged. "I tell you what. Why don't you close your eyes for a minute while I answer my impatient associate?"

She decided to play along. "Okay." She put her head back while Roger went back to the desk.

Janine's mind was racing. Is Roger just being nice? Is this a seduction? She kept thinking about Miriam's reaction. Brent's warning could have just been a macho thing. But Miriam's? Poor Miriam.

Roger came over quietly. She was ready to respond to a kiss. He stood over her for a second. He touched her arm. "Justine?" She hesitated. He snapped his fingers over her. She hesitated. "Justine? Justine?" She was confused by his actions and disappointed he'd forgotten her name.

She heard Roger move away. She heard him open the door. "C'mon in."

"Is she out?" said a strange voice.

"Yeah," replied Roger. "Set up right away. I've got the restraints."

Janine stiffened. Oh God, she thought. This can't be happening!

She felt someone sit next to her. He pulled her leg up, removed her shoe, and placed a strap around her ankle. She did not resist. He pulled her other leg out and placed a strap around it. Still she stifled her revulsion and played dead. He placed a strap on each wrist.

The other person entered the room. "Okay, the camera's ready. Can we get started?"

Now she knew why Miriam and Brent had warned her. She had to get out. Is this why Miriam cringed at the sight of Roger? Miriam deserved revenge. She had to get to her purse and the pepper spray.

"Let's put her in the chair," said Roger. "Help me."

Janine felt hands on either side lifting her up. She could take no more. She opened her eyes. "What are you doing? Let go of me!"

"Whoa!" said the strange man, falling backwards on the couch.

"What the…?" said Roger.

Janine shook off Roger. She grabbed her purse.

The strange man ran out the door into the hall. "I'm gettin' out of here!"

"Janice!" said Roger with surprise. "It's not what you think." He stepped toward her.

She rummaged through her purse frantically. "Is this what you did to Miriam?" She began to panic until she felt the spray can. "What were you going to do, you pervert!"

"Janice, it's not like that…"

She sprayed him in the face while covering hers. The pepper spray stung her eyes. "It's Janine! And it IS like this!"

Roger fell to his knees. He was choking and coughing.

Janine ran to the bedroom. She turned on the light. A camera was now mounted on a tripod. She found a strong box open with Miriam's passport on top. She took the safe and all the papers nearby. She pulled the camera off the tripod and went back to the couch.

She looked at Roger on all fours and discounted him as a threat.

Janine emptied the contents of the strong box into her purse. She jammed the papers in on top. Janine grabbed her shoes, purse, and coat. She moved toward the door. She looked back. Roger was crawling toward the washroom gagging and coughing.

Janine peeked around the hall. She could hear Roger puking in the bathroom. She ran out of the apartment barefoot. Not wanting to chance the elevator she took the stairs. She moved through the lobby warily. Outside she took stock of herself. She put the pepper spray in her purse and donned her shoes and coat. She scanned the street, looking for the strange man. She walked to the corner trying to be casual. A dog walker past her without an acknowledgment. She saw some tall bushes and ducked behind them.

With her back against the wall, she covered her mouth to mask her heavy breathing. She was shaking. She stood as still as possible scanning the street. When she heard voices coming, she grabbed the spray and stood ready. An elderly couple walked past oblivious to her.

What to do? She wanted to get back home. She wanted refuge.

Suddenly, it was Eric's voice in her head. "You can call me anytime, I'll come get you. No questions asked."

Janine rummaged around in her purse until she found the phone. She hit Eric's quick dial number. *C'mon, pick up.*

Several rings went by. "Janine?" came Eric's voice. "Are you alright?"

"No. Come pick me up."

"Okay. I'm on my way."

Janine hid in the bushes, shaking. She became aware that she was thirsty and needed the bathroom.

A police car pulled up. A bright spotlight blinded her. "Come out of the bushes," called an amplified voice. She seemed frozen in place. She heard two car doors close.

"Lady, what are you doing in the bushes? Come out of there."

Stiffly, Janine moved out from behind the bush.

"Ma'am, are you alright?" A female officer stepped forward. She looked Janine in the eye. "She's in shock." The officer sniffed. "And she smells like pepper spray. Honey, did you get sprayed?"

Janine shook her head no. She showed her the spray in her hand. The cop stepped back.

"Honey, you'd better let me have that." The officer took the spray.

"She's got restraints on her ankles and wrists. Did she escape from somewhere?" said the other cop.

Just then Eric pulled up. He got out. "Officers, what's going on?"

As he approached, Janine fell into his arms, crying.

"Sir," said the male officer. "What can you tell us about her? Is she an escapee?"

"Escapee? No, she was on a date." Janine clung to Eric. "Apparently a very bad date."

"Sir," said the female cop, "can you identify her?"

"Sure, sure." Eric looked Janine in the eye. "Please give the nice police officers your ID."

Janine nodded yes. She broke her embrace and opened her purse.

"And you sir, ID please," said the male cop. "Do you know if she's into...bondage?"

"I don't know," replied Eric. He handed the cop his ID. He helped Janine find her ID.

"Just a minute," said the male cop. He took the IDs back to the car.

"Honey," said the female cop, "have you been raped?"

Janine had resumed her position wrapped around Eric. She shook her head no.

The female cop looked Eric in the eye and pointed at the restraining strap on Janine's wrist. Eric nodded acknowledgement.

The male cop returned. He handed Eric the IDs. "Okay. Are you going to take her home?"

"Yes, sure," replied Eric.

"Get your daughter some help," said the female officer.

"Let's go home." Eric led Janine to the car.

"Bathroom first," said Janine.

"Sure thing."

Eric pulled into a twenty-four-hour McDonalds. Janine made a dash for the restroom. Eric ordered coffee and tea. He was waiting when she finished in the lady's room.

When they returned to the car, he noticed that Janine had removed the restraints.

"I put some ice in your tea. It should be drinkable."

She sipped the tea. "You put sugar in my tea?"

"Yes, I did."

They did not speak again in the car.

The house was quiet when Eric and Janine returned. They both carried their half-finished drinks to the kitchen table. Neither said anything.

Olivia came in. "Mom, are you alright?" She hugged her mother. Janine hugged back.

"Yea, yes I'm...okay."

Olivia looked over her mother. Her hair was messy. Her dress was unevenly buttoned. Her feet were muddy. "Were you on a picnic?"

Janine shook her head negatively. "I'm alright."

"I'm going to get ready for bed," said Eric. He finished his coffee. "I'll see you in the morning."

"Why don't you ask me?" said Janine. Her voice was quavering. "Just say it!"

Eric sat down and took a long breath. "Janine, I'm not your father. You don't owe me an explanation. I told you that if you needed me to come get you, I would. No questions asked. I'm not asking anything."

Olivia stepped forward and wrapped her arms around her mother. Janine turned in her chair and buried her face in Olivia body. She began weeping.

Eric took a long breath again. "Okay. Let's hear what happened?"

Olivia sat down next to her mother.

"It started out so nice. Dinner was…elegant." She blew her nose. "And then it turned so…so…evil."

Eric listened to Janine's tale expressionless and silent. Olivia let out small gasps. Janine omitted her swiping the camera and the strongbox contents. She did not know what she had.

"…and the police thought Eric was my father." Janine looked at Eric and made an appreciative smile. "You were so right. Why should I have trusted any of Brent's friends? I was so stupid."

"Oh, Mom," said Olivia with another hug.

"You weren't stupid," said Eric. "You trusted him just enough. You protected yourself. That's important. I'll get you some more pepper spray. Were they were going to rape you?"

"Oh, Mom," said Olivia with another hug.

"No, no, I don't think so. They wanted something else." She smiled at her daughter. "Can I have another cup of tea?"

"Sure," said Olivia. She put water up to boil.

"Eric, can I ask you a question?" asked Janine. "When you warned me about Roger, was it because…because…" She looked away.

"Because what?" he said.

"Because you wanted me?" She looked directly at Eric. "Why haven't you made a pass at me? A girl's got pride. Or am I...too damaged."

"Maybe I should go," said Olivia.

Eric turned toward Livy. "No, stay. There should be honesty." He looked at Janine. "Dear, lady. You have had a world of crap dumped on you. I offered you the sanctuary of my home. What kind of a man would I be if I said you had to sleep with me? I won't victimize you.

"Now, if you want to change our relationship, we should talk about that. But certainly not rebounding off a bad date." Eric rose, hugged Livy. "Good night." He walked up to Janine and touched her face. "Get some sleep. We'll talk tomorrow."

With that Janine rose and bear hugged Eric. She kissed him on the cheek.

"Good night, dear lady." Eric left the kitchen.

Olivia smiled at her mother. She refilled two cups of tea. "Do you want to talk?"

In the morning after the kids went to school, Janine told Eric that she had taken the camera and the articles from the strongbox.

"Okay. Do you still have the camera?" asked Eric. "We should see if anything is on there."

"I think so." She opened her purse and dumped it out on the table. She handed the camera to Eric.

"Why didn't you mention it yesterday?" asked Eric.

"I...I didn't want to scare Olivia. And...I wasn't sure I wanted to share it. I think he killed Miriam."

Eric froze. "You think so?"

She nodded.

Together they watched the recordings on the camera.

The first images were of a bruised blonde woman. She was duct-taped to a chair.

An off-camera voice asked, "Where did Lawrence put the money?"

"That's Roger," whispered Janine.

"Lawrence?" asked the woman. She seemed to be drugged. "Lawrence? He…we took some money to Vegas."

"You took some of the money to Las Vegas? What did you do with it there?"

The woman tried to smile. "Gamble, baby."

"You gambled all of it?"

"Naw…Nope. He put great big wads in the bank."

"Is that all? Where else did Lawrence put money?"

"Money…Lawrence…Oh, he sent money to that broad in… Europe."

"Europe, who did he send money to in Europe?"

"That broad…Monica something. Monica Stein."

The video went blank. Eric stopped it. "Do you recognize her?"

Janine shook her head slowly. "No. I don't know her." She looked at Eric questioningly. "Could she be talking about Lawrence Gawn?"

"And who is Lawrence Gawn?"

"He's Brent's boss. The head of the firm." She bit her lip, thinking. "He's always looking for the next big deal. He's a major player. I wouldn't trust him near my money or my daughter. If Brent and Lance are gone, I bet he's gone too."

"You didn't check?"

"I never had his number."

They both thought a moment in silence.

"Let's see if there is anything else on this camera," suggested Eric.

He activated the camera. Another woman was restrained in a chair. She too appeared to be drugged.

Janine gasped, "It's Miriam!"

"Where did Lance keep the money?" asked an off-camera voice.

"In the safe. He kept money in the safe."

"Miriam, what's the combination of the safe?"

"Combonation…combitation?" A hand slapped Miriam's face. "What's the combination?"

"His lucky number…09, 19, 29."

The video stopped. The video restarted. Miriam's head was down. A hand lifted her head. "Miriam! Miriam! Wake up!"

"So sleepy," she replied groggily.

"Miriam, where did Lance take the money?"

"To…the bank."

"What bank?"

Miriam struggled for consciousness. "Citys…Cittzeys… Citicezbank."

"Citizens Bank?"

"Cizzenzenz Blank," she said, slurring.

The video went blank.

Janine was crying. "They killed her." She looked at Eric. "They killed her."

Eric put an arm around her. "I think they did. And they might have killed you too."

"Oh my god." Janine had a long cry. Eric held her.

Finally, Eric said, "Maybe we should have a look at the rest of the stuff you boosted."

"Yeah, alright." Janine dried her eyes and blew her nose.

"Let's see," said Eric. "Here is Miriam's passport with her Social Security card tucked in it. Here is an old driver's license. Here are a couple of pictures of the family. Here is a wedding picture. This a key ring with several keys." Eric handed her a greeting card envelope.

Eric examined the driver's license and the passport. "You know, with these pictures you could pass for Miriam." He held the license up near her face. "Did anyone ever mix you two up?"

"Um yeah. Once or twice."

Janine pulled a card out of the envelope. Sorry Dear, said the front of the card. The inside read: I Won't Forget Next Year, Happy Birthday! The card was signed Lance. There was a date written on the upper left corner. "The idiot forgot her birthday," said Janine.

Eric looked at the envelope. "He was in Vegas."

Janine handed him the card.

"This is kind of odd," said Eric. "You don't usually put a date on your wife's birthday card. Maybe an occasion like a graduation, but not your wife's birthday. And why would she keep a card to remind her he forgot her birthday?"

"Let me see that," said Janine. She pointed to the date, September 19th 1998. "Miriam's birthday is near Father's Day. We went to a house party there." She looked at the passport. "Her birthday is in June not in September."

"What did Miriam say in that video? His lucky number was 9, 19, 29?" said Eric. "September 19th is 9/19. Maybe this is some kind of code? It must have been important."

"What does it mean?"

"I don't know," said Eric. "But maybe we should keep some of this to ourselves. I'll make a copy of the video. We should give the video to the police."

Janine looked at him and said, "You think so?"

"Absolutely. Do you think it has something to do with Miriam's suicide?"

Her eyes widened.

"We don't need anyone coming after you. We keep the rest to ourselves," said Eric. "There's a lot more going on here than there seems."

The next morning, Eric and Janine went to the police. Initially a community relations person took her statement. She mentioned being in the bushes and the officers she encountered. Janine did not mention the articles from the strongbox. She was asked to wait.

"Hi, I'm Detective Long. I'd like to go over this incident with you, Ms. Piersen. Please step into my office."

Detective Long listened to her tale without comment. When she finished, he asked, "This man is known to you as Roger Preiss? Is that right?"

"Yes."

"I see," said the detective. "You actually have no proof of this... assault, do you?"

"I have the restraints." Janine pulled them from her purse. "And I have the camera." She pulled it from her purse.

"Camera, I see. But you weren't actually filmed on it, were you?"

"Me, no. But there are some others."

The officer put the camera down. He motioned her to wait while he made a call. "I need an evidence team here now." He made another call. "Vince, it's Long. I think your case just walked in the door."

They took Janine's statement that she had taken the camera from a unit in the building, and she had it all night.

Janine was called in to the station the next day by Detective Long. She was shown to a conference room.

There were lots of people with badges. There were lots of questions: How did she know Roger? Why did she suspect criminal intent? Had she viewed the tape? Did she recognize anybody? How did Roger know Brent?

Janine answered the questions as best she could. "Can I ask some questions? What is this all about?"

The inquiring officers all nodded at Long. "You do deserve some answers.

"We've been looking for this guy for a while. Roger Preiss is not his real name. We suspect he has done this kind of drugged interrogation for about twenty years. We have a lot of information, thanks to you. You really helped us by pepper spraying him.

"We think he's dangerous. We don't think he'll be a danger to you. We think he has left the area. But if you do encounter him, please call the police.

"We may need you to testify at some point in the future. But that is all I can share with you today."

ANOTHER DATE

When the kids had gone to school, Janine sat opposite Eric at the table.

"Eric, we need to talk."

"I guess we do."

There was an awkward silence for a few moments.

"About us?" said Eric. "There seems to be a lot of tension around us."

"Are you mad at me because I went on that…date?"

"No. I have no claim on you."

"I owe you so much."

"Janine, let's put that aside. That's a business agreement family to family. I expect that whatever happens you'll honor the monetary debt. That's a point of honor between us."

"Okay. But it bothered you that I went on a date."

"I guess it did a little," he said.

"I thought, I mean the way you've acted, that you weren't attracted to me?"

"I never said that." Eric took a deep breath. "Look, I find that I have as much ego as any man. You are young, attractive, and here. But I can't, I won't victimize you. I can't help feeling that a relationship would be... predatory."

"Okay, I get that. I'm not the wide-eyed fool I once was. I appreciate your saying that you won't take advantage of me. But you do have feelings for me. And not like a daughter."

"I have both, actually," he said.

She smiled at him. "When Saundra was here, she kept asking about you and me. She made me realize what a great husband you would be. You have taken better care of us than Brent ever did. My mom would say you're a steady, reliable man."

"Now just wait a minute," he said. "There are other issues besides attraction and availability. If Brent comes back, what then?"

She sat back and thought. She shook her head slowly. "He used me, our family, and my children. I don't want him back." She looked Eric in the eye. "I'm done with him."

"Okay, I'll take that." He shook his head and smiled. "And then there is our age difference."

"What does that matter?" she asked earnestly.

"When you saw a late-middle-aged man with a younger woman, what did you say to yourself? They always go for the younger ones?"

She nodded affirmatively. "Yes, yes I did. But this is different. Is that what's bothering you? It's not like I'm just out of high school?"

"No, no you're not. But I'm not a young guy." He searched for words. "I might disappoint you."

Janine looked at him and smiled. She reached out and held both his hands. "No, you won't."

Eric looked at her and smiled. "Well, we'll see. But anyway, let's start out where we should start out.

"I have tickets for the symphony tomorrow night and you're not working. I usually go with Lana; she was one of Peg's friends. We used to be a foursome with Lana's partner. Then Peg died and Lana's partner died.

Anyway, I still go with Lana, but she's laid up right now. Anyway, will you go to the symphony with me, Janine? It's a jacket and tie evening. I will take you out for dinner."

"You are asking me out on a date?" She smiled at him. "Tomorrow night? I'd love to." She looked at him quizzically. "Why haven't you told me about Lana?"

"Since you guys have been here, I haven't been going."

"But you and Lana?"

"Me and Lana?" Eric smiled slowly at her. "Oh, me and Lana. I'm definitely not her type. But you might be."

Janine spent extra time on her hair and nails. She was glad the dress from her ill-fated date was wearable.

Olivia appeared after school. She watched her mother's routine. "Where are you going?"

"Dinner and the symphony with Eric," she replied.

"Oh, okay."

She looked at her daughter. "What would you think if we dated?"

"Is he going to propose?"

"Livy! No. We're trying something new. This might be a disaster."

"It's okay, Mom. He'll forgive you."

Janine gave a short laugh. "Not that kind of disaster. I'm not sure I can be what he wants."

"I don't understand," said Livy. "He loves you."

"Livy? You don't know that? It's complicated."

"Not so much. I mean with Dad and all, yeah. But the way he watches you, he loves you. He even had the car washed!"

Janine smiled. "We'll see." She gathered up her wrap and purse.

Olivia accompanied her mother to the living room.

Eric was looking at the paper. He rose. "Are you ready?" Eric was wearing a suit and tie.

"Uncle Eric, look at you," said Olivia.

"Yes, look at you. You look handsome tonight," said Janine.

"Of course," said Eric. "When you take a lady out, look your best. Shall we go?"

Olivia watched them walk down the drive. Eric opened the car door for her. She watched them drive away.

Eric dropped Janine at the door of a downtown restaurant. She waited inside while he parked the car. She noticed several older couples talking. The men were in black tie. Janine wondered if she and Eric weren't under-dressed.

When Eric turned up, he led her to the hostess. He had made a reservation. They were seated immediately. "We haven't seen you in a while, sir," said the hostess.

"They seem to know you," said Janine.

"Yes, we've been using the theater package for years. They'll get us a timely dinner. We'll get the bus and be in our seats before the overture."

Janine motioned toward the couples in formal wear. "Black tie?"

"Yes, sure. The Dress Circle crowd. They probably donate heavily to the symphony." He looked at her. "You've never been to Orchestra Hall?"

"No, never. Brent never wanted to go anywhere…cultural. Mom and I went to concerts in the park."

She looked at the ladies in expensive dresses and jewelry. "Do they always go to the symphony like that?"

Eric noticed her eyeing the elegant couples. "Sure. And the opera and the museums. The institutions don't run on bake sales."

Janine ordered a petite steak, asparagus, and had really good wine. "The food here is excellent."

"I'm glad you like it. If you didn't go to cultural events, where did you go as a couple?"

She was taken aback by the question. "Mostly the country club."

Eric laughed. "A man of letters, no doubt." He looked at her and said earnestly, "You look elegant tonight."

She flushed. She changed the subject. "Did you bring your wife here?"

"Sure, absolutely. She loved the symphony."

"You loved her, didn't you?"

"I did. But she's gone now. A pleasant memory." He looked at her. "Time for new memories."

Janine finished her dinner feeling warm and comfortable.

Waiting for the bus, Janine was standing near an elderly lady. "We were wondering if your dinner partner had lost his wife. We haven't seen her in a while. She was very nice."

Janine was taken aback by the lady's comment. "Yes, he did."

The elder lady reached out and touched Janine. "You take care of him, honey. Good men are hard to find." She smiled at Janine and joined her own party.

Eric joined her after paying the bill. "Are you ready?"

As they moved through the lobby of Orchestra Hall, Janine was struck by several things. She had been to many popular concerts, but this was strikingly different. First of all, there was no shoving or jostling. It was polite and gracious. There were many ladies wearing tasteful expensive dresses. She had seen them in the catalogs.

When they took their seats, Eric said hello to a couple of people. Janine surveyed the stage. The orchestra seemed disorganized, each playing something different. The men wore black tie. The women wore black dresses.

Eric sat to her left. "Are you okay? Comfortable?"

"Yes, fine," she replied in a hushed voice. "At the restaurant, that lady asked if your wife had died."

"Did she? Peg was always talking to someone." Eric looked over the program.

Not knowing much about classical music Janine chose not to look at the program. Instead, she scanned the hall and the audience. She noticed a few families with a few children. But she kept noticing the women and the jewelry.

When the house lights blinked, everyone settled down. The house began to hush until the conductor came out.

Janine let the music play without hearing it. There was nothing interesting to watch on the stage. A bunch of musicians playing their instruments. She began to watch the audience.

Most of the audience seemed focused on the musicians. There were some looking at the walls and ceiling. When she shifted in her seat, she crossed her legs. Out of the corner of her eye she noticed Eric was looking at her legs.

She let her mind drift. The piece ended and everyone was applauding. The conductor left the stage briefly and then returned. The orchestra began playing again.

Janine was scanning the audience. She noticed a silver-haired man in a tux looking at her. She scanned the audience for a while. When she looked back the man was watching her again. She shifted in her seat and crossed her legs the opposite way. Both Eric and the stranger were looking. Janine let her wrap fall down behind. She had worn a sleeveless dress cut low. She noticed that Eric had noticed. She reached over and held Eric's hand. She scanned the audience for a while. When she looked back the silver-haired man was looking again. Janine moved closer to Eric.

The music stopped. The audience rose and applauded. Eric looked at her. "Intermission. Let's stretch our legs." As they entered the lobby Eric said, "Ladies room is over there."

Halfway to the restroom Janine looked back. Eric was watching her. He smiled back.

On her return from the ladies lounge, Janine spotted the silver-haired man. His eyes followed her across the lobby. She found Eric with a small glass of white wine. "Share a wine with me?"

"Yes, please." She sipped and passed it back. "You watched me walk away."

He smiled. "You caught me."

"Why?"

"You look really nice tonight." He looked away. "Besides, you might find someone else to go home with."

"Mister Eric," said Janine, "I have some serious competition in this room. There are a couple of grandmas over there with some serious bling. They'd love to take you home."

"Well," said Eric playfully, "why don't you come back to my place after the concert?"

"Will you buy me a cup of coffee?"

"It's a deal."

Janine held Eric's hand for most of the remaining concert. She caught his glance several times as he looked at her. Now listening she let the music carry her thoughts to mostly pleasant places.

Janine hooked her arm around his as they walked out of the hall.

When they sat on the bus Eric asked, "Did you enjoy it?"

"Yeah," she replied. "At first, I wasn't into the music. I was looking at the people. After the break I really felt the music. Yeah, I enjoyed it."

When the bus returned them to the restaurant Eric asked, "Do you want desert?"

"Could we just go home?"

"Sure. Why don't you wait inside while I get the car?"

"Wait, come here." Janine pulled Eric into the lobby. She pulled him close and kissed him. She felt his arms encircle her. It was a long passionate kiss.

Eric stopped kissing and looked at her. He still held her. "That was nice." He stepped back a bit. He touched her cheek with the back of his hand. "That was very nice. But…I should go get the car."

Janine watched as Eric disappeared out the door. She looked around.

The restaurant hostess smiled at her. "Good concert?"

Janine did not reply. She waited at the door for Eric's return. When he pulled up, she entered the car before he could help her.

As Eric drove away Janine looked straight ahead. "I'm sorry."

"Sorry for what?"

"It was a lovely evening and I wrecked it."

"Dear lady, no evening has ever been wrecked by a heartfelt kiss."

"You're mad at me. You asked me to go slow and I…"

"Okay, let's talk. Why do you think that I'm mad? I'm not mad. I was a little surprised."

"I shouldn't have done that. You think that I'm…"

"I think that you are lonely and hurt. I think that you expressed what you felt. That's okay."

"You have reservations about me. I'm trouble."

"Well, don't worry about trouble. That doesn't bother me. I know exactly where your troubles are. I'm paying the lawyer. Forget that." Eric hesitated. "I'm not scared about you. I'm…scared about me."

"What? What do you mean, about you?"

"Look, Janine, I haven't…been with a woman in a long time. Peg was sick for a couple of years. And you are young and beautiful. I'm not sure I can…"

"Okay, wait. You're scared of…you have performance anxiety?"

"Oh, it sounds worse when you say it."

"Eric, that kiss was electric. I just need to be held and kissed. I need to feel wanted for me." She was crying. "Can you hold me tonight? I just want to be held."

"Sure. Sure, I can do that. I would like to do that with you, Jan."

When they returned home Olivia was waiting. "How'd the evening go?" Her face fell when she saw her mom had been crying.

"Okay, fine," said Janine. She ducked into the bathroom.

Olivia looked at Eric quizzically.

"I thought it went well," he said without emotion. "Tell me when she's out of the bathroom." Eric went into his room.

Olivia waited for her mom in the bedroom. "Mon is asleep," she whispered. "Are you okay?"

Janine began deal with her clothes. "Yeah, I'm okay. It was an emotional evening."

"Did Uncle Eric do something?"

"Uncle Eric is a gentleman. He would never do anything."

Olivia watched her mother hang her dress, put her jewelry away, and remove her makeup. She heard Eric leave the bathroom. He went to his room and closed the door.

Janine went through her night routine without a word. She put on her night gown, sat on the bed, and brushed her hair.

Olivia sat in a chair with her laptop. She watched her mom wordlessly.

Janine finished with her hair. She put cream on her hands and legs. She stared emotionlessly. She put the lotion and brush on the nightstand. Then she sat on the bed motionless for several minutes.

Finally, Olivia could wait no longer. "Mom, are you alright?"

"Yes honey, I'm fine." She stood up and put on her robe. "I'm going to spend the night in Eric's room." She kissed her daughter and left.

"About time."

Janine roused when Eric came into the bedroom. The morning sun had brightened the room. He sat on the bed facing away from her.

"Are you okay?" she asked him.

"Yeah, I had to go to the bathroom."

"That's not what I meant."

He turned and caressed her face. "I'm fine. Did you sleep well?"

"Better than in a long time. What time is it?"

"Five fifty. The kids will be up soon. What will we tell them?"

"Will I be sleeping here from now on?"

Eric nodded. "I hope so."

At the breakfast table Olivia kept smirking.

While they were eating Janine spoke, "Kids, from now on I'll be sleeping in Eric's room." Janine looked at Olivia.

Olivia smirked and said, "Okay."

"Whatever?" said Alan.

Monica seemed not to care.

In the late morning Eric was sitting on the couch. Janine sat down next to him. She hooked his arm and kissed his cheek.

"I slept better last night than I have in months." She put her head against his shoulder. "What about you?"

"Not so much. I kept feeling your warmth and smelling your... scent. I kept wondering if it was a dream. I watched you while you were sleeping. I won't forget it."

"If you thought last night was good, sex is going to be fantastic."

"You know I'm a little uncomfortable with talk like that. I've only had one lover you know?" He looked at her.

She broke her hug and looked him in the eye. "You only made love to Peggy?" She smiled at him. "I believe that. You had a special love. I respect that. If you want to...just sleep together, I mean without sex, that's okay."

"No, it's not!" He looked indignant. "I never said that. I don't mean that. I only mean that we were just kids starting out. We learned everything together. We enjoyed each other. If she was disappointed in some way, she never said." He smiled at her. "I do want to be...intimate with you. You'll promise to tell me if I...fall short? I want things to be good for you." He smiled at her. "If we're going to live in sin, we should enjoy it."

"You never cease to amaze me. Brent never asked once what I wanted. He did what he wanted when he wanted. He never thought about my needs. And I...suppressed them." She closed her eyes. "He used me there too. I was his...puppet."

Eric hugged her. "You aren't anyone's puppet anymore."

She hugged him again. She had tears in her eyes. "And I have you to thank for that. I can stand up for myself."

He handed her a tissue. "I make all the women cry."

"Don't say that," she said, wiping her eyes.

Janine stood up. She reached out her hand. "Come on."

Eric stood up. "Now?"

Janine led him to the hall. "Now."

"What about my feelings?" he said.

Janine took him to the bedroom. She closed the door. "We'll discuss them later."

Eric called for a family meeting after dinner. Eric pulled two chairs together. Eric and Janine held hands.

"Kids," Janine said, "Eric and I are going to live together as a couple. We need you to know it."

"Will Uncle Eric be my daddy now?" asked Monica.

After looking at Janine, Eric spoke, "Monica, Brent will always be your father. Nothing can change that. I'm not sure if or when I could adopt you; it's complicated. I think for now I have to be Uncle Eric. You know I care for you, but it will have to be Uncle Eric."

"But I want you be my daddy," said Monica.

"Me too," said Alan.

Janine looked at Eric. "Why can't you be daddy here at the house? But outside, kids, it has to be Uncle Eric. Okay?"

"Kids," said Eric, "your mother is lonely. I'm lonely. We want to live as a couple." He looked at the children. "What it means for is that this is your house now. This is your home. You are not homeless anymore."

"Oh wow," said Olivia.

Janine started to cry.

Monica sat in Eric's lap. She hugged him.

LADIES NIGHT

Janine continued working the two jobs through the winter. Two graveyard nights and Sundays at Denny's. At least two nights a week at the casino.

Now she only worked as a drinks hostess. She often worked alongside Marlene. Their brief conversations were work related: Those two are already drunk, He's robbing the cradle, Cougar at table six, etc.

It was a slow wintery evening when Marlene and Janine began talking relationships. Marlene got Janine to admit moving in with a man while still technically married.

"He took you and your kids? Some man."

"He is," she replied. "So…you're between men right now?"

"I'll say!" Marlene said. She spied a customer and moved off.

When next they came together Janine inquired, "Aren't you looking for someone else?"

Marlene did not answer. She just smiled and shrugged.

At the end of their shift Marlene said, "I'm having a girl's night at my place Saturday. Why don't you come?"

"Maybe, I'd have to see."

Janine talked to Eric. "A girl's get together with Marlene from work."

"There's nothing going on here," said Eric. "You decide."

"Are you sure?"

Eric looked at her. "Sure, what can happen?"

Janine arrived at Marlene's apartment with a bottle of wine. She never did get the names of Marlene's two friends.

The four were drinking from several bottles of wine. The cheese and crackers were plentiful. One of the women lit up a joint which they all shared. The conversation in general was man bashing. Marlene had worked with the other two at some previous time not explained.

Janine went to the bathroom. She washed her face. She felt warm and fuzzy.

When she returned Marlene's two friends had lit another joint. Janine sat down on the couch. They offered her the joint. She breathed it in deeply. It sent a warm glow down her body.

Marlene started another round of man bashing. It was accompanied by another bottle of wine. Janine lost all sense of time.

Janine came home in the wee hours. She sat in the car for a few minutes before going in.

The house was quiet and mostly dark. It was there that she first noticed the smell of "reefer" in her hair and clothes. She bagged her clothes and showered.

When she crept into the bedroom, Eric was asleep on one side of the bed. On the other Monica slept on top of the covers clutching her giraffe. Monica had been having bad dreams. Janine decided to sleep on the couch.

"Mom, Uncle Eric says you'd better get up of you'll be late for work," said Monica, shaking her.

Janine jerked awake. "Okay, I'm up." She followed the girl into the kitchen.

"Coffee?" asked Eric. "You got in late last night."

"Yeah, late." She could not look Eric in the eye. She put cream and sugar in the coffee. She went to the bedroom to get dressed.

She went to the kitchen in her waitress uniform. Someone had washed it for her. "I've got to go. Bye kids."

"Be careful," said Eric.

"What?"

"It's been snowing out there," said Eric. "Be careful out there."

"Yeah," she replied.

"We're going to build a snowman," called Monica.

Janine sleep-walked through her shift. She felt a little guilty about getting high with the girls. She wouldn't want the kids to know. What about Eric? What would she tell him? She'd better wash those clothes right away.

Elaine, her manager, asked if she was alright. She shrugged. "Yeah, late night."

When Janine came home, she saw the snowman on the front lawn. When she went in, she was greeted by Monica and Alan, "Did you see the snowman, Mom?"

"Yes, yes. Best snowman ever." She kissed and hugged them both.

She found Eric straightening in the kitchen.

"Everything okay?" she asked. Janine felt a great tension between them.

"Everything's okay here." Eric looked at her. "You okay? You want coffee?"

"No. I'm headed for bed. I'm tired. I just have to throw some things in the machine. I need a clean uniform." Janine went to the clothes pile to retrieve her pot-infused clothes. She couldn't find the bag.

Janine went back to the kitchen. Eric and Olivia were at the table.

"Did you wash clothes for me?" she asked Eric.

"I sure did. You have a clean uniform on the line," Eric said matter-of-factly.

"Well, don't do that anymore." Janine went to the bedroom.

Olivia looked at Eric. "What's wrong with her?"

"I don't know yet," said Eric. "I must have done something."

Janine was waiting on the bed when Eric came in.

"Jan dear," said Eric, sitting on the bed, "what have I done? Is this about Monica?"

"What? No." She was sobbing. "You washed my clothes because of how they smelled."

"Okay," said Eric calmly. "Why don't you tell me what this is all about?"

"I had a night with the girls. We drank some wine and smoked a joint. Is that a crime?"

"No. Just tell me it's not a regular thing. I won't have it in the house." He walked around the bed to face Janine. "I love you. You let off some steam."

"We were man bashing. I didn't defend you."

"I'll survive as long as you bashed Brent!"

She was smiling now. "I am so lucky." She thought for a second. "I've never asked what you want."

Eric sat down and pulled her into his lap. He brushed the hair out of her face. "Unless you made love with Brent or shoot someone, I will love you."

"Are you sure?"

Eric looked into her eyes. "Did you shoot Brent?"

Janine started to laugh. "No."

"Then we're good. Let's get some sleep. I had to do extra laundry today."

"You make a pretty good maid," she said with a laugh.

Eric made a hush sign with his finger. "But I keep sleeping with the guests!"

The next day after school Olivia asked Uncle Eric if they could talk.

"What's up, Livy?"

"Uncle Eric, Julie and I want to take a Saturday course at the Art Institute school. Her mom says she can only go if you drive us down. Will you, please?"

"Sure, no problem. I'd like that."

Olivia clearly had something else to say.

"Okay Livy, spit it out?"

"Is Mom in love with you?"

"Okay," said Eric. "Honestly, I don't know. I don't know that I should talk to you about this." He looked into her eyes.

"Right now, she's with me," said Eric. "That's all I can say."

Eric arranged with Janine to attend his Credit Union Dinner Dance. "It's the guys from work and their wives. Peg and I always went," he told her. He told her it was a jacket and tie affair. Sensing it was important to him, Janine spent extra time on hair, nails, and a dress.

Arriving at the banquet hall, Janine realized that Eric had lived in a different world. In her country club life Blacks and Latinos were service staff. Here they were the guests.

Eric greeted several Black couples with jovial handshakes and fist-bumps. One lady threw her arms around him and hugged. "It's so great to see you!" Eric always introduced Janine as his friend. Several Latinos stopped speaking Spanish to greet Eric. She knew that the greetings were legitimately warm.

One man greeted Eric with mock distain. "Who let you in here?" He looked past Eric to Janine. "Is this your date? Honey, you can do better than this." He took Janine's arm and led her to table. "This is Eric's date. Now can't we get her a better guy here somewhere?"

A woman stood up. "Now hush!" She took Janine's hand "Don't worry, honey, we've got your back! You sit down here!" Everybody laughed. The men all stood and shook Eric's hand.

They sat at a table with Whites, Blacks, and Latinos. She could not help but think that the country club set would refuse to sit.

After dinner and some speeches, a DJ set up. Eric always seemed to be talking to someone. A Black lady sat next to Janine. "Are you serious with Eric? He's a good man. His wife was a good lady. We were worried about him, being married so long."

"Did you work with Eric?"

"I sure did."

"It seems like everybody liked him."

"Everybody who counted!" They both laughed. "Take care of him, honey."

Eric returned. He looked at the ladies. "It looks like you're planning something."

"I told her that if you don't behave, I'll kick your ass."

"See," said Eric, deadpan, "I have friends everywhere. Jan, honey, how about a dance?"

Eric and Janine danced a few slow numbers. Eric suggested they get going.

In the car she had to tell him about her country club thoughts. She wondered about what they might think.

Eric made no comment.

"Honey, we lived a half mile away, but it is a different world," Janine continued. "All we ever seemed to care about was how good someone looked or how much money they spent. We avoided the city like the plague." She looked at Eric. "Those were nice people. They cared about you. They cared about me and they'd never met me before."

Eric made no comment.

THE OFFICE

When Janine's phone rang, she dreaded answering it. Since she transferred her old number into the new phone, she had received regular calls from bill collectors and law firms looking for Brent. Some agents were aggressive and insulting. So, when the phone rang that winter morning, she steeled herself before answering.

"Ms. Piersen?" said the man's voice. "Is this Ms. Janine Piersen?"

"Who's calling?"

"Oh hello," said the voice warmly. "This is Peter Waverly with Loop Management. I manage the office property. Yours is the only number that seems to be working."

Janine was bewildered. "What property? I don't own any property."

"Oh, sorry," said Waverly apologetically. "I'm calling about the Gawn office suite in our Loop building. I'm trying to contact someone about the break-in at the office suite. Can you contact Mr. Brent Piersen or one of the other lease holders?"

Janine was bewildered by the message. Hadn't they kept up with events? "I'm sorry, Brent is out of town. I don't know if I can contact any of them right now." Her mind was collating the facts. "There was a break-in at the office?"

"That's right," said Waverly. "We need someone to meet with the police and assess the damage. Can you come in?"

"Me? I don't know. Hold on." She muted the phone.

Eric stood a few feet away. "What's up?"

"There's been a break-in at the downtown office. Brent's office. They want me to go down there." She shook her head negatively. "I don't want anything to do with it."

Eric shook his head affirmatively "I understand. But…maybe there are some clues about Brent or Lance that might help you."

Janine thought about Miriam and her own eviction. "Mr. Waverly, I will come right down."

"Eric dear, will you look after the kids?"

"You know that I will."

Janine stood outside the downtown building for a few seconds. She hadn't been here since that terrible day she knew that Brent had deserted them. She steeled herself and walked through the revolving doors.

At the lobby desk she identified herself. "Oh hello," said the woman. "Mr. Kimbark will be right with you."

After a couple of minutes, a late-middle aged man appeared. He seemed familiar. "Hello again," said the man jovially. "I remember you now. You're Ms. Janine." He held out a hand. "I let you in the building that day years ago."

Suddenly Janine remembered. Brent was out of town and needed information he had left on his desk. The man let her into the office. "Oh yes, Mr. Kimbark. How nice to see you."

Kimbark led the way to the elevators. "It's Horace," he said, entering the cab. "We haven't seen anyone from the Gawn Group since the police raid."

"I wouldn't think so. They still have a lease?"

"Oh, yes. For another two years."

"Who's paying for it?"

"You know, I don't know. We charge a credit card account, and the payment is always good. Until the payment stops or the lease runs out it belongs to Gawn Associates."

The elevator opened and Horace led her to the suite. As they passed another suite two women peeked out.

The doorway to the Gawn office had been pried open. The yellow "Police Line Do Not Cross" tape lay on the floor. Horace pushed the door open. He turned on the lights. "Well, I guess somebody's paying the electric bill too."

They stepped inside. The office looked rifled through. Papers were scattered everywhere.

"If you need me, I'll be back in about half an hour," said Horace. "The locksmith should be here soon."

"Okay," said Janine. "I'll be here."

Janine looked at the receptionist's desk first. The computer keyboard and screen were there. The computer had been removed. The file drawers were open and empty. All the desk drawers were open.

Not seeing anything of interest, she went to Lance's office. It was the same. There was nothing there.

Reluctantly, she went into Brent's office. The room, which had always smelled fresh, was stale and dusty. She wiped off Brent's chair and sat at his desk. The blank screen and severed keyboard seemed odd. Stuck on the side of the screen was a Post-it note with the words "69 Mustang" on it. On one corner of the desk was a framed picture she had given him. It was a family portrait she insisted on taking. She looked at the five smiling faces and remembered a perfect day. There was a piece of scotch tape on the glass with the date 9/19/1999 on it. She put the picture and the Post-it note in her purse.

She found nothing else of interest in the office.

She heard the locksmith working at the door. He told Janine that his repairs would take some time. The damage to the door was extensive.

When Horace reappeared, she said that she could find nothing missing besides the computers.

On their way down to the lobby, Horace said she could get the keys to the suite at the desk next time.

"Oh, by the way," said Horace, "will you be taking the boxes of mail for the suite?"

"Boxes of mail?"

"Sure, mail comes every day or so. We throw it in a box. I'll have Luther carry it to your car."

"How many boxes are there?"

"Three full ones. He'll use a hand truck."

"I'm parked in a lot."

"That's alright. Just pull up. He'll load it for you. Nice to see you again."

Janine and Eric put the boxes of mail in his room overnight. They didn't want the children reminded of their father. The next day, while the kids were at school Eric brought the first box into the living room. "Let's see what we've got."

They began to sort the mail. Eric brought a bag for recycling. They began piles for correspondence and bank records. They agreed to sort all three boxes before opening any of the mail. In the end two boxes were obvious recycling. Eric took them out to the bin right away.

"Correspondence or bank records?" asked Janine.

"Why don't you open correspondence while I sort bank records?"

Janine began going through letters. There were some requesting more information on their investments. There were two from the Illinois State's Attorney requesting tax and accounting records. There was a letter from the Nevada Attorney General requesting information. Janine put them all in a pile.

There were two personal letters. She opened the letter to Lance first. Inside was a note suggesting another erotic encounter. Inside was a picture of a naked woman in a beckoning pose. She stuffed the contents back in the envelope making an icky face.

"What is it?" asked Eric.

"An erotic invitation for Lance." Without looking at Eric she said, "Men are pigs."

Janine held the second letter for a few seconds before opening it. It was addressed to Brent. She wondered for a second what Pandora's Box could be in the letter. Finally, she opened it. The letter was a renewal lease for an apartment in Henderson, Nevada. She handed Eric the lease. "Where the heck is Henderson, Nevada?"

"It's a suburb of Las Vegas," said Eric while reading the lease. "Did you know you had a place in Nevada?"

"No, I didn't."

"That's funny because you have a bank account in Henderson too."

THE CLUB

"Honey, one of the girls from the country club asked me to come out for a tennis match," said Janine. "I told her I'd think about it. I'm not going to go."

"Why?" asked Eric.

"It's not my life anymore. I can't look back. They're from some dream in the past."

"Jan honey, if you want to go play tennis with some old friends, go ahead. It isn't an insult to me or your current life."

Janine thought a second. "Do you think so?"

"I do," said Eric. "Who is this?"

"It's Tina. I used to play with her from time to time. She says her regular partner is out of town. I'd have to play a weekday semi-final and again over the weekend."

"If you feel that you're up to it, go."

"Up for it? My calves are like rocks. My arms look like I've been lifting weights."

"Yes, I know," said Eric with a smile. "You are very fit. I meant with work and the country club attitudes."

"Screw their attitudes. They can't hurt me anymore. As for work? I'll be fine." She hesitated. "You think I'm fit, do you?"

Eric nodded. "Yes, I do. Say, why don't you try on that tennis outfit, just to make sure it fits?"

"Why, you dirty, old…voyeur."

"What do you mean old?"

Janine arranged to meet Tina at the country club. After their doubles match they would have lunch.

On her way in and out of the locker room she ran into several familiar women. They all asked, "How are you?" in a way that suggested her response might be juicy. Janine always responded, "Fine. Good, really." No more, no less.

She caught up with Tina on the courts. Their first match was really no contest. She remembered Tina to be a moderately good player but lacking any drive. They easily beat the first two.

Janine had played many times with Brent. He always played with "sporting aggression." She now found that she had more muscle for a forehand shot. She also found a new exhilaration in aggressive play.

Tina found Janine for the second sets. This round they faced Roxanne and Sue. Although these two were regularly friends with Tina, Janine suspected they wanted to embarrass her. She had seen them humiliate others before.

On the court Janine channeled some aggression against "Roxy and Suzy." Tina played moderately well. They won handily.

Janine showered, dressed, and met Tina in the dining room. They sat with Roxy and Suzy.

"So, I hear that you're a working girl now," said Suzy.

"I'm working two jobs right now," replied Janine. "I had to support my children."

"Working? Where?" asked Roxy.

Janine felt tension at the table. "I waitress at Denny's and the Casino. I don't have a man paying my way anymore."

"We heard you were living with some retired guy," said Suzy.

Their food came. Janine took the moment to strategize her position. "I was lucky enough to find a good man."

"It must be quite a way down from your husband," said Roxy.

"Brent? No, you couldn't get much lower than him." She had a bite of salad. "You know, now that I think of it, the FBI asked me to list all of Brent's…associates. I'll have to add you two to that list."

Roxanne and Sue froze in place.

Tina broke the tense moment. "So, Janine, how are the kids? Do they like their new schools?"

"They're getting used to them," replied Janine. "It was a bit of a shock." She directed her attention on Tina. "How are yours? Your son is in junior high now?"

"Yes, yes he is."

"You know," said Roxanne, "I think I should be getting home." She pushed her plate away.

"Me too," said Sue. "It was nice seeing you."

"Was it?" replied Janine.

Roxy and Suzy left quickly.

"I'm so sorry," said Tina. "I didn't know they would…I mean…"

"That's okay," said Janine. "I'm not taking crap from a couple of bitches anymore." She looked at Tina. "Why did you invite me here? It wasn't the tennis."

Tina looked confused. "Well, it is and it isn't. I did need a partner and you are good. Have you gotten better?"

"I had some tension to work out. I unloaded on them." She looked at Tina. "Well?"

"I need you to talk to my aunt." Tina looked a little sheepish. "She's in the governor's room."

"Your aunt is upstairs in the governor's room waiting to see me?"

"That's right, come on."

Tina led Janine upstairs to an impressive oak door marked Governor's Room. Tina knocked and led her in.

"Come in, dears," came the voice of an elder woman. Two ladies sat in lounge chairs by reading lights. Both women were of advanced years. One woman was knitting.

Tina stepped forward and kissed the non-knitting lady. "Aunt Hester, this is Janine."

"How do you do, girl. And this is Helen." Helen nodded while counting stitches. "We are going to have tea. Why don't you girls join us?"

"I really have to go," said Tina.

"You will stay, won't you, Janine?" asked Hester.

"I can stay for a bit."

"Good. Pour yourself a tea," said Hester. "Let's have a talk."

Sensing an interrogation coming, Janine decided on an unemotional response. "What shall we talk about?"

"My dear," said Helen, putting her knitting away, "we were hoping to enlist your help.

"We believe that a change in the club's management is imminent. We would like you to be part of the new management."

"The club manager is leaving?"

Hester shook her head. "It has not been made public yet."

"And you want me?"

"Actually," said Helen, "we were thinking of assistant club manager. Have you ever run a club?"

"No. My work experience is limited to waitress and drinks hostess."

"It sounds like you'd be perfect for kitchen and catering manager."

Janine looked from one to the other. She did not doubt their sincerity. "Why are you talking to me? You don't know me."

Hester looked at her and smiled. "You don't remember me, do you? You showed up to help at my League of Women Voters event. Your child was in a stroller."

"Oh, yeah," said Janine, remembering. "Saundra roped me into... sorry, signed me up to help. And then she didn't show."

"That's right, dear. And you soldiered on, toddler in tow. I have not forgotten." Hester looked at her quizzically. "You do know that Saundra was hospitalized the night before? There was in incident with her husband."

"I didn't know." She thought for a minute. "People here won't be happy if I'm on the staff."

"Because of what your husband did?" asked Helen. "We all assume that since he left you, you had no part of his actions. Is that true?"

"I had no idea what he was doing. Are you two sure about this?"

"Oh, yes, dear," said Helen. "We've seen many women misused by their husbands. Some sink into despair like young Miriam. Some get stronger, like you. We'd like to harness that strength. There is a decided lack of women running clubs like this. We'd like you to come work here."

"If you would like to work here," said Hester, "we believe that we can get you in. You would be able to play tennis and use the pool.

"There is, of course, the unwritten rule: no fraternizing with the members. You are young and attractive so the men will try. We cannot bend on this; no affairs with the members or staff."

"Men or women?" asked Janine provocatively. "That wouldn't be an issue. I am living with a man that I love."

"Oh, really?" said Helen. "Good for you, dear."

"Janine," said Hester, "please think about it. Talk it over at home. Here is an application."

Janine looked at these grand dames sipping tea. "You think that the manager is leaving?"

"Oh, yes, dear," said Helen. "Remember the part about no fraternization?"

"There is something else we'd like you to do," said Hester. "We have a private investigator looking into improprieties in in our club's management. Some of those improprieties involved your...estranged husband. We need you to work with the agency while they sort out these...happenings."

Janine thought for a few seconds. "You think I'm involved in these issues, don't you?"

"Nonsense," said Helen. "You have been already cleared. We are convinced that you too are a victim."

Hester looked Janine right in the eye. "Anything you hear, anything you find, call the investigator. We trust you."

Janine recounted her day at the club to Eric. He listened intently. When she finished, she asked him, "Well?"

Eric thought for a few seconds. "Well, I have a couple of observations. Firstly, you must explore all options. It does no harm to apply at the club.

"Secondly, I thought you applied for management training at the casino. What happened to that?

"Thirdly, whatever you decide, you must discuss with the kids.

"Lastly, we have yet to discuss our long-term relationship."

"Eric, what do you mean?" she asked. "I thought we were, we are a couple. Today I told those ladies that I love you, I mean that."

"When you get your divorce, if we marry, will you continue to work?"

"Eric, I love you. I thought we were going to get married?"

"I do want to marry you. But I need to know if you plan to stop working?"

"Eric, how much money do I owe you now?"

"Upwards of $50,000."

"Eric, you have always been straight with me. I have to be straight with you. I will pay back every nickel you spent on us. I'd rather do it married to you. But you must know that I will pay it back no matter what."

"Janine sweetheart, I love you too. I won't marry you for better or worse so long as you pay me back. It's a matter of honor for you, I understand. So long as you can support yourself from now on. I'll support whatever decision you make."

"Okay, then that's agreed," said Janine. "I'll find out what's happening at the casino. And tomorrow I'll call the lawyer about my divorce."

Janine made an appointment to see the personnel office at the casino. Ms. Wilson showed her into her office. "I'm glad you called. I just received a background report on you. There seems to be some troubling issues."

"Issues?"

"Yes. First there is an open FBI file on you. Some financial dealings with a Brent Piersen"

"My estranged husband."

"Yes," said Ms. Wilson. "And also, the state of Indiana is investigating a financial issue associated with you.

"I'm sorry, Janine. The company cannot train management who have open FBI files on financial issues. Your training request has been turned down."

"Ms. Wilson, I listed those issues on my initial application. It should be no surprise."

"Your current work record is exemplary. Perhaps at another time."

Janine thought about making a scene or telling Ms. Wilson off but did not. "Thanks for seeing me."

Janine called Eric before her shift. "The casino training is off. Some issue with the FBI."

"I know," replied Eric. "They want to see you tomorrow."

FBI INQUIRY

When Janine returned home from her shift the FBI was waiting. They put her in a car handcuffed. When she was taken into the interrogation room, Janine had a flashback of Miriam.

She was now used to the routine. Left alone in the interrogation room she settled back and closed her eyes.

"Miss!" Someone was shaking her. "Miss, wake up!"

Janine focused on the two men sitting opposite her. She replied to the usual questions in a daze. It was a rerun so far.

"Have you had any contact with Brent?"

"Not since he left us in Wisconsin."

"Do you recognize this card?" The man held out a greeting card.

"No."

The man opened the card. There were no preprinted words on the inside. In script was written: See you soon, Love Brent.

"Do you recognize the handwriting?" asked the agent.

Janine looked at the script. "It could be Brent. I'm not sure."

"You're not sure?" said the agent. "I'm sure. I think he wants to see you."

"Well, you can meet him. I will not. I don't want anything to do with Brent anymore."

"He's still your husband."

"Estranged husband. As soon as I get my divorce decree, I'm changing my name back to my maiden name. If you find him, keep him. I don't want to see him."

"Why does he want to see you?"

"I don't know. I don't want to know. I'll tell you the same thing I told those guys from the mob. If you find Brent, I don't want him back."

Both agents stiffened in their chairs. "What guys from the mob?"

"Two guys came to the house. I told them what you told me."

"Why would you do that?"

"They were polite and respectful. They asked me without handcuffing me first."

The two agents whispered between themselves. "What do you know about a safety deposit box in Valparaiso, Indiana?"

"Do they call Valparaiso Valpo?"

"Sometimes."

"Brent had a phone call from someone. They were to meet in Valpo. That's all I know."

"When was this? On your Wisconsin trip?"

"No before. Meet in Valpo he said."

"You have never been to Valparaiso?"

"I don't know. Is it near South Bend? My aunt could have taken us there. But I don't remember for sure."

"You never went with Brent?"

"No. Never."

"Is this your signature?" The agent held out a bank form.

"No," she said. "Let me show you my signature." She wrote it several times. "See, no match."

The agents left the room. Janine settled in for a nap.

The door opened. "Come on, Ms. Piersen, let's take you home."

KAT

When Janine got her SNAP food benefits card, she always went to a bulk grocer far away from the house. Janine had hoped to never meet anyone she knew at first. Then it was just a habit. On one benefits shopping trip, Janine saw a young woman who sat near the door with a baby in a stroller. She looked a little shabby. The mother raised her face and smiled as Janine passed by.

While Janine shopped, the image of the young mother ran around in her head. She felt that she knew her from someplace. It nagged at her while she shopped. It nagged her even more when exiting, but the woman was gone.

At the dinner table everyone told of their day. Monica announced that she was invited to a sleep-over birthday party. Could she go? Alan asked if he could join a Park District basketball league. Olivia announced that she was taking driver's education. Janine brought news that she would have to attend a number of court appearances for her divorce and bankruptcy cases. She had also applied for a managerial position at the country club.

Janine also recounted the story of the shabby mom and her stroller. On her way to her legal meetings, she intended to go past the grocer hoping to find the woman again.

Eric announced that he was invited to a retirement lunch of a friend.

Janine and Eric took Alan to a Park House gym to register for his basketball league. While the adults were dealing with officialdom, Alan was bouncing a ball with some other boys. When Janine went to corral her son, another mom was doing the same.

"Oh, hi," said the woman. "You're Janine from Denny's." She held out her hand. "I'm Marge." Seeing no recognition from Janine she said, "Officer Marge?"

"Oh hi," said Janine, recognizing the woman. "Which one is yours?"

"Jeffery! Let's go!" said Marge.

Alan and Jeff came over. Both women hoped to see each other again.

On her way to the bankruptcy hearing, Janine saw the young mom and stroller. They were huddled in a doorway out of the rain. She pulled over and got out of the car.

"I know you from somewhere, don't I?" said Janine. She leaned over to look at the toddler in the stroller. She was startled by the look of the child. It was like seeing Olivia at that age. Now she knew where she'd seen the mom before. She had been a waitress at the country club. "This is Brent's baby, isn't it?"

The woman started crying. Janine hugged her. "He got you pregnant, didn't he?"

Janine looked at the girl. She was thin and pale. Her clothes were dirty. "Are you living on the street?"

The girl was sobbing hard. Janine could barely make out, "They threw me out."

Jan looked the girl in the eye. "Are you homeless?"

Sobbing, the girl nodded yes.

"And this is Brent's baby?"

Sobbing, the girl nodded yes.

"Get in the car," ordered Janine. "We've got to get some warm food into you both."

Janine called Eric as she sped home.

"No problem," said Eric. "I'll be ready."

Rushing as fast as she could, Janine met her lawyer outside the hearing room.

"This guy likes punctuality," said the lawyer. "You'll have to apologize."

Still breathless, Janine and lawyer entered the hearing.

"We have a lot on the docket," said the judge. "We don't like to be kept waiting."

"I am sorry, your honor. I had to stop and help a homeless mother and her baby."

The judge looked up and locked eyes with Janine. Still breathing hard, she kept her stare.

The judge nodded slowly. "Of course, you did," he said less formally. "Let's proceed."

As the lawyers talked, Janine's mind drifted. She thought about the homeless girl and her baby.

She felt her lawyer nudge her. "The judge is talking to you!"

"What, I'm sorry."

"Aren't these proceeding important to you?" asked the judge.

"They are. But I don't understand all the legal terms. I can only hope everything works out."

There was a titter in the room. The judge smiled at her. "Your candor is remarkable. But I need to ask you some questions. You are stating that your husband deserted you. Is that correct?"

"Yes."

"Further, you assumed debt that he left behind?"

"That's right."

"And you have no means to pay?"

"He left us penniless, your honor. We were evicted."

"You are homeless?"

"We, my children and I, were taken in by a friend. I have shelter but no home of my own."

"You reside at the address listed. Is it a relative?"

"No. I pay him rent from my salary to stay there."

"And the credit accounts? You used them?"

"I did until they stopped. I did not know we had money problems."

"Your husband did not inform you of financial troubles?"

"No. He took us up to Wisconsin to keep his plans from me. He drained my trust funds. He drained my children's trusts. He scammed my aunt's funds in Indiana." She looked the judge in the eye. "And then he took off with his secretary."

"Is there a warrant out for his arrest?"

"Yes, your honor." Janine's lawyer handed a document to the judge. "This is the latest indictment."

The judge looked at the document for several seconds.

"Your honor, may I see that?" asked one of the other lawyers.

The judge handed the document to the lawyer. "It seems that your husband was a busy man. I assume that you have been interviewed by the FBI?"

"Estranged husband. Yes, I have been interviewed many times."

"You are divorcing him?"

"Yes, your honor."

"You are not suing him?"

Janine looked at the judge quizzically. "Your honor, I don't have the resources for that. I don't have the resources for this. I am raising three children, fighting bankruptcy, and divorcing on credit. I can't ask my friend to fund another legal battle."

There was silence in the room. The judge looked at some papers. "Are you working?"

"I work as a waitress at Denny's and a drinks hostess at the casino."

The judge nodded. "And you stopped to help a homeless mother and her baby?"

"Yes, your honor. I'm sorry about that."

He smiled at her. "I would like to see all the relevant representatives. Everyone else clear the room."

Janine went out into the hall. She sat on a bench. A middle-aged woman in business/court attire sat next to her.

"This is unusual," said the woman. "You tell a compelling story. The judge believes you. He's heard a lot of wacky stuff. You were devastating. I hope it all works out for you."

"Whose side are you on?"

"Oh, we're suing you. But if you'd like a piece of advice, ask for a jury trial. Tell 'em just what you said today. Just the way you said it. We wouldn't have a chance."

"Whose side are you on?"

"I represent the people who pay me. It's business. I have a family to support and loans too. Anyway, I just wanted to say you were courageous in there. Good luck."

When Janine was recalled to the courtroom, the judge stated some legal jargon Janine couldn't follow. Then the judge hit the gavel. "Court adjourned."

"What happened?" asked Janine.

The lawyer said he'd send her a summary when he knew more.

Baffled, Janine left the hearing and headed home.

When she entered the house, she heard a crying baby. Olivia, Monica, and Eric were calming the toddler unsuccessfully.

"Where's Kat?" she asked Eric.

"Showered and asleep on our bed," he replied. "Clothes in the dryer. How'd it go?"

"The hearing? I think okay." She watched them dealing with the child and then met Eric's look. "How long 'till dinner?"

"Half an hour, forty-five minutes."

Janine stopped at Alan's door. "Hi, honey, I'm home. Dinner in 45 minutes."

"Okay, Mom."

At the door to her bedroom, she steeled herself. She knocked and entered. Kat was sprawled on the bed. She was wearing Janine's robe. Her hair was still wet from the shower.

As Janine changed, Kat awoke. Janine put on sweatpants and a sweatshirt. "Dinner's in forty minutes or so." She sat down facing the woman. "We need to talk."

Kat sat up and looked at Janine. "You're mad at me. I'll just take Little Al and go."

"Alright, hold on," said Janine. "If I was mad at you, would I drop you here in my home? I don't think so. I would like to know about your son and why you're living on the street?"

"I stole Brent from you. That's why he left you. We were in love."

"Oh honey, you are so wrong. Brent did not love anybody. He was screwing half the women at the club."

Kat started crying. "He loved me. He said he did. He had me call him by his special name, Alan."

"I know, he told me the same thing. You know, I wonder something. Brent was pretty careful. How did you get pregnant?"

Kat started to answer.

Janine cut her off. "You know, that's not important right now. How did you end up on the street?"

"My family wanted me to…get rid it. I told them Brent was coming back for me. He…" She started sobbing. "And then that other man from the club said he was going to arrange a video chat with Brent.

"He set up the video and we had a couple of drinks." She started sobbing. "And then, I don't know what happened. I think he drugged me." She was sobbing.

"You mean Roger, Roger Preiss. He tried that with me." She looked at Kat. "What happened next?"

"Somebody sent the video to my dad. They asked me where Brent was keeping the money. I didn't know what they were talking about. They asked where I went to have sex with Brent. I told them it was a motel. They asked about the money again. I still didn't know. Then they asked me about sex with Brent, what we did..." Kat stifled her upset. "I can't believe I said those things. They had me explain all the things we did, how..."

"That's alright," said Janine, stopping her. "Go on."

"My dad was...I've never seen him so angry. He hit me. I told him I'd been drugged. Not even my mom believed me. I had to leave."

"And you've been living on the streets since then?"

Kat nodded. "I had the baby at county. I named him Alan like his father. I always called him Alan." Her sobbing subsided. "Did you kill Alan?"

Janine looked at the woman and smiled. "Not yet. Let's get ready for dinner."

Little Al sat on Eric's lap while everyone else ate.

Monica recounted her perfect grades on a math test Uncle Eric helped her study for.

Alan talked about his new friend Jeff from basketball.

Olivia said she and Allie were collaborating on a project for art class.

Janine recounted her long day of bankruptcy hearings. Then she mentioned that she had found Kat and Little Al.

All the time they were eating, Kat had been gobbling down food. When Janine mentioned her name, Kat stopped abruptly. She looked around the table startled.

"It's alright, Kat," said Eric. "Why don't you slow down a little and chew your food. There's more if you want it.

"I've enjoyed playing with your little man here," said Eric. "I just hope you both don't catch cold."

"You're being very nice to me," said Kat. "You know that he's your brother."

"What does she mean, Mommy?" asked Monica.

"She means that Brent, your father, is Little Al's father too." Janine looked at Kat with a sigh. "It means that you have a half-brother."

"I don't understand," said Alan. "Did Dad marry her too?"

There was an awkward silence before Janine spoke. "No. They just made a baby. They were in love."

"I thought Daddy loved you," said Monica.

"I thought so too, pumpkin. But men who love their families don't run away. They don't steal from others."

"He loved me!" said Kat. "I know he did! He's coming back for me!"

"Kat," said Eric, "Brent is wanted by the FBI, Illinois, Indiana, and organized crime. If he does come back, he'll be in prison until hell freezes."

"Is that true, Mommy?" Monica asked.

"Now, we should make Kat and Little Al comfortable tonight," said Janine.

When Janine came to bed, Eric was reading. "What are the sleeping arrangements?"

"Alan has temporally given his room to his new brother and his new stepmom." She looked at Eric. "You have not commented."

"When you saw that the baby was Brent's, you had to help them. I get that. I am a little uneasy about Kat's street experiences. Is she a drug user? Hard to tell. She's in denial about Brent, that's for sure."

"Can she stay a while? She's a lost soul," said Janine.

"Well, I'm not looking forward to sharing the bathroom with another female. But this is your home too. She stays if you want it."

"You are a good man, Uncle Eric."

"You know my life was a lot quieter before you got here."

"It probably was. Do you regret it?"

"No. I'm a lucky man twice over."

Janine snuggled next to him. "Thank you for saying that. I love you."

Janine took Kat to see Detective Long. Kat identified pictures of Roger Preiss. She recounted her tale of being drugged. A vice detective wanted Kat to view a video. Kat insisted on Janine accompanying her.

Janine held Kat's hand as they watched. A woman was restrained on a chair. Initially blindfolded, several men questioned her.

Kat was shaking.

One of the men pulled her blindfold off. It was clearly Kat.

"This is you, isn't it?" asked the detective.

Kat was doubled over, crying. Janine said, "I think we've seen enough."

"Sorry, I have to ask, that is you?"

"Yes," said Kat, crying. "That's me."

They returned to Long's office. "I'm sorry, but you never reported the incident. We have no record of your incident. Give us as much information as you can, maybe we can get this guy."

Janine helped Kat through the interview.

It was watching the video and seeing Kat's reaction that sparked a thought for Janine. When she talked to Roger that night at the party, Miriam shrank away.

"Detective, I wonder if a friend of mine wasn't a victim too. If you can get a picture of Miriam Porter, you can compare it with your files."

"Okay, I'll check it out."

On the way home Kat was still snuffling.

"Kat, do you suppose we call your parents? The police can show what happened is not your fault. Maybe you can reconcile and have a family again?"

"You think?"

Janine arranged a meeting with Kat's parents, John and Ruth Donahue, at Eric's home. She also arranged for the detective to be present.

When Kat's parents arrived, Eric explained the Kat was a victim of Brent and Roger. He turned the meeting over to the detective.

Detective Long showed them his badge. "We believe that Kat Donahue and many other women were drugged, restrained, and shot up with inhibit releasers. We believe that initially Roger Preiss was working with Mr. Brent Piersen making these videos of Brent's victims. The tapes have embarrassing personal events that the victim would not want revealed.

"At some point there is a falling out between Roger Preiss and Brent Piersen because in the later videos, the questions Roger asks are about where Brent is hiding or concealing the money, the loot.

"Apparently, Roger thought that young Kat was a scam victim and not just a sexual conquest. Not convinced by her story, he sent the taped interrogation to you hoping for something on Brent.

"We were able to piece together photographic evidence. I'd like to show you pictures of the restraining and drugging victims. It was Janine, here, that managed to get away from one of Roger's interrogations and provided us with important evidence."

"We are building a case. We have not found the perpetrator, but we will."

The officer stayed while Kat and Little Al came in. There was a lot of crying and hugs.

The detective asked to talk to Janine as he was leaving. They stepped outside. "I believe that you are right. Your friend, the late Miriam Porter, appears in a staged bondage video. Can you come down to the station sometime? I know it's a little rough. But it would help."

Janine returned inside. Kat and her mother were locked in a crying embrace. Kat's father sat silent, staring off.

Jan looked at Eric. He looked worried.

"Momma, can I come home?" said Kat.

Her mother touched Kat's face. She turned and asked her husband, "Can she come home now?"

"Daddy. Can I come home?"

The man looked briefly at his wife and Kat. His stare returned to some far-off place. "Why don't you go get Al?" said Eric.

When Kat left, her mother sat next to her husband. "John?"

"Ruth, she was carrying on with a married guy. Nothing changes that."

"She made a huge mistake; she believed a man. She's not the first."

"She could have dumped the baby and moved on. God knows what she's been up to?"

"John," said Janine, "I believed that man too. I believed him to the tune of a house, three kids, and deserted destitution. So many people believed him that the FBI has me on speed dial. Your daughter and your grandchild need your help."

John was red faced. "Ruth, how did we get here?" He stood up. "Ruth, let's go." He walked out without looking at anyone.

Ruth kissed her daughter and grandson. "Thanks," she said, leaving.

KAT'S ESCAPE

The next couple of weeks for Janine were filled by three issues: Kat, Miriam, and the club.

Janine seemed obsessed with making Kat's life better over the next few weeks. She took Kat and Little Al to visit Ruth while John was at work. She took Kat shopping for new clothes. She talked to Kat about career opportunities.

Kat was reluctant to apply for work anywhere. She used her baby as excuse. "He might need me," she said. Janine tried to explain that her parents would find her more promising if she was employed.

Janine confided to Eric that she thought the parents were losing interest in repatriation. Kat had a bad encounter with both her parents. Her father wanted to know about Kat's future, how would she support herself. Kat had hoped her parents would take her back and decide on a livelihood later. Kat returned to Janine's house perplexed and disappointed that her parents wouldn't welcome her back.

Janine spent all night talking to Kat about her experiences. Work and self-support were necessary. Janine stressed the appearance of responsibility. Kat seemed to understand.

Jan was at work when she received a text from Eric: Call when you can!

"Only have a few minutes, what's up?"

"It's Kat," said Eric. "Her parents, the Donahues, have called in Child Services. They are petitioning for custody."

"Oh my god!"

"Yeah, it's ugly. There were deputies and Child Service workers here. Kat had to be pulled away from Al. Then she attacked the Services worker. They took Kat away in cuffs."

"None of the kids are home, are they?"

"No, just me." Eric fell silent. "I'm going to bail her out if I can. Call you later."

Janine called Eric at the end of her shift. His phone went to voicemail. Janine went home.

The kids were unaware of Kat's issues or Eric's whereabouts.

Janine monitored homework assignments half-heartedly.

Ruth, Kat's mother, stopped in. "Have you heard what's happened?" she asked Janine.

Janine asked the kids to let them talk alone.

"Child Services came here and took Al if that's what you mean? Eric went to bail Kat out of jail."

"Oh," said Ruth. "So, Child Services has Al? And the police took Kat?"

"I guess there was a scene."

Ruth was clearly distressed. "We just want...We want what's best for our grandson. You see that, don't you?"

Janine did not answer for some seconds. "Ruth, we're in the middle of this. But I want what's best for both of them."

Ruth looked at Janine for sympathy. She found none. "I'd better go."

Janine showed her the door without a word.

The kids all came in when they heard the door close. "What's going on? Where's Al?"

"It looks like Kat's parents brought in Child Services. The grandparents want custody of Al. Child Services took Al away from Kat. Kat was arrested. Eric has gone to get Kat out of jail."

The kids looked at their mother in stunned silence.

"Can they take Al away from her?" Olivia asked.

"Yes, they can. This is going to get ugly."

"Is there anything we can do?" asked Olivia.

"Well, we'll get a lawyer and see if we can help Kat." She smiled at her children. "In the meantime, let's get ready for bed. Tomorrow is a school day."

Eric returned home past eleven. He went right to the kitchen. He dropped a bag of White Castle burgers on the table. He put a cup of coffee in the microwave.

Janine and Olivia came to the kitchen. The three hugged.

Eric took his coffee and sat at the table. "I didn't get dinner. I'm starving."

"No Kat?"

"No. No Kat."

"Was it bad?" asked Janine.

"Yeah," said Eric between bites. "It started off okay. The social worker just wanted to examine the child. Kat became defensive and hostile quickly. Kat had to be pulled away from Al. Al was crying. Kat had to be pulled off the social services worker. The cops cuffed her and put her in the squad. She kept screaming, 'You can't take my baby.'

"It took me a while to track her down. There was a bond hearing. Kat assaulted and bit another officer. She started screaming, 'You can't take my baby!' in the hearing. They restrained her and sedated her. She'll be in the psych ward for a while."

"Ruth was here," said Janine. "She seemed very upset. They only want what's best for Al, she said."

"Not what's best for both of them?" Eric had a swig of coffee. "She's going to need a lawyer."

"Yeah, she is."

Eric shook his head. "We ought to be getting a group rate by now."

Janine made an appointment to see her divorce attorney, Levi. After an update on her situation, she brought up Kat's situation.

"I have an associate here who deals with family custody matters. Let me see. This Kat Donahue fought with the social worker, assaulted an officer, went berserk at her bond hearing, and was restrained and sedated. Wow."

"Please do what you can?"

Janine stopped in to see Detective Long. "Oh, hi. Vince will be right with us. I hear on the grape vine that one of your husband's associates was caught in Nice, France."

"Will it get me any of my money back?"

"I doubt it."

Vince brought them into a conference area. "I'm going to show you a video that I think has your late friend Miriam Porter in. Tell me if this is her."

He started the video. The woman was restrained and gagged. Someone removes her gag. "Lance, Lance, please stop!" she yells. The image stops.

"Is that Miriam?" askes Vince.

"No, it's not her."

"I'd like to show you parts of this video with men in it. I'd like you to try and identify them. Is that okay?"

Janine looked at the image of the trussed-up woman. "Go ahead."

A man put her gag back on. Another man entered the frame. He had on a mask. He began to shake her.

"Wait," said Janine. "Can I hear the voices? Is there sound?"

"There is. I didn't want to upset you."

"If I can hear a voice, I might be able to recognize it."

The video restarted. The shaking man said, "You've been holding out on us!"

"Stop!" Janine's hands clenched. She felt her heart race. "That's him. That's Roger Preiss."

"You're sure?" asked Detective Long.

"I'm sure. I'd know that voice anywhere."

"Okay," said Vince. "Ms. Piersen, there are two more men in the video. If you can tell me who they are?"

"Okay. I'll try."

The video restarted. The shaking man, Roger, said, "Here, take my place." The man with the gag started yelling at the woman, "You're holding out on us."

The woman drooped in the chair.

"She's fainted," Roger went off camera.

Another man entered the frame. He had a face mask. He had a syringe. "Why don't you use this?"

"Stop!" Janine's fists were clenched again. She was shaking.

"Are you alright?" asked Det. Long.

"Was that too upsetting?" asked Vince.

Janine closed her eyes and sat back. She tried to control her anger.

"Ms. Piersen," said Longtooth softly. "If this is too hard, I'm sorry."

"No. No, it's..." She pointed at the frozen picture. "That is Lance... And that," she pointed at the man with the syringe, "is Brent!"

"That's Brent!" said Vince. "Your husband? Are you sure?"

Janine shifted her stare from the video to the officer.

"Of course, you're sure," he said apologetically.

"Could you turn that thing off?" asked Detective Long.

"Sure," said Vince. "Ms. Piersen, are you alright?"

Janine started crying. "No I'm not."

"I'm sorry," said Longtooth. "I really am."

Vince was thinking out loud. "That means Roger and Lance and Brent are all tied together."

"Quiet," said Long. "Ms. Piersen, is there anything I can do?"

Janine pulled out a tissue. "No, there isn't anything you can do. My husband, my husband...thief, forger, liar, philanderer, embezzler, and now..." She gathered her things. "If you'll excuse me, I'm going home to have another cry."

Janine came home and went straight to the bedroom. Eric came in and sat with her. He held her head in his lap while she recounted her experience.

"How could I love a man so evil?" She looked at Eric. "You must hate me? How could I be so stupid?"

"No, no," said Eric, "you are still a good person. You have a good heart. You are a great mom. I love you. However bad he was, you couldn't see it. Miriam could not take any more. But you are stronger. You have endured." Eric hesitated. "You are woman, you are invincible..."

Janine started to laugh. "Oh, come on. I deserve a good cry."

"Yeah, you probably do. Didn't you ever suspect Lance, Roger, and Brent were up to something like this? How many of the wives and girlfriends did they exploit?"

"I don't know. I'm afraid to think about it."

"What did the lawyer say about Kat?"

"He said he will look into it, but it looks bleak. Maybe I should have stayed out of it."

"Kat is damaged and not thinking clearly. If she wanted to live on the street, that is one thing. But a toddler on the streets? That's a whole different thing. The child must be protected."

"Eric, I don't think I've adequately thanked you for protecting my children. That could be me."

"No, I think you're stronger than that."

"I don't know. When we were being evicted, I was useless. You and Saundra saved the family. I was lost." She snuggled closer to him. "How many women are there, deserted and lost? Not knowing where to go or what to do? I know that terror. It's crippling. That's where Kat is, lost and terrified. I have to help her."

"I know you do. That's why I love you."

"I didn't help Miriam. I can help Kat."

"Maybe you're helping Miriam now?"

"You know, I'm going to encourage my girls to go to law school."

"Will you visit me in debtor's prison?" Eric shook his head in mock derision.

Janine went to visit Kat. The secure psychiatric ward was deep in the hospital complex. Jan exited the elevator into an anti-room with secure doors and multiple warning signs. An attendant took Janine's purse and keys. The man "wanded" her. "You're okay. Follow all instructions. Kat Donahue will be with you in a few minutes."

Janine waited on a couch. Kat was escorted in. She was wearing a bath robe over pajamas. She sat dejected. She looked at Janine without emotion.

"Kat, are you okay?" asked Janine.

"I'm locked up. How do you think I am?"

"I don't know. I have arranged a lawyer for you. We are hoping you'll be released soon."

"Why can't I see Al? I want to see Al now. I need my baby boy."

"Right now, the doctors say you're too agitated to see Al. If you are calm and your evaluation goes well, there will be a hearing."

"And then Al and I can go!"

"No. No matter what, Al will be supervised."

Kat's head sank.

"Look, Kat, you've been through a tough time. Talk to the counselors. Listen to the doctors and the counselors. My lawyer will help you. But know that it can get better. It will get better. I can help."

"We were doing fine. Just me and my Little Al. Then you came. Now I'm locked up and I don't have my baby!"

An attendant came over. He spoke to Janine. "She's getting agitated. You'd better leave."

"Yeah, you leave me alone!" yelled Kat.

Janine was escorted back to the anti-room. She was given her things. She felt badly as she returned to her car. She sat in the car and shed a few tears. She hoped that Kat would find the strength to compose herself and regain her son. She really hoped so.

When Janine activated her phone, she had a message from the club. It was the club secretary asking her to call.

"Ms. Piersen, hello. We are in the process of hiring a new club manager and assistant club manager as well. I have received your application. After reading your application, I see that you have no current experience as a manager. I do believe that your application would be suited for the assistant position. Can you come in for an interview?"

Janine agreed. The club would send a confirmation letter and details of interview.

Janine spent the next weeks working and visiting Kat.

Kat remained in the psych ward until her hearing. She came in dejected and head down. She scanned the courtroom for signs of her son. Not seeing Al, she answered all questions in monosyllables.

Janine's lawyer got Kat's assault charges neutralized. Kat would be released into Janine's care.

Kat was summoned to a meeting at Child Services. Kat, Janine, and the lawyer waited in an interview room. When Ruth and John entered with Al, Kat lit up. She hugged and kissed her son.

Finally, a hearing officer, Ms. O'Dell, came in. She informed everyone she was taping the interview.

Ms. O'Dell read excerpts from Kat's psychiatric evaluation. "Katherine Donahue has delusions of a lover, Brent, caring for her. Katherine has no clear plan for the shelter and care of her offspring. Katherine believes that her love alone will sustain mother and child. It is recommended that sole care of the offspring known as Al Donahue not be given to Katherine."

Kat seemed not to hear what was being said.

Janine's lawyer brought up the fact that Kat was distraught. She had cared for her son until the intervention of the State.

Ms. O'Dell asked Kat if she had a job. Did she have a permanent address? Was she in job training?

Kat did not verbally answer any of the question. She just nodded no.

"Then it is the findings of this officer," said Ms. O'Dell, "that the child known as Al become a ward of the State. Said child is remanded to his grandparents for care and welfare until such time as his mother proves competency. Further, this Office grants Katherine supervised visitation three times a week. This hearing is closed."

As everyone stood, Kat stood holding Al. Ruth moved to take the child.

"No," said Kat, clutching the child. "He stays with me."

"Kat, haven't you been listening?" implored Janine. "Al stays with your parents until you're better."

"Nooo," said Kat pathetically.

John stepped forward. "Katherine, Al's going home with us. You can come visit him there." He pulled the child away. He turned his back on Kat and strode out of the room.

Ruth stood undecided whether to console her daughter of follow her husband.

"Come on, Ruth," called John.

"Sorry," said Ruth, exiting the room.

"Janine," said the lawyer, "this outcome was the best we can do. I'm sorry, I have to go. I have another hearing."

"Okay, thanks."

Janine and Kat were the only two left in the room.

Kat was crying. "I just want my baby."

Janine held her. "I know you do." She held for several seconds. "Come on. I'll take you home."

At the dinner table Kat sat like a zombie. She ate a couple of forks full. She did drink some hot sweet tea.

Eric engaged with the kids on their daily reports. Janine couldn't focus on the kids. As dinner finished Kat left the table and crashed on the couch.

After dinner Janine and Eric finished in the kitchen. They settled at the table to talk.

"Will she be okay?" asked Eric.

"I don't know. If she wants Al back, she'll have to work for it."

"I hope she's strong enough for that."

"Me too. I'll try to get her a job at Denny's. She will have to show self-sufficiency to fight her parents."

"You have your own self-sufficiency to think about. There's a letter from the club." Eric handed Jan the envelope.

She opened it and read it. "It says that I have an appointment to meet with the board about the position. It also says we are invited to a 'Get to Know the Candidates' drinks gathering a week from Friday."

"We?"

"Yes. It says plus one."

"Oh, I get to sit with the wives. That'll be fun."

"Down, boy. Behave yourself."

Kat seemed to sleep-walk through the next week. She moped around the house and slept a lot. Her only enthusiasm came when she visited Al at her parents' house.

Janine talked to Kat about waitressing. Kat showed great reluctance to do anything. She was taking medication.

Eric took Kat to a required doctor visit. Kat left the doctor's visit angry. "She wouldn't release me. I'm much better and she wouldn't release me."

Eric tried to reason with her back in the car. "Kat, it might take some months before they will release you. You will have to be patient."

"You don't want me have my baby either!" she screamed at Eric.

"I know that you're frustrated, but you will just have to be patient. You must be calmer and engaged to retain Al."

"You don't think I'm a good mother, do you?"

"Kat, I think you are a dedicated and loving mother. However, right now, I don't think you could adequately care for either of you."

Kat grew quiet. "You hate me, don't you? You are just a man."

"Kat, if I hated you, you wouldn't be in my house. I think you need some help right now. We are really trying to help you. If you don't trust me, that's okay. Trust Janine. She's on your side."

Kat grew quiet. "Janine."

Kat returned to her routine. On days when she did not see Al, she moped around the house in a bath robe. On visiting day, she showered and dressed immaculately.

Janine and Eric hoped for the best.

On her next shift at the casino Marlene invited Janine over for a lady's night. Janine mentioned it to Eric in bed.

"You thought of this while we're in bed?"

"I shouldn't go, should I?"

"Jan, I'm not going to be the jealous husband here. If you want to go, go. Satisfy your curiosity or don't. But don't blame me either way."

"I do enjoy bashing you men."

"Well, some of us deserve it."

Janine arrived at Marlene's "Ladies Night" with a bottle of wine. With Jan, there were six. They ate cheese, crackers and drank wine. They "bashed" men gleefully.

Janine was intent on staying relatively sober. On this occasion Marlene had her sights on Olga, a blonde Polish girl. As the evening wore on Jan noticed that there were only four. As Marlene was getting closer to her target, Jan began talking to Maria. They stopped talking when Marlene began seriously kissing Olga. Marlene rose and led Olga off.

Jan and Maria continued to talk in general about kids. Maria was a single mom with a son. They agreed that boys were totally different from humans. When pleasure noises could be heard from the bedroom, Jan signaled enough.

"You know, I think it's time to leave. I'm going for pie and coffee," said Jan.

"I think I'll join you," said Maria.

When Janine came into Denny's she was met by Emma. "Hey girl! You can't stay away from this place."

"Just coffee and pie for my friend and me. How about a small booth?"

"Sure, honey."

As Janine sat, she scanned the dining room. There was a table with three male officers. At the counter was a lone female officer. It was Officer Marge. Janine went over and invited Marge to join them.

"You know her?" asked Maria.

"Sure, she has a son also."

Janine asked Marge if she was comfortable with the male officers.

"They're old buddies. They'll be less inhibited without me there." She looked at Maria. "Are you a single mom too?"

"Yes," she replied meekly. "He didn't like being a father."

"Yeah. They don't mind starting a family. It's being in one they don't like." Marge laughed.

The other policemen were rising. "Well, gotta go," said Marge, rising. "Say Jan, thanks for dropping Jeffery off after the games. It takes a load off."

Janine replied, "Okay. No problem."

After the police left Janine looked at Maria. She had become nervous.

"Maria, are you alright?"

She nodded negatively.

"Are you afraid of the police?"

Maria nodded yes.

"Oh, no," said Janine. "Are you illegal?"

Maria did not nod, but her eyes told the tale.

"I'm so sorry."

"I better go," said Maria. She moved casually through the doors.

Emma came over. "They leave you with the bill, honey?"

"It has been a strange night."

"Honey, every night here is strange. You know that."

When Jan cane home there was a note on the table from Eric— Wake Me!

Janine checked the bedrooms. All her children were asleep. She got ready for bed and then woke Eric. "Eric, honey, what's up?"

"Did you talk to the police?"

"No, why?"

"It's Kat. She took off."

Jan thought back. The lack of Kat in the house had not alarmed her. "She's gone?"

"Yes, she's gone. And she took Little Al with her!"

"What!?" Janine thought a minute. "How'd she do that?"

"She made a bogus phone call supposedly to her mother. She made sure I heard it. She would bring the stroller and let Al get some air. I left her off at Ruth's. I came home. Kat loaded Al into the stroller and joined the after-school parade of families.

"Ruth called me. She had no car. Kat and Al were gone. I went over. Ruth called the police. Finding a particular woman in the after-school crowd was impossible. Kat was gone. She took over $600 from my wallet that I didn't notice. She hasn't been taking her medications. She packed the diaper bag with clothes for Al and her. She's gone.

"We'll have to talk to the police tomorrow," said Eric. "She certainly planned it out."

"She really did," said Jan with a yawn.

"You're home early," said Eric. "No swimming in the lady pond?"

"The water was too chilly." She smiled at him. "Move over. You can warm me up."

The phone rang first thing in the morning.

"Have you seen Little Al?" Ruth's voice seemed frantic. "She's kidnapped the child!"

"We haven't seen either of them," replied Janine calmly. "They haven't returned?"

"No, she's stolen him!"

"Ruth, if we hear from them, we'll call you." Janine hung up on her.

Janine called the lawyer handling Kat's case.

"Hello Janine, what's your question?"

"Kat seems to have kidnapped her son from the grandparents."

"No, that can't be possible."

"I'm telling you she's gone with the child."

"That might be true. But I had the judge revoke the custody order when she was released. Kat is free to take her child anywhere."

"Why did you do that? Kat is still on medication."

"You called my office and asked me to."

"I never called your office. She tricked you and me. You'd better have a copy of the court order. The police will want to see it."

It was a couple of hours later that the doorbell rang. Two police officers were on the porch.

"Hello, I'm Officer Barnum and this is Officer Bailey. We are looking for a Kat Donahue...Oh hello! You're Janise something?"

"It's Janine. Good to see you two again. Why don't you come in?" She motioned them in.

Eric came in. "Ah, old friends."

"Sir, we are looking for a Kat Donahue..." said Officer Barnum.

"We know," said Janine. "Nether Kat nor the toddler are here. Go ahead and look."

Officer Bailey walked down the hall peeking in the rooms.

"Officer, I am informed by Kat's attorney that the court reinstated Kat's custody of her son. Here is the attorney's number. I think that you'll find Kat can take Al anywhere she wishes."

Officer Bailey returned, nodding no.

"Court order?" said Barnum. He held up the paper with the attorney's number. "Okay. Sorry folks."

Officer Bailey looked at Janine. She moved a finger between her and Eric. "Are you two an item now?"

Janine did not answer.

Officer Bailey smiled at her. "That's okay. I was just asking. The kids okay?"

"They're fine." Janine smiled.

"Good," said the woman. "I'm glad to hear it. Goodbye."

As Officers Barnum and Bailey were leaving, Detective Longtooth and Vince from Vice were pulling up.

"Problems?" asked Vince.

"Are these two regulars?" asked Bailey. She looked back at Janine.

"Informants," said Longtooth.

As Janine served coffee to the officers, Eric's phone rang.

"Hello. No, everything is alright over here. Just some inquiries. Okay, thanks for calling."

"Busybody neighbor?" said Longtooth.

"You may know Captain O'Neil. He lives across the street."

"Ms. Piersen, look at these pictures, please? Tell me if you recognize any of them?" Vince handed her photos.

She examined each picture carefully. There were two women she recognized. "I've seen this woman before. She was at a party at Miriam and Lance's. I don't know if I ever caught her name." In the men's pictures she did not recognize any of them. "That's it. Sorry?"

Janine deliberately did not tell them about the second woman she recognized. It was Tina, her tennis partner. She decided to talk to Tina about it privately.

"Okay, well thanks," said Vince. "What were the other officers here about?"

"It's Kat Donahue," said Janine. "Apparently she has taken her son and disappeared."

"She was out of the hospital?" said Longtooth.

"Oh, yes. I wouldn't count on her participation any time soon."

"Any chance we can get you in one day next week?" asked Vince. "There are some task force people I'd like you to talk to."

"Actually," said Janine, "I have to go to South Bend next week. There is a court hearing about my aunt's estate. You know, the one Brent drained? Anyway, some DA wants to crucify me about it."

Vince looked at Longtooth for a second. "Can I see your court summons?" said Vince. "It may bear on the case we're building against your…estranged husband."

"Sure. I'll get it."

"I'll get it," said Eric. "You look at those pictures again. Maybe something will come to you."

While Eric retrieved the summons, Janine looked over the pictures again. "Sorry, just the one."

Vince photographed the summons with his phone. "Alright, well thanks. We'll be in touch."

Eric showed them out. He came back and looked at Janine. "Are you alright?"

"Those pictures make me sick to my stomach."

THE CLUB'S RECEPTION

Janine and Eric went to the reception at the country club in Eric's car.

"Your Buick should be easy to find among all those Lincolns and Cadillacs," said Janine wryly.

"The valet will probably park it with the staff's."

In the lobby, Janine pulled Eric aside. "You look very sharp tonight, sir."

"I have to. Being with a lovely woman makes a man feel good." Eric looked her in the eye. "You look great. You are great. Your family's proud of you. Knock 'em dead."

"Eric, don't let anyone bait you."

"There you are worrying about me. I'll be fine. I won't let you down."

Janine leaned over and kissed his cheek. "You never have, and you never will."

He looked at her and smiled. "Let's go meet the enemy."

When Janine and Eric walked into the reception, several heads turned. Janine's tennis partner, Tina, came over.

"Janine, I'm so glad you could make it," said Tina loudly. She shook Janine's hand. "And this must be Eric." She shook Eric's hand.

"Nice to meet you," said Eric politely.

Tina escorted Janine and Eric around, introducing them. Many did a double take when introduced to Janine. This continued until they met the club secretary.

"Ah, Janise," said the secretary, "I'd like you meet the managerial candidates. Please come this way." He dragged her away from Tina and Eric.

"I'm sorry," said Tina.

"It's quite alright," said Eric. "I'll be fine."

"Actually," said Tina sheepishly, "there's some people I'd like you to meet."

The secretary led Janine to a corner of the room. "Now that I've got you all in one place, we can make the formal introductions."

The secretary stepped up to a mic. "Attention everyone! These are the candidates for club manager: John Smith from Snooty-bottoms, Duncan McReynolds from Over-Rated and Elizabeth Lessor from High-Moor. Let's have a round of applause. Now also tonight we have a candidate for catering manager and first assistant manager Janise...no Jemma, no... what is it? Janine?" There was clapping.

Groups descended on the managerial candidates. Janine was left alone.

Janine wandered out into the crowd. No one seemed to want to speak to her. She looked for a friendly face. She found herself at the bar. She ordered a scotch.

"Well, well, well." A man came up to Janine. She recognized his face from a party at Lance's. "So, you're coming back as part of the staff?" He looked her up and down a bit lewdly. "You haven't changed much."

"Oh, yes, I have."

"Well, if you're available some evening..."

"I am not."

"Oh, I see." He nodded toward Eric. "You're living with your dad now. Can't get away?"

"He's not my dad," she said defiantly. "He will be my husband."

"Really? Quite a step down from Brent."

She smiled at him. "You don't know what you're talking about. Anything is a step up from Brent."

He laughed. "Really, Jan? I knew Brent."

"I didn't catch your name?"

He reached out a hand. "Phillip Aslov. Call me Phil."

"And you knew Brent well, did you?"

"I did. And do you know what he said about you?"

"Well, Phillip Aslov, I hope he told you I was a smart woman. Because you are going to regret this conversation."

"And why would that be?"

"Because Special Agent Wilson, over at the FBI, has asked me to refer all of Brent's friends to him. Apparently, there are a lot of loose ends to be tied up. Nice meeting you, Phil." Janine left the bar with her scotch.

Janine found Eric seated with her two elderly acquaintances, Aunt Hester and Helen. There was a white-haired man seated with them. They stopped talking when Jan approached.

"Come on over, Janine," said Hester. "We were just talking with your paramour here. Eric is an interesting man." She motioned to an empty chair. "Janine, this is Judge Johnson. Like us, he goes way back with the club."

"How do you do?'

"Fine," said Johnson. "But your presence here has caused quite a stir. I think most people would like to forget…Brent. He has caused several people to leave the club."

"Judge," said Eric, "we have found that Brent had his fingers in many pies. He didn't scam the club too?"

"Oh yes, he did. He was pals with the accounts clerk. He took us for thousands."

"But," said Hester, "the insurance covered the losses. We are now under financial scrutiny."

"Then surely no one is going to vote Janine onto the staff," said Eric.

"Not so," said Helen. "Many of the women sympathize with her troubles. We have all followed the scandals. Janine has weathered the storm admirably."

"Besides," said Johnson, "we don't know how many other scandals are beneath the surface. If Janine would be free to mediate these issues, we would appreciate it. We don't need any more negative publicity."

"I think that there may be more sex scandals coming," said Janine. "I wonder who else was involved."

"You see," said Hester. "We need her on the inside."

Judge Johnson looked at Janine. "Talk to me about the sex thing later."

"Now, why don't you kids mingle," said Helen.

Eric and Janine reentered the crowd. There were polite hellos but no conversation. Eventually, Elizabeth Lessor came over.

"Alright, explain what's going on," Lessor said. "You are a shoo-in for assistant. I always hire my own assistants."

"I guess this time you'd have to accept the assistant with the job."

"I don't think I do," said Elizabeth.

Eric said softly, "There's a hidden agenda going. You see those three elderly people in the corner? They want Janine no matter what. Take it or leave it."

There were four phone calls the next day for Janine. One from Elizabeth Lessor, one from Judge Johnson, and two with the police.

Janine called Detective Longtooth. "I had an encounter with a man at the country club by name of Phillip Aslov. He told me he knew Brent quite well. He seemed to think that he knew something. I don't remember him, but you might want to check him out?"

"Okay, Janine," said the detective. "We might have some more pictures we'd like you identify. Is that okay?"

"Sure. Call me."

Judge Johnson called Janine. "I know that it is an imposition, but I'd like to sit down with you and our private investigator. We'd like to discuss a few things?"

"At the club?"

"No, no," said the judge, "at the investigator's office."

"It would have to be in the early afternoon. I can meet with you for say two hours? Then I have to go to work. Say Thursday?"

"I'll call you back."

"Hello Janine, this is Elizabeth Lessor. I would appreciate getting together with you soon. I would really like the manager's position at the country club. There seems to be things going on I don't understand. Are you free for lunch?"

"It's starting to be a busy week, but I'll fit you in."

Janine met Judge Johnson and Private Investigator Tracey Richards at his law office.

"I don't have to tell you that your husband has brought a lot of... unrest and suspicion to our organization," said the judge. "I truly believe you to be innocent of these things. You are innocent, aren't you?"

"I am as appalled as you are," replied Janine. "I was totally unaware of Brent's activities. I guess I should have seen them, but I did not."

"Do you think there is more left undiscovered?"

"I know of someone else who may have been a victim."

"Do you want me to get involved?" asked Richards.

"I'd prefer just talking to the person. I'll let you know if there is anything you need to know." She hesitated and then asked, "I'd like to know more about Brent's swindle of club funds?"

"Apparently," said Tracey, "he convinced the accounts manager to side-line some money. They invested in a short-term deal, made some cash, and returned the original funds. They did that a couple of times. Then Brent convinced him to side-line a substantial amount. It was to be a killing. That's when Brent took off with the money. A classic swindle."

Janine absorbed what they said.

"But," said Tracey, "we are also getting hints of a blackmail scheme involving Brent and Roger. I can't get anyone to confirm what it was all about."

Janine thought whether to share what she knew. "Apparently Roger would tape a sex romp. Then he would threaten to release the tape. From what I've seen he may have gotten blackmail money and released the tapes as well."

"Porn blackmail?" Tracey exhaled. "With members of the club?"

"I expected something like this," said Judge Johnson. "And you think there might be more?"

"I'm afraid so."

"You're not in any of them, are you?" asked the judge.

"No," replied Janine. "I don't think Brent would give anyone a chance to blackmail him."

Judge Johnson looked at directly Jan. "Ms. Piersen, I want you on the staff over there. I know that things have not been good for you. I hope you will take the job. I will find a way to supplement your income there if you'll do it. Anything you hear you share with Richards here. Okay?"

"I do need the position. It would be nice."

"Okay," said the judge. He rose and shook her hand. "Thank you, a lot."

TINA AND BOBBY

Janine called Tina. Could she come over for tea?

Eric let Tina in. He went out.

Janine brought tea. She tried to size her up. Tina came from money. Not flashy but expensively dressed. Fine jewelry but not too much.

"Did you get the job?" Tina asked.

"I think so. Thanks. Your aunt is something!"

"She sure is."

"Tina," said Janine, "I asked you here because I ran across something. I've been working with the police on some dirty dealings by Brent and Roger."

Tina stiffened. She hid her expression behind the teacup. "Oh?"

"Tina…did they tape you in a…some kind of…porn movie?"

"Oh god." Tina put her cup down. "Did you see it? Is it on the web?" She covered her mouth with her hands.

"I did not see it," replied Janine. "Nor do I want to. The Vice officer showed me some pictures of Roger's. I recognized your face."

"Oh god." Tina began to sob.

Janine moved next to her. She put an arm around her to comfort her.

"Oh god," said Tina. "It was supposed to be a movie for me and Bobby. He wanted a movie of us to keep for when we were older. We were supposed to have the only copy. He promised us. No other copies."

"And then he comes over…"

"Roger?"

"Yes, Roger. We used his place. His set up. Then he shows us, he shows us the tape on his phone. He wants $5,000. Bobby was screaming. Roger says it goes to the web. Bobby goes to the bedroom. He comes back with his pistol. He puts it in Roger's ear. If he sees the video anywhere, he'll blow Roger's brains out. Bobby takes Roger's phone. He throws Roger out."

"You didn't pay him?"

"No. Bobby won't pay him." Tina sobbed some more. "You think it's on the web?"

"I don't think so," said Janine. "Tina, I have to ask you a couple of questions. I've been working with the police."

Tina nodded. "I know."

"Okay. First, have you heard from Roger?"

"I haven't, but Bobby might have. He went on a hunting trip with some guys. Bobby has never hunted."

"Do you know where he went?"

"No."

"Okay. You haven't seen your…tape on the web?"

"No."

"Do you know anyone else that Roger might have been blackmailing?"

"Miriam, I think. And maybe Chase."

"Chase? Saundra's husband? Why do you say that?"

"It's what Bobby said when he had a gun to Roger's ear. He said something like 'You'll bleed us like you're bleeding Chase.' I didn't understand it then."

Janine handed Tina a tissue. "It's okay. Everything will be okay."

Tina looked at Jan. "Do you think so? What if my family finds out?"

Janine hugged her. "Honey, you didn't do anything illegal. You had sex with your husband. It's a little embarrassing but not illegal." Janine thought for a minute. "Besides, there are two things. First, do you think your aunt watches porn? And why are your family members watching porn?"

Tina laughed through the sobs. "That's funny. Auntie watching porn."

"And secondly," said Janine, "your aunt does understand blackmail. She is aware of some of Roger's scams. You should tell her some of this. She'll understand."

"I don't think I can. How can I tell her?"

"You can tell her that you're a victim. You wanted to record an act of love between your husband and yourself. It got perverted by a blackmailer." She looked the sobbing woman in the eye. "You are a victim. I should know."

"Things," said Tina, "have not been the same with Bobby and me. Since the Roger thing, he won't touch me. He wouldn't…"

"Oh no," said Janine. "We can fix this. We need to get together us four. Get it out in the open."

"You think so? I can have you over for dinner." Tina began to cry again. "I love Bobby so much. Can we fix this? Can we?"

"It's okay. We're going to try."

They drove up the semi-circle to the entrance of the estate. As Eric got out, he looked back and forth.

"What are you looking for?" asked Jan.

"There must be a parking valet here somewhere?"

"Cut it out!"

Bobby answered the door. Janine's knees got a bit weak. Bobby was box-office-idol-type handsome, in a Superman kind of way. In a polo shirt, with his biceps bulging, it took her breath. All the women at the club envied Tina.

"Hello, Janine." He held out his hand. He was taken aback when she kissed his cheek. "And you must be Eric. Nice to meet you."

Tina came into the foyer. "Hi, Jan." They hugged. "Eric, thanks for coming." She shook his hand warmly. Tina led them into the front parlor.

Tina led Janine to a corner where they could talk. Bobby pointed Eric to a set of chairs. "What are you drinking?"

"Whatever you're having."

"Twenty-year-old scotch."

"Fine. Make mine neat."

Bobby asked Eric general questions: Are you on pension? Are you a widower? How are the kids doing?

Tina took Janine on a tour of the house.

As soon as the ladies left, Bobby's demeanor changed. "Look pal, I don't know what this is all about. I don't need you sticking your nose in our business."

Eric let him vent without reacting. He sipped his drink to formulate a strategy. "Bobby, we don't know each other. But Janine knows you two. When she was asked if she recognized Tina from the porn pictures, she told the police no. She wanted to protect her from scrutiny. I assume you want the same?"

Bobby did not reply. He glared at Eric.

"Janine did not want to be mixed up in this mess. But she is. And she's concerned about Tina and you. She's been through hell. She doesn't want anybody else to follow."

"Dinner's ready," called Tina.

A cook served the four of them at an elegant table. The dinner conversation was general and light. After an excellent dinner Tina led them back to the front parlor. The conversation stayed light until the dining room was cleared.

Janine changed the mood. "I want the two of you to know some of the things I've been through in the past year. Our mutual…acquaintance, Roger, tried to interrogate me. He tried to drug me and record me."

Both Tina and Bobby were shocked.

"Apparently Roger has been making a living blackmailing people. I've been working with the Vice Units to identify victims. I'm pretty sure my…Brent was in on it.

"So, when I saw Tina's picture, I denied knowing her."

"Oh god," said Bobby.

"He scammed you, didn't he?" asked Janine.

"That bastard," said Bobby. "It was just for us. I wanted it just for us." Bobby put his head in his hands. He looked at Tina with tears in his eyes. "Lil' bit, I'm so sorry. I'm so sorry."

"Bobby," said Eric calmly, "you have been scammed. But it's not your fault. Don't let it ruin your life. Don't let it ruin your marriage. You still have each other. Don't lose that."

Bobby hid his face in his hands. "I'm supposed to protect her. I'm so sorry."

Tina moved over next to Bobby. "Sweet man, I love you. I'll always love you."

Bobby looked at her with tears in his eyes. "I let you down. I should have killed him!"

"Sweet man, you couldn't kill anyone." She held his head near to her. "It's alright. We have each other. We'll be alright."

"How can it ever be alright again?"

"Bobby," said Janine calmly, "I lost everything I had. I lost my husband, my house, my life. I got tossed out into the street. I get food stamps. My children are on welfare. I've been arrested so many times I know the drill. I know the cops. You have each other. Cling to that. I had to find someone to cling to. I got lucky."

"Lucky?" Bobby looked at Janine.

"Lucky," said Jan. "With Eric's help I kept my kids. We put a new life together. We could be living in cardboard boxes, but we got lucky." Janine looked at Bobby with a reassuring smile. "And you're lucky too. Ask Tina if she blames you."

"Sweet man," said Tina, "we both did the video together. We both wanted to do it. We got scammed together. It's not your fault."

"But I'm supposed to protect you."

Tina raised his head. "You wanted to kill him, didn't you?"

"I would have…"

"I know. But I couldn't let you do that." She smiled at him. "I need you here with me, not in a jail cell. We'll weather this together. Together, okay?"

Bobby nodded. "Okay."

There were a few moments of silence.

Bobby looked at Janine. "You were arrested?"

Janine nodded. "Yup, in two states and the FBI."

"Brent's wanted by the FBI?"

"That's right. My ESTRANGED husband is a fugitive."

"How are your kids taking that?" asked Tina.

"Well, we've been honest with them right along. We told them most of the things that Brent did." She hesitated. "We did not tell them about the porn stuff. Maybe someday but not now."

"You keep saying 'we,'" said Bobby. "It's like you've been a couple for a long time. How long have you been married?"

"We're not," said Eric with a wry smile. "Janine is proceeding with her divorce. She's abandoned, you know. Once she's free, I hope she'll marry me."

"You had to go to court to get a divorce on abandonment?" asked Bobby.

"That's right. And bankruptcy. He left me penniless."

"That's why you're working at the casino," said Tina. "Or is it Denny's?"

"Both actually."

Bobby looked at Janine and then to Eric. "Let me see if I got this?" He looked at Janine. "You are working two jobs: waitressing jobs. You are essentially homeless. You get food stamps. Your children are on welfare. You are both abandoned and bankrupt. You live…with Eric. And you tell me you're lucky?"

Janine nodded her head. "I'm not begging on a corner or living in a shelter. I have my kids sheltered." She looked at Eric. "And I have a proposal from a good man. I'm very lucky."

"How about some tea and coffee?" said Tina. "I bought a cake."

"Let me help you with that," said Jan.

Eric and Bobby sat in silence for a few seconds.

"She's really been through a lot," said Bobby.

"It's been difficult."

"Eric," said Bobby, "I'm not usually…"

"Bobby, what's said here stays here. I just hope you kids can bond together."

"Did you see the…?"

"I did not. And I don't want to." Eric thought for a moment. "If anyone ever asks you about it, don't deny it. Don't confirm it either. Just say relations with your wife are nobody's business."

"You think so?"

"I do," said Eric. "And one more thing, tomorrow you stop and get Tina flowers. Don't order them, pick them out. It's the little things that let them know they're loved."

SOUTH BEND REVISITED

Janine travelled to South Bend alone. Eric had to tend to the kids. Her mind wandered as she drove. Was there some new scandal? Is some new DA going to make a name for himself? Had Aunt Sarah's niece, Naomi, reneged? Too many possibilities.

Janine arrived in South Bend early enough to have breakfast. She tried to relax. She scanned the local paper for anything she might need to know.

Janine reported to the court clerk half an hour before her hearing. Minutes before her hearing, four men entered and approached the clerk. She recognized Vince from Vice among them. The clerk showed the men into the back. About ten minutes later the clerk asked Jan to accompany him.

Janine was led to a room marked Jury Room. Inside was Vince and three other men. The clerk left the five of the alone.

"Janine Piersen," said Vince, "this is Special Agent Dean, FBI, Mr. Yoder of the Indiana Attorney General's office, and Lieutenant Malcom of the Indiana State Police. We are all involved the tangled web your husband Brent Piersen spun. I believe these organizations are requesting your assistance."

"Ma'am," said Yoder, "there are several sealed trust accounts here in Indiana we would like access to. We believe that they are key to unlocking a ring of blackmail, thefts, fraud, and money laundering by your estranged husband."

There was a silence. Everyone was looking at Janine.

"Okay, go ahead," she said. "Why tell me?"

"You see," said Vince, "the accounts are joint sealed accounts in Brent's name and yours. We have no compelling evidence to get a warrant. But you can access the accounts for us."

"Why can't you get a warrant?" she asked.

"Because," said the special agent, "these accounts pre-date our current investigations. The courts have clamped down on wide ranging warrants. It would take a solid year of evidence gathering to build a case. You, on the other hand, could grant us access today. We'd like to nail Brent Piersen as soon as possible."

"And," added Vince, "prove your innocence."

"You do believe I'm innocent?" She looked at the three. There was no resounding response.

Janine thought for a minute. "If there is money in those accounts, whose is it: yours or mine?"

"That depends," said Agent Dean, "on when was it put there and how?"

"I see," said Jan. "I've been called here today to answer for the theft of my aunt's funds. Now you say that there are accounts you have no access to. The easiest thing to do is to tie the accounts to the theft of my aunt's funds and pin it on me."

"Miss, you have to see how this looks?" said Agent Dean.

"I do," said Jan. "I'd need that charge to go away before I cooperate. I need you to indemnify me or I go no further."

Jan noticed the four men stiffen. "I'm going to the lady's room. You boys talk."

Janine went for a walk to the washroom furthest from the meeting room. When she returned only Vince was there.

Vince had a grave face. "They won't indemnify you."

Janine looked Vince in the eye. "I hope you nail Brent, the rat bastard. As for me I have a court date."

Janine went to the court clerk's office and told them she was ready.

Janine was shown to the Judge's Chambers. Mr. Yoder of the Indiana Attorney General's office and Lieutenant Malcom of the Indiana State Police were there. After the opening ceremonies Mr. Yoder stated his claims against Janine. He used phrases like willful misuse and fraudulent actions. Janine zoned out.

After her last encounter in South Bend, Jan remembered something her father had given her. For some reason she never put it in a safe or bank box. She had it with her diary. In the tumult of eviction and temporary housing she had kept her diary close. Now it would pay off.

"Madam," said Judge Wilson. "What have you to say to these charges?"

"Your honor," said Janine matter-of-factly, "I'd like to show you this. Ten years ago, my father had Aunt Sarah sign a power-of-attorney in my name. I believe I had every right to move my aunt's funds at will."

Judge Wilson took the paper, eyeing Janine suspiciously. "Ms. Piersen, you are just producing this now?" He began to read the affidavit. After finishing he held it out to the DA.

"Your honor," said DA Yoder, "first this woman claims that someone else did it. Now she claims that she had every right to do it. Which is it?"

"Well Ms. Piersen, which is it?"

"Your honor, in the last year I have been abandoned, swindled by my husband, evicted, and nearly raped. It took me some time to locate this affidavit."

"Your honor, I object!" said Yoder.

Judge Wilson raised his hand to silence the DA. "My good God." He looked at Janine to gauge her sincerity. He looked at Lieutenant Malcolm. "Is any of this true?"

"Your honor, I understand that it is essentially true. That's pretty much what the Vice officer told me."

"Ms. Piersen, you understand that the court is obliged to protect all our citizens. This sheds a different light on the situation. I will order verification this document. It will be returned to you forthwith.

"This hearing is suspended until further notice."

Janine returned home well after dinner. Eric, Alan, and Monica were in the front room. Alan was doing his math problems. Monica and Eric were working on a picture puzzle.

"Kids, it's bedtime," said Eric. "We'll all catch up tomorrow." Monica and Alan gave their mom a hug.

"Livy is at Julie's," said Eric once the kids had left. "Listen, honey, I got two bad news phone calls."

"Can it wait?" asked Janine. "I'm tired."

"We got a call came from the senior's complex. Phyllis has fallen. She's in a coma."

"Will Mom be alright?"

"They didn't say," said Eric. "My guess is they don't know."

"I'd better plan on going there," said Janine. "What was the other bad news?"

"Oh, it's Ilana, Peg's friend. She's in a bad way. She wants to see me."

"What does she want?"

"I'm not sure. But I think I should stop over there when I can." He looked at her and smiled. "Was it a hard day?"

"Yes. Come to bed and hold me."

In the morning, Janine started packing in case she had to stay near Phyllis. She sat with Eric before leaving.

"What's going on, anything?"

"Busy weekend. Monica's got that sleepover party. Alan is going with Jeffery and his mom to a basketball tournament. The boys will be bunking out at Officer Marge's place. Olivia, Julie, and Allie are going to some art show in Rockford. Allie has booked rooms for them there." Eric looked at her with mock surprise. "I guess I'll be abandoned. Wow, the house to myself."

"Maybe you should catch up with Ilana?"

"Yeah, I should do that. You be careful now. You are irresistible to senior men, you know."

Janine tracked her mother to a hospital. Phyllis was in the intensive care ward. Behind the oxygen mask and hooked to the monitors she was barely recognizable.

Eventually a doctor came to talk to her. "I'm sorry, Phyllis has had multiple strokes. Her recovery is questionable. The next twenty-four hours will tell us everything."

Janine sat holding her mother's hand. She began recounting everything that had happened to her. When a nurse came in to service Phyllis, Jan went to the rest room. When she returned, the nurses were changing the bed clothes, so Jan went to the cafeteria for soup and tea.

When Janine returned Phyllis lay inert as before. Janine held her hand. She began recounting all the trips they took together. The hospital arranged a place for Janine to sleep. She slept restlessly for a few hours.

When Janine returned to her post the doctor was there. "Your mother's condition is deteriorating." He tapped on of the monitors. "Her brain is shutting down. I'm afraid she has only hours to live."

Janine resumed her watch. She held her mother's hand. She recounted all the family highlights she could recall, out loud to her mother. When the nurses came in Jan would relieve herself. She ate quickly in the cafeteria. She returned to the death watch.

The blare of alarms woke Janine. She had dozed off holding Phyllis's hand. A doctor came in. He looked at the monitors. He listened to her heart. He looked at Janine. "I'm sorry. Phyllis has passed."

Janine was shown to the office of a grief counselor. Janine heard the usual words of condolence in a haze. "I have to arrange for the funeral," she heard herself saying.

"According to this, your mother's arrangements and burial are prearranged," said the counselor.

"They are? Okay, good." Jan thought for a minute. "Is there anything else? If not, I'm going home."

Now she focused in on the counselor. She was a grey-haired woman in a clerical collar. "No, there is nothing else. But I suggest you spend a few minutes in the chapel. I will pray with you if you'd like."

"No. No, thank you. I'd just like to get back to my family."

"Are you okay to drive? Just be careful."

"I lost my mother a long time ago. I've been grieving with her since I got here. I'll be okay."

"Most people are not used to this level of trauma," said the counselor with heartfelt sincerity.

"I've been through a lot recently," said Janine. "This is just one more event. Thanks."

When Janine returned home the house was dark and empty. She had called Eric several times, but his phone went right to voicemail. She called each of her children to check in and tell of Grandma's passing. She asked Olivia if she knew where Eric was.

"He said something about his wife's friend, Lana," Olivia said. "Isn't he home yet?"

"Not yet. Don't worry about it. Say hi to Julie and Allie. Love you. Goodnight."

Janine had a shower. She had a bite to eat and went to bed.

Janine woke about 6:30 a.m. She walked the house. Eric had not returned.

Janine tried to sleep. She kept wondering what Eric was up to with Ilana. Had he been seeing her all along? What was their deal?

Janine's phone woke her. Eric was calling at 7:45. "Janine, sorry I missed your calls. My phone was off."

"Just what have you two been up to all night? Why was your phone off?"

"Jan, I'm sorry. I'm so sorry about your mom."

"Never mind that. I want an explanation. I go out of town and you're cavorting all night. She's been waiting to bed you, hasn't she?"

Eric was silent on the phone.

"She's taking you from me, isn't she?"

"Why don't you come over here and ask her?"

"I might just do that. Where are you?"

"At the hospital on Dempster. I'll be in the cafeteria." Eric hung up.

"Oh no!" Janine had let the green-eyed monster do the talking. She called Eric back. His phone went to voicemail. "Eric, I'm so sorry. Please forgive me?"

Janine got dressed. She left a note for the kids and went to the hospital. She found Eric in the cafeteria reading the paper. She sat down opposite him.

Eric reached out and took both of Janine's hands. "Honey, I'm so sorry about Phyllis. Was it peaceful?"

She looked at Eric with concern. "Eric, honey, I'm so sorry. I…"

Eric put a hand up to stop her. "As long as you're alright." He smiled at her. "You know, I got this phone call from this crazy woman looking for her husband. She was really confused."

"Maybe she thought he was going to get a better deal elsewhere?"

"Why would she think that? Had he ever complained about the deal he had?"

"No. No, he had not." Janine looked into his eyes. "He's been remarkably loving and patient."

"Then it must have been a stress related crank call."

"Yes, it must have been." Janine looked around the cafeteria. "How is Ilana?"

"She's run down. Iron deficient, they tell me." He leaned forward as if to impart a secret. "I think its change-of-life related." He leaned back. "They're going to give her a tune-up. New plugs, wires, and a filter. She'll hum like a vintage model." He looked at Janine and smiled. "Why don't you get some breakfast and sit with me? They won't let me see her for a couple of hours."

Janine got some breakfast and rejoined Eric.

"What does your mother's passing mean?" asked Eric.

"It closes a chapter in my life. I'm alone now, family wise, I mean. Mom and Dad are gone. Aunt Sarah is, for all purposes, gone." She ate and thought a bit. "With Brent gone that means all the ties of my old life are dead." She looked at Eric. "You are my new life. More independent, more self-reliant, and loved for it. You know, I could be a happy woman now. Not just going through the motions but happy."

Eric had a look of surprise on his face.

"What? Surprised you made a woman happy?"

"Well, I guess so." He smiled at her. "I'll take all the accolades I can get. But I was asking about your mother's affairs. What will you have to do for her?"

"Oh that. Apparently, Dad fixed all the funeral arrangements up years ago. Some lawyer is going to call me."

Eric made a face of concern. "Jan, what would make you think I was sleeping with Lana? When we started…being together, I told you that there was no one else."

"I'm so sorry. There's been so much deceit. So many deceptions. I guess I'm getting gun-shy." She smiled at Eric. "I'm sorry, my mind is playing tricks on me. There are only two men in my life that have not deceived me: you and my dad. Please promise me that you'll never deceive me."

Eric thought for a minute. "I know we haven't talked about our married lives very much. I loved Peggy very much. We had our ups and downs, but I never seriously considered straying. Ilana came to me twice over the years and asked for sex. Not love but lust. What she wanted was physical contact she wasn't getting. She didn't get it from me. I never told Peg.

"I never thought I would feel for anyone the way I felt for Peg. You have replaced her in all but my fondest memories. Yes, loving you has been a bumpy ride. You make me a happy man every day. Whatever comes, I'm here for you. I love you, Janine. You and only you."

They both visited Ilana later that morning.

PHYLLIS'S LAWYER, DAD'S SURPRIZE

It was the second morning after Phyllis's passing that a lawyer called. Wren Sterling made Janine an appointment to discuss her mom's affairs. She would see him the next morning. The same morning Eric was to take Lana home from the hospital.

Although Janine arrived fifteen minutes early, she was shown in to see Attorney Sterling immediately.

After the amenities Attorney Sterling produced papers showing the arrangements for Phyllis's funeral. Janine nodded approval. "As to the trust for your mother's care at the home, we can negotiate a settlement. The home will claim the bulk of the trust, but you shall receive the balance."

"Balance?" asked Janine. "I can get some of the money?"

"Certainly. I think we can safely say you are due upwards of $20,000. Not a lot of money, but something."

"That's great!"

"There are three other issues."

Janine felt the earth slipping away. "What issues?"

"First, there is the land in trust. There are two properties. The first is a parcel of undeveloped land in a vacation development. The trust has kept the taxes current. We have had several inquiries about selling the property. I believe that the property can only be sold through the development. We could try to fight the clauses, but it would be expensive."

"But we can sell it?"

"Certainly, once your parent's trust is processed through probate."

"Probate, I see."

"And that brings me to the other property assigned to your sister."

"Sister? I have no sister."

"Ah, I see," said Sterling. He held out an envelope. "You had better read this." The attorney left the room as Janine opened the letter.

My dearest daughter,

It may come as a surprise for you to know that you have a sister. Her name is Janelle.

I had to keep my relationship with Doreen a secret. My partners would have run me out if they knew. Our daughter is a few years younger than you. You should meet her. She is wonderful.

Janine, Pooh Bear, by the time you were born your mother and I were out of love. We agreed to stay together for your sake. Please don't blame Phyllis, it was all my fault.

If you are reading this, we are both gone and the trust evaporates. The property Janelle lives on will be hers if she is still alive. You had to know.

I can only hope that you, Brent, and the kids are happy.

Sorry if I let you down, love, Dad.

Attorney Sterling returned in time to hear Janine say, "Goddamn it!"

"I take it you did not know?" asked Sterling.

"I did not."

Wren handed Janine another envelope.

"What's this?"

"A letter of introduction to your sister." He looked at her questioningly. "Will you meet her?"

"I don't know." She sat back and closed her eyes. "This is very…"

"Distressing? I'll bet. Is there anything I can do for you?"

"Actually," said Jan, refocusing, "you'll be doing some work for me, right?"

"Yes. Probate work, unless you object."

"No, I don't object. I have another issue I'd like you to investigate?"

"And what would that be?"

"I have been informed that there are three sealed trust accounts in my name and Brent's. He's my estranged husband. These accounts are in Indiana."

"Why don't you and your estranged husband look into this yourselves?"

"Two reasons. First, I didn't know about these accounts until recently. My husband must have set them up. Secondly…my estranged husband is an international fugitive."

Attorney Sterling looked at her without comment for some seconds. "And what do you expect to find in those accounts?"

"I really don't know," said Janine. "But three branches of law enforcement would like to find out too."

Attorney Sterling assessed Janine for a few more seconds. "Why don't you and your law enforcement friends look into this yourselves?"

"Right now, my law enforcement acquaintances are being unfriendly. They are not playing nice." She looked Sterling in the eye. "I'd like to know what's there before our next pow-wow."

"I see. So, if I accept your instructions, I could expect a visit by… whom?"

"Attorney General Indiana, Indiana fraud squad…and maybe the FBI."

"Well," said Sterling, "your estranged, fugitive husband must have been a busy guy?"

"You can say that again."

Eric picked up Olivia on his way to the hospital. She had a half-day at school. Eric was to take her shopping for art supplies. He had to pick up Ilana at the hospital first. She was going home.

At the hospital, Olivia retreated to the back seat and zoned in on her phone.

A hospital aide helped Ilana out of a wheelchair into Eric's car. She didn't notice Olivia in the back.

As Eric pulled away, he glanced at Ilana. "Are you okay? Are you feeling better?"

"Eric, I want you move in with me. I'm better for you than some hussy with a pack of kids."

"Ilana!"

"No, I'm going to say it. I've loved you all these years. You protected me from Gilbert, but I wanted you."

"Ilana?" Eric glanced at Oliva in the rear view. She was frozen in the back seat.

"No, I'm going to say it. Leave that gold digger. I know what you like. You'll never satisfy a young woman. She only wants your house. Don't be fooled."

Eric glanced at Olivia again. She was covering her mouth.

"Ilana," Eric said patiently, "I was never going to pair up with you. I think of you as a sister. I always have. That's why I turned you down before. I couldn't have sex with you while Peg was alive, and I won't now."

"If I can't have you, I'm going to move in with Phil."

"You're brother-in-law?"

"That's right. He might be dull, but he's fire in the sack."

"Ilana, I didn't know that you felt that strongly. Maybe it's best if we don't see each other again." Eric pulled his car up to Ilana's building. "Let me help you into your unit."

Eric came around and helped the woman out of the car. He braced her as she walked unsteadily into the building.

All the while Olivia sat motionless in the back seat, stifling her laughter. Once they were inside, she moved to the front seat. Eric returned to the car twenty minutes later. He looked at Olivia with a blank face and said, "No, we did not have a quickie."

"Oh wow!" said Livy with a giggle laugh. "Did she know I was here?"

"I don't think so."

Eric drive silently to the art supply store. As he parked, he motioned to Olivia. "How about we get the supplies and then we get a cup of coffee. The café is right there."

Olivia led them to a table by the faux fireplace. "Uncle Eric, I didn't know what to do. She just started talking…"

"I know. Don't worry about it."

"I mean, she just came onto you like that?"

Eric composed his thoughts. "Livy, she used to hide out with us when she'd had a confrontation with Gil. They used to fight. They'd yell at each other. A couple of times he punched her.

"Anyway, one time she came over, knocked on the door. Peg was away. I made us some coffee. Ilana comes out of the bathroom naked. She sits down next to me, almost on me. She starts kissing me. She took my hand and…" He looked at Olivia's rapt stare. "Well, you get the idea. I said, 'Whoa there!'"

"She wanted you to sleep with her?"

"She wanted…intimacy that she was not getting. Ilana stayed over several nights when Peg was sick. Peg drifted off to sleep. Lana and I talked well into the morning. I went to wash up for bed and there she was naked. She tried to lure me into the side bedroom. I declined then too."

Olivia was following every word in rapt silence.

"Apparently, I'm irresistible to women," said Eric to break the mood. "Ilana said some things that I don't want your mother to hear."

Olivia shook her head negatively. "Don't worry. I won't tell her anything. It's our secret."

"No, that's not what I mean. Feel free to tell your mom most everything. We have no secrets." He paused and looked at her intently. "No, I don't want Jan to hear the comments about her being a gold digger. That she used her proximity and youth to seduce me. Janine seems to be sensitive about it. She would find it hurtful. She'll spend the next week questioning me about my feelings."

Olivia nodded her head positively. "I think you do love Mom. I won't tell her that part. But the rest is kind of funny."

Livy thought for a few seconds. "One time I crept downstairs and watched my parents having sex in the front room. I don't think they ever knew. Dad was…he was pulling the clothes off Mom. She kept saying to stop. She didn't want to wake us kids. Dad was very…he was…like an animal. He was grunting. He was on top of her. She kept saying to go gentle. He let out a huge grunt. He settled back on the couch. Mom said he hurt her. He should be more gentle with her. He had torn her blouse. He said she'd take what he gave her and be happy with it.

"I will never forget it," said the girl. She looked at Eric. "I heard you two the other night." She turned red and looked away. "It was totally different." She leaned forward and whispered, "She really liked it!"

Olivia sat back, red faced. She avoided his face. "I think you both love each other."

Eric smiled at the girl. "Well, thank you. We'll have to get a radio or something. But now Uncle Eric wants to ask a question. Is Olivia interested in this Beau guy? At the exhibition he couldn't keep his eyes off you."

Livy's face turned red again. "Really?"

"Olivia, my dear, why don't you invite him over. He seems like a nice guy. Art lover, artist lover?"

"He's never asked me out."

"He may not. Guys are stupid that way. Besides Julie is usually pretty close. He may find that intimidating. Ask him over for a joint art project. Tell him it's an art project with someone you don't know well." Eric looked at his watch. "We should get going."

Janine drove home from the attorney's office wondering what to do. She would be getting some money from her mother's estate. How much? Some but not enough to change their lives. Should she share this knowledge with the kids? With Eric? Or should she wait to see how much it amounted to?

Would she contact her newfound sister? Should she tell the kids they have an aunt? Damn, her dad was a rat-fink too!

Can't any men be trusted? Can she trust Eric? He does seem attentive and loving. He should be. He'd never get a woman like me. He's spending a lot of time with Livy. She's an impressionable young girl. He can't be that depraved, can he?

When Janine entered the house, Eric was working with Alan on his math homework. Monica was across the table doing her homework.

"Jan, honey," said Eric, "now that you're home, we'll start some dinner."

Janine nodded and went to her bedroom. She changed into a tee shirt and sweats.

Olivia came in. "Mom, you alright? Did everything go alright with the lawyer?"

"Yeah, okay," said Janine, distracted. "Livy, do you like it here?"

"What do you mean?"

"Maybe we shouldn't stay here?"

"Mom," said Livy, concerned, "where would we go?"

"I don't know," replied Janine. Suddenly she focused in on her daughter. "Olivia, you would tell me there was something going on, wouldn't you?"

"Like what? I don't understand?"

"Eric," said Janine abruptly. "Has Eric…done anything to you?"

"Mom!?" Olivia moved over and took her mother's hands. "Mom, he loves you. He never touches me. Today Ilana wanted him to move in with her. He chose you." She looked into her mother's eyes. "What's the matter?" She searched her mother's expression with her eyes. "I thought you loved him?"

"I do," said Janine. She closed her eyes to compose herself. "I do. It's just that…"

"What, Mom? What's happened?"

Janine looked into the eyes of her daughter. Her concern was evident. "Something at the lawyer's office upset me. I need to digest it." She reached out and touched Livy's face. "I'll be alright."

Janine really didn't hear what the kids said at dinner. She declined coffee, showered, and went to bed.

Janine came awake at 4:17 a.m. She was alone in bed.

She found Eric asleep on the couch. She shook him. "What are you doing here? Come to bed."

"I was asleep," grumbled Eric, getting into bed.

"You belong here with me." She snuggled next to him. "I got scared when you weren't here."

"I thought you wanted to be alone."

"Stop thinking and hold me."

"I am irresistible to women."

"Go to sleep. You're dreaming."

Janine got the kids ready for school. Eric processed breakfast. After the kids were gone, they settled at the kitchen table.

"I heard you got an indecent proposal yesterday," said Janine.

"I did. I guess I'll need a new…BFF?"

"Don't you have any guy friends?"

"I do. I did. That's why I gave up golf. My foursome broke up in the second year." Eric thought for a second. "Now that I think of it, Curt wanted me too. Apparently, I'm just irresistible."

"That's enough of that or you'll be sleeping on the couch a lot more," Janine said in jest. Then she looked at him seriously. "Why did you sleep on the couch?"

"You were clearly upset. I thought you might like the space."

"If I need space, I'll tell you. What I need the most is knowing that you're next to me." Janine sipped coffee. "I was very upset when I left the lawyer's office. My father was keeping a woman and daughter in secret." Janine began to sob. "I have a sister."

Eric reached out and held her hand. "Oh my…" He pulled a tissue for her. "Oh, I see. The lawyer had to tell you because of the estate."

She shook her head no, still sobbing. "Dad left me a letter. He wants me to meet her."

Eric held her hand. "So that's why you were so upset last night."

Jan looked at Eric imploringly. "Tell me you never…"

"Jan, honey, I was a working stiff. Working men love the woman they're with or get divorced. Only rich guys can afford two families. No, I never seriously thought of straying. Ilana offered several times."

"Eric, I'm so sorry," she said through increased tears. "I'm so sorry."

"Why? You're having a secret sister means nothing to our relationship."

"When I left the lawyer my worst fears…All the men in my life. My dad and his lover, his daughter? My cheating, bastard, criminal husband." She wiped her tears. "I thought of you here, with my kids. With Olivia. I kept thinking…And then I come home and you're doing homework with…How could I?" She began to sob heavily. "Tell me you'd never…"

Eric came around the table. He put his arms around her. He pulled a chair next to her. "It's okay. Let's air those fears and we'll put those demons to rest." He put a hand under her chin and looked her in the eye. "Peg has a place in my heart, but I love you here and now. I love Alan, Monica, and Livy like I love my son. I can't imagine how it…destabilizes your foundation to find out about a sister. But you have to know that I would never…take advantage of any of you. If you seriously believe that, then you should pack up now."

"You promise me?"

"Yes, I promise."

"I know, I'm so sorry." Janine renewed her tears.

Eric held her. "It's alright. If anyone should entertain their demons, it's you."

"Don't ever not come to bed with me," she said through tears.

Eric smiled and let a small laugh. "Yes, ma'am."

She fake-punched him. "What do you have planned for the rest of your day?"

"My day is yours." He looked around as if someone could hear them. "We could repair to the boudoir?"

She smiled at him. "Okay."

"That reminds me, we have to get a radio in there."

PHYLLIS'S FUNERAL

Janine hastily found a black dress. She had the kids wear their best clothes. They arrived at the funeral home in the early afternoon. It was the same place as her father's wake all those years ago.

In a few quiet moments Janine looked around the room. She remembered her dad's wake. She had wondered at that time why her mom did not cry. Now she knew. She wondered if her new sister attended her father's wake.

A pair of elderly couples interrupted her thoughts. They were old family friends who she barely remembered. One lady inquired about Brent. Jan replied that they were no longer together.

The other lady updated Janine on her children. Jan barely remembered them.

A group of seniors arrived at one time. The bus from Mom's senior's home brought them over. There seemed to be a parade of walkers, canes, and scooters. They all told Jan some anecdote about her mother. It all seemed a blur.

In a quiet moment Eric called Jan out. "Why don't you use the washroom and freshen up?"

She hugged him. "Thanks."

When she returned from the restroom, Aunt Sarah and Naomi were at the coffin. Eric gave Jan a look of surprise.

Jan came up from behind as Sarah peered into the coffin. "Is she dead?"

"Yes, Sarah," said Naomi. "It's her funeral."

"Who is she?"

"It's your sister Phyllis."

"Oh, my." She reached out and touched her sister's face. She looked at Naomi. "She's dead."

"Yes, she is. Come on, dear." Naomi led Sarah to the chairs. Once seated, Naomi glared at Janine.

Janine greeted some more people until the pastor arrived.

Janine watched the funeral service through a kind of haze. She kept thinking about the trips she took with her mother. That they were a rouse so her dad could be with his other family now obsessed her.

She looked at her mother and wondered how lonely she must have been. She reached over and held Eric's hand. At least she was not alone.

As the service broke up Naomi came over. "I'm sorry about Aunt Phyllis. The police tell me that you will not be prosecuted. They say Brent stole everything. I helped him. That is to say, I sent him to the bank. When the bank called, I told them that he was...alright." She looked Janine in the eye. "He fooled me too. When Sarah dies, don't come down. I never want to see any of you again."

Janine watched as Olivia tried to engage Aunt Sarah in conversation. Sarah smiled at the girl but was not comprehending anything.

Janine talked to several people whose relationship to Phyllis remained unclear. She spied a woman sitting alone, not interacting with anyone. The woman was snuffling into her hankie. Jan decided to talk to her.

"You don't remember me," said the woman. "I'm Sylvia. I was your father's secretary for years."

"Oh, yes. I remember now. Did you know Phyllis well?"

"Oh dear," said Sylvia. She seemed to be struggling with something. "Dear girl, I knew both of your father's wives. I arranged the trips, the vacations." She looked at Jan intently. "I had to know if you were alright."

Janine thought about what Sylvia said. She enabled her father to live two lives. She helped him deceive his daughter. Her father the bigamist. Janine was exasperated and emotionally exhausted. Did she need to know about the double life her father led?

Janine opted for not wanting to know more. She simply looked at Sylvia and said, "Thank you for coming."

THE INTRUDER

It was a busy evening for the family. Olivia was over at Julie's. Alan and Monica did their homework while Eric and Janine attended parent teacher conference. As their conference broke up, they ran into Jeffery and his mother. Officer Marge offered to take the boys out after her conference. Janine had to go to the casino for a shift.

Eric and Monica returned home together. Monica wanted Eric to play a game with her before bed. Monica was talking as they entered the house. Eric noticed a light on in his room. She was still talking when he thought he heard a noise.

Suddenly a man came up from the bedroom. Before Eric could react, the man held out a gun.

"Just stay right there!" The man aimed the gun at Eric.

Monica clung to Eric, burying her face in his stomach.

"Easy now," said Eric. "What do you want?"

"I want the envelope. It's not in the dresser."

"What envelope? What dresser?"

"I know it's here. Brent left it behind."

"Brent who?"

"Uncle Eric?" said Monica, clinging to him.

"It'll be okay, Mon. Just stay quiet. Let Uncle Eric do the talking."

"Keep the kid quiet. You know who I mean, Brent."

"This is my house. There has never been a Brent here."

"Don't lie to me, old man."

"I know the Brent you mean. Same last name but I never met him. He's never been here."

The man stepped closer. "They told me she's here!"

"Look, you're scaring my granddaughter. We're the only ones here."

"There's ladies clothes in those drawers!"

"My wife died."

"Gimme your phone."

Eric handed the man his phone.

"Get over there!"

Eric moved with Monica wrapped around him. She was crying.

The man walked out the door.

"Monica, it's alright? He's gone now."

"I'm scared," she said, sobbing.

"Yeah, me too." He looked her in the eye. "You were a brave girl. It's all over now." He stood up. "Come on."

He led her to the kitchen. He picked up the landline telephone and dialed 911. They waited in the kitchen for the police to arrive. He called Janine's number. It went to voicemail. "Jan, honey, there was an intruder here. Monica and I are alright. Be aware, he's looking for you."

Eric and Monica sat in the kitchen while the police searched the house.

Finally, a detective came to talk to Eric. He held up Eric's phone in a plastic bag. "Whoever it was dropped your phone out front. We'll dust it for prints and return it to you. He seems to have pulled out all the dresser drawers in the house. Any idea what he was looking for?"

"He said something about an envelope. Then he said some guy's name I didn't recognize. I told him that this is my house. He took my phone and left."

"I'll need you to come down to the station tomorrow to finish my report. Okay?"

"Sure."

"How'd you call in if your phone was outside?"

Eric pointed to the phone. "Landline."

Just then the phone rang.

Eric answered, "Hello?"

"Are you alright?" Janine's voice was very concerned.

"We're okay. The police are here now. We're just finishing. Will you be home soon?"

"I'm coming home now."

Janine came home as the police were leaving. The detective stopped her. "Can I just see your ID, please?"

"I live here."

"Okay," said the detective. "I'm just trying to figure this out. ID, please?"

She gave him her ID.

He looked at the ID and returned it. "You his daughter?"

"No." She left him and entered the house.

"Baby, are you okay?" Janine hugged Monica.

"The man threw my clothes on the floor," said the girl.

"Alright, well, let's go clean it up." She led Monica to her room.

Janine and Eric exchanged glances of serious concern as she accompanied Monica to her room.

After an hour of restoring order, Eric and Janine met in the kitchen. Eric poured coffee.

"She's finally asleep," said Janine. "I don't know that I'll be able to sleep soon. Are you alright?"

"Well, I had to check my pants. I haven't had a gun aimed at me for a long time."

"What did he want?"

"He was looking for some envelope that Brent had left in a dresser. I told him Brent had never been here. I told the cops I didn't recognize the name of the guy."

"Why?"

"Jan, we put some of your furniture in storage, right? Maybe we should go have a look. It's been a while. We should probably check it out anyway."

"Why didn't you tell the police the truth?"

"Did you get the immunity in Indiana?"

"No."

"Do they believe you're innocent?"

"I don't know."

"Why don't they think you're innocent?"

"I don't know."

"Maybe there's something we should know that we don't. Let's check out the storage."

The next Saturday all five of the family went to the storage locker. They had not accessed the space since the eviction.

Janine gave each of the kids a box. They could retrieve anything as long as it fit in the box. Eric helped Jan put summer clothes in a box.

"Livy, why don't you take your brother and sister down to the car? I want to bag up your dad's things for the trash."

Once alone, Eric and Jan worked their way back to the dresser in the rear of the enclosure. They pulled out all the drawers from the dresser. They looked at all the interior surfaces with a flashlight. They found nothing.

The top drawer had men's socks. "He was very particular about his socks," said Janine.

She bagged all of Brent's clothes for the trash.

Eric looked at small tray with cuff links and pins. "Why did he have a drill bit in here? Did Brent do carpentry?"

"No. Not that I know of," replied Jan. "That's a pretty small drill bit. It's just larger than a pin."

Eric looked at the empty drawer. "Why does this drawer have a different bottom than that drawer?" He pointed to another empty drawer. He pulled the sock drawer out and examined it. He turned it over. "Look here, four small holes." He took the drill bit and inserted it. "It fits!" He pushed the bit in each of the holes, pushing the false bottom out.

An envelope and a CD fell out. Neither of them moved to touch it.

"What is it?" asked Eric.

"I don't know." She looked at Eric. "Do you suppose this is the envelope he was looking for?"

Janine's phone went off. It was a text from Olivia: Police Here!

"They followed us," said Eric. "Gimme those." He took the false bottom, envelope, and CD. He moved down the corridor opposite their entrance.

Moments later the police arrived. "Stop right there. Ms. Piersen, we have a warrant to search your belongings."

"Okay," said Jan, stepping back. She took the warrant.

"This is going to take a while," said Detective Wilson.

"We're pretty much done here, aren't we, Jan?" said Eric.

Janine nodded. "I'm done."

"Well, Officer," said Eric, "why don't you lock up when you're done. We'll get going."

"Wait a minute," said the detective. "Please empty your pockets first."

Eric and Janine pulled everything out and showed the officer.

"Good enough?" asked Eric.

The detective looked at Janine. "What have you taken from this locker?"

"The boxes downstairs containing clothes and the kid's possessions. That's all."

"We searched them." He looked at Eric. "What about you?"

"Officer, I swear I don't have anything on me from that locker but dust."

"Okay, you can go."

"Promise you'll lock up?"

"Sure."

In the freight elevator Janine whispered, "What happened?"

"I put it under the door of my locker. You know I have a locker here too. I'll stop by some other time."

When they returned home two letters were there for Janine. Both were from law firms.

"I have to make an appearance in my bankruptcy case. There seems to be some issue about the Indiana accounts," said Jan, perusing the first letter. "I'm going to have to go to Indiana about the trust accounts. This is a mess."

"Do you need me to come with you?" asked Eric.

"I don't think so. But you might check out the storage locker tomorrow."

INDIANA ACCOUNTS

Janine went down to South Bend early in the day. This time she met with Mr. Yoder of the Indiana Attorney General's office and Lieutenant Malcom of the Indiana State Police.

"We have examined several accounts here in Indiana," said Mr. Yoder. "Your name and Social Security numbers have been associated with each. In the case of Citizens Bank of Chesterfield, we were able to attain video evidence of a transaction. The woman in the video is clearly not you. This woman's signature matches the signature of the other accounts that you deny knowing about.

"These three accounts were used to move funds to offshore accounts in the Cayman Islands disguised as mortgage payments. Although none of the accounts has your exact signature the interest statements were attached to your income taxes. You did sign off on your tax forms. This is your signature, is that correct?"

"Are you saying that Brent paid taxes on the funds he was embezzling?" Janine asked. She examined the forms in front of her.

"I don't think that's the point. You signed off on accounts with embezzled funds. Are you claiming that you had no knowledge of the source of these funds?"

"Gentlemen, I am guilty," said Janine, "of trusting in my husband's honesty. As far as I know, he paid the taxes he was supposed to. As for these accounts," she held up the paperwork, "I know no more than what it states here. If there are accounts opened by someone impersonating me, go get her. If not, I'll have to file charges of my own."

After a moment of silence, Lieutenant Malcom spoke. "Janine, are you telling us your husband never mentioned anything about his dealings in Indiana?"

Janine thought for a few seconds. "I am advised by council that conversations between my husband and myself are, or were, private. I can testify that I never conspired, discussed, or planned any embezzlement or theft. I am embarrassed that my name was associated with any of this."

"Ms. Piersen," said Mr. Yoder, "will you testify in court?"

"I am advised by council to request immunity," said Janine. "With immunity from prosecution, I will gladly testify in any actions involving my name."

"I see," said Yoder. "And if we charge you as an accomplice?"

Janine thought briefly about unloading on the men. After all the humiliation and grief, to be charged as an accomplice? She took a deep breath and said, "Are you charging me?"

The men looked at each other without comment.

"I would like to ask you about your relationship with Roger Preiss," said Lieutenant Malcom.

"Relationship? Why?" Janine wondered where this was going.

"He made several deposits into an account here in Indiana. I would like to know what your relationship was."

She thought for second. "I met him several times briefly with my husband. I did not know the extent of my husband's relationship with him. About four months ago I ran into Roger. He offered me dinner out. I accepted. After dinner he made up an excuse to get me to his apartment. It was there that he tried to drug and rape me."

Both men startled. They glanced at each other. "Are you telling me," said Yoder, "that you were one of Roger Preiss's victims?"

"Almost. I pretended to be drugged and escaped."

"So, you were not one of his accomplices?" asked Lieutenant Malcom.

Now Janine was mad. "What! You think I was an accomplice? I helped him rape and blackmail women!?" She took a deep breath. Her fists were clenched. "I'm…done here. Charge me or let me go."

Yoder looked at Malcom. They both nodded yes. "You can go," said Yoder.

Janine left the interview room without a word. She made her way to the lady's room. There was no one in the rest room.

Janine stood at the sink shaking with rage. "Goddamn it!" She began to calm herself. She ran some cold water over her wrist. She wiped her tears. She entered a stall.

Janine heard someone come into the lady's room. She sat on the toilet until she felt calm. When she exited the stall, a uniformed officer was washing her hands. "Are you okay?" said the cop. "Yeah," replied Janine. "As good as…I'm okay."

HIDDEN EVEDANCE

Eric retrieved the DVD and envelope from his storage locker. He kept it out of sight until he and Janine were alone in the house.

"Did you look at it?" asked Janine.

"No. It's yours. I wonder why Brent left it behind."

"Maybe he just forgot."

"That doesn't sound right," said Eric. "He sure planned things out well. I don't think he forgot. He either left it for you or it was no longer important."

Janine opened the envelope. Inside were two packs of one-hundred-dollar bills. They were marked $10,000 each. "It's hard to think this isn't important."

"It's hard to believe that it wasn't important enough to take along. Unless…"

"Unless what?"

"Unless he wanted to incriminate you."

"I still don't get it?"

"We need to see what's on this disc."

"Okay. But I still don't get it."

They put the disc into the laptop. The disc would not open without a password.

"Now what?" asked Janine.

"Now you keep plugging in phrases, birthdays, and names until it unlocks. Get a pad and write down all the things you try."

"Birthdays?"

"Yeah. Birthdays, anniversaries, and nicknames are usual."

"Yeah, like Brent could remember the kid's birthdays. I had to remind him of our anniversary."

Janine spent two hours plugging in possible passwords with no success. Finally, they agreed to put the money and disc away. She agreed to note any possible keys.

Janine heard from the country club. Elizabeth and Janine had tea in the Founders Room.

"I wanted to touch base with you now that I will be the manager," said Elizabeth. "I would like to be able to confirm you at the next board meeting. We need to settle the boundaries of responsibility here." She poured tea.

"I see," said Janine. "What do you have in mind?"

"I see you running the catered events. They would be yours to arrange and manage."

"I see," said Janine. "And my position title would be?"

"I think Catering Coordinator. At Grand Hills we had a Catering Coordinator. Her salary was paid by the event."

"I see." Janine thought for a bit. "If I were to accept your position, I would have to give up one of my jobs. I would need some sort of base salary."

"I understand, by the awards in the case, that you are proficient at tennis. We could use someone on staff to act as tennis pro. You could manage our tennis events more formally."

"As a salaried staff person?"

"Yes," said Elizabeth. "Now, I understand that your estranged husband was involved in questionable financial dealings with this organization. I believe that you, personally, have been…cleared of responsibility in those dealings. Is that correct?"

Janine sat back and tried to assess the woman. "I have been interviewed by the club's agent. I am working with law enforcement as we speak. They have not found me guilty of anything except being duped by my former husband."

Both women were stiff and wary.

"Look, Ms. Pierson, in any other organization I have dealt with, you would not be allowed on the property, guilty or not. The owners are divided about you. They want you here but don't want you near club resources. I've been tasked with giving you limited responsibility and monitoring you. I am not happy about it. You can understand that, can't you?"

"I see," said Janine with a sigh. "You can't know how much I've lost. How embarrassed I am about my…about Brent's crimes. I know that there will always be a cloud over me. But I need to support my family. A position like this is…a godsend. But I do understand your dilemma. What can we do about it?"

Elizabeth cocked her head. "This isn't going as I anticipated. But let's think. I could keep you away from the finances. That would satisfy one of the concerns."

Janine nodded. "I'm okay with that."

"You would have to satisfy one of my concerns."

"And what's that?"

"You're going to have to tell me everything you know. I need to know what I'm dealing with. I need to know that I'm not going to get surprised by hidden issues."

"Well…" said Janine, thinking. "Okay, but you may be sorry. This is going to take a while. Can we have some more tea?"

"How about if I order some sandwiches too? Chicken salad?"

Eric woke up from a nap with a thought. He fed the disc into the laptop. First, he fed in all the combinations of the word dresser. He then fed in "$10,000"; the disc program opened!

The first images are of figures in a notebook. The next images are of Roger and another man carrying a woman to a chair. The men bound her. Then there was a gap in the recording. When it resumed, they kept asking her where the money was. She babbled incoherently. They kept slapping her face to rouse her. Suddenly she coughed heavily and convulsed. She began to gasp. "What's going on?" asked a voice off camera. A hand lifted her head. Another hand slapped her face. She continued to gasp. Then she went limp. "What's going on?" said a voice. A hand felt her neck. "She's got no pulse. Oh shit! It can't be?" The video stopped.

When Janine and Eric had a private moment, he told her about the disc. "I think Brent gathered evidence to protect himself. You don't have to see it if you don't want to."

"I think I'd better see it. We'll have to decide if we're giving the disc to the police."

"I don't see how we can't. It's a film of an assault and fatality."

Eric and Janine watched the disc in their bedroom. Janine was crying and shaking at its conclusion.

"Vince from Vice told me that they hadn't found a video with Roger in it. He is clearly in this one. The other man who assaulted me is in this one too." Janine was crying. "How could Brent stand by and let those animals kill her?"

Eric hugged her. "I don't know, dear. I just don't know. Did you recognize the woman?"

"No, I don't."

"I'm concerned about the notebook and the numbers. They clearly mean something. I haven't seen any account numbers like that in your files." Eric held her.

Janine was shaking. "That woman was drugged, like they were drugging me. I hope that she's alright." She looked at Eric. "Men are bastards—except you."

Eric leaned forward and kissed her forehead. "There are lots of good decent men. Let's just make sure your son is one of them."

"Will you hold me tonight?"

"You know I will."

Eric was on his way to pick up Olivia from Julie's house. He stopped at an intersection to let a fire truck pass. He hesitated because he could see the lights from another emergency vehicle. He followed the fire equipment with curiosity. The brigade stopped at a house he knew well. It was the house Janine had been evicted from. He parked his car and walked as close as he could.

Smoke wafted through the windows. Flames licked the roof at the back. Fire hoses sprayed through the windows. Eric moved close to the fire chief. A newsman had a microphone near the official.

"…we're going to get the arson investigators out," said the chief. "It looks like a suspicious fire."

Eric walked back to his car as calmly as possible. *First the intruder in my house, now the old house is on fire. Someone wants the hidden messages.*

Eric had just started the car when his phone rang.

"Uncle Eric, will you be here soon?" asked Olivia. "Julie's dad is here to pick her up."

"Be there in a minute."

Livy was outside waiting for Eric. "Julie's dad was early," she said, getting into the car. "We didn't have time to eat."

"Well, let's stop. Coffeehouse, okay?"

Eric filled a mug of coffee and chose a table while Olivia waited for her food. A man sat at the table opposite Eric. With a deadpan face he said, "Hello."

Taken aback, Eric stared for a moment. "Hello, Tony. I was just thinking about you."

"Were you?" replied the man, deadpan. "How come?"

Olivia came to the table with her tray. "Oh, you've got a friend." She pulled up a chair.

"Olivia," said Eric, "this is Tony. We went to school together. Tony, this is my niece, Olivia."

"Hi," said Olivia hesitantly.

"Niece?" said Tony, eyeing the girl. "Sure."

"Anyway," said Eric, "we had an…unexpected visitor the other day. He seemed to think we had a message from…our mutual friend." Eric looked at Livy and motioned a finger to the lips.

"Friend?" Tony looked at Livy. "Sure, friend." Tony's expression indicated impatience.

"Anyway," said Eric, "we looked around and sure enough we found the…message. It doesn't make any sense to me. I made a copy. Maybe you can decipher it for us."

Eric had made a printout of the notebook pages. He pulled out his wallet and produced the copy. He handed it to Tony. "Maybe you can figure this thing out."

Tony looked at the sheet. "Is this all of the…message?"

"There were some…home movies. But this is all the message he left."

Tony folded up the paper and put it in his coat pocket. "Are you going to pass the message on?"

"We have an appointment for the day after tomorrow."

Tony looked at Olivia. She had been eating and had said nothing. Tony looked her up and down. "You gunna take care of your…uncle, are ya?"

Olivia swallowed with a gulp. "Uncle Eric? He takes care of me."

Tony looked at her with a lascivious smile. "I'll just bet he does." With that, Tony got up. He looked at Eric deadpan. "Two days." He held up two fingers. Tony disappeared out the door.

"Wow," said Livy, "he's scary." She looked at Eric. "Did he think we were…"

"The thought crossed his mind."

"Uncle Eric, that was about my father, wasn't it?"

"Yes."

"Was my father…with guys like that?"

Eric nodded. "Yes."

"Are we going to be okay?"

"I think so."

"Are you and Mom okay?"

He smiled at her. "Very okay. Is it okay with you, your mom and me?"

Olivia put her head down. "My dad was…a bad…he was…bad." She looked at Eric. "Please tell me you won't hurt Mom?"

"I'll try not to." He smiled at her. "What a thing to say. I love Janine."

"Will you marry Mom?"

"That's a complicated question," he said. "To be honest I would like to. But your mom's…legal situation would make that very difficult. I can't let your family's debt drain us." He smiled at her. "I can't let future problems endanger my house. You don't want to be homeless again, do you?"

She nodded her head no. "No, I don't." A small smile crossed her face. "Did he really think you and I were…?" she whispered.

"Why not? You are an attractive young woman, and I am a handsome man." Eric straightened up into a pose.

Olivia giggled. "Uncle Eric!" She was embarrassed.

SETTLED ACCOUNTS

Janine heard back from her mother's lawyer, Wren Sterling, by phone. "Wow, you weren't kidding. I have been interviewed by the FBI over your husband's accounts. As near as I can tell the accounts were a conduit for funneling money offshore. Whatever is there or was there has been seized.

"As for your mother's estate there will be upwards of $30,000 left for you. I hope that will suffice."

"Can you hang onto the money for a bit?" replied Janine. "I have some things to work out here."

"It will take a few weeks to settle things. Is that okay?"

"Fine, thanks."

Janine summoned her children into the girl's room. "We have to talk about money. Mom's estate, your grandmother's estate, has left me some money. It's not a lot, about $30,000. There are so many things we could do with it, but I need to pay back a debt. Eric's put out so much money to help us. I promised that I would pay back every cent he spent. He deserves the money.

"I think that I'll be working at the country club soon. That means we'll have more money."

"Does that mean I can get a smart phone?" asked Alan.

"I don't know, honey. We'll have to see. We all have things that we want, but I promised Eric I'd pay him back. He deserves to be repaid first. Okay, my darlings?"

"Eric, we have to talk," Janine announced as they sat at the table. "Mom's estate has upwards of $30,000 left over. I want to apply it to our debt to you."

Eric looked at the committee. "Wouldn't that money be better used for rebuilding the kid's funds?"

"It wouldn't be enough," replied Janine. "That's not the point. I promised you that I'd repay everything you put out supporting us, remember?"

"I do. It's a point of honor, is it?"

"Yes, it is. You've done so much for us."

"Well, okay. Sure."

"That's settled then."

When Janine came to bed, Eric was reading. He put his book down. "We have to talk." Eric's expression showed his agitation.

"Yes, my love?"

"You didn't have to do that. It's no longer about the money. We're a family except…"

"Except we're not," said Janine in a soothing way. "We may be playing house here, but we both know the legal issues. Besides, I made you a promise. Of all the things that happened, you've been a rock. I can't ignore the promise I made. It would eat away at our relationship. That money is less than half what I owe you. But more than that it means a bond of trust between us."

Janine reached out and took his hand. "This is great between us. I've never felt more loved or wanted. But I've learned that trust and respect is just as important. I trust and respect you. It's so important that you trust and respect me."

"You know that I do. I don't want this money to be a point of friction between us."

"Me either, so you'll take the money. Besides…"

"Besides what?"

"You know I have a hearing about my bankruptcy coming up. Maybe it's best if you hold the money anyway."

Eric smiled at her. "Okay, okay. You know people think I'm taking advantage of you, don't you?"

"That's funny. I get the feeling people think I'm taking advantage of you."

"You know I don't feel that way."

"I hope you do. I do love you."

"I know. I love you too. Taking care of each other is part of a loving relationship." Eric changed expression to a playful grin. "But just in case, get in this bed and take advantage of me."

"Oh no," she replied in a teasing voice. "It's your turn to take advantage of me."

"Okay, we'll do it your way. Just turn on the radio."

Janine went to her lawyer's office. She met briefly with her Attorney Levi before they went to a deposition hearing. They are meeting with the Illinois States Attorney and members of law enforcement.

After being sworn in, the States Attorney officer, Hugh Egot, grilled Janine. "Ms. Piersen, you want us to believe that you knew nothing about the three accounts, in your name, in Indiana?" "I have sworn that I knew nothing about those accounts," said Janine.

"Large amounts of cash moved through those accounts to offshore banks," said Attorney Egot. He hesitated for effect. "And you want us to believe that you knew nothing about that either?"

Janine had a quiet word with her lawyer. "I have sworn that I knew nothing about those accounts," said Janine. "I have been made aware of the accounts in the last few weeks."

"Furthermore, the accounts in the Cayman Islands have your name on it," said Attorney Egot.

"I have sworn that I knew nothing about those accounts," said Janine. "And furthermore, my passport shows that I have never been to the Cayman Islands."

"You want us to believe that you were ignorant of your husband's dubious financial affairs?"

Janine and Levi had quiet words between them. She glared at the attorney. "I have sworn that I knew nothing about those actions."

"You want us to believe that you were ignorant of your husband's blackmail schemes?"

Janine and Levi had quiet words between them. The lawyer responded, "My client denies all illegal wrongdoing. Further, her estranged husband's alleged illegal activities were beyond her knowledge at that time."

The States Attorney handed Levi several sheets of paper. "And your client denies that this is her signature?"

Janine and her lawyer talked quietly between themselves. Attorney Levi replied, "My client has already stipulated that she signed documents for her husband without ascertaining their intent. She believed she was signing forms for a retirement tax shelter. She clearly had no further dealings with these organizations."

"You signed documents for your husband supplied without ascertaining their significance?"

Janine steeled herself. "I signed the documents that my husband asked me to. At that time, I trusted him without question." She locked her stare with Hugh Egot's. "Do you trust your wife?"

States Attorney broke his stare. "Thanks for coming in. That's all."

Eric and Janine went to see Detective Long.

"We've found some things," Janine told him. "We found these in a dresser we had in storage." She handed the officer the disc.

Detective Long put the disc in the computer. Eric recited the password to open the program. He started to watch the image of the men binding a woman to a chair. He stopped the video. "Have you seen this?" He turned to look at Eric and Janine earnestly. "This is serious evidence. Do you recognize the woman in the video?"

"No, we don't," said Janine. "But play some more and we'll see Roger and the guy who assaulted me."

Detective Long played the disc to the end. He remained motionless for a few seconds.

"That was my husband Brent's voice at the end," said Janine.

Detective Long looked at Janine askance. He looked at the ledger sheet. "Have you got any idea what this means? Whose ledger is it?"

"I don't know. I've never seen it before."

"Apparently, I'm going to have to share this with some people. Leave it with me." Long looked at then both with a nod. "Thanks for coming in."

Janine drove to the country club with mixed emotions. She stopped the car within sight of the main entrance. She had always felt special going through that door.

Now Jan drove around to the employee's lot. She went through the side entrance. Instead of oak lined walls with portraits, she found painted cinder block. She passed the time clock and went to the manager's office. She signed in on the sheet affixed to the wall.

Janine went to the catering office. There were piles of papers strewn across the desk. She put her purse in a desk drawer and started to organize the clutter.

Elizabeth Lessor appeared in the doorway. "Good morning, Janine. Can you be in my office in twenty minutes?"

"Sure. Okay," replied Janine. She continued organizing until she had to go.

Elizabeth and Janine went over upcoming events together. There were two anniversary parties and a wedding reception upcoming. Janine made notes. Elizabeth informed her that she had arranged some tennis lessons also.

Janine's afternoon was filled with detail phone calls.

At the end of the day, Janine looked around her office and smiled. She had accomplished one more positive thing. She smiled as she turned out the lights and closed the door.

SECRET SISTER

Janine's stepsister came to the house by arrangement.

Eric answered the door. He welcomed Doreen in for coffee.

Janine was sitting in a corner of the couch. She nodded and said a subdued, "Hi."

"I was hoping to meet your kids," said Doreen, sitting on the other end of the couch. "Now that my son's in service I feel like I don't have any family left."

"I see," said Eric politely. "You don't have any family on your mother's side?"

"No," said Doreen. "Mom and Dad were my only family. Dad travelled so much...or so I thought. It was Mom and me most of the time. But we had such great vacations." She produced an album from her purse. She held it out to Janine.

Janine was sitting frozen on the couch eyeing Doreen. Her body language read revulsion. She took the album and opened it slowly. She was shaking.

"So, Doreen," said Eric, "what do you do for a living?"

"I work in an insurance office. I also work in a beauty shop part time."

Janine was looking at the family photos. There was her dad, arms around a strange woman. Janine had no photos of her dad in a like position. And then there were photos of Doreen with her dad at Disney World. She closed the album. She was shaking.

Sensing her upset, Eric moved between the women on the couch. He took her hand. "Jan? Are you alright?"

Rage was welling up inside Janine. She could not speak.

"Doreen, is there something you wanted to say?" asked Eric. "Is there something you want?"

"We shared a father, a loving father. I thought we might share... family?"

Janine struggled for control. "No. No, we didn't share a father. You had a father. I had an absent dad. He spent his vacations with you. I spent my vacations with my abandoned mother."

Janine looked at Eric. "I'm sorry, I can't do this." She fled to the bedroom.

Janine collapsed on the bed. She opened her nightstand drawer. She pulled her album out. Her vacation pictures were of Phyllis and herself. She only had her college graduation with Dad in it.

Janine heard the front door close. Eric opened the bedroom door and poked his head in. "Can I come in?"

Janine reached out her arms for him. When he sat on the bed, she clung to him. "I'm sorry," she blubbered. "Is she gone?"

"Yes. It's alright now. That was hard." He soothed her face. He took a Kleenex and wiped her tears.

"I couldn't hear anymore," she said, crying, "I couldn't take any more. She had a father. I had..."

"You were provided for. Your parents loved you."

"No, Dad loved Doreen's mom. Phyllis was empty. It was a sham. My marriage was a sham. Until I got evicted my whole life was a sham. I was living in a dream. I don't...I don't know what love is."

"Now wait a minute," said Eric. He looked her in the eye. "No mother ever loved her children more than you. Through this whole odyssey you have given them strength through your love. And I truly believe in our love."

She collapsed in his lap. "Do you mean it?"

"I do. If I didn't, you'd be sleeping on the couch."

"Will you hold me for a while?"

"Sure."

"On the couch?" She sat up and looked at his face. "I...am a semi-lucky woman!" She kissed him.

He looked her in the eye and smiled. "Semi-lucky?"

PUZZLE PIECES

Janine couldn't sleep. She kept thinking about bank accounts, ledgers, and Brent. If Brent could steal all that money, why couldn't he have left something behind? Ten thousand dollars and numbers on paper was not much of a legacy. Why had he left the numbers behind? They must mean something.

I was so stupid trusting that bastard. I was lulled into routine and contentment while Brent was screwing around. How could I have been so blind? He gave me almost everything I asked for, that's how.

Everything in my life has been a sham except for my kids and Eric. My dad was a two-timer living for a woman he didn't marry. Did he ever show up at a school event? Did he ever visit ne at college? No.

My husband was a two-timer too. My whole married life was a cover for Brent's scams. What a fool I am?

Stupid, stupid, stupid! Why did I let them do this to me? I WANT IT BACK!

Brent left that stash in my dresser as an escape plan. A route to another life. That's it! The ledger is the key to another life. It's an escape plan.

Janine shook Eric. "Wake up! I want it all back, at least the parts I can."

"What? Who?" Eric sat bolt upright. "Who took what now?"

"Brent, Daddy, stupidity. I'm going to get back everything I can."

Eric rubbed his eyes. He tried to focus. "Okay…okay. Get what from who…whom…who?"

Janine sat up. "They left quick! Brent left more behind. I'm going to find it!"

"Oh," said Eric. "You want your life back."

"Don't you see?" She sat up on the bed facing him. "Brent left an escape plan. He left the money in the drawer in case he had to get away. It's safety insurance. There's more than $10,000 stashed away. That's what the burglar was looking for. That's why they burned down my old house. Don't you see?"

"Okay," replied Eric, scratching his head. "Let's just say you're right. These are nasty guys. If you are going after…loot left behind, you are not alone. They want it too. And so do the feds. You'd have to be very careful."

"Eric…I can't do it alone. Will you help me?" She reached out her hands and took his.

Eric let a sigh. "Okay, on two conditions. No, three conditions. Firstly, we have to insulate this house and my finances from whatever we do."

Janine nodded. "Of course. I'm not going to be homeless again."

"That means that we'll probably never get married," he said. "I'm sorry."

"Me too." Janine shrugged. "But living in sin isn't so bad, is it?"

"So far it's been great," he said with a smile. "Secondly, we have to insulate the kids. They cannot know or be hurt in any way. We must be very careful."

"Agreed," she said with a nod. "We cannot harm the kid's life further. What else?"

"Thirdly," said Eric gravely, "and I cannot stress this enough, if we're going to have these late-night strategy meetings you have to warn me. I'll take a nap in the afternoon. But right now, I've got to get some sleep."

"You go back to sleep. I'll start planning." She kissed Eric and got out of bed. She opened her nightstand. "I know there's a pen in here somewhere."

GROUNDWORK

Janine and Eric began sorting out all the pieces that had been collected. They only worked when the kids were absent. Eric called it Team Janine.

Janine started her own journal. First there was the cash and ledger from Brent's dresser drawer. Then she itemized the contents of Miriam's strong box. Then she categorized the bits she had collected from the Gawn office.

Janine began to wonder if Brent had information on his email accounts. Could she hack in to those?

Every time they investigated the trove of clues Eric would end by saying, "How can we access anything without implicating ourselves?"

Some nights Janine would review the journal before bed.

Janine woke Eric in the wee hours. "I've got it!"

Eric sat up. "Another revelation?"

"I just dreamt I saw Miriam withdrawing money from a bank. Don't you see?"

Eric looked at her blankly. "Was it a zombie bank?"

She slapped him playfully. "No silly, it was me. I was Miriam. I was disguised as Miriam."

"Whoa," said Eric. "How could that work?"

"You said I could pass for Miriam."

"Yes, I did. We'd need some documentation." Eric thought for a few seconds. "We know Miriam is dead and the police know Miriam is dead. I wonder if the DMV knows she's dead. We have her passport and Social Security card. What else would we need?"

"If I went in with no makeup and pulled my hair back, do you think it would work?"

Eric thought for a few seconds. "It's my experience that they don't question middle-aged people too much, especially women. Besides Jan, honey, dead people vote in Cook County all the time!"

Team Janine decided that the easiest way to reestablish Miriam's identity would be to keep her old address. In order to do that they would need a current utility bill.

Janine drove past Miriam's house. She had avoided that street since that awful day. There was a For Sale sign on the lawn.

Team Janine decided to call the realtor and ask to see the house. Maybe they could find a utility bill.

They arranged to meet the Real Estate agent, Wanda, on an early afternoon. Eric played the skeptical husband while Janine played the enthusiastic shopper.

The house had been emptied of everything Janine knew. She kept up her act of, "What's in here?" She even opened drawers.

After half an hour of poking around the empty house Janine was stumped. She caught Eric's eye and nodded no.

"So," said Eric, gazing at the empty space, "what's it take to heat this place?" Eric had maintained the skeptical husband act throughout.

"The house has the latest efficient heating and cooling," replied Wanda with a smile.

"Do you suppose I could see a gas bill?" asked Eric. "This must be a monster to heat."

"You know," said Wanda, "I think that there might be one here." She led them to the front hall. Inside the closet was a cardboard box full of mail. She rifled through until she found a gas bill. "I'm sure we can take a peek."

Wanda opened the bill and handed it to Eric. He tried to focus on the bill. "It's too dark in here. Can we step outside into the light?"

When Eric and Wanda stepped out on the porch, Janine grabbed several pieces of mail and thrust them in her purse.

"Well, this doesn't seem too bad," said Eric. "What are the taxes again?"

"But honey," said Janine, stepping out onto the porch, "it's such a pretty house." She turned and looked back into the hall. "I could be happy here." She reached out and touched Eric warmly.

Wanda replied automatically, "I'm sure you and your family could be happy here." She handed Eric the info sheet. "The taxes are listed here."

"Right, right," said Eric. "Well, I've seen enough. How 'bout you?"

"I guess so," said Janine, looking back into the hall. "Thank you."

"Please give me a call if you have any questions," said Wanda.

As Team Janine pulled away from Miriam's house, Janine began to cry. "That was so hard."

"I know it was," said Eric. "You did great. What'd you find?"

"I can't look. Can we just go home now?"

At home, after a cup of tea, Eric sorted the envelopes. "Bingo! A water bill."

Team Janine went to the DMV. Janine, sans makeup, asked to renew Miriam's license.

"This is an old one," said the receptionist.

"My purse got stolen."

"Did you report your license stolen?"

"No…I guess not. You see I lost my husband and…"

"I'm so sorry," said the receptionist, interrupting. "Go to line 6." She nodded over her shoulder. "Next!"

"Can I help you?" asked counter man 6.

"My purse was stolen, and I've lost my license." Janine handed the man the old license she had.

"I see," said the clerk. "Do you have any other forms of ID?"

Janine fumbled through her envelope. "You see, my husband's gone now, and I had my purse stolen. Here," she said, handing the clerk the envelope. She blew her nose. "This is very distressing."

"I'm sorry to hear that," said the clerk, looking through the envelope. "Passport, Social Security…what's this?" He opened the water bill. "Uh, okay. Your license still has six months on it. You can renew it for three years today if you want."

"Oh, could we?"

"Yes, Ms. Porter. You have no violations. You just have to take the eye test. Please step over here. Do you wear glasses?"

Janine nodded. "Just let me put them on."

Janine put the costume eyeglasses on. "Okay."

She aced the eye test easily.

"Thank you," said the clerk. "Just step over there and pay the cashier and have your picture taken."

"Oh really? Can't we use the old picture? I didn't have time to do my hair." She ran fingers through her hair.

"Sorry. Unless you come back and do this at another time."

"No, no," protested Janine. "My friend drove me over in case I had to take a driving test."

The clerk smiled at her. "Not this time. Just pay the fees and take the picture."

"Oh, you're so kind," said Janine.

Eric was sitting in the waiting area. Janine sat down next to him.

"Hello…Miriam. What's going on? Do you need a driving test?"

"I am an excellent driver," said Janine. "Let's go."

The next step on Team Janine's plan was to set up an email account for Miriam. Once the G-mail account was established, Miriam applied for a credit card. That effort was stalled when they realized that Miriam needed a cell phone.

Janine bought a minimal phone and service with cash using Miriam's old address. She had the billing sent to Miriam's email account.

Now all Janine had to do was intercept the card sent to Miriam's old address.

Janine went to the post office and had the mail held for "Vacation." The clerk looked at Miriam's ID twice. Now Janine had makeup on. The clerk initiated a two-week vacation hold.

Miriam collected her mail, including her new credit card, the next week.

So far, so good.

Late one evening, Janine sat on the bed with her laptop. She had periodically tried to open Brent's email accounts. She harrumphed.

"Still trying to get into Brent's account?" said Eric, working on his crossword puzzle. "When I had an office, I kept my passwords on notes near my monitor screen."

"The screen?' Janine visualized Brent's office. "There was a note attached to his monitor. What's it say? 69 Mustang?"

Eric stopped looking at his paper. "Did he have a '69 Mustang? The one in your pictures is a 2000 something Mustang. Did he ever have an old one?"

"I don't think so."

"Then maybe it means something. Plug it in and see if it opens his e-mails."

"It said '69 Mustang." She opened the laptop. "'69Mustang' worked! I've got it!"

Her expression fell. "Oh shit. Test questions. Best Man? Danny. Oh shit. Not Danny? What was his nickname? Oh, yeah, Danno, like Book-em-Danno." She punched it in. "Pet name?"

"Did he have a pet?" asked Eric.

"I don't remember. Pet name? I'll have to think on that."

It was the next day at the country club when Janine found the answer. Someone had made an appointment for a tennis lesson but had left no name. Elizabeth asked Janine what was on her schedule. "I have a lesson with no-name!"

Having said it, it struck her. "No name."

Janine remembered that Monica had once been offered a puppy. She was all excited. Brent adamantly said no. No pets! Monica pleaded. Brent got mad. Monica cried. Brent got madder.

When Janine asked him about it later, Brent revealed a nugget of his boyhood life. Someone had given Brent a puppy. Brent was trying out names for the dog. His mother had a violent allergic reaction. Brent went to the vet with his father. His dad had the puppy put down. When asked for the dog's name, Dad said, "No Name."

That night Janine opened Brent's email again. Best man, Danno. Pet's name, No Name. The account opened. Janine took a deep breath. What would she find here?

The first thing she found in Brent's account was twelve thousand inbox emails. This was going to take a while. Eric suggested that Brent had abandoned the site. However, there might be information worth having.

Janine spent a week sifting through emails.

Janine had to spend two evenings at parent-teacher conferences. She was able to schedule Monica's and Alan's meetings for the same night. Eric sat in on both.

Monica's teacher said that she seemed like a well-adjusted, happy girl. The teacher commented that "Uncle Eric" had helped Monica become an A+ math student. The teacher clearly wanted to define Janine's and Eric's relationship. They left her unclear.

Alan's teacher reported that the boy was moody. Not overly so for a boy his age. He was polite and studious. He had few friends. His grades hovered at B+. This teacher believed Eric to be Alan's grandfather. They did not correct him.

Janine had been called in to a meeting at the high school with Olivia. There was a counsellor and Vice Principal Crenshaw in attendance. Apparently, Olivia had been caught making inappropriate statements to a boy. Olivia claimed that she was being bullied and was retaliating. They were sensitive to the fact that the family had been evicted and forced to transfer into city schools.

Janine tried to make the case that Olivia was a sensitive girl and would not initiate bullying.

There had been reports of her being bullied.

Eric had listened quietly through most of the proceedings. "I'd like to say something."

"Off course," replied the vice principal.

"Olivia," said Eric, "if you're going to retaliate, it must be when adult witnesses are not present."

"Now wait a minute!" said the Vice Principal Crenshaw.

"These guys have a job to do," said Eric, ignoring the VP. "And you have to live with that."

Olivia was suspended and had to take an online course in sensitivity.

When they got in the car, Janine was fuming. "Eric, how could you! You only made things worse!"

"Mom!" said Olivia. "He was great! I thought Crenshaw was going critical!"

Eric looked at Olivia and smiled. "You're insensitive. But I love you anyway."

"Gee thanks," replied the girl.

Eric looked at Janine. "I love you too."

Janine tried to remain angry at Eric. "You did raise that man's blood pressure." She chuckled. "You enjoyed that. You are an evil man."

"You are right. Olivia, you are guilty as charged. As a penalty you get your choice of pie or ice cream."

"You are a very evil man," said Janine.

"What? I'm paying."

Team Janine spread out all the collected information on the kitchen table.

"Well, what do we know?" asked Eric.

"Okay," said Janine. "There are three bank accounts in Henderson. Brent had one and Lance had one. Both accounts had us wives as a secondary. Both accounts are in the same bank."

"That would be the Community Bank of Henderson?"

"That's right. Brent's account has $150,000 in it." Janine held an account sheet. I hope I can access the account on my signature. It might be better if I had a death certificate for Brent.

"Lance and Miriam have an account with a little over $50,000 in it. They also have a safety deposit box. The box is rented through the bank account.

"The third account is a Gawn company account. It has $2.5 million. It's paying several monthly accounts. One of those accounts is the downtown office lease here in Chicago. Another is a property management company for $1,500 a month. It must be an apartment."

"Wasn't there a letter in the Gawn stack asking something about an apartment lease?" asked Eric.

"You're right. There was."

While Janine sifted through the Gawn correspondence, Eric referenced Brent's dresser drawer ledger.

"You're right again," said Janine. "This property manager is asking for an increase on the apartment lease."

Eric was comparing the drawer ledger with the bank sheets. "Look, this account that you say is Brent's matches these numbers. The second set of numbers match the Gawn account numbers."

"Okay," said Janine, "but the third numbers don't match any of these."

"And," said Eric, "if these account totals are accurate, the third account has $150 million."

"One hundred fifty million," said Janine sotto-voce. She looked at Eric, eyebrows raised.

Eric had a worried look.

"What?" asked Janine.

"This is the kind of money people kill for. If Lance and Brent left this money untouched, they're either hiding or dead."

"You're scarring me."

"Good. I just want you to know that the stakes are really high."

"Well, maybe we could just get some of it?"

Team Janine decided to make some phone inquiries with the banks and property manager in Nevada.

Janine called the bank from the downtown Gawn office. She introduced herself as Miriam. She said that she was now the office manager at Gawn and asked about the accounts. The bank officer in Nevada said she couldn't discuss the accounts without written confirmation from Gawn.

Janine found some stationary with Gawn's headings. She also found some letters with Lance's signature. She had practiced signatures of Lance and Brent at home. She wrote the letter and forged the signatures. She tucked the letter in her purse.

Janine called the property manager who requested the increased rent. Mr. Wylie was eager to talk to her. As she was calling on the Gawn phone system, he assumed that she was legit. Janine asked Wylie the particulars about the suite. She said that she would soon visit but couldn't find the key in the office.

"Of course not," replied Wylie. "Mr. Porter left the key with the super as always. All you have to do is leave me twenty-four hours' notice, and we'll be there to let you in."

"You are so kind. Thank you," said Janine.

She turned off the office lights and moved to lock the door. A man was standing outside the office.

"Hello," said the man, expressionless.

"Hello," said Janine. She stood in the doorway, half in, half out. "I'm locking up."

"May I come in?" The man produced a badge. "I'm Agent Fellows, FBI. Can I look around Ms...?"

"Janine. Janine Pierson. Sure...have a good look."

Janine stepped in and turned on the lights.

As Fellows talked, he peered into empty rooms. "You are Brent Pierson's wife. You stated that you nothing to do with Gawn Associates. Is that right?"

"That's right," said Janine.

The agent focus on Janine. "Then what are you doing here?"

Jan took a breath. Her eyes moved around the empty office. "I come down here to think if there's any clue where Brent is. I come down here to remember when things were...better. When I had my own home." She looked at the agent. "What did you come here for?"

Fellows nodded. "We got a report that someone was accessing this office. Have you had any contact with your husband?"

Janine tried to look pitiful. "No."

"Lance Porter?"

"No."

"Anyone else from this office?"

"No."

"Can I look in your purse?"

"Have you got a search warrant?"

Fellows said nothing. He turned and walked out of the office.

Janine waited until she heard the elevator door close before locking up the office.

THE PLAN

Team Janine met to plan.

"Jan, honey, I want to state that there is danger here. I don't know how Brent stashed two million dollars, but it can't be yours. If you are able to tap into it, how would that work? You can't carry a bushel of money out of the bank. And you can't reveal the accounts as assets, or it will foul up your bankruptcy."

"I know honey, I know. But some of that is mine. It's my house, my kid's future, my life. I'll take back what I can and leave the rest."

"I just don't want to lose you," said Eric. "Please, please be careful."

"I will."

"It seems to me that we have a couple of problems. First, we have to get you in and out of Las Vegas without anyone noticing. Next, you'll have to switch identities on the fly. Third is communication."

"Communication?"

"Yes. You'll have to leave your cell phone here. It can be traced."

"Okay, I see that. What else?"

Eric looked at her for a few seconds. "We have to figure out how to move funds from there to here without anyone realizing."

"Okay, where do we start?"

"Actually, I have a couple of ideas," said Eric with a smile. "I want you to meet somebody."

Eric welcomed Cheryl and Billie into the house. He introduced Janine and the kids as they settled into the living room. The two women settled warily on the couch. Janine offered them wine which they accepted. The kids disappeared into the kitchen to finish preparing dinner.

"Cheryl, it's been a long time," said Eric with a smile. "I am glad to see you and finally meet Billie. I hope you two are happy together."

Cheryl reached out and took Eric's hand. "Thank you, we are. I was sorry to hear about Peggy. I liked her."

"Thank you," said Eric. "Dinner will be in a little while."

Cheryl looked at Janine. "Your children are charming. They must be a blessing."

Janine smiled. "They really are."

"So," said Eric, "are you still in theatre?"

At dinner Eric continued his usual routine. He asked Monica about her day. She told of learning a song. She said she made a new friend at the math class.

Cheryl and Billie seemed amused.

Eric asked Alan about his day. He said that he liked playing basketball in gym class. Eric asked how the math test went. "Oh, yeah," said Alan, "I passed the test."

"Good work," said Janine. "You need to keep up with the math." She looked at Olivia. "What about you dear?"

"Well…" said Olivia, "Julie and I worked on our art project for the school art fair." She looked at Billie. "We're doing a collage of city views."

"I'd like to see that," said Billie.

Eric looked at Janine.

Janine smiled. "Today I had to see my lawyer and sign papers. And then I had to do some shopping." She looked at Eric.

"Well today," said Eric, "I visited an old friend. He's in a home now. He won't last long. But I've been looking forward to being here with guests tonight." He smiled at Cheryl and Billie.

Cheryl looked around the table. "Well, today was my volunteer day at the woman's shelter. I took a woman to her court hearing on her order of protection. Her husband, her estranged husband, threatened her in court and got locked up. She's been beaten many times."

Billie looked around the table. "Today I taught a ceramics class. That was this morning. Then I aided a class of refugees in English." She looked around the table. "I...I didn't want to come here tonight. Cheryl made me. But I really am glad I met you all."

After dinner, Eric suggested the adults settle in the living room. He promised that tea and cake were coming.

"Eric," said Cheryl, "I always wanted to thank you for standing up to the theater guild that way. I know it cost you some friends."

"It wasn't right, Cheryl," he said. "You had led us so skillfully. Firing you because of your lifestyle was wrong. And I said so. The uptight conservatives couldn't take it. And I suspect some were hoping that your husband, your ex-husband, would come back."

"Well, that wasn't going to happen. Besides," she said, taking Billie's hand, "I had a new life to live."

"Actually," said Eric, "I have a favor to ask you. But first I'd like you to hear a story. I'd like you to hear Janine's story."

"What!" said Janine.

"Jan, honey, I'd like you to give them a quick version from the Dells to the police investigation."

Janine started with being left high and dry in the Dells. She covered the eviction and moving in with Eric. She mentioned the bankruptcy and divorce proceedings. She mentioned that she was routinely called in by various police divisions.

All the time Janine told her tale, Cheryl and Billie let out little gasps. They kept looking at each other, shaking their heads.

By the time Janine was finished, she was in tears. Cheryl motioned Janine over to sit between them on the couch. The three women hugged in tears.

"You brave, brave girl," said Cheryl. She looked at Eric. "What is it…how is it I can help?"

Olivia came in with a tray. She served tea and cake all around.

Eric waited until Olivia left the room. "Years ago, I helped backstage at a play you were in. You would leave the stage, change costumes, and return as a different character a few seconds later."

Cheryl smiled at Eric slyly. "And you peeked at me every time."

"Uh…" Eric flushed. "I…I was admiring your stagecraft."

"That's not all you were admiring," said Cheryl. The ladies shared a laugh. "It's called quick-change."

"Okay, well," said Eric, "what we need is some of your stagecraft. Without going into too much, I'd like you to teach Janine quick-change."

"Why," asked Cheryl, "so you can ogle this girl too?"

"No, so she can recover some of what her husband took from her."

Suddenly the mood changed.

"What!" said Billie.

Cheryl looked at Janine and then at Eric. "Are you serious?"

Eric nodded his head. "There is a chance that she can recover some of what was taken from her. But she will have to be able to disguise herself once or maybe twice to do it. She can't be Janine when she gets it back.

"Now," said Eric gravely, "I can't reveal more than that. I can't let you know too much. But I am asking for your help. We could call it acting lessons. You could be teaching her costuming or something."

Cheryl looked at Janine. "Is he forcing something on you?"

"No. This is my idea. He's never forced me to do anything."

Cheryl patted Janine on the hand. "I can't find it in myself to trust men these days. Promise me that this wasn't his idea."

Janine took Cheryl's hand. "Everybody in my life used me…except Eric." She looked at Eric and smiled. "He said we don't have to do this. He says we can survive without the money."

Janine rose and sat in Eric's lap. "No one ever really asked me what I wanted before Eric. He's saved my family. But now I want to get back some of what that bastard husband stole from me and my children.

"Eric's right, we don't want to implicate you in anything we do but if you could help, we'd appreciate it. If you want to walk away, that's alright too. We'll try something else."

Cheryl looked at Billie. Billie scooted over next to Cheryl on the couch.

"We need to talk," said Cheryl.

"Of course," said Eric.

"What's there to talk about?" said Billie. "These are the three things that you like best: helping out a sister and teaching quick-change. You're going to do it. Don't pretend."

She turned to face Eric. "Now," said Billie, "why don't go get us more tea and let us girls talk for a while."

"Yes, ma'am," said Eric.

"What's the third thing?" asked Janine.

Billie looked at Janine and Eric with a sly smile. "Screwing over an ex-husband, of course."

Later that night, when Janine came to bed Eric was reading. "I liked your friends," she said.

"Good. I'm glad." He continued to read.

"Did you really peek at her while she changed?"

Eric put down the book. "Not so much peek as stood there… admiring what was there to be seen. She knew it and I suspect Peg knew it."

"You were a married man."

"Are you telling me you never did any…comparison shopping?"

"Well…"

"And you never flirted with anybody?"

"Okay, okay. What did you mean by disguising me once or twice?"

"It occurs to me that we might be able to pass you off as that secretary at Gawn. If we could get a debit card from the bank, you could start tapping into Gawn funds. Who's left to object?"

"You want me to pretend to be Charlene Wilcox?"

"Why not? It might be good practice?"

"How would we get a debit card?"

"You go down to Gawn and call the bank. Tell the bank you are Charlene. Tell them you need a company debit card. See what happens. You can figure this out."

"What happened with Cheryl at the theater?"

"Peg loved to act in plays. Cheryl and her husband Harris were the resident actors at a local theater group. They had had a quick-change act for years. I used to help out as a stagehand sometimes.

"I was there when Harris announced that he was leaving Cheryl. It was at the wrap party. It really put a damper on the evening."

"You put up a fuss about that?"

"No. It was the next season. Harris turned up with his new 'squeeze' and Cheryl turned up with her new life partner, Billie. The sponsors threw a shit fit. They fired Cheryl at the second rehearsal. Her 'lifestyle' was unacceptable. That's when I objected."

"Do you think it will work?"

"The disguises? If anybody can make it work, it's Cheryl."

While Janine spent available time learning costume changes from Cheryl, she managed her twin duties at the country club.

Janine had been coaching Kate, who was using tennis as exercise/rehab for a leg injury. Kate had suggested a foursome as a test of her newfound skills.

Kate invited Thomas and Stephanie for the match. Janine had met them before and found them aloof. Janine partnered with Kate for the first set. Then Thomas and Janine partnered for the second set.

Kate had arranged a luncheon for them afterward. After showers they met in the dining room. Janine did not usually eat in the dining room since she was on staff, but she acquiesced.

After a few minutes of match replay and ordering, Thomas got serious.

"Do you hear from Brent anymore?" he asked.

Janine not realized that this "foursome" was more than a sports outing. "No. I haven't heard from him since he deserted me. Why?"

"He scammed our families out of a lot of money," blurted out Stephanie. Her gaze fell to her plate.

Janine looked around the table suspecting an attack from all sides. "Do you think I had anything to do with that?" She looked at Thomas and Kate. No one looked her in the eye.

Suddenly Stephanie looked at Janine. "I don't understand how they let you work here. After all the things Brent did? I don't understand."

Janine summoned patience. She spoke even voiced. "Do you realize that Brent scammed me too? He left me and my children homeless and penniless." She put her napkin on her plate. "The club offered me a job in exchange for me not suing them. They didn't want the publicity. There is a private investigator working on the case. I'll have him call you."

"I'm sorry," said Stephanie. "I didn't mean to hurt your feelings."

"Feelings? What do you know about feelings? Have you ever been evicted? Seen your things carried out to the street? Stood in line for food stamps? Been interrogated by the police? I don't have any feelings left."

Janine looked around the table. Stephanie was crying. Thomas was soothing her. Kate stared back at Janine stone faced.

"I've spoiled your lunch," said Janine. "You'll excuse me."

Janine left the table and went to her office.

Thomas came to the door and knocked. "Can I come in?"

Janine hesitated and then nodded.

Thomas sat down. "Can I ask you a question? It's about your husband."

"I no longer think of him as my husband, but go on."

Thomas hesitated. He shifted in the chair. "We had Brent over. We thought you were coming too. Anyway, we had a couple of drinks. And then...I don't know what happened. I woke up on the couch with a blinding headache. Stephanie...well, she woke up...in the bedroom. She doesn't know how she got there. And then...there was...our debit cards were missing. Our accounts were drained."

Janine looked at Thomas. "You were probably drugged. Did you report it to the police?"

"No," he replied emphatically.

She wrote a number on a note and handed it to him. "Here is the number of the Fraud Squad. Tell them your story."

Thomas shook his head negatively. "She thinks she was...violated. He, Brent, said there were...pictures. We can't, we won't go public."

"Why tell me?"

"If you find anything," he implored, "can you...?"

Janine looked into his eyes. She could see the desperation in his face. She nodded slowly. "If I find anything."

Thomas nodded. "Thank you." He departed.

Eric kept up with all the kid's school activities.

Alan was participating in a basketball league with the Park District. Eric made sure that Alan was at all the practices and games. Sometimes he had Monica in tow. Janine only attended games when her schedule permitted. She confessed to Eric that practices were boring. They agreed that if she had the time, games were better for attendance.

Monica seemed happy to be part of a tween gaggle. They seemed to swarm from house to house giggling along the way.

Janine came home late-evening to find Eric and a strange woman in the living room. "Hello?"

"Oh, hi," said Eric, rising. "I'll make a fresh pot of tea. Meet Tammy."

Just then two tween girls scampered out of the bedroom and into the kitchen. "S'mores!"

Suddenly Janine realized it was pajama party night.

"Hi," said Tammy, standing to greet her.

"Sure. Hi," said Janine. She hung up her coat.

"Hi, Mom!" said Monica, scurrying into the kitchen with two other girls.

As the women shook hands they sat.

Tammy smiled at Janine. "Dolly said that you were…that only your uncle…was here. I thought I'd stay until you came home."

"Sure, of course," said Janine with a smile. "You're welcome to stay. I'm sorry I'm late."

"You know how it is," said Tammy. "I was just catching up with… Eric. We haven't seen each other since…Anyway, he sure is good with the girls. A lot of patience."

"Yes, yes, he is. As I said I'm sorry I was late. I got held up at work."

Eric returned with a pot of tea.

"Actually," said Tammy, refusing more tea, "I'd better be going. Al's taking me to the Moose Hall tonight." She rose and moved toward the door. "I'll leave you to the screaming hordes. Good luck."

Eric let out. He looked at Janine. "You were late."

"Since when is this pajama party night?"

"What!" said Eric. "It's on the calendar. Big letters!"

She pulled out her phone. "See next week."

"I don't care what your phone says. Look at the calendar in the kitchen."

Monica bounded in. She threw herself into a big mom hug. "Hi, Mom. Uncle Eric, can we have *The Princess Bride*?"

"Of course. I'll be right there."

Monica bounded out.

"I was so looking forward to a quiet evening," said Janine.

"Don't worry, they'll run out of gas soon. That was the last of the s'mores."

"Oh, you silly old dear."

Olivia and Julie were immersed in their art studies. Eric instructed them on how to use public transportation to access the downtown area. After their classes at the Art Institute, they spent the afternoon at different sites along the lakefront. Sometimes they toured the galleries and sketched. At the appointed hour, Eric would retrieve them and drive home.

Eric was also letting Livy practice driving for her license. She seemed at times reluctant. "Why should I get a license? I'll never be able to buy a car."

"Driving is a life skill. Where would your mother have been without it?"

"Okay," replied Olivia. "But I'll never be able to own my own car."

"You never know," said Eric. "You never thought that you'd be in a class at the Art Institute. Be prepared."

THE VEGAS DECEPTION

Eric and Janie walked up the stairs to the front porch. Eric pushed the bell. The porch light came on.

A woman opened the inner door. She looked at Eric quizzically.

"I'm here to see Howard," said Eric.

The woman frowned. She pointed toward the left. "Down the gangway and in the basement." She shut the door.

Team Janine made their way down the shadowy gangway to the back of the building. They carefully climbed down the uneven cement steps to the basement landing. A piece of paper was taped to the door with the name Howard Arliss handwritten on it.

"This is the guy that's helping us?" asked Janine.

"You bet," replied Eric.

Eric searched for a doorbell but found none. He knocked. No answer. Finally, he opened the door himself.

Team Janine entered a dimly lit utility area with clothes hanging on lines.

"Hello!" called out Eric.

A door opened, shedding light into the area.

"Eric?"

"Hey Howard," replied Eric. "Good to see you."

Howard held out his hand. He shook Eric's hand vigorously. "It's good to see anyone. Come on in."

"Howard, this is Janine."

Howard looked at Janine and smiled. "Well, hi." He looked her over. "We haven't met, have we?" He motioned his guests toward a tired couch.

"No, we have not." She looked around the dingy room. A couch, a bed, a dresser, a wide-screen, and the recliner. The walls were bare wood paneling except for a torn Bears Super Bowl XX poster.

Howard settled into a tired recliner. He looked at the two of them. "Hard times. My sister lets me stay here because I bought the house with my winnings." He scratched his unshaven chin and looked at Janine. "He tell you my story?"

Janine smiled at Howard. "Only that you won the lottery."

"Huh," grunted Howard. "Worst day of my life." He motioned upwards. "I bought this house for my sister. Now she's had to mortgage it to pay my bills. That's about all that's left. Except what Val got in the divorce."

Janine could only nod at the story. She was speechless.

"Actually," said Eric, "that's what I wanted to talk to you about. When you won the lottery, you chartered a plane to Las Vegas. You invited me, Rusty, Mop-up, and our wives for the trip. You put us up at that casino hotel for the weekend."

Howard closed his eyes and sat back in the recliner. "That was sweet."

"Howard," said Eric, "I need you to rerun that trip."

"That would be great," replied Howard. He seemed to be reliving a dream.

"I'm serious," said Eric.

Howard's attention now focused on Eric. "Sorry, man. I couldn't buy a trip to St. Louis by bus. How could I charter a plane to Vegas?"

"I'll front the money," said Eric. "What I need is a two-way charter party plane to Vegas."

"It's okay by me. Charter yourself a plane."

"Well, see, that's the point," said Eric. "We need it not to be my name or Janine's name on the charter. We need this trip to be…clandestine."

"Clandestine?" said Howard incredulously.

"Definitely off the record."

"I don't understand?"

"We need Janine to get in and out of Las Vegas unnoticed," said Eric.

"What!" said Howard.

"Look," said Eric, "we need Janine to do some business in Las Vegas without being seen travelling there."

"And you think I can do this?" asked Howard.

"When we travelled with you, on that charter flight, all those years ago they just took our names. No ID. No proof. If she travelled under an assumed name, who would know?"

"Okay," said Howard skeptically. He looked at Eric and then Janine. "Are you doing something illegal?"

"Illegal? I don't think so." Eric looked at Janine and then back to Howard. "We are trying to recover money stolen from Janine by her husband. He abandoned them but left money in Vegas. She wants some back, but the feds want it too.

"We need you to take her to Vegas under an assumed name and bring her back. We'll supply the cash for the charter and hotel stay. We'll even supply you with gambling money. Maybe we can get Rusty and his wife to go too. We want it to look like the party group that went last time."

"You won't be there?" asked Howard.

"No. I have to cover the home front and make it look like Janine is here."

Howard looked at Eric while he thought. "I get to fly the party plane, gamble in Vegas, and fly home on your dime. All I have to do is take this lady with? I'm in."

"Are you sure? Nobody else can know who Janine is," said Eric.

"Sure, sure," said Howard. "I wish you'd be there but hell yes. I'm in!"

KAT'S RETURN

When Janine came home from work, Kat stepped out of the shadows. "Help me," she whispered.

"Kat! Oh my god." Janine hugged the girl. "Where's Al?"

Kat pointed to the shadows. The stroller was barely discernable.

Janine thought fast. "Take the stroller through the yard and into the alley. I'll pick you up there. They're watching the house."

Kat disappeared into the shadows. Janine walked casually back to the car. She scanned the block to see if anyone was watching. She pulled out her phone and acted as if she had a call. She got back in the car.

As Janine drove around the block to the alley, her mind was racing. She really did not need police scrutiny at this point in her plans.

With Al buckled into the back, Kat got in the front. Janine drove away.

"Kat, everyone is looking for you. You've kidnapped Al!"

"How could I kidnap my own son? They took him away from me! We were just fine," replied Kat. "You've got to help me. He's your son too."

"How can I do that? The police are all over me," replied Janine. "They're going to find you. And if they do, you'll never see Little Al again."

"I'll go somewhere where they can't find me. Lend me money for the bus. I'll go far away." Kat was pleading for help.

"I'd like to help but ..." Janine went silent.

"What!?" asked Kat. She smiled and looked back at Al. "She's going to help us."

Janine pulled the car into a motel. "I'm going to put you up here. I've got some plans to work out, but I think we'll be alright."

Janine helped Kat get Al out of the back seat. "Listen, when we get in the office, I'm Miriam, your mom, and you are Sarah and Eli Porter. Got it?"

"I'm Sarah and he's Eli. I got it."

When Janine returned home again, they were all eating dinner. Eric gave her a quizzical look but asked nothing. After dinner, Janine asked Eric if he could meet her in the bedroom.

Sensing something was important, Eric made a joke about her request. "Well, okay. Don't let it ever be said I turned down a lady."

Once they were secluded in the bedroom Janine began to talk quietly. "Kat was here."

"Here, where here?" asked Eric.

"She was outside. I put her and Little Al in a motel."

Eric cocked his head. "Why?"

"She was begging me to help her. They took away her son. It isn't right."

Eric slowly nodded his head. "Okay, I get that. Now what?"

"I'll take her and Al to Vegas and leave them there. No one will ever think to look for them there."

Eric stared at her quizzically. "Kat is a fugitive. Aren't we playing with fire here?"

"Not if she's disguised as someone else. I'm going as Miriam; she can go as Miriam's daughter and grandchild. All we need are IDs."

Eric sat trying to find words. "IDs?"

"Miriam's youngest daughter, Sarah, is just a bit older than Kat. I went to the wedding, nice girl. Then I went to her son's Christening about six months later; he's Eli."

"Eli," said Eric.

"I'll take them both for birth certificates as Miriam."

"Birth certificates," said Eric.

"Then I'll take them to the DMV and get Kat, Sarah, a State ID."

"State ID," said Eric.

"Then Sarah and Eli can fly to Vegas with me."

"Fly to Vegas," said Eric.

"I'll try to set something up for them while I'm there."

"Set something up," said Eric.

Janine sat next to Eric on the bed. "It's a perfect plan."

"Perfect plan," said Eric. He bit his lip. He took in a long breath and cocked his head. "It's an ambitious plan. I think it endangers what you are trying to do…but we're in this deep anyway. What's a few more deceptions along the way. Kat is wanted. If she's recognized, it could blow your whole plan. That being said, I'm in. Just keep me in the dark about the details. I need some level of deniability."

Janine kissed him. "I couldn't do this without your support. How can I ever thank you?"

Eric gave a little laugh. "By staying out of jail. I don't think I would want to break in another wife."

THE VEGAS TRIP

Eric and Janine told the kids that she would have to go to South Bend for another session in court. Because it was going to be Monday through Friday, they would have to stay at home with Uncle Eric.

Janine drove off after waving goodbye to the kids. She drove around for an hour, making sure no one was following her. She pulled up in the alley behind Howard's place. Howard pulled out his car and Janine put her car in its place. Janine changed into her Miriam disguise, grabbed her suitcase, and got in Howard's car. Howard closed the garage.

Miriam and Howard drove to the motel where Kat was staying. Kat, Little Al, and the luggage were loaded into Howard's car. The four now headed to the airport.

Pal-Waukee airport is basically a small private concern. There are small charter flights leaving from there.

Howard unloaded the car and locked it up in the lot.

Rusty and Pam Waggoner were waiting in the airport diner. Howard introduced Miriam, her daughter Sarah, and her grandchild Eli to the Waggoners.

After checking with the charter agent, Howard said they were ready to depart. They all grabbed their luggage and moved down a hallway.

"Howard," called out Pam, "I thought Eric was joining us?"

"He had to cancel last minute," said Howard.

The six left their luggage with the attendant at the jet's stairway. The settled into the cabin.

"Hello, I'm Mike, your co-pilot." The man had a blazer and striped tie. He held a clipboard. "I have to take names and check IDs."

"We didn't have to do that last time," said Pam.

"Sorry," said Mike. "There are regulations." He looked at Kat/Sarah. "Will the baby be comfortable in the air?"

Sarah handed him her ID. "I put him on a juvenile dose of Dramamine. He seems to be falling asleep already. He's Eli Porter and I am Sarah."

The pilot scanned her ID and wrote down the names. He reached out for Miriam.

"I'm Miriam Porter," she said.

Rusty and Pam handed their IDs to the pilot. He wrote the names down. "Okay. It looks like we're ready to go."

Miriam/Janine looked at Kat/Sarah with a thankful nod.

"So far, so good," said Miriam under her breath.

As soon as they were airborne, Howard, Rusty, and Pam began to play pinochle. Miriam and Sarah sat together holding hands. Mercifully "Eli" settled down quietly for a nap.

Rusty and Howard were talking old times and work acquaintances as they played the card game. Howard was in a very good mood.

In a lull Pam asked Howard, "I thought that this was Eric's idea? We were hoping to see him and his new lady."

"Uh…" said Howard, "he cancelled last minute. Said they couldn't come."

Pam nodded toward Miriam. "Who's your friend?"

Howard was stuck for an answer.

Hearing the question, Miriam came over to the table. "I'm an old friend of Eric and Peg. That is to say, Eric and Lance were friends. I only met Peg a couple of times. What a shame. They were the nicest couple I knew."

"We were sad about Peg too," said Pam.

Miriam continued. "I have to settle some business in Las Vegas. My late husband left me a mess. Eric was kind enough to offer me and Sarah his place on the trip."

"Well, that explains it," said Howard. "I wasn't too sure."

Miriam returned to sit with Sarah.

"This is great!" whispered Sarah. "They'll never find me."

"It isn't over yet," replied Miriam in a hush. "And don't forget to call me Mom!"

At the airport, a limo was waiting. The five of them piled in. Young Eli was just beginning to stir.

At the hotel Howard was the first to the check-in counter. "Have my things sent to my room," he told the clerk.

Howard faced the other four. He slapped his hands together. "Well, this is where I leave you," he said with a smile. "You know where I'll be," he said jubilantly. He moved spiritedly into the adjacent casino.

"Oookay," said Rusty, shaking his head. "Some things never change."

Pam registered and held the keycards to their rooms. She shook her head and motioned toward Howard. "It's like déjà vu."

Miriam registered Sarah in her room. "We're all set."

"Why don't we get some dinner down here in an hour?" said Pam.

"Sure. Why not?" replied Miriam.

Once they were in the room, Miriam/Janine sat Kat down. "Look, it is extremely important that no one starts asking questions about us. I've got to do a thing to help get back some of the money Brent stole from me. And you don't want Al taken back, do you?"

"No!"

"Then from now on answer to Sarah and call me Mom. Okay?" She smiled at Sarah/Kat. "We'll figure out your situation as time goes on."

Miriam, Sarah, and Eli met Rusty and Pam already seated in the restaurant. Rusty seemed affable and kept looking toward the casino.

Pam did most of the talking. She was suspicious of the trip, Eric's absence, and Miriam. Miriam fended off most inquiries by sticking to the scenario Janine and Eric had written. "…So, tomorrow we are all having dinner with here Mike and Mary…"

"Mop-up!" interjected Rusty. "Good ol' Mop-up."

"Yes, sorry," continued Pam, "Mop-up and Mary. They live out here now. Why don't you join us?"

Miriam was caught off guard by the invitation. Eric had given her some background info on them. "Sure, why not? If we're welcome?"

"Sure," said Pam, sensing a coup. "I'll let them know."

As the meal broke up, Rusty escaped to the casino. Pam invited Miriam to join them gambling.

"I think I should help Sarah get the Eli settled down," said Miriam. "We'll see you tomorrow."

Back in the room, Janine called Eric on their new burner phones. Janine's regular phone was off at home. They would only communicate with Miriam's phones.

"Is everything alright?" asked Eric. His voice showed concern.

"It pretty much went according to the script," replied Janine. "There are a couple of glitches. First, I've been roped into dinner with Mop-up and his wife at their house."

"That shouldn't be much of a problem," replied Eric.

"I don't know. Pam is very suspicious. I'm holding up so far, but she wants to know more." Janine let a sigh. "This sneaky business is hard."

"I know," replied Eric. "You'll be alright. I love you. You can do this."

"There is one more thing," said Janine. "That young friend of ours, with the baby, made the trip with us."

There was a long silence on the phone. "Eric, are you still there?"

"I'm here."

"I just thought they could use a trip." She tried to sound hopeful.

"I see," said Eric. "That lends a new dimension to your trip. It also explains the phone calls I've been declining this evening. Ah oh, doorbell's ringing. Gotta go. I love you."

Janine took her Miriam wig off and kicked off her shoes. She pulled out her plan and sat at the table.

Kat came over. "I'm making trouble for you, aren't I?"

Janine smiled to reassure her. "This whole trip is trouble. You're no more trouble than me pretending to be Miriam. Besides, if I can help you find a life for you and Al, I will have done something."

"Thanks. You guys have really been good to me." She nodded. "What can I do to help?"

"Nothing," said Janine. "Well actually, why don't you order us some tea? I've got to study for tomorrow."

Janine reread her Tuesday game plan while Kat changed into a Tshirt and shorts. When the room service came, Janine put her plan away.

Kat laid out the tea on the table. "Who is Miriam?"

Miriam left Sarah and Eli in the dining room after breakfast. She took a cab to a casino/hotel halfway to Henderson. She played the slots for twenty minutes unsuccessfully. She found the ladies room. In the handicap stall she changed costume into Charlene the Gawn "secretary."

Janine had scoured Charlene's pictures to get a profile of her. Although most of the pictures had her in a pencil skirt, she had a picture of her in slim slacks, a white blouse, and open jacket. At an outdoor event she had worn a pink White Sox hat. A pair of sunglasses were an essential part of Janine's "Charlene" outfit.

Janine made her costume change in minutes. She exited the restroom as Charlene Wilcox.

Charlene took a cab to the apartment complex in Henderson. She rang the bell for the superintendent. No answer. She walked around into the courtyard. A man was watering flowers. As she approached, the man smiled at her.

"Ah, Ms. Wilcox. Good to see you again. I have your key right here." He dug in his pocket. He handed her a key on a fob. It had the number on it.

Charlene coughed a bit. "Sorry, I think I got a cold on the plane." She took the key. She smiled at the man. "Could you open it for me? The last time the door stuck, and I had a hard time with it." She put a hand on his arm coyly.

"Sure, miss," he said with a smile. "This way." He led her to a stairway. He motioned her up first.

Charlene knew that he would be admiring her derriere, so she added as much wiggle as she could.

At the top of the stairs, he moved past her and opened a door. "There. No stick." He reached in and turned on a light.

"Thank you sooo much." She smiled at him. "Oh, where is the car parked?"

"Right out back." He pointed to the rear of the apartment. He pointed to a set of keys on the table. "There are the car keys. Gassed and ready to go. And your mail is here." He pointed to a box on the table.

"Again, thank you so much. You are a dear." She handed the man a $100 bill. She nodded and closed the door.

Janine put her shoulder bag on the table and collapsed in a chair. "Phew!"

Well, she had successfully fooled the janitor into believing she was Charlene. Now would the bank buy it?

Charlene began to search the apartment. The unit was essentially bare. A few pieces of clothing hung in the closets. In the bedroom closet was a safe. She wondered what would be there. She tried the magic numbers 9, 19, 29, and it opened.

Charlene found the key to the Gawn safety deposit box, $500 in cash, and the bank agreements. She also found another envelope. This one was an agreement for a locker at Stor-A-Lot. There was a key with a tag. The tag gave entry codes to the facility. This was unexpected. She took the envelope.

Charlene drove the car to a casino. She played the slots for twenty minutes and then went to the ladies' room. Charlene entered; Miriam emerged. She took a cab to the Community Bank.

Miriam first went to the safety deposit box area. She signed in and showed her ID. The clerk questioned her access to the vault. She produced papers showing Miriam's and Lance's joint account. She showed them the key. "Lance needs me to access the box," she said. "That's why he left me the key."

After asking her a few questions, she convinced them of her validity. Miriam was led to the vault. She turned her lock with the key she found in Miriam's house. She let the teller put the box on a table in a booth.

Once Miriam closed the curtains, she donned rubber gloves. She opened the security box to find $10,000 in cash, passports for Lance, Brent, and Charlene, and a heavy 8"x 4" box. Inside the box she found a pistol. She returned the gun-in-box to the vault box. She put all the other items in her shoulder bag. She closed the security box and removed her gloves. She signaled the clerk to return the box to its vault.

She said that she wanted to see a bank officer. She introduced herself as Miriam Porter. She wanted to transfer $50,000 from the Gawn account into her personal account.

The bank officer, Anthony, a twentyish man, had her sign a withdrawal slip, a deposit slip, and took Miriam's ID. Miriam waited while Anthony met with two other more senior staff. Anthony returned a few minutes later. "I am sorry for the delay. We'd like to verify your request with the account holder. Can we call them?"

"Please do," said Miriam. "I'll wait."

Janine had redirected the Gawn Associates number to a cell phone in Eric's possession. Eric was answering all Gawn phone calls while Janine was in Vegas.

Anthony punched in the Gawn number. After a few moments he responded. "Yes, this is Anthony Aimes at the Community Bank in Henderson, Nevada. Can I speak to someone about your account please? Thank you?"

After a few seconds he responded. "Yes, this is Anthony Aimes from Community Bank in Henderson. That's right. I have a Miriam Porter here from Park Ridge, Illinois, who wants to transfer $50,000 out of your accounts…that's right…okay, okay. And you are Lance Porter? Of course, sir. We just wanted to verify such a large transfer. Thank you, sir. Goodbye."

Miriam waited a few more minutes while the transaction was completed. "Thank you, young man. You are very thorough. I'll tell them that. Now, can you call me a cab? I must get back to my hotel."

Miriam took the cab back to the casino where the car was parked. She snaked her way through the slot machines and entered the rest room. She changed again into her Charlene disguise. She drove to the casino hotel across from hers. She parked the car. She entered, snaked her way through the slot machines, occasionally lingering. She entered the ladies' room and emerged as Miriam.

She hailed a cab. She had the cabby head back toward Henderson. As they went, she told the cab driver that she had forgotten her phone. Could they go back? He turned the cab around and headed back. She tipped him generously. She played the slots for a while before leaving the hotel and crossing the street.

Miriam returned to the room exhausted. Sarah and Eli were out. She began off-loading her purse into the table. She kept the money with her. She loaded the passports into her suitcase.

Janine removed her Miriam wig and kicked off her shoes. She now realized how much nervous energy she had used. She sat back in the chair, took a deep breath, and unwound.

When the door opened, Janine roused. She had been sleeping in the chair.

Sarah and Eli were in swimwear. "Hi," said Sarah/Kat. "We were at the pool. Do we have time for a bath before dinner?"

"Dinner?" Janine tried to focus. "Oh, yeah, dinner with the locals. I remember."

While Kat and Al were bathing, Janine called home. Eric picked up on the second ring.

"We were hoping you'd call," said Eric in an upbeat voice. "Monica wants to say good night."

"Good night, Mommy," came Monica's voice. "I miss you. Come home soon."

"I'll try. I love you too. It's bedtime. Uncle Eric and I have to talk."

Eric returned a few seconds later. "How are you doing?"

"I'm exhausted," she replied. "But we're on schedule. How are things there?"

"The police were here looking for Kat and Al," replied Eric. "They even interviewed the kids. I texted your phone that the cops would be looking for Janine."

"We didn't think of that."

"I think we've got it covered," said Eric. "What are you going to do about Kat?"

"I don't know yet. I'm working on it." Janine hesitated for a moment. "This is hard. I wish you were here."

"I love you too," replied Eric. "Phone's ringing. I got to go."

Eric put down the Miriam phone and answered his regular phone. It was Janine's number. "Hello, sweetheart. I hope you girls are enjoying Indiana?"

"Oh, we're having a great time," came Cheryl's voice. "Has anybody found Kat yet?"

"No, no word here."

"Yeah, the police were here at our B&B this morning. I was just out of the shower. They're getting irritating."

"Sorry they bothered you," said Eric. "I don't want to keep you. You girls enjoy your trip. Love you."

"Love you too. Bye."

Eric sat back relieved. Yesterday he had texted Janine's phone that their friend Kat and her toddler were missing. Police might seek them out. It was a good thing that he sent Cheryl and Billie to Indiana with Janine's cell phone and credit card. With Cheryl disguised as Janine, they went on a B&B tour, purposely leaving a false charge and phone trail of Janine in Indiana.

Miriam sat through the dinner with all of Eric's friends without enthusiasm. Joining the group were Mike and Mary who lived in Henderson. The general discussion was about how Howard scraped up enough money for a return trip to Vegas.

Howard was in particularly good spirits. He claimed that his old lucky gambling streak had returned, and he was way ahead.

The women had congregated at one end of the table. Miriam sat next to Sarah with Eli, in a highchair, on the far side. Mostly the women's conversation nearby was comparing children and grandchildren. Eli had been interacting with most of the woman with a smile. He had been very pleasant.

Sarah told Miriam that she had to use the restroom. She started to take Eli when Pam shooed her away. "He's fine. We'll keep an eye on him."

After Sarah had been gone for a few minutes, Mop-up Mike came down the table. He reached out a hand and Eli took his finger. "Hi, big guy. You need to come visit the men." Mike unstrapped Eli and hoisted him eye level.

Eli cooed and grabbed Mike's nose.

"C'mon, little fella." Mike returned to his seat at the man's end. He put Eli on his lap. He handed Eli a spoon. Mike reentered the conversation, occasionally interacting with the tot.

When Sarah returned, she stopped dead when she saw Eli's highchair empty.

Miriam pointed at the tot in Mike's lap. "He decided to join the guys."

"They all stick together," said Pam jokingly.

"Kids just love him," said Mary. "Any kid, any time. They just love him." She motioned for Sarah to sit back down. "Say, why don't you all come over tomorrow night to the house? We'll throw some steaks on."

"Well…" said Miriam, "we don't want to intrude."

"Nonsense," said Mary. "We'd be glad to have you. And bring that child too."

When Eli began to fuss, Sarah excused herself. She would take him up to bed.

Miriam excused herself also.

When the bathroom was free, Janine had a hot shower. When she came out, Kat was watching TV with the volume way down.

Janine pulled out her plan and sat at the table. She went over tomorrow's plan. She packed her bag carefully. Tomorrow was going to be a tricky day.

After breakfast in the dining room, Miriam left the hotel on foot. She walked across the street to the hotel/casino. She played twenty minutes of slot machines and then went to the ladies' room.

Charlene exited the ladies' room. She walked out to the parking lot. She walked back and forth a few times, seeming to be lost. Finally, when she was sure she was alone, she got in the car she had parked there yesterday.

Charlene found the Stor-A-Lot. She entered the code on the key fob. The gate opened. She drove along until she found a loading area. She parked the car.

Inside the storage building she found a map near the elevator. The storage space was on the second floor. She walked up the stairs and followed the signs. Overhead lighting came to life as she walked. She saw no one. When she found the unit, it looked like any other. She tried the key in the padlock. It opened. She pulled back the bolt. She opened the door. She reset the bolt so that she could not be easily locked in.

Inside was an office desk and two filing cabinets. Charlene looked both ways down the hall before she entered. She put rubber gloves on. She opened the top drawer of a filing cabinet. Inside was a clear plastic bag jammed with money. The bag had a jumble of denominations: $20's, $50's and $100's. She closed the drawer. The lower drawer had a similar bag full of money.

Charlene's/Janine's heart was pounding. She knew what Eric would say, "People will kill for this kind of money."

Charlene opened the second cabinet. This one only had one bag of mixed denomination bills.

Charlene opened a desk drawer. There were neat, bundled stacks of $100 bills.

What to do? After a few seconds she decided. She took six bundles of $100's, marked $10,000, and put them in the bottom of her purse. She closed the desk drawer. She closed up the locker. Her hands were shaking.

Charlene walked as casually as she could, although her knees were shaking. She peaked around the loading area. No one was there. She got into the car and left as casually as she could.

Once out of the Stor-A-Lot, she drove until she saw a McDonalds. She ordered a hot tea at the drive-thru and parked. Her heart was pounding, and she was shaking. She sipped the tea and collected herself.

Once Janine was calm, she consulted her notes. Charlene entered McDonald's restroom. Janine emerged. No one seemed to notice.

Janine drove to the Community Bank of Henderson. Here she wore Janine's clothes with Charlene's sunglasses and pink baseball hat. She asked to see someone about closing her account.

While she was waiting, Mary and Mike came in. They walked up to a teller.

Janine tried to dodge their glances. A personal banker, Bill Sommers, led her to his cubicle.

"Hi, I'm Janine Pierson. I wish to close my account." She handed the agent a bank statement and an Illinois State ID.

"I'll have to make a copy of this," said Sommers. "And how would you like this money? I can't give you $150,000 in cash."

"Certainly not," said Janine. "I want it transferred to this account." Janine handed the agent a letter.

The agent disappeared with the documents.

Janine sat alone in the cubicle for some minutes. She felt silly in a pink ball cap and sunglasses. Janine wanted to appear to look like Charlene. When she went to get the State ID, she had tried to look as

Charlene as possible. Cheryl had helped Janine with the makeup and hair style.

As for the transfer, Janine wanted the money to go to the escrow account from her mother's inheritance.

After a while a second agent came into the cubicle to verify the transaction. He repeated all the questions that the first agent asked. Janine repeated the answers with a tinge of disgust. Then the second agent intentionally misstated her birthday.

Janine cranked up her disgusted/snide voice. "That is NOT my birthday." She stated her birthday with slow distain.

Eventually Janine took $20,000 in cash and transferred the rest into the escrow account.

Janine walked back to the car feeling like she was under scrutiny. When she got in the car, she scanned all around to see if anyone was watching. She drove up and down. She drove through parking lots. When she was sure she was not being followed, she headed toward the Gawn apartment building.

In the Team Janine game plan, she was to abandon the car at the apartment building. As she neared the apartment building, Janine pulled over for two police cars that came by with mars lights flashing. The cars seemed to turn where she was going. Janine felt her stomach drop.

Janine passed the street where the building was. She circled around the building. There were police cars all around the Gawn apartment building. Janine drove away from the area. She pulled into a food store parking lot. She sat in the car for a few minutes. What to do?

Janine took a deep breath. What are the priorities? Misdirection! Get out of Janine persona. Get into Charlene costume and dump the car.

Janine pulled the car to the back of the lot where it was empty. She changed into her Charlene costume. She did not don the sunglasses or hat. She drove the car into the crowded part of the lot and parked. She gathered everything from inside the car. She pulled out a hand wipe and gloves. She had practiced this many, many times at home. Janine wiped down the steering wheel and the whole front of the car.

Charlene walked through the lot and crossed the street. She waited for a bus. She spotted a garbage truck coming down the street. She dumped the pink hat, sunglasses, and car keys in the can. She watched the garbagemen empty the can.

The bus came. She paid and asked the driver how to get to the "strip." It seemed to Janine that the bus ride was lasting hours. The driver called out the strip.

Charlene walked into a casino in the middle of the block. She played the slots for a few minutes. Alarms and flashing lights made her jump. She expected to see police. Instead, a floor manager was congratulating her.

"You won the big prize! Congratulations!" The man smiled. "What's your name, dear?"

Janine had to think. "Charlene Wilcox."

The floor manager pulled her over to the cashiers. He handed her a placard and wrote in $11,609 and her name. They posed. A picture was taken. They handed her a pre-loaded gift card. It had all happened so fast.

There was no chance of changing in the rest room unnoticed now. Charlene went out the front door of the casino and flagged down a cab.

She went to the casino across from her hotel. She played the slots for twenty minutes. Charlene entered the ladies' room. Miriam emerged. She walked out of the hotel and crossed the street.

Miriam returned to her room exhausted. She kicked off her shoes, pulled off her wig, and flopped on the bed. She was asleep almost immediately.

"Janine. Janine, are you alright?"

Her eyes focused on Kat. She held Al on her hip.

"Are you joining us for dinner?" asked Kat. "Rusty and Pam are taking us to a show later."

"Dinner sounds good," replied Janine. "I'll just be a minute."

Miriam, Sarah, and Eli came to the table together. Rusty and Pam were already there. Sarah recounted how Pam and Mary had spent the day with her and Eli. They were just ordering when Howard came to the table.

Miriam was trying to listen to them but all she wanted was to talk to Eric. Sarah intruded on her thoughts. "Are you going to the show with us?" asked Sarah.

"No," replied Miriam. "I had a long day. I just want to take a hot bath." She rose to leave.

"Don't forget," said Pam, "we're all going to Mike and Mary's for dinner day after tomorrow." She made a circular motion with her finger.

"I won't forget," replied Miriam.

When Janine got to the room, she ordered a pot of tea. She hung up her clothes for tomorrow. Then she unpacked her purse. She counted all the cash. Sixty thousand dollars from the storage locker. Twenty thousand dollars from Brent's account. And $500 from the strong box at the Gawn apartment. Plus, the gift card for $11,609. She had recovered $97,109 of her life that day.

After the room service arrived, Janine took off her Miriam clothes and wig. She poured herself a hot tea. She called Eric.

"Honey, it's so good you called," said Eric.

In the background she could hear Monica's voice, "Mommy, Mommy."

"Can you say good night to the kids?" said Eric.

"Can I please?"

Eric put them on speaker phone. "Kids, I miss you."

"Mommy, we love you," said Alan and Monica.

"I love you all so much. I'll see you all Friday. Sleep tight."

"Good night, Mommy," they said.

After a few seconds Eric came back. "Sweetheart, how'd it go today? Are you alright?"

"Oh, honey," said Janine. She hesitated. She choked up. "It's so hard."

"It's alright," said Eric warmly. "Take your time." He waited a few seconds. "How did it go at the bank?"

"Okay, okay," said Janine. "The bank went according to our plans. I have Brent's and Gawn's accounts transferred."

"Okay, well that sounds good," said Eric. "Did you get scared?"

"Yeah," she said, choked up. "I got scared. When I went to park the car at the building the police were there. I parked the car in a grocery store lot. I wiped it down like we practiced. I had to take the bus home."

"They didn't see you, did they?"

"No, no, I don't think so," said Janine.

"You made all your costume changes?"

"Yeah. That went well."

"What didn't go well?" asked Eric. "Did you get to the storage place?"

"Eric," she said, "it's full of money."

"What? What do you mean?"

"There was a desk and two filing cabinets," she said. "There must be a million there. Bundles and bundles of money."

"What did you do?"

"I took $60,000," she said. "And then I locked it back up and got out of there. I thought about what you said."

"What I said?"

"Yeah," she said, "that's the kind of money people kill for. I got really scared."

"Okay, honey. You'll be alright." He hesitated. "You don't have to go near the bank or storage place again. You should be alright."

"I wish you were here," she said.

"I can't wait until you're back," he said to reassure her. "What's on for tomorrow?"

"We're supposed to go to a show or something. And we're invited to Mike and Mary's for dinner."

"Okay. Rest well. I love you."

"Me too." Janine hung up the phone. "Now for a long hot bath."

THE ORGANIZATION COMPLICATION

Eric was washing up the dishes after seeing the kids off for school. The doorbell rang. Eric opened the door to find Tony on the porch. He pushed past Eric into the front room. Eric closed the door. "Morning, Tony."

Tony looked Eric in the eye. He put his right index finger on Eric's chest. "Be at Angelo's on Grand in Elmwood. One o'clock sharp. You got it?"

Eric nodded. "Angelo's, on Grand at one."

"Good. Don't make me come get you." Tony turned and went toward the kitchen. "I'll go out the back."

Eric walked into Angelo's a little before one. He stood near the door, removed his glasses, and put them in his pocket.

Tony came over. "You got a gun?"

Startled, Eric replied, "No. Do I need one?"

Tony harrumphed. "Naaa. Better you don't. Cell phone?" He held out his hand.

Eric gave Tony his phone.

Tony led Eric to a side room. At a large round table where four people sat, Tony pointed to an empty chair and sat on the other.

A grey-haired man sat opposite Eric. On his right were two stony faced men. On his left was a young woman obsessed with her hair.

The grey-haired man sat back and assessed Eric. "So, you must be Mr. Pierson. Mister Eric Pierson. You're Tony's friend."

There had been no introductions. By their body language, Eric surmised that the grey-haired man was Mr. Big around there. Eric nodded. "We seem to have renewed our friendship lately."

Mr. Big waived a forefinger at him. "You are a very smart man."

"I try to be," said Eric.

A waiter appeared at the table. "Can I take your order, sir?" he asked Eric.

"Please order something," said Mr. Big.

Eric shrugged. "Okay, lasagna, please?"

"Can I bring you a glass of wine?" asked the waiter.

"No, thank you. I'll have coffee if I can get it."

The waiter disappeared.

"Now," said Mr. Big, "Tony says you got a new girlfriend at your house. He says you did real good."

Eric nodded. "I guess so. Her husband was running a scam. The bastard left town and left his wife and kids on the street. I have no respect for someone that screws over his own family." He leaned back. "She's a nice lady."

Mr. Big had Eric locked in his gaze. He nodded slightly. "You found some...home movies." He hesitated for effect. "They belonged to my ex-wife."

Eric felt an accusation. "I'm sorry. If I had known it belonged to you, I would have sent them to you. I didn't know who it belonged to. If you want a copy, I'll make one."

Mr. Big put both hands up in a stop motion. "That's unnecessary. I don't care about the movies, except for two things. Firstly, she's missing." He hesitated. "Not that I care so much but my kids are…distressed."

Eric nodded. "I can see that."

Mr. Big looked at the woman sitting next to him. "No, I don't care that she's gone as much as she took some things from me. Many, many things. Things I'd like to get back."

Eric was trying to decipher the conversation. He knew he there was danger here. He knew he had to be careful.

The waiter brought Eric's food and coffee. He left without a word.

Eric suddenly knew what to do. "It's funny you should say that. My lady friend went off to find things that were taken from her." Eric looked at his audience. All eyes were on him. "She says that she found what was lost. She says that there was more there than was hers. Perhaps some of what you're looking for is there too?"

Mr. Big nodded slowly. "Really?" He hesitated. "This is your friend in Nevada?"

"That's right," Eric continued. "She says that there is more there than she could possibly carry. She says it would take a mover to bring things back home. Perhaps you could recommend one?"

"What are we talking about?" asked Mr. Big.

"Two filing cabinets and a desk. They're kind of heavy," replied Eric. His throat was dry. He sipped his coffee. "You could have it shipped to you. If some of the things are yours, and I bet they are, you could… recover yours and pass the rest on to us."

Mr. Big locked his stare on Eric. "And this arrangement would be just between us?"

Eric nodded. "Absolutely. We have no wish to share our findings with anyone. There is no reason anybody else has to know. I assume you don't either."

Mr. Big nodded. "So, I should take what's mine? What if it's all mine?"

Eric shrugged his shoulders. "Then we won't have any more or less than we had before." He looked at Mr. Big. "I'll trust your judgement. A gentleman's agreement."

Mr. Big looked at everyone at the table with a little nod. "I said you were a smart man. Enjoy your lasagna."

Mr. Big and his entourage left the table.

Eric sat back and exhaled with a "Phew." He was sweating.

By the time the entourage returned, Eric was halfway through his lasagna. They all resumed their original seats.

Mr. Big spoke in a matter-of-fact voice. "Contact your friend. Tell her to expect a call about nine tomorrow morning. She can make sure that the items are properly loaded. Capiche?"

Eric nodded. "Sounds okay."

A waiter put glasses and a bottle on the table.

"You'll share a drink with us to seal our deal," said Mr. Big. He poured and handed a glass to everyone except the woman. "My cousin makes it. My grandfather used to call it dago red." He raised his glass. "Salute!"

All the men took a sip. They all looked at Eric.

Eric took a sip. "Very nice. I haven't had it in a long time."

Mr. Big finished his drink. "Leave Tony the phone number. Finish your lasagna. Take a dessert home." Mr. Big rose, and the entourage left except for Tony.

Eric pulled out his Miriam phone. He put his glasses on.

Tony entered the number into his phone. "You did good here. You know not to come here again."

Eric smiled. He took his glasses off. "That's a shame. The food is really good."

After dinner Eric sent Janine/Miriam a text to call. She was supposed to, but he needed to make sure.

Janine called later in the evening. After a round of good night with the kids, Eric took the phone to the bedroom and shut the door. "Sweetheart, I had a get together with our friend Tony and his family."

"Ooh," replied Janine.

"Yeah, oh," replied Eric. "This is what I need you to do…"

Miriam was dressed and having breakfast with Sarah and Eli before 8:30. As Miriam left the table, Sarah handed her a tote bag.

Miriam played slots for a few minutes and then entered the ladies' room. Miriam emerged from the restroom as a tourist. She had a casino logo sweatshirt, sweatpants, and a baseball hat.

At 9:00 Janine received a text confirming her Uber driver was waiting outside in a white Lexus.

"Where to?" asked the driver.

Tourist Janine directed the driver to the Stor-A-Lot. When she got out to access the security gate, she noticed a white van immediately behind her car. She let both vehicles in and reentered the car.

The Uber driver said he'd wait until she was done. Two men from the van followed Tourist/Janine into the building.

Tourist/Janine opened the unit and stood back. The two men wordlessly began taping the filing cabinets and desk drawers closed. When they moved the three pieces out into the hall, Miriam secured the unit again.

Janine watched as the men used dollies to move the pieces into the van. As they closed the van one man thrust a clip board at Tourist/Janine. "Sign on the bottom." She signed Miriam's name.

Tourist/Janine reentered the white car. She had to exit the Uber car to activate the gate again. The van disappeared through the gate. She was hoping the Uber car was not going to abandon her. He did not.

When she was returned to her hotel, she held out a $50 bill for the driver.

"Sorry, I can't take that. Have a nice day." The white Lexus pulled away.

A young couple looked incredulously at Tourist/Janine. "Wow. How'd you get a Lexus? We got a Honda."

"You've got to know the right people," replied Tourist.

Janine called her room and spoke to Sarah. Tourist/Janine played the slots until she saw Sarah go into the ladies' room. In the ladies' room Sarah handed Tourist Janine a tote bag.

Miriam exited the restroom and played slots while Sarah went back to the room.

THE LUNCHEON

The room phone started ringing. Sarah picked it up. "Hello, yes," said Sarah. "She's just come in." She looked at Miriam. "Will we be ready in ten minutes?"

Miriam nodded.

"Okay," said Sarah.

The six Illinoisan's were picked up by Mop-up driving a club van. Rusty loaded everyone else in the back and sat up front with his buddy. Howard sat behind them and added comments from time to time.

The ladies sat in the back quietly for some time.

"Did you get your business done okay?" asked Pam.

"Yes. I think so," replied Miriam.

Mike pulled into the driveway of a low flat ranch house. "Here we are."

Mary greeted them at the door. They congregated in the large dining area. Beer and lemonade were passed around.

Mary took Sarah by the arm. "There's lots of toys in our grandchildren's room. This way." She led Sarah and Eli into another room. By the time Mary returned, the women had congregated at the dining room table. The men had settled around the TV area.

Miriam/Janine was half listening as the women talked about the "Vegas Experience." She occasionally caught laughter among the men. She watched the easy banter among the men and wished that Eric was there.

A voice intruded upon her daydreams. "…Miriam? We were just wondering how Howard arranged all this." It was Pam. "I thought he was living in his sister's basement."

"What? Oh yeah, me too." Meriam smiled at the women. She wanted to change the subject. "Mary, you have a nice home here. How long have you been out here?"

"We've been out here almost six years now," replied Mary. "We came out on Howard's celebration trip and liked it. We moved six months later. We love it here." She looked at Miriam. "I hear that you had some business here. I hope it wasn't shares in a gold mine."

All the women smiled at the joke.

"I wish," said Miriam jokingly. "I think my husband bought shares in a sand bar."

When the smiles stopped, Mary called out. "Mike! Why don't you start the grill? Everybody looks hungry."

"C'mon guys," said Mike. "You've got to see this set-up."

As the guys made their way to the patio, Miriam sought out Sarah. The playroom had toys for all age kids. Eli was happily playing with two trucks on the floor.

Sarah was looking out the window. A cactus grew in the corner of the yard. "I like it here," she said without turning to look.

"It is nice," said Miriam.

"I like these people," said Sarah. "They don't judge me."

Miriam watched Eli mutter as he played with the trucks. She missed little people's noises.

Mary appeared in the doorway. "How do you like your steaks?"

Sarah turned to face Mary. "I don't eat meat."

"Well, there's lots of salad."

Miriam looked at her and smiled. "Medium rare for me, thanks."

Miriam followed Mary to the kitchen. The women were setting the table. Mary called out orders for Mike. The smell of meat grilling filled the air.

They all stood around the table as Mike and Mary said grace. As the plates were filled, they all sat in jovial spirits. It was then that Pam shattered Miriam's disguise.

"So, which is it, Miriam or Jeanette or Janice? We'd like to know. Just how are you scamming Eric?"

Janine choked momentarily.

Pam looked around the table. "At the dinner dance, she was Eric's lady friend Janice. Now he's not here and she's Miriam. What gives?"

Miriam took a gulp of lemonade and took a deep breath. "Okay, it's Janine. And Eric knows I'm here. He's watching my children. He's very good with them."

"I told you," said Rusty. "I knew she was the one from the dance."

"Yes, it was me."

All eyes were on Janine. "Okay, well I guess I should explain a few things. Eric and I planned this whole trip so that I could get in and out of Las Vegas without attracting attention from the authorities."

Everyone at the table looked at each other in disbelief.

"That doesn't sound like Eric," said Pam.

"Alright," said Janine. She opened her purse. She punched in Eric's number. "Hi, honey. I'm here with your friends. We're on speaker phone."

A simultaneous "Hi," filled the air.

"Honey," said Janine, "your friends have been working on a puzzle. They think that you have the missing piece. They know that I'm Janine. We met Rusty and Pam at the dinner dance. They think I'm scamming you."

"Well, you can tell everyone that we needed to get you in and out of Las Vegas as Miriam," said Eric. "Miriam had to do the business to keep it away from the tax man and divorce lawyers. You can share with my friends and give them my best wishes."

"Alright, honey. I'll call you later." Janine hung up.

There was silence around the table for a long time.

"Honey, there's got to be a good story behind this," said Rusty.

Janine told them the saga of abandonment, eviction, integration with Eric, bankruptcy, Miriam's death, and an abbreviated list of Brent's crimes. She said that misdirection was the only way to recover anything of hers without it being confiscated. Janine ended by saying that she didn't want to deceive Eric's friends, but she didn't want them to be implicated in any way.

There was a long pause when she stopped. Finally, it was Rusty that broke the silence. "Wow!"

"And that's why you were in the bank looking like someone else," said Mary.

"That's right," said Janine. "I need the bank to believe I was someone else pretending to be me."

"Wow," said Rusty again. "Aren't you afraid of being caught?"

"Of course," said Janine. "That's why I need you to keep calling me Miriam."

Pam looked at her quizzically. "Are you with Eric? I mean…his girl…his lady?"

Janine smiled. "I sure am. He's been so good to me and the kids. I love him so much." She smiled at the crowd around the table. "But I don't know if we'll ever be able to marry."

"Aww," said Mary. "Why not?'

"I'd have to get a divorce from…that bastard husband of mine." Janine looked at the faces around the table. "Unless he turns up, I'll have to wait quite a few years for a divorce in absentia."

"Just trying to get my head around this," asked Mike. "Is Sarah your daughter?"

While Janine had been telling her tale, Sarah/Kat quietly took her son to the playroom.

"No, she's not," said Janine. "She's a homeless single mom I'm trying to help. I thought that she could use a trip away."

"Wow," said Rusty again. "That's the darndest story I ever heard. But if Eric wants it that way, we won't tell anybody."

When Mary and Pam served coffee and dessert, the men retreated to the TV area. The women remained at the table. They sat silently for a long time.

"I think that if I were evicted, I'd die on the spot," said Mary. "They put all your things on the curb?"

Janine nodded. Her eyes welled up. "It was so hard. I kept crying. I didn't know what to do."

Both the women looked at Janine teary eyed.

"I thank God that Eric came by," said Janine. "He…saved us."

Pam and Mary each reached out a hand and took one of Janine's. They sat immersed in their thoughts for a few minutes.

Howard came over. "Hey, we should be getting back."

Janine went down the hall to find Kat. She was looking at a children's book. Al was sleeping on the divan.

Mary came in behind Janine. "Aw. The little guy's asleep." She looked at the child and smiled.

"You can stay here tonight if you want. Let him sleep."

"I don't want to bother you," replied Kat.

"It's no bother," replied Mary. "That couch folds out. You can sleep here. We'll bring you back in the morning."

Kat looked at Janine.

"It's alright with me," said Janine.

"Good," said Mary. "I'll get you some sheets."

Janine donned her Miriam wig again. She smiled at the reduced party. "Miriam's ready to go."

Miriam/Janine entered the hotel room alone. She called down for a serving of tea. She began packing while she waited. She checked her plan and nodded. She had accomplished so much. All she had to do was get home. She packed her purse with clothes changes just in case there were issues.

After the tea was delivered, she removed all her clothes and the wig. She had always wanted a hotel room to herself but now it seemed hollow. She desperately missed Eric and the kids. She called Eric.

"What? Oh, are you alright?" Eric said sleepily.

"I'm sorry. I didn't realize it was so late. Were you sleeping?" she asked.

"Yeah," said Eric, "but I had to get up to talk to my wife."

Janine had never heard him call her his wife. She began to tear up. "I'm just missing you and the kids. I'll feel better when I'm back home with you."

"Were my friends upset?"

Janine thought about the answer. "No. No, I wouldn't say that. Bewildered, yes. Supportive, yes. Angry, no. They were…understanding. They trust you."

"Okay," said Eric. "I'll feel better when you're back too. Oh damn…"

"What's wrong?"

"I seem to be sleeping with a giraffe and his little girl," said Eric.

Janine smiled. "Yeah, sometimes they sneak into bed on my side."

"Now you tell me. Just come home safe."

"I'll try." Janine hesitated. "You called me your wife."

Eric hesitated. "Yeah, well, I think of you that way. Otherwise, why would I have your demon giraffe in my bed?"

"I love you," Janine whispered, "more than ever."

"Me too. Godspeed. And now I have to go wrangle a giraffe herd back into its pen."

"Why don't you just let them sleep there?"

"No way. They're hogging the bed."

Janine had a fitful night's sleep. When she heard some knocking at a door in the hall, she woke in a panic. Were the cops here? She moved quickly to the door. She couldn't see anyone through the peep hole.

When she opened the door and looked outside, a man was holding an ice bucket entering another room. He looked at Janine and said, "Sorry."

Janine then realized that she had not thought to bring any reading material with her. She turned on the TV. She kept changing stations until she happened upon the *Mary Tyler Moore Show*. The comedy remined her of evenings on the couch, snuggled against her mom. She would be happy to be home, snuggled with her family.

Janine had finished packing her things and was packing Al's when Sarah knocked on the door. Janine put on her Miriam wig and answered the door.

Sarah, Mike, and Eli came in.

"Hi. I've almost got you packed," said Miriam.

Sarah/Kat hugged Janine. "I've got news. We're going to stay here with Mike and Mary," said Sarah.

"What?" said Janine.

"It's true," said Kat.

Janine sat on the bed. "Mike...Mike, you should know more about Kat before you decide this."

Kat began packing where Janine had stopped.

"You mean about Kat heisting her son from her parents?" said Mike. "We looked it up online last night. They think she's gone to Indiana."

"We'd like her to stay with us. We'll help her out," said Mike. "We do some sheltering for illegals trying to get back to their families. They owe us a favor or two. We'll get Sarah," he made parenthesis marks with his hands, "all the papers she'll need. Nobody will ever find her with us." Mike held Eli while Sarah packed.

"Okay," said Janine. "It sounds like two less on the plane."

"Three," said Mike. "Howard's staying too. He's up $150,000 and he doesn't want to go back to his sister's basement."

"Okay," said Janine with a laugh. "I hope you know what you're getting yourself into."

Mike and Howard insisted on driving Rusty, Pam, and Miriam to the airport.

Howard helped Miriam with her luggage. "Say thanks to Eric, will you? Good luck." He hugged her. "Take good care of yourselves."

"I will."

Mike shook her hand. "Nice to meet you, Miriam. Come when you can stay longer."

"I will."

The three entered the plane. The pilot looked around. "Only you three?"

Miriam/Janine sat by herself during the take-off. She watched the land slip away as the plane gained altitude. What a strange trip it was. She had pulled it off. She had ripped off Brent, the bastard. She looked at her bag with the thousands of dollars in it. Would she be able to keep it? How would she explain deceiving banks to her kids? Would Eric's friends keep her secrets?

"Miriam?" It was Pam. "How about a couple of scotch on the rocks and a round of pinochle?"

Miriam/Janine focused in on the woman. "Yeah. Fine. I'm in."

After a few hands of cards, Rusty leaned forward and whispered, "I gotta ask, how many women did you pretend to be?"

Janine let a small laugh. "Four, counting me."

Pam put a hand on Janine's arm. "Honey, we all hope it all works out. And you and Eric too."

After another hand, Rusty leaned forward again to whisper, "And don't worry. We won't tell anybody. I can hardly believe it myself!" He belly-laughed.

HOMECOMING

At the Pal Waukee airport, Miriam accessed Howard's car. After dropping of Rusty and Pam, Miriam was alone in the car. She drove to Howard's house. She ducked into the garage and changed into Janine. She pulled her car out and put Howard's car in.

While she was loading her luggage, Howard's sister appeared. "Where's Howie?"

Janine handed her Howard's car keys. "He stayed in Vegas. I don't think he's coming back."

"Really?!"

Janine headed home.

When Janine pulled up to the house, she noticed Eric's car was not there. When she entered the house, her kids smothered her with hugs. They sat in the living room while Monica and Alan peppered her with their week's stories. Olivia brought tea.

When Eric came in Janine rose and hugged him. They kissed.

"Ooo," said Monica and Alan simultaneously.

Eric ordered pizza so they all could sit and eat at the table. It was past eleven when Eric suggested it was time for "little ones" to get to bed.

It was past midnight when Eric and Janine were alone in their room.

"I think we did it," whispered Janine. She pulled bundles of $100 bills from her purse.

"Turn the radio on," said Eric. "The walls have ears."

Janine turned on the stereo. "Why weren't you here when I got home?"

"I had to retrieve this." He held out Janine's phone. "Cheryl says to remind you that you enjoyed the bed and breakfasts, the boutiques, the antique shops, and dinner at Amish Acres."

"You know, I think I have been there," said Janine. "I have a lot to tell you."

"Tomorrow," said Eric. "Tonight, I just want you."

Janine and Eric were still having coffee when the doorbell rang. Olivia answered the door.

"The police are here," said Olivia.

Eric and Janine went to the living room. There were two uniformed and two plain clothed officers. "Eric Pierson and Janine Pierson, we're taking the two of you in for questioning in the disappearance of Katherine Simmons and Alan Simmons. Please come with us and bring your cell phones."

Eric was seated in an interrogation room alone. He knew he had to be extremely careful what he said.

The ununiformed officers came in and sat down. "I am Detective Pippin. This is Detective Laughlin and Special Agent Ware."

Eric took a pen and paper out of his pocket. "Let me see those badges, fellas," he said. Eric examined each ID and held the picture up to the man's face. Then he wrote down the name and badge number.

"Now, officers, what can I do for you?" said Eric.

"We are looking for Katherine Simmons who kidnapped a child Alan Simmons," said Detective Pippin. "What do you know about it?"

Eric shook his head no. "Well, I know that Kat's parents muscled her child away from her. I know that the police are or were looking for the two of them. Still haven't found them?"

There was a moment of silence. "We're going to get a court order to search your phone," said Detective Pippin.

Eric looked at them and shrugged. "Here." He handed the detective his phone.

"When's the last time she called you?" asked Laughlin.

"I have no idea," said Eric. "I don't know that I ever talked to Kat on the phone."

Detective Pippin opened Eric's flip phone and searched the calls.

"When's the last time you saw her?" asked Agent Ware.

Eric sat back. "A week ago, Thursday maybe. She was over at the house. She was going to visit her son in the next few days."

"You mean to kidnap him?" asked Pippin.

Eric shook his head. "She didn't say anything about taking him. She was going to have dinner or lunch with her mom. That's all I heard."

"Are you sure about that?" asked Laughlin.

Eric stared the officer down. "That's what I said." He looked at all three men. "And I do not know where Kat or Al is."

Det. Pippin responded abruptly, "I believe your wife took Kat and Al to Indiana last week."

Special Agent Ware's gaze turned abruptly toward Pippin.

Eric thought for a second. He looked the detective in the eye. "My wife didn't take Kat anywhere."

Detectives Pippin and Laughlin eyed each other. They rose and offered their seats to Agent Ware.

"Just a minute," said the special agent. "Janine Pierson is not your wife, is she?"

Eric looked at him. "No, she is not. But I do not think that Janine took Kat to Indiana."

The two detectives left the room. Agent Ware opened a file. He put a recorder on the table. "This is being recorded. Special Agent Ware and Eric Pierson…"

Eric steeled himself. If this wasn't about Kat, it must be about Vegas.

"Mr. Eric Pierson, why did you have lunch at Angelo's last Wednesday?" asked the Agent.

"I was invited by my friend Tony."

"I see," said the agent. "I don't think you just had lunch with Tony."

"No," said Eric. "There were others there."

"Who were they?"

"I don't know. I wasn't introduced."

The agent made a face. "You had lunch, but you didn't get names?"

"That's right."

"How many of them were there?

"Besides Tony, four."

"Could you recognize them if you saw them again?"

"No," said Eric. "I took off my glasses when I went in. They were blurry."

The agent pursed his lips. "You didn't want to recognize anyone in there, did you?"

Eric nodded. "You got it."

"What did they want to talk about? Or did you have earplugs on too?"

"They wanted to know if we'd heard from Brent. They asked about the broad that took off with Brent, Carrie or Charlotte or something. They asked what I knew anything about the woman on the video we found."

The agent looked puzzled. "What video?"

"The one we found of Brent's. The woman all tied up. We gave it to Detective Long," said Eric. "He should have it."

The agent made some notes. "Okay, so what did you tell them?"

"At Angelo's? Nothing. I didn't know anything about those things."

"And then what?"

Eric looked at the man and smiled. "They fed me lasagna and I left."

"That's it?" said Ware. "That's what they asked?"

Eric nodded.

"Let me ask you about your relationship with Tony," said Ware.

"I helped Tony get through high school. He was not interested in school, but his father and grandfather said he had to graduate. We used to play ball in the street as kids. I knew his family.

"Anyway, we made a deal. I get him through his classes, and he taught me a few things. I'd go over to his house and help him with math and general science. His momma fed me.

"So, I got him through to graduation. His family was happy. I said goodbye and I thought we were done. But I ran into him recently."

"You met Tony's grandfather, Carmine?" asked the agent.

"Sure. I think there's a picture of us at the graduation."

Agent Ware assessed Eric carefully. "And what did Tony teach you?"

"All kinds of stuff. How to hot wire a car. Where to get a gun. And he showed me how to enter a house so that no one knows you've been there."

Agent Ware looked at Eric. "For the record, Janine is not your wife. She's your niece."

Eric looked at the agent. "You guys are really sharp over there."

Eric and Janine were dropped off at home later that day. Before they went in, Eric stopped her. "Don't tell me what happened to Kat or Al. They really wanted me to tell them something. What I don't know I can't tell. Okay?"

"Okay," replied Janine. "I had to swear that I did not take Kat to Indiana."

"Oh, yeah. I had to swear that my wife didn't take Kat to Indiana!" He held her from kissing him.

Janine smiled at him. "They thought I was your wife?"

"Only some of them," replied Eric. "The others think you're my niece,"

Janine leaned close and whispered, "I think we fooled 'em."

Eric smiled. "Me too. Let's take the kids for ice cream. Okay?"

Team Janine decided to keep their "caper" quiet and return family life to normalcy. They had only two pressing issues to cover.

Janine wrapped up all her disguises. Eric dropped the costumes off with Cheryl. She would keep them in case Janine needed them again.

The other issue was the cash. They packed Eric's small safe with cash. They agreed to use cash whenever possible and bank their incomes. Eric would report gambling winnings on his taxes. Janine would report higher tips.

By being careful they thought no one would take any notice of their newfound affluence.

THE REWARD

Eric had made a stop at the coffeehouse a weekly occasion. Eric filled a mug of coffee. He had to dodge a workman with a ladder to choose a table. No sooner had he sat down when the power went off. Since he had his coffee and sweet roll, Eric decided to stay in the darkened dining room.

A man sat at the table opposite Eric. With a slight smile Tony said, "Hello."

"Oh, hi," said Eric. "I wasn't expecting you."

"Uh ha," said Tony. He scanned the restaurant. "My cousin found what he was looking for." He nodded affirmatively. "You did good, you and your...friend. She did really good. She's a keeper."

"I think so," said Eric. He sipped his coffee.

Tony sat back. "I hear you had a meeting with...some other guys." Tony nodded. "I hear you're a tough guy, straight up." Tony leaned forward and grinned. "They think that Brent guy and his girlfriend ripped off some banks in Vegas. What do you know?"

Eric nodded. "That so? Well, it's a good thing me and mine were nowhere near there."

Tony nodded.

Eric looked around the still darkened restaurant. "I wonder when the power's coming back on."

Tony nodded toward the workman on a ladder. "He'll be done in a few minutes. I think there's something wrong with the security cameras."

Tony looked back and forth. "Why don't you and your lady stop by Momma's house on Sunday? She'd like to see you. How about two o'clock?"

Tony stood up and walked out. Eric watched the man until he disappeared around the corner. The restaurant lights came on one minute later.

Eric told Janine that they were going to visit an old neighbor. Eric drove down a street lined with brick bungalows. He pulled over in front a house, seemingly identical to the rest. "This was our house." He stared at the building for some seconds. "We're going over there."

Eric pulled the car across the next intersection and stopped. When Eric got out, Janine did too. He led her up the cement steps to the entrance portico. The inner door opened, and a man pushed the storm door open. "C'mon in," he said.

As they entered Eric thrust his hand out, "Hello, Tony."

Janine stiffened as she turned to greet him. "Hello," she managed to choke out.

The living room was lined with people, but they were all focused on Eric and Janine.

"Hi everyone," said Eric cheerfully with a wave. "I'm Eric and this is Janine."

They all nodded but said nothing.

"This way," said Tony. He led them through the dining room where more people were sitting. Tony took two left turns and led them into a small bedroom.

Janine was now aware of several things. Firstly, she was shaking. Eric had not prepared her for an encounter with Tony. He was a large man with an expressionless face. He exuded a kind of harnessed power that Janine felt threatening. Secondly, the assembled crowd watched them and had not broken a welcoming smile.

The bedroom was dominated by a hospital bed. An elderly, frail woman lay seemingly motionless. As they entered an attendant left the room.

Tony leaned over the reclining woman. "Momma. Momma. I've brought a friend to see you. It's Eric." Tony reached over and pulled Eric closer.

The woman's eyes opened and her head turned. "Eric?" She feebly reached out a hand.

Eric smiled and took her hand. "Hello, Mrs. M. I had to stop by and see you."

"Eric," she said weakly. She nodded slightly. "You're a good boy. I'll get you something to eat."

"That's alright," said Eric. "You take it easy. They'll feed me in the kitchen."

Janine was suddenly aware that the house was full of cooking smells. She began to notice the room. There were pictures on the walls and a large crucifix. She looked at Tony whose eyes dared between Eric, his mother, and herself.

The bedside meeting lasted only about two minutes. Eric turned to Janine and pointed to a picture near the door. There were two boys in blue graduation robes and a crowd of adults. "That's me and Tony, graduation day. They had a huge party over here." Eric led her out of the room.

Tony led them through the kitchen to the back porch. There was a couch and two chairs. A grey-haired man sat facing them. He motioned toward the couch. "Please sit down."

"Oh, hi," said Eric, recognizing Mr. Big. He held Janine's hand as they sat on the couch.

"You two," said Mr. Big, nodding negatively. "You two." He looked at Janine. "I don't know what to call you: Janine or Miriam or Charlene. That was first class, you two. Very, very good."

"You got your...package?" asked Eric.

"Like I said, very, very good." Mr. Big looked at Eric. "And what do you say when you're interviewed about today?"

"I've just come to pay my respects to Mrs. M. She was always good to me," said Eric.

Mr. Big held out a key by the tag. "This is for you."

Eric took it. "Thanks."

"You should clean out your locker in the next few days. I think some of your things are still there. And," said Mr. Big, "don't bother to come to the funeral. Capiche?"

Eric nodded and pocketed the key. "I think we should be going." Eric rose and shook Tony's hand. "It was nice to see your mom."

Tony wordlessly showed them out the back door.

After Janine had left for work and the kids were off to school, Eric went to a U-Haul depot. He purchased four banker's boxes with cash.

On the key tag was the address of a storage facility. It was some distance away. The security gate code numbers were on the tag. Eric assembled one box and put the rest in it. He opened his car trunk and grabbed for some rubber gloves.

Inside the storage house Eric found a cart. He put on his gloves, loaded the empty boxes in the cart, and searched for the locker. As he walked down the deserted halls, automatic lights activated darkened sections.

Eric found the designated locker. The key opened the pad lock. The only thing in the space was a filing cabinet.

Eric stood for a second looking at the cabinet. All alone in the room it reminded him of the monolith in 2001.

Each of the two drawers of the filing cabinet were secured with duct tape. Eric pulled out his pocketknife and cut the tape loose. He opened the top drawer. Inside was a large clear plastic bag. Packets of bills were helter-skelter in the bag.

Eric took the bag and stuffed it into a cardboard banker's box. He opened the lower cabinet drawer. In it was another clear plastic bag with various denominations of money. Eric assembled another box and stuffed the bag in.

Eric closed the cabinet. He closed and secured the locker. He pushed the cart to the elevator. He pushed the cart to the car. He put the banker's boxes in the back seat. Eric drove home. He put the boxes in his bedroom in the corner.

He and Janine would count the money during their alone time. All the money that Eric had loaned Janine was repaid and then some.

In the weeks that followed, Janine and Eric were questioned several times by the police. The questions were always about Brent and Charlene. Janine and Eric vehemently denied any contact with either.

TEN YEARS LATER

As the memorial service went on, Janine's mind strayed. She thought about the terror she felt when Brent abandoned her, and they were evicted. She remembered the bewilderment of empty bank accounts. She remembered the anger she felt discovering Brent's misdeeds. And all the time Eric was there like a husband/partner delivered by a guardian angel.

Janine tried to focus in when Olivia began to speak her part of the memorial. She spoke of "Uncle Eric's" support and encouragement in her art. She would be forever grateful. Janine recalled Eric dragging her to an art show she really didn't have the energy for.

Livy had come in from the West Coast. Thankfully she had helped organize the reception and was Janine's deputy throughout.

Monica came up from U of I Champaign for the service. She spoke of "Uncle Eric's" tolerance of pajama parties and chaperoning concerts. Janine vividly recalled Eric and Monica at the table doing her homework.

Alan spoke of "Uncle Eric's" attendance at numerous sports events. He spoke of working with Eric on numerous home projects. Janine visualized Eric and Alan rebuilding the back fence. And now Alan was nearing the end of his apprenticeship as a carpenter.

Janine looked at Paul, Eric's son, seated next to her. Paul had been so gracious planning Eric's service around both families.

Paul got up to speak. He spoke of how lucky he was to have had a father like Eric. He had always felt supported and loved by his father.

Paul recounted how his father said he was such a lucky man. Eric, he said, had loved two of the finest ladies ever. He had married the love of his life with Peggy. Eric felt that his life was pretty much over when she died. And then he found Janine. Courageous and loving, she made his last years precious.

Paul's words struck Janine through the haze of her grief. She would miss Eric so much.

After the memorial service, many people stayed for the reception. Many people told Janine that Eric had been such a great guy. Janine spotted several of the people from Eric's workplace. She also spotted several members of law enforcement.

When "Mop-up Mike" came over to Janine, he had Sarah/Kat with him. "I had to come," said Mike. "You remember my daughter, Sarah."

"I do," said Janine. "It's nice to see you again. How's that son of yours?" She held Sarah/Kat's hand a few seconds.

"Oh, he's fine," said Sarah.

They both locked eyes for a few seconds. They needed no words between them.

"Thank you both for coming so far," said Janine.

Olivia came up and looked at Sarah/Kat quizzically.

"You do remember Sarah, don't you?" said Janine. "She and her baby son stayed with us for a while."

Olivia's eyes got wide. "Oh, sure. How are you?"

Alan came over. "Mom, you remember my friend Jeffery and his mom Marge?"

"Of course, I do," said Janine. "How are you?"

The boys drifted off. Marge sat down close to Janine.

"I've been assigned to cold cases," said Marge. "I'm a detective now."

"Oh," replied Janine.

"I was watching some old surveillance footage of Brent's girlfriend in Las Vegas," said Marge. "Did you know that they tried to implicate you? She disguised herself as you. They even put some money in your account to throw us off."

Janine tried to look surprised. "Are you closer to finding them?" She shook her head slowly in the negative. "But if you do…don't give HIM back to me."

Both women chuckled. Marge moved on.

By prearrangement, Paul and Sheila arrived at Eric's house in the early evening after the memorial service. While Olivia set out coffee and tea, Janine brought Monica and Alan into the living room.

"There are some things I need to explain to all of you," said Janine. "I will only say these things once, but you all need to hear what happened."

Paul pulled a letter out of his pocket. "Does this have anything to do with this? Dad left me a letter that says you are going to explain why you couldn't get married."

Janine nodded. "Olivia, pass some coffee around."

Janine settled back and took a deep breath. "First of all, I loved Eric so much. He saved me. He saved my family. I would have married him in a minute. But we could not."

"Because of Brent?" said Paul. "I thought you got your divorce?"

"I did," said Janine, "but there's more. We promised each other that we had to protect this house and Eric's estate. He was determined to leave a legacy to you, his son. Whatever happened, we had to insulate Eric from the Brent issues."

Paul and Sheila nodded to each other. "We don't want to leave you homeless again," said Paul. "Dad left me lots of money. He made me promise to take care of you."

Janine nodded. "Thank you. But actually, I'm financially sound. To that point I'd like to buy this house from you. I know it's your family home, but it's become my family's home."

Paul looked confused. "Buy it?"

"That's right," said Janine. "Why don't you let me tell all of you how I recovered my family's resources?"

Janine explained how she and Eric put together the clues of the Las Vegas connection. She told of a charter flight to conceal her whereabouts. She told of multiple disguises. She told of shipping the cabinet back. She told of using small amounts of the money at a time.

Janine did not tell them about Kat and Al. She did not tell them about Cheryl and Billie driving around Indiana to establish an alibi. She did not mention the involvement of the mob.

"So, you see," said Janine. "We had to keep Eric and his finances away from mine, just in case."

"Mom, you really did all of that?" asked Monica.

Janine nodded her head. "I had to get back what Brent took from us."

"Great going, Mom," said Olivia.

"You're the best," said Alan.

Paul and Sheila had been whispering to each other. Paul looked at Janine and said, "Wow. I mean…wow. Dad helped you with this?"

Janine nodded. "Yeah. He did."

"Go Uncle Eric," said Olivia.

"How much money did you find?" asked Paul.

"I can't and won't tell you that," said Janine.

Paul and Sheila held hands. "We were going to let you stay in the house," said Paul. "You made Dad very happy."

"Thanks," said Janine, "but I'd rather buy it from you. I've never had a place of my own."

Paul looked at his wife and nodded. "I think that'll be okay with us."

"Just one thing," said Janine, "none of you can repeat my story outside of here. The police cases are still open. Agreed?"

They all nodded.

Paul looked at Janine. "I'm taking a week off. We'll get together after our vacation to work out the details."

"Okay," said Janine. "Where are you going?"

"We've rented a vacation chalet in the Wisconsin Dells," said Paul.

Janine's face fell. "Don't go!"

END

www.ingramcontent.com/pod-product-compliance
Ingram Content Group UK Ltd.
Pitfield, Milton Keynes, MK11 3LW, UK
UKHW021433240125
4283UKWH00041B/591